Hypnos

Jon Biddle

Clink
Street

London | New York

Published by Clink Street Publishing 2019

Copyright © 2019

First edition.

ISBN: 978-1-913136-97-0 paperback
978-1-913136-98-7 ebook

Please hit this link in the e-book to receive my FREE
BOOK and join my mailing list.

https://jonbiddle.uk/get-my-free-book-troll/

Troll -Have you checked your account settings,
are you safe from a Troll?

ARE YOU SURE?

The bodies of two teenagers have been discovered, from
different universities, but they went to the same school.

A Serial killer is on the loose in London and
Alex Brown is investigating.

Alex uncovers a narcissistic killer hell bent on destroying
everything that they have come into contact with. Stalking
his victims, they all trusted him, and now he pins them to
the floor with a nail gun and takes everything from them.

A prequel to the Harvester, the 1st episode in Jon Biddle's
Broc series, this story pulls no punches and makes you
read the book behind the safety of the cushion.

It will make you think about everything
you do on social media.

Watch out, there is a troll about.

https://jonbiddle.uk/get-my-free-book-troll/

To Jorden and Devon – For being the best children you could possibly be, you have become the best people you can possibly be. The corner stone of my inspiration is your achievements always striving for a better world and better life, I simply love you both forever, thank you.

1

Jamal was thinking that if time could be reversed now, this would be the time to do it. His right hand was gripped in a vice in his dad's old shed, with a lunatic screaming in his ear. He watched the South African reach for the lump hammer on the shed wall, leaving a white outline showing where it should always belong.

Like a golfer, Van Den Jong, or Jongy to his mates, took couple of dry swings to the tips of Jamal's fingers. On the fourth swing it connected. The middle finger was the first to snap, followed immediately by the ring then the forefinger and finally the little one.

Jongy stood back. "Fuckin' 'ell eh, look at that eh," he said to Errol. "The little bastard pinky finger Errol, only bashed the top of it, eh."

Errol shuffled on his feet. A small Zulu from Bulawayo peered at the hand trapped in the vice. Jamal was hanging from said vice, trying to support his trapped arm. Screaming, the pain searing through the limb like a hot needle. He daren't look at the vice, eyes fixed to the floor, sweat pouring down his face.

Errol reached for a pair of pliers that was marked out next to the lump hammer, felt the weight, like a plier connoisseur.

"What are you doing?" Jongy asked Errol, who looked at

him, showed him the pliers and then motioned to the little finger, still standing proudly next to the other smashed digits.

Jongy looked at Jamal. "Errol just wants to tidy up your hand, your little finger isn't as smashed up as he would like, eh."

Jamal looked up. "Fuck you! I'm connected you know, I know people."

"Oooooo," Jongy taunted, before tapping Errol who laughed as well.

Errol turned and Jamal screamed as the pliers came closer.

"Errol, the boy has been through enough eh, let's see if he cooperates."

Errol nodded and moved out of the way, Jongy crouched. He looked at the hand, which was turning dusky blue around the edges of the vice.

"Tut tut," he said, he grabbed Jamal's hair and pulled his head up with it.

"You only have to agree to our terms and I'll let you go," Jongy said.

He was well dressed, cropped hair, six foot three and made of what Jamal could only assume was human steel. There was a coldness to his attitude that was unnerving. Well turned out, he didn't fit the usual reprobate he dealt with. His South African accent was menacing and threatening. Jamal fought a hard corner. He knew he had a winner, he just needed to hang on a bit longer.

The week previous, Jamal had been hacking American government files and had come across a file marked, 'Gamma top secret.'

The details of the file were titled HYPNOS. After deep searches on the conventional web and the dark web, he finally made it to the locked vaults of the CIA in Langley. Within minutes, he had download the entire HYPNOS file including the software driver, still not knowing fully what he had. Files and software that had this much security often meant secrets that shouldn't be made public, or access to software drivers that could be used to aide further his criminal behavior.

When Jamal opened the file, it seemed unbelievable. A software program that could upload instructions to the receiver and the receiver could be made to do whatever the operator wanted. All the software needed was an app-based game, which used eye movement to control the game and soundtrack. This caused a triad of hypnosis to the user, opening the brain-waves for the software to be uploaded.

"Bollocks," he said out loud.

He quickly found the game that fitted the parameters of the software on the app store, and invited his friends to play the game. Jamal had already hacked most of his friend's phones, using their location signals to baffle the police for ongoing jobs he did for the criminal underworld. They agreed to play and when he knew they were playing the game, the software did everything else.

Rufus, Jamal's longtime friend from school, was playing the game in the local pub. Watching him, he had access to the front camera, he could see the progress that he was making while playing it and uploaded the software. Jamal hacked into the security camera at the back of the bar.

With free text, Jamal typed, 'Steal some beer from the beer tap, and drink it in front of the landlord.' The software ran algorithms. A few seconds later, the information was being uploaded to the game.

Not more than five seconds later, Rufus put his phone down and walked off. He came into view of the CCTV camera and stopped. He turned almost robotically to the bar, took a step, picked up a half full pint of beer and tipped it on the floor.

The owner of the pint took a step back, demonstrating his anger at what Rufus had done, being quickly held back by the man's friend.

Rufus didn't even skip a beat. Leaned over the bar and pulled on the tap. The beer, clear in the footage, was filling up the glass. The beer drinker now incensed. Jamal stifled a laugh.

When the glass was almost full, Rufus took it and started to drink, leaving the tap on, spilling beer all over the floor. At this point, the landlord came into view and was remonstrating. Rufus stood back and drained the beer while sticking his two fingers up at the bar. It was at this point Rufus was wrestled to the ground and dragged out of the bar by the bouncers.

A more sinister exercise – Jamal's cousin Salma. She worked in the bank as a cashier. He instructed her to steal one thousand pounds secretly, in a way no one would ever know. Deliver it to one of his dead drops by 9 pm that night. Jamal went to the dead drop, scoped the area, then reached into the bush by the phone box. His fingers found the bundle of notes, his heart quickened as he touched them. Pulling them out, he didn't need to count it. He knew he was on to a winner.

Back in the garage, with Errol and Jongy. Jamal now regretting ever clamping his eyes on HYPNOS.

"Give us the software and we'll leave you alone," Jongy said.

"Don't believe you," Jamal replied, the pain was searing through his arm, the ulnar and radius grinding together in the vice.

Jongy laughed. "He doesn't believe us, Errol, what's that all about, eh?"

Jamal was soaked in sweat, his knees hurting, he tried

to get to his feet, but the pain in his hand was unbearably painful. Just moving irritated the nerve receptors trapped around the vice.

"Does your friend speak?" Jamal asked.

"Who, Errol?" Jongy turned and looked at Errol, pulling drawers out and tipping them on the floor.

"No, some kaffir cut his tongue out when he was a boy, the good thing about that is that he doesn't say a fuckin' word, eh?" Jongy said, trying to help Jamal up.

"Fetch that stool there, Errol, the boy needs a little comfort." Errol stopped, looked at Jongy, nodded and walked over to the stool. He kicked it over.

"Now, we have got the unpleasantries out of the way, why can't you just give me the software my boss wants, eh?"

"You won't be able to run it," Jamal said.

"How so? It's like Pacman, right?" Errol laughed. Even Jongy turned to look.

"I don't get to hear that that often eh, eish, tell me more."

"The algorithm is difficult to interpret," Jamal screwed his face up, the pain still building. He was trying to keep things under control.

"Then teach me," Jongy retorted. It was Jamal's turn to laugh.

"You think I'm some sort of rock spider? You be careful there, young man. I'll clap you right out, eh."

"I wasn't trying to offend you." Jamal's breath was getting shallower, clearly in more pain. "The algorithm is complex, it took me a few hours to figure it out, and before you say anything, me figuring it out is not me being able to teach you in a few hours."

Jongy stood, his back was hurting. He scratched his head and looked at Errol. Nothing.

"Jawelnofine, we're running things from here, and you is the man, yesh."

"Do I still get paid?"

"Haibo, fuck no, you cheeky loskop, you'll be grateful we don't kill you in the process."

Jongy unwound the vice, the hand flopped out, Jamal catching it before it hit the floor.

"Right, get your arse over to the computer and do your thing for me."

There was a sound from the front of the house, and Jamal slumped his shoulders. Someone had just returned from work.

Errol grabbed Jongy's hand and yanked it toward the door.

"I know Errol, go sort that fuckin' noise out eh, be quick."

"What do you mean 'sort that noise out'?" Jamal asked. "That's my mom!"

"Shut up, man."

Errol disappeared. There was a shuffle, then a banging, a scream, then silence.

"There we go, man, all's well. Let's get on with it." Jongy stated.

"What do you mean, it's all sorted?" The pain in Jamal's hand had disappeared.

"You just concentrate on dealing with that, I'll go and see what Errol is up to, eh?"

Jongy walked to the door, which was slightly ajar. Jamal got up and followed him, holding his battered hand with his good one. He peered through the door.

"What the fuck, man? What are you doing you filthy kaffir? Get off the woman! What the fuck, man, eish."

Jamal followed into the kitchen, which was connected to the garage. Errol was molesting Jamal's mother on the floor. Jongy grabbed Errol by the collar and pulled him off, Jamal came closer and then realized that his mom had been decapitated. Her head had been tossed into the sink, a large pool of blood forming around the jagged mess of flesh, bone, and skin, her leg still shaking. Sinking to the floor, Jamal sobbed.

"For fuck's sake, Errol, look what you've done!" Jongy clocked Jamal sobbing on the floor.

Holding out his hands in protest to Errol, who was wiping the machete on a tea towel, his penis still hanging out of his pants.

"Seriously, man, 'take care of it' meant bringing the lady into the garage so she could be with her son, not cut her fuckin' head orf and then fuck her carcass. When they cut your tongue out eh, they should've kept cutting til yours fell orf to."

He turned to Jamal. "Come on, boy, let's go back to the room, you don't need to see this."

He looked back at Errol. "And put your dick away, eh, you'll scare the fuckin' cats."

"Fuck you and your dumb sidekick, I ain't doing squat for you, you…" Jamal didn't know how to continue.

"Fuck it," Jongy said, walked up to Jamal on his knees and grabbed his face. His free fist smashed into the bridge of his nose, knocking Jamal clean out.

"Right, take care of this," Jongy said, as he started dragging Jamal back into the garage. "And that means, bring the body into the garage, man, and get a mop and bucket, eh, and clean this fuckin' mess right up, you doos."

Errol nodded, and came over and started helping Jongy take Jamal back into the garage.

It took Errol an hour to clean the mess up, when the door opened and closed again.

"Hellloooo."

Both Errol and Jongy exchanged glances. "That'll be my dad," Jamal said. His face swollen, his fingers hanging by their skin, barely lifting his head.

"Izzit, I'll go sort this shit out, eh, you stay and guard the boy."

"Please don't kill my dad?" Jamal pleaded feebly.

"Eh, sorry, boy, we're a bit late for shit like that, leave me be and I'll have this sorted in a jiffy, eh."

Jongy left the room, seconds later he came back following Jamal's dad, who had his hands on his head.

"What have you got yourself messed up in now, Jamal?" The booted and suited man said. Late fifties, professional type, well-spoken.

Jamal looked at the floor. Sobbing, his shame apparent. "Where's your mom?" The man asked.

"About that, eh." Jongy pivoted around the man, holding a Nighthawk custom 9mm pistol.

"She bumped into my kaffir friend, Errol." Jerking his head to the black man in the corner. He was wearing his trademark flat cap, Pringle golfers, black sweater, a loud Hawaiian shirt poking out the top and the bottom. Dirty Farrah pants with snake-skinned slip on shoes. Errol was so lazy that even the slip-on bit was a bit much, the backs of the shoes had worn down and were more like slippers.

"What do you mean?"

"They killed her, dad," Jamal said, his sob heavy. His dad finally saw the hand and the fingers, and registered his son's battered face.

"You see, if things had just gone smoothly, we wouldn't have had to resort to doing things like this." The report of the gun was dull but loud. Jamal's father stared Jongy in the eyes, almost knowing his fate. The round smashed through the father's face and out the back of the head, smattering the wall behind with its contents.

"You fucking animals, you fuck–" He was cut short. Jongy punched him again, then again and then again. His face was a mess, his body slumped against the office chair, gently rocking the unconscious body as though it was going to sleep.

"Clean this fucking mess up, eh." Errol looked at Jongy in disbelief.

"I know I made the fuckin' mess but you're the kaffir, do as you're fuckin' told man." Holstering the pistol.

Jongy pulled his phone out. Found the number he needed, hit dial. The line answered immediately.

"Things have gone a bit crap here, we need to get a clean-up team in, and get me, the kaffir and the boy wonder to the location." He nodded as the other end was talking, then the line went dead.

"Okay, we go, let's get ready. Box all this shit up, the clean-up boys will be here to get rid of the bodies and we're going for a little trip."

They surveyed the room, "What a fuckin' mess, eh?" Errol nodded.

2

Tock, tock, tock. No tick. The carriage clock was on the shelf next to a vast array of books relating to psychology and family education, all neatly rowed in size order. Most likely alphabetized as well. No tock, that was grinding Alex's gears!

Alex sat in the sumptuous chair, enveloped by soft leather. The smell of lemons hung in the air, natural light flooding the room, which had an incredible view of the River Thames.

Jenny had been coaching and treating Alex for some weeks now – on the insistence of Broadstone, her new boss.

Following the sheer horror of the Troll case, then Broc coming into her life and the killing of her partner Renton Davis, and now with the kidnapping of Devon, Alex's daughter, Alex was emotionally broken.

Her isolation drove a wedge between her and her husband Simon, who just couldn't take the stress of her job and blamed her for Devon's disappearance, her obsession with the case had broken the barriers and hurt the sanctity of the family.

Alex recounted it like a bad nightmare, triggering her negative thought process. Watching the moment Devon was taken, re-living this over and over in her mind. Going home and telling Simon was the hardest thing she had ever had to do. He didn't take it well. A few weeks had gone by and the atmosphere had only become more and more sour.

Alex had checked out of the relationship, blaming herself as much as Simon did. When she packed her bags without a word one morning, Simon watched her from the bedroom door and said nothing. The memory was biting at her and making her heart break all over again.

When will it end?

"Sorry, Alex, you wanted to say?" Jenny said.

"I was just thinking," Alex was staring out of the window, watching the tourist float go by on the barges of the Thames, the people looking very happy.

"I could see you were thinking, what was it?"

"When will it stop?" She bit the inside of her lip to try and stop the tears, she was successful, but her eyes still glistened as she turned back to Jenny.

"When will what stop, Alex?"

"The pain, I didn't mean for any of this, is this a test? Why?"

Jenny shifted in her chair, looking back at her with a steady gaze, knowing the deeper sentiments behind Alex's words.

Pagans always spoke in pidgin tongues about their beliefs. Historically, one would be burned at the stake or drowned for suggesting a deeper connection with the universe. Today, the same tactics are used to avoid ridicule. Nutters worshipping the sun and not working for a living, walking around draped in long flowing frocks and hanging around towns with powerful lay lines. The stereotype was very real, but there was nothing was further from the truth.

"Alex, you know why you're here, I'm a clinical psychologist and I'm here to help you make sense of how you're feeling. The trauma you have suffered emotionally will have an underlying effect on your life if you can't find a coping strategy to deal with the PTSD, your mind won't be able to move on from the trauma. Together we will be able to work with that, but I'm also a spiritual therapist." She motioned to the necklace around Alex's neck.

Alex touched it, then clasped it for strength, her eyes screwed up.

"The pendant you wear, it's the tree of life enveloped in a pentagram – do you follow the Craft?" Jenny asked.

Alex nodded. "Not as much as I want to, but I do believe, yes." Her voice cracked, the emotion getting the better of her.

"The universe is on your side, Alex."

Alex's face felt numb, it hardened as she looked back out over the Thames. "It doesn't feel like it."

"This too will pass, Alex, you're surrounded by light and your guides are with you. Work with them, they're there to help you get through this, you only have to ask."

"Why does it have to be so difficult?" Alex asked, feeling frustrated.

"Have you been regressed?" Jenny's voice was soft, non-confrontational, and comforting.

"Yes," Alex said, grabbing another tissue. "This is my fifth time. I've been regressed three times now and I've been told that this is my fifth time on Earth."

"Which is why life is hard for you, Alex. You still have much to learn about yourself, and the lessons that this life can give you. You're a special being, Alex, and the lessons you learn here will all be for a higher purpose."

Alex could feel the tears and felt overwhelmed with a sense of relief, the inner knowing enveloping her like angel wings. Her body crumbled, the tensions holding her together leaving her as she started to cry. The silent tears turned into sobs, and she hid her face in her hands. Alex brought her knees up and perched her feet on the edge of the seat like an upset child. She leaned forward and started to howl, her body racking out the pain in a deep pitiful sound.

Jenny left her to cry for a moment, allowing the full impact of her grief to filter into every nerve ending and the cell memory of her being. Alex then felt Jenny's hands. Warm, healing, and heartfelt, they squeezed. Jenny was now at her feet.

"Renton is here, he's sitting behind you," Jenny said. Alex instinctively looked behind, but she knew there would be no one there.

"He loves you, Alex, none of this was your fault. He wants you to know that he will be with be with you always, you must call on him when you need him."

"I'm sorry, Renton," Alex said and sobbed more. "So sorry."

Jenny looked over Alex's shoulder and nodded. "There's nothing to be sorry about. You will have justice, and he will guide you."

Jenny got up, her lithe yoga-toned body walked over to a large wooden chest, pulling open the right drawer, she pulled out a small box wrapped in black silk. She brought it back to the table in front of Alex and pulled out a pack of cards.

"Do you use the tarot?" Jenny asked.

Alex nodded.

"Pick three cards for me," Jenny said.

Jenny spread of cards on the table like a magician. The random choice that could tell you of your past, your present and helped define your future.

"Okay, we're just looking at your future," Jenny said.

Alex pulled the first card. The artwork exquisite – the High Priestess. She fingered the cards and felt the need to pull out the next, turned it over – the Tower.

"One more," Jenny said.

The Hangman.

"Beautiful." Jenny scanned them. "The High Priestess is feminine, it's a great card for you right now. Great rewards are in store for you, with understanding. The future is good, but with the Tower, there will be obstacles and high hurdles to navigate. The Tower has crumbled down, and you are standing amongst the ruins. There will be rebuilding, new beginnings, you will see how the walls have tumbled and the lightning is destroying what has already been built. There will need to be a moment of recovery, which I believe is now; and then you will start to rebuild your tower bigger and better than ever before. The High Priestess means you are about to embark on a journey of self-discovery, which again, compliments the Tower." Jenny paused, rechecked her channeling. Alex was sat, captivated, the tears still falling freely off her reddened cheeks.

"The Hangman is telling me that there are many things unknown to you, so you need to plan," she considered. "Schedule you days minutely and think nothing but good thoughts, be positive. Along with the Tower, what you have experienced will hold you in good stead for the road ahead."

Jenny pulled another card.

Justice. Jenny smiled, Alex closed her eyes.

"In Justice, we have karma, when it's all said and done, you will get what you truly deserve. It's about finding balance and the knowledge that, in time, you will find balance."

Jenny piled the cards and replaced them.

She turned back to Alex. "You need to take comfort in the cards, Alex, you are loved, you are blessed and anointed, you will prevail and you will get what you deserve." Jenny squeezed her hands again and got back up, heading to back to her chair. "Remember, you choose this life because you're strong enough to live it."

"What about Simon?" Alex asked.

"How do you feel about Simon, and the way he has behaved towards you?"

Alex pursed her lips, she thought for a moment. "I guess I'm pretty mad, he's my soulmate, we've been through so much together and in this time that we need to be together, he's turned his back on me."

"Do you believe that, Alex? Do you truly believe that?"

"It makes me feel really sad, he's at home, hurting like me." Alex wiped her eyes. Crying had become her primary emotion since Devon had been taken. Nothing. No sightings, no communication, no calls, not even a ransom, was she even still alive? The only thing to do was cry.

"That's the truth, Alex. Simon is hurting, just like you. He's as emotionally traumatized as you. He can't express it in the way you can. He is as isolated as you but his love for you hasn't changed. He will heal from this, whatever the outcome. You need faith. You are protected by the angels, Renton is by your side. Have faith, Alex, that's what they're telling me." Jenny's voice was soft and tender.

"Is that bergamot orange I can smell?" Alex queried, looking for the oil burner.

"Indeed – citrus aurantium var. It has many properties, particularly as a relaxant and anti-depressant, it tends to change the moods of my clients, I need them to leave a bit happier than when they arrived," Jenny said with softest of smiles.

Alex laughed.

"You have a beautiful smile Alex. You are a truly beautiful woman. Your aura is of the most whitest of lights, I feel honoured to be of acquaintance with you."

Alex flushed, her smile broadened, and she moved her hair from her right ear. She felt embarrassed.

"Why the embarrassment?" Jenny asked.

Alex moved the hair again. "I feel like I don't deserve your platitude, Jenny."

"I wasn't being trite or dull, I genuinely mean it, Alex. You're a good person, you need to feel joy in your life, your way to…" Jenny trailed off to find the right word that wouldn't leave a negative impact.

"Frigid, cold and frigid, and I don't mean that in a bad way, Alex. Are you okay with me saying that?"

Alex laughed out loud. "Frigid, gosh I haven't been called that before."

"I haven't upset you have I? You're okay with me saying this?" Jenny asked.

"No, erm, I mean, not at all, but why do you say that?" Alex asked, wiping her nose and gently trying not to disturb her already ruined eyeliner.

"You're way too consumed with work, you're addicted to it. Let me be clear, you're not addicted to your job exactly, but work. If you worked in an estate agent, you would as consumed in exactly the same way, do you understand?"

Alex nodded.

"What you need to do is find balance, and that goes back to the cards again. Your life needs to be governed by balance. Addressing your work could shift your addiction to sex, drugs, alcohol, even food. And addiction is isolating, trying to separate you and ultimately destroy you. It's part way there already."

"How come?" Alex asked. She was dialled in, the comment resonating, shedding her clarity on things she already knew.

"Your marriage. Look at your marriage. What happens if we don't address that your marriage is failing and how will this affect you?" Jenny left the question hanging in the air, making Alex wince inside. She shrugged.

"Now, this doesn't mean that you will get back together with Simon. What this means is that the end result won't affect you or your husband in a way that could further isolate, separate and destroy. So, if the final act is to reconcile and make another go of things, then great. But if the final act is to reconcile, and then go your separate ways, then again, awesome." Jenny waited, Alex nodding.

"So, Alex, tell me, what is the key here?"

Alex mulled over the words that Jenny had just said. Reconcile.

"Yeah, I get it. We have to make things right, whatever the outcome."

"Perfect, see, you know these things."

Jenny closed her notebook. She reached for a bowl – in the bowl was a pile of small cards, like the wisdom notes from a fortune cookie.

"Angel cards, Alex, I want you to pull one and use the wisdom they bestow each day."

Alex reached and rummaged briefly, pulling a small card out.

"Read it," Jenny said.

"Silence, be still and listen to your silence, let it fill you with joy." Alex read the card, stopped, and let the words wash over her.

"Silence, your inner silence, Alex. Quiet the chatter and enjoy the joy of silence. Find a time today to do this?"

Alex nodded. "I will, I promise."

Jenny reached in the drawer and pulled out a box. "These are for you, your own set of cards. To break your addiction, and to help yourself, I need you to go out and have fun."

Alex looked at her. "I don't know what you mean."

"Go out with some friends, socialize. Go to an art gallery. Do something for yourself. Love yourself.".

Alex looked confused.

"When was the last time you touched yourself, like, really intimately touched yourself?"

Alex thought for a moment. She was a passionate woman who loved sex. She had it whenever she could with Simon. She realized that she hadn't even thought about sex for the last six months.

"I can't remember," Alex said.

"Loving yourself is as important, I feel, as going out and having fun. Candles, bath, favorite music and love yourself. Your soul needs love to find healing, and sexual energy is the best cure for this. Enjoy yourself," Jenny said.

There was a pause. Alex, surprised that she hadn't considered sex for months.

"Okay then, Alex, until next time." They both got up at the same time, Jenny came over to her and hugged her. The embrace was warm, the energy Alex felt from Jenny instantly charged her. Alex suddenly felt better. She returned the embrace. "Thank you, Jenny," Alex whispered.

Jenny released Alex and cupped her face. "No, thank you for bringing light to my day, keep saying to yourself that 'you love you,' say it every time you see yourself in the mirror, have fun and love yourself physically."

"I will, I promise." Alex suddenly felt the vibration in her jeans. Work had been calling.

Alex pulled her phone out – Ricky.

"Do you need to get that?" Jenny asked.

"No, just work, I'll text them, going there now so no dramas."

Alex went to leave, grabbed her Angel cards and her coat, then turned and looked at the view.

"What a view." She paused, then she was gone.

Jenny paused for a moment too. Extraordinary woman, she thought.

3

Jamal had been driving for some hours. The back of the van was cluttered and dirty, with no light whatsoever. The constant fight against the urge to throw up was palpable. His mind was racing and the pain was traveling up his arm. He gingerly touched his ruined digits. The weird shapes through the rough bandaging made him feel even worse. He reflected on the last few weeks.

After the initial experiments with the software, he had posted the evidence on the dark web and had received a few offers. The entrepreneur in him saw a market in the software. He would hire out its capabilities to the highest bidder – making the payments and processes all incognito. A South African man had been in touch a few days earlier and insisted that there was to be a meet. The guy wanted to do things with the software that would make a lot of money fast, but he wasn't prepared to do the whole transaction anonymously. A meet was required with a taster of five hundred grand deposited in the bank. Jamal thought that this was someone who could be trusted so made arrangements.

Little did Jamal know that he had become a target, and the day before the scheduled meet both Jongy and Errol knocked the door. Four hours later, his entire world was boxed up, thrown into a van. People murdered in front of him, and he was trying desperately to keep his smashed hand up and off the grubby van floor. There was a constant taste of blood in the back of his mouth. His tongue explored the inside of his mouth, two of his bottom teeth were loose. He winced then weirdly, although it hurt, kept probing the wobbly teeth, causing him more pain. He realized that the pain in his mouth was less searing than the pain in his hand. So, he kept pushing around his swollen gums.

The van turned and the road surface changed from smooth tarmac to something bumpy. The odd slosh and crunch of gravel told Jamal that they were now off the beaten track and the journey would soon come to an end. He had a feeling that he wasn't going to die. His knowledge was too important. He had protected the data with his own set of encryptions, making him the only person that could operate the program. He still had a trump card, although knowing how cold-blooded and sadistic Jongy and Errol were, he knew he was going to be in for some more pain.

True enough, the brakes made a squeal as the van came to a stop. It slid a bit on the gravel surface. The door clicked open in unison and then thumped shut, the springs of the van causing it to rock. The back door opened.

"Hey, man, I thought you would've thrown up by now," Jongy said. He grabbed him by the collar and Jamal snapped it back.

"Why do you have to keep pulling me about? Where the hell am I going to go?"

"You have a fair point, I guess. Old habits die hard, eh," Jongy said. He then launched himself at Jamal, grabbing him by the throat. His breath was fetid, a bit of jerky stuck to his teeth. "Don't you ever second guess me or think that your millennium bullshit works here, you are fuckin' two steps away from having your brain shot out, eh!"

Jamal looked at him, fighting the urge to capitulate, but he knew he still had that trump card.

"Will you fuck. I don't dance to the tune of the monkey. Take me to your organ grinder."

"Cunt!" Jongy snapped his head forward, headbutting Jamal in the face, reopening his previous injuries and knocking him clean out. Jongy dropped him on the van floor, his unconscious body lying awkwardly against the van's side. His mangled hand was too tempting, and Jongy stamped on it. "Disrespectful."

Jamal stirred, the pain invading his senses. His hand was horribly blue and the fingers pointed in different directions.

Jongy got out of the van. Errol was stood by the back, enjoying the view of the Cambridgeshire countryside. Spring had sprung in March. So green, he thought.

"Errol, don't just stand there eh, get the boy out of the back and get the bastard in the house, then empty the van. Get it set up in the garage. I'll go and speak to the boss."

A smartly-dressed man was walking across the courtyard in a gray fitted suit. Blond hair, mid-forties. Six foot five, and a back row kind of guy with hands like shovels.

"Jongy, eh, how's it going?" His South African accent was even stronger than Jongy's.

"Mr Veshausen, things got a little heated, my apologies eh, the kaffir accidentally killed his mother and then we had to dispatch the father. We brought the boy and all of his belongings."

"How did the mother die 'accidentally' when her head was being taken off? When are you going to stop defending that incompetent kaffir, and get rid of him. He's a liability to you. Which makes you a liability to me, eh."

Jongy was looking at the floor. He had no defence, Errol was stupid, but he still felt responsible for him.

Errol was helping Jamal out of the van and Veshausen clocked him.

"And holy fuckadoo, how the fuck did the boy get in that state? I said no drama." He walked over to Jamal, his face grisly and ghastly. His hand wrecked.

"He's going to need a doctor, and how will that happen?" Veshausen shook his head. "You're both a pair of monkeys, seriously, the money I pay you, I deserve better!"

Jongy swallowed, he hated being a disappointment. Errol looked at the view again, he didn't give a shit.

Jamal was helped into the house. The smell of a family home, and not the van, filled his nose. The kitchen was modern, high end. He was helped to a seat at the table. Veshausen took a seat opposite.

"Welcome, I first must apologize to you for your treatment at the hands of my–" He paused – "associates." Jamal dropped his head, a clotted gelatinous string of blood hanging from his mouth.

"Why?"

"I am sorry," Veshausen said.

"Why did you bring me here? For the right price, I would've driven here myself and done whatever you wanted me to do. Right now, your associates have killed my parents and messed me up. The only thing you have to do for me now is dig a shallow grave once I give up my software."

"You can go," Veshausen said to Jongy. Jongy practically clicked his heels, nodded his head and strode out of the kitchen. His head still down, Jamal's eyes watched the feet leave.

"They have their purpose," Veshausen said, getting up. He opened the fridge and removed some food and a bottle of soda.

"You need to eat, eh?"

He placed the food in front of Jamal and re-took his seat opposite.

"I accept your points about what has occurred, and I have already apologized. That will be the last time that I apologize to you." Veshausen pursed his lips and reached for his laptop. Opening it, he scrolled. "I've done my homework on you, Jamal. You're an interesting character. The criminal world's go-to guy for anything that requires a computer which, in today's world, means literally anything. The most interesting thing about you is that your parents died when you were young," he stopped, glanced at Jamal. "Those people my associates killed weren't your parents!" He returned to the screen.

"You bounced from foster home to foster home and had a difficult childhood. Yet you excelled in anything relating to science. A gifted genius, and thanks to the criminal underworld, you turned to crime to make your money. I get the people that you were living with fronted as your parents because you've been spinning a dark web in the physical world as well as the digital world. Am I in your ballpark?" Veshausen asked. He left it there, hanging in the air.

Jamal thought for a moment, how the hell did he get all that information? He's got me, but I still have the trump card.

His silence told Veshausen that he was right. He closed the lid of the laptop.

"Talk to me about the software. Is it true?" Veshausen asked

"I'm not saying a word until I have concessions and demands made. Just so you're aware, the software can't run without me. I've protected the algorithm."

"How?"

Jamal laughed. "You're right, I live in spun webs of deceit and sleight of hand. I knew the commercial value of this software to people like you, which is why I've ensured my safety."

"Tell me?"

Jamal picked up some food, placed it in his mouth. His lips were barely able to separate to get the morsel in, but the bigger problem was the chewing. Jamal winced. Veshausen winced as well. "We need to get a doctor to tend to your wounds. I know a man."

"That man being a bona fide medical professional?" Jamal asked.

"Of course. Tell me about your encryption." Veshausen pushed.

Jamal knew that Veshausen needed to know to keep him alive. Jongy or Errol would snuff him out at the earliest opportunity. Telling him everything was going to be in Jamal's best interest.

"The software has been deleted from the digital vaults of the CIA. There's no way to hide that. So, they will be looking."

"How does that impact me?" Veshausen asked.

"Well, if you do something silly, like make one million people run down Pall Mall naked, they'll get a whiff of it. Digitally, it doesn't exist. No one will find it, only the outside has the potential for it to be discovered."

"You say that you're the only one that can operate it, how is that? What's stopping us from getting my people to just copy you and then I get rid of you? Which I know is was you're thinking, eh." Veshausen leaned forward.

"I have bio encrypted everything. Even my keyboard for each keystroke will work by fingerprint recognition. My voice and facial movements are tracked by the camera and will only allow me to access the software, while biometric feedback is sent to a remote server, bouncing back the facial movement to confirm recognition. My heart is also monitored, constant EKG readings are a physiological fingerprint, we all have different cardiac signatures." Jamal took a sip from the soda.

"The hint of cold, sore throat, fluctuations in my normal

body temperature. My heart rate, if it's different, the software will shut down. The user then has ten minutes to biometrically log back in. If this doesn't happen, then my location, the location of the software, everything the software has done to date will be uploaded to the authorities and every single social media site on the planet."

Veshausen pondered. He nodded.

"That makes us business partners then."

He stopped there. Jamal considered what Veshausen had said.

"I want ten percent of whatever scam you're running, no negotiation."

Veshausen leaned in further, bringing his hands up to his chin in deep thought.

"And if I don't accept your terms?" Veshausen said.

Jamal leaned forward on his damaged hand – the wrist still had his smartwatch on. He held his arm out, the pain was excruciating, and the fingers were sickeningly disfigured. With his good hand, he hit the screen, the watch beeped and vibrated.

"What have you done?" Veshausen asked, suddenly becoming worried.

"You have five minutes, the CIA will be contacted by automation as well as the police of this location. Which will include the content of the software as well, if you check your cloud storage files, they will be littered with child porn."

Veshausen picked up his smartphone and started scrolling through.

"Even if they can't charge you with software infringement, because no doubt none of you are clever enough to have hacked it, and, of course, you will have already killed me in a fit of rage. But every person in your contacts, including any social media as well as the police, will know you're a pedophile." Jamal took another sip from the soda.

"Which means, in this country, you will face a minimum of ten years at Her Majesty's pleasure."

The realization of what Jamal had done shot across Veshausen's face, and Jongy came running in. "Boss, fuckin' hell!" He exclaimed, holding his phone.

"Very good," Veshausen said, scrolling through the thousands of porn images on his phone. "Very good."

"Tick fucking tock, Mr Veshausen," Jamal said. Jongy clocked the attitude, and was about to deal with it.

"Stop, Jongy." Jongy stopped with a look of amazement.

"Jamal, you have a deal. Twelve percent, I guarantee."

Jamal thought, two percent extra. Always the entrepreneur. In the legit street, he would've been devastating. But this deal was about to become sweeter.

"Now, it's your turn to tell me your plan," Jamal said.

Veshausen leaned back and thought for a moment.

"What I am about to tell you breaks national security, eh. My employer is a high-ranking government official who needs to, at this point, be kept secret." Veshausen stood, walked to the fridge. He pulled out a soda for himself, opened it and drank some. He belched violently.

"Heartburn," he said.

"You need to drink milk?" Jamal asked.

Veshausen paused, considered his comments. Then sat back down.

"I need to know what I'm getting into," Jamal said. He took some food, the pain slightly easing. Either the pain was getting better or he felt stronger because he understood the position he was in.

"I will need to speak to my employer first. You might suspect that this room is rigged with microphones and cameras." He motioned around the room.

"I did think about that, and can we consider that your employer is now my employer?" Jamal asked.

Veshausen thought, he nodded.

"I shall return in the morning, can I make sure that you don't give Jongy and Errol any bother?" He said while getting up.

"As long as they keep their distance, and that they go and get me pizza for my dinner."

"Jongy?" Jongy stiffened.

"Yes."

"Make sure that Jamal's needs are met, and please do not make him feel uncomfortable."

"Of course, Mr Veshausen." Jongy shot a glance at Jamal, he smiled back at him, making his piss boil inside.

"First, we need that doctor to come here and take care of you," Veshausen said.

"Who were those people that Laurel and Hardy killed?" Veshausen asked.

Jamal took some more food. "They were nobodies, people I hired for the front I live. You're right, My life is a tangled web, and that's how I like to keep it."

Jongy stepped forward.

"What is it, Jongy?" Veshausen asked.

"Where is the boy sleeping?"

"He'll sleep in the house, Jongy, where did you think he was going to sleep, eh?"

Jongy contemplated for a second. "Wouldn't he be better off in the garage, boss, under lock and key, eh?"

"He's not a prisoner, Jongy, your methods of bringing him to me were suspect to say the least." Veshausen looked at Jamal. "He'll be no trouble, will you?"

Jamal nodded.

"Go and get that doctor!"

4

Alex found the entrance to the club. It was late, and heels weren't her thing either. They were already biting the arches of her feet. She grabbed the wet wrought iron rail and head down the steps. Three men watched her come down, and she took extra care, one slip and she would have been on her ass at the bottom. Her Angel card that morning said she needed hope, and that the universe wanted her to have her heart's desire. As she clumped down the steps in her heels, the only hope she was feeling was agony. The card also told her to ask her angels for help in finding what she wanted. But she wasn't sure that being at a sex club was the best choice right now.

"Evening," said one of the guys. All three in black, the doormen. She suddenly felt even more nervous and queasy.

This was the tenth club Alex had been to. But the last nine had been under the guise of a police officer. Brandishing her warrant card and scoping the place out surreptitiously in the hope of finding her daughter.

This was all done given the nature of her last protagonist, Dale Broc – the sociopathic liver surgeon. He frequented clubs like this in the search of nubile young girls to dominate and use. Pragmatically, Alex felt that Devon was heading for that scene in a capacity Alex shuddered to think about.

Alex wasn't used to going out. No real social friends that

she could escape to, the clubs, oddly, seemed a great place to meet people that struck her as being honest and open.

"Hi, guys," Alex said.

"Just yourself then?" the same guy asked.

Alex looked over her shoulder. "I think so," she answered.

"It's a busy night in the club, you look after yourself. Any strife, look out for Alfie or Baz." He pointed to the two guys and they smiled. "They'll sort you out, okay? Take no nonsense either, remember, no means NO."

"I'll bear that in mind," Alex said. She felt good with tight jeans and a nice top. A little light makeup too. She remembered to show a bit of cleavage, and red heels that were to die for. Alex never really understood the heel thing, until she put them on. She strutted like she was in *The Devil Wears Prada*, she felt invincible.

She stepped into the doorway and entered the club. A small Chinese lady was sat on a stool behind a desk.

"Just the one?" She asked without looking up, flicking through a *TV Times*.

"Yes, thank you," Alex said, she felt the nerves singing at her clothes.

"Wanna towel?" The lady said.

"No, thank you."

The lady looked up. "You bin before?"

"Nope, first time, I brought my own," Alex said holding up a clean crisp white towel.

"Ahh, you clever girl, dressing room first on the left." She went back to reading her magazine.

Alex was told on a few occasions that when you go to a club, always take your own towel. The ones you get at a club are worn out, and often not cleaned properly. Plus, they're always a little too small for the women, making them more revealing. The row of off-white, chewing-gum colored towels paid dividends to that nugget of advice.

Alex entered the dressing room. It was small, and a couple who Alex took as a husband and wife were there, already in a state of nakedness. The woman had a broad Northern Ireland accent, it stood out to Alex as she had served multiple tours with the Royal Military Police in the province. Her husband was much shorter but well stacked. They looked good together.

"Evening," he said, looking up.

"Hi," Alex replied. Her mouth was dry. She wasn't sure if she should wait or just start getting undressed. He was stood, naked, scrolling through his phone.

"Switch it off, Ray, for fuck's sake, I'll bury you with that phone." Her accent was harsh, abrasive, but at the same time gentle. Alex liked it. The lady threw a glance at Alex, she held it, Alex too, they smiled. Ray looked over his shoulder, clocked Alex, he smiled and threw the phone in the locker before turning and walking out naked.

The girl quickly followed and Alex was alone. She stripped. When she got to her underwear she hesitated, what the hell am I doing here? She thought.

She took her bra off and then peeled off her panties. She caught a glance of herself in the full-length mirror. She was in good shape. She had originally feared that two children, Devon who was the younger, and her son, also at university, would have taken their toll on her body, but she kept herself fit. Her breasts were not too big but still had their shape, her waist tucked in, giving her the classic hourglass figure. She hated it, but Simon loved it. Simon, she thought. She paused at the open locker naked, feet cold on the wooden floor, and considered getting dressed and going home, but something was keeping her there.

She grabbed her towel, wrapped it around herself, covering her and then some, closed the locker and walked out.

The dressing room opened into a large space. Opulent

sofas and armchairs, separated by tall indoor ferns, made natural barriers, sectioning off the room into quieter spaces. Above the bar NO MEANS NO – NO EXCEPTIONS.

Alex got to the bar, took a seat. The barman came over, well, sort of. He was a twenty-something wearing only an apron saying DA BOSS on the front.

"Watcha drink?"

"Just a coke," Alex said.

"Leaded or unleaded?" he asked.

"Sorry," Alex said, looking confused.

He let out a laugh, "No, I'm sorry, diet or full fat?"

"Oh, I see what you did there, very funny, I need some sugar, give me the leaded."

"Coming right up, new face, first time?" he said while he brought a can up.

"Er yes, it is. Is there a glass coming?"

"Oh yes, sorry, most of the clientele here don't bother, just go for the can, I like a woman with class. Are you here to play?" he asked.

"Not really, I'm here to check things out, not sure if it's my thing, really," Alex said, pouring her own drink while he leaned against the bar watching.

"Shame, you're hot," he said.

Is this dude for real? He's barely out of school, she thought. "Thanks."

Alex turned on the stool. The couch in the corner was occupied by three men and one woman, she was draped over them, her head bobbing, one of the men clearly enjoying the action while the other two just sat and chatted. On another sofa was a couple, her straddled, hips gyrating, the guy's head resting back.

She turned back. "What's the deal here, can you give me a guided tour, it seems a big place but there doesn't seem to be anyone here?"

"You're joking, right? The place is heaving. There must be at least 100 people here, squirrelled away in the private rooms, gloryhole rooms. The BDSM suite. We also have the swarm on tonight."

"The swarm?" Alex asked.

"Yeah, I've done it once. It's awesome, I might do it again tonight, that's if my boss let me, but I can show you around – only take five minutes to get your bearings?"

"Cool." Alex jumped off the stool, and filed in behind.

"I'm Tom, by the way."

"Alex, I'm Alex. You seem very young to be here?"

"I'm at uni here, but I grew up around the scene. My parents were, I mean, still are, into swinging, so it doesn't bother me. I'm looking for my own pet."

"Pet?" Alex asked.

"Yeah, I'm a Dom, so yeah, always on the lookout for a sex pet."

"What constitutes a sex pet then?" Alex said.

"Well, a young nubile girl that's very submissive and wants to be used, used sexually that is."

Alex was feeling a little shocked. She had read up about the sex scene, but the scene was become like what the Zookeeper had talked about when she met him in prison. The sex scene was evolving at such an alarming rate, the need for labels was insatiable.

"Is there such a thing?" Alex asked.

"This is the gloryhole room, bit busy in there." Alex peered in, the room was packed with a combination of women and men. The next room was the freestyle room – it was a series of beds where people were swapping and sharing each other, again the room was rammed. Hardcore hetero-sexual pornography was being screened on a projector.

Tom carried on, "Yeah, I mean, I've had two girls serve me."

"At the same time?" Alex asked.

"Well, kind of, they sort of overlapped. I'd sit for hours watching them play with each other, kinda hot, right?"

"If you say so, Tom," Alex said, furrowing her brow.

"This is the wet room, not a piss room. There are a couple of hot tubs, and a sauna, the steam room is more than a little hot, if you see what I mean."

Alex peered in. There were four people chatting obliviously to what was happening opposite them. Two women 69ing on the bench, dripping in sweat, their bodies glistening in the light. "Shut the fucking door!" the woman on the bottom shouted, "it's bloody draughty."

Tom pulled Alex away, almost losing her towel. "Oops," Tom said, helping her secure the towel, his hand lingering for longer than it should.

"The next room is normally called the Pit, but today it's called the Swarm."

Tom opened the door, and Alex was hit with the smell. It was pungent. Hot, moist. She had to breathe slowly through her mouth so as not to cough. Her lungs had to acclimatize to the sudden change in atmosphere.

"Hey, beautiful," said a tall, muscular Afro-Caribbean man with long dreadlocks. Also naked. Bangles on both wrists, rings on every finger.

"This is Tray, he looks after the swarm."

"That I do, Tom." His smile was wide and welcoming.

"Would you like to enter the swarm with me, darlin'?" he said.

Alex felt Tom's hand push the small of her back, and she didn't fight it. She felt weirdly at peace in the room.

Alex nodded.

"This is Alex, Tray. First timer."

"Oh." Tray laughed. "You're gonna love the swarm darlin', just go with it, and open yourself to the spirits, they will entice you to sexual oblivion, darlin'." He gently curled his arm around her, Alex felt safe, and she walked with him. Her heart was racing, pumping in her chest and neck, and she could feel herself perspire. The air was heavy, and the smell was amazing. The room was dark apart from low red lights casting shadows. The music was low. A deep drum beat.

"What's the music?"

"What's that, me darlin'?"

Alex checked herself, she had to raise her voice. "The music, what is it?"

"Ahh, these are Native Alpha drums that get your conscious mind onto a theta wave, runs at 432 megahertz, opens the inner chakras and gets you sexually charged. Access your inhibitions, darlin', it means you can access your sexuality as a whole."

Tray guided Alex over to a brass bowl – smoke was billowing out of it. "Place your head over the bowl and breathe deeply, me darlin'."

Alex complied. Narcissus, she recognized the smell, the other was neroli oil, but she wasn't sure of the other note. The fourth was the unmistakable scent of cannabis, the smoke billowed into Alex's face, she breathed in, and again, and then again. She felt her sensations shift. Her thoughts went from the structure, and order, to being carefree. She bent in again. The smell was intoxicating. The rhythm of the drums caused her legs to sway. The chanting of the Buddhist monks in the background of the music vibrated through her body, she leaned in again and breathed in. She felt her towel slide off her body. The euphoria was spreading through her like a warm glow. She leaned in again, more smoke. She kinda heard Tray speak, but she ignored it, her face still in the smoke. She felt his strong hands around her waist.

"Come with me, darlin'." He gently pulled her away, Alex's head lolled. She felt his body against hers. She had the urge to touch him. He didn't complain, he just gently pulled her hands down by her side.

Alex looked down where she stood. The mass of bodies below her squirming together. It was ethereal, exquisite. Alex's conscious mind would never have allowed this, but she surrendered. At that moment, her conscious mind gave in to the sensations that she was feeling. Tray started rubbing her back with warm oil. In a trance-like state, she enjoyed the big Caribbean tonic, he turned her and continued to wipe her breasts, legs, abdomen. He placed his hands over her vagina. Her head lolled back, his strong hands catching her unsteadiness. Alex was wet, the man's hands strong and powerful on her femininity, she parted her legs to invite him in further.

"Oh no, darlin', I ain't here for that, you go find that in the swarm." His smile was broad and friendly.

He made her sit on the warm wet floor, and gently guided her into the swarm of people. Her body disappeared into the abyss in sexual ecstasy. She drifted in and out of conciseness, she felt women's vaginas, men's penis's, breast of varying shapes, sizes and softness. Her femininity was probed. Her clitoris fondled, rubbed, kissed, licked, sucked. She came twice, her body wracking in complete ecstasy. Then she found the lips of a woman, her breath sweet and warm. Her lips were full, and her tongue probed her mouth. Fireworks exploded in her head, she gushed between her legs as the women inserted her fingers into her vagina. The drumming and chanting were coursing through Alex like electricity. She hadn't experienced anything so profound, the only people in the world right now were Alex and the mystery woman. She felt a oneness she had never felt before. It was as though the rest of her body had been missing, and at that moment, she was complete. She didn't want this moment to end, ever.

Then suddenly it was over. Alex thought that the whole time was about ten minutes. In fact, two full hours had gone by as people started filing out of the pit.

The narcotics and essential oils wearing off, Alex suddenly felt awkward. She brought her knees up as soon as they became free from the tangled mess of limbs and bodies. She sat waiting. The woman in the dressing room came over, sat next to her. Alex instantly recognised the smell. It was the women that Alex had kissed for so long.

"I thought it was you," said the strong Irish-accented women. She was stunningly beautiful, her body muscular and toned. "What was that all about? Bejesus, I've never been kissed like that."

Alex smiled, cocked her head and rested it on her hands. She shrugged, feeling a little coy.

"Come, let's go for a shower and a drink."

The woman helped Alex up and they followed the crowd into the shower room. The shower was communal, it didn't matter though. People were chatting and counting the two hours in the swarm.

Alex got under the free showerhead, the warm water rinsing the sex and oil off her. She didn't feel anything other than exuberance to what had just happened. Her inner glow was blazing. She then felt hands on her, the smell of lavender filled her nose.

She turned, the Irish lady was washing her down. She stopped, looked at Alex. "Do you mind if I do this?" she asked.

Alex shook her head and turned. She loved the connection. This connection was different. In the swarm, the feeling was like dynamite, right now, the feeling was like a low current of electricity running through her body every time the woman touched her.

The woman washed her down, her hands cleaning every inch of her, even her feet and toes. It was as though she couldn't get enough of Alex.

"Swap," said the lady. Alex jolted out of the moment, took the soap. The lady turned, grabbed the back of her long hair and moved it to one side. Alex started to clean her, the low current running through her again. Her tummy doing somersaults every time she felt it. She copied the Irish women. When finished, they stood staring at each other, it took a few moments for them to realize that the room was empty.

The Irish women looked about, then smiled at Alex. Alex could feel her penetrate into her soul, she felt as though she had found something very precious in her life, it was inexplicable. Beyond rationalization, yet it felt so right and perfect.

The woman smiled again, no words needed to be said, and she guided Alex over to a tiled ledge coming out of the shower wall. Sitting Alex down, the women kneeled at her knees. She placed both hands on them, still smiling at Alex, right in the eye. Not even Simon looked at her like that. Alex didn't need any encouragement. She had never had sex with another woman. She parted her legs and shifted her bottom so she could lean back. "Sweet Jesus, just look at that, it's so beautiful," the women said, and then buried her head between Alex's legs.

5

Alex skirted around the women who had already taken a seat at the bar. Tom was stood waiting to take the order.

He smiled. "How was it, Alex?"

"Yeah." She looked at the lady, who was smiling too. "It was definitely something I enjoyed."

She looked at the lady again, their stares spanning the rifts in time. Time stood still as she stared into the emerald eyes of this women she had just met and with who she had had the most erotic, sensual sexual experience of her life. Alex's nerve endings were tingling.

"I don't even know your name," Alex said.

"Siobhan, my name's Siobhan, and you?"

"Alex." The staring continued. Siobhan was resting an elbow on the bar surface, chin on her palm, just looking. Smiling like they were reconnected long lost friends. The connection unfathomable and beautiful.

"Wow, some energy here, ladies," Tom said, breaking the connection. Siobhan burrowed under Alex's towel and rested a hand on her bare leg. The low current was fizzing exquisitely on the touch, travelling all the way up the leg, making Alex's heart swell. She flushed.

"You feel that?" Siobhan asked.

"Yeah, I do, what is that?" Alex responded.

"I dunno, I never felt it before," Siobhan's accent was deep, harsh, yet reinforced with a gentleness. Alex had always loved the northern Irish accent, especially in women. She combed through her memories, she had never had feeling towards another women before. She didn't even feel this connected to Simon after so many years of marriage.

"Two cokes, leaded, Tom." Siobhan ordered.

"Coming up."

Alex placed both hands on Siobhan's knees. "Tell me everything about you, I just need to know everything about you. I mean, we just had sex, something I've never done before, I have this burning need to know everything about you."

Siobhan took a drink, and squeezed Alex's leg. "Well, I'm married, you saw my husband Ray, we have a couple of kids. I met Ray when he was in the forces in Belfast."

Siobhan continued speaking, and the time just flew by, it didn't matter. They told each other everything. Like a catch-up, yet they had never met before. People came and went from the bar, at one point the bar was very busy but the space they occupied had its own exclusion zone. Even when Ray came up for a beer, he didn't bother them. They chatted, laughed, cried. They became entwined in each other.

"So, what's the deal between you and your husband?"

"We're very promiscuous, he sees me as a hotwife." Alex frowned. She had heard the term before but didn't really understand it.

Siophan noticed her confusion. "The lifestyle has so many subgenres and labels even I find it hard to keep up."

"What is it?"

Siobhan took a drink.

"Well, I get to have sex with whomever I choose, I have a string of boyfriends."

"Isn't that a bit complicated? I mean, your husband is here having sex with other women, not sure I could do that."

"Ray is the most amazing husband, lover, father and provider. He's a strong man, so he is," she paused and leaned forward. "The trouble is with Ray, there's something I can't give him."

Alex thought for a moment, she couldn't think of anything. Siobhan was gorgeous, sexy and willing to do anything. She broke Alex's train of thought and motioned behind her. Alex turned – Ray was chatting amongst some guys, all naked.

"I still don't get it," Alex said.

Siophan laughed, almost more of a giggle. "The one thing Ray wants and I can't give to him is a dick up the arse, so it is."

Alex jolted, turned and looked, she noticed Ray's hand resting on the thigh of another man.

"Oh shit, your husband's gay?" Alex thought for a moment. "Oh."

"I know, right? So, we have an open relationship. Some of my boyfriends are bi, so they get both Ray and myself. It's actually very liberating."

"And us? What's the deal with us? Have you done it with a women before?"

Siobhan thought for a moment. "No, a couple of liaisons in a swingers club up north, but nothing like we have." She smiled at Alex. "Tonight was, I mean IS, something special, I've never experienced that before."

"Does that make us lesbians?"

"Sweet Jesus, no it doesn't, the big man up there won't allow a God-fearing woman like me be a *lezzer* now."

"So, are you a cup or a plate?" Alex asked. Siobhan stopped, stared back in disbelief then burst out laughing. "I haven't heard that for years, Alex, holy shit that made my heart glow."

She took a drink. "You may not be pleased to know, but I'm a cup. But I don't follow the cloth, the big man upstairs needs to sort his own shit out before he judges my arse."

Alex thoughts went back to Londonderry, the Bogside. The kids running around would ask the soldiers if they were cups or plates. Cup meaning Catholic and plate meaning Protestant. In the bogside, if you weren't a cup, then you were either spat at, bricked or petrol bombed.

"This thing we have," Alex asked, "what is it?"

Siobhan pulled a face. "Back to the labels and lifestyle genres, this, Alex, is called pansexuality."

"Oh, we're pansexual?"

"Umm, yeah, I know you're gonna ask, lovely, so I'm gonna tell ye."

Alex took a drink, she felt a chill but it didn't matter, time meant nothing right now.

"With bisexuality, you are sexually attracted to either men or women, it's physical thing. Ray is a gay man, anything to do with my vagina makes him feel yucky, how the hell we managed to have kids is a miracle in itself, fucking me was like you eating your least favorite food, it's off putting, so it is. With pansexuality, you love the person irrespective of their sexual presence or being. That's what we have, Alex."

"Amen to that," Tom said, interrupting the conversation.

"Any chance of a three-way with you gorgeous women?"

Alex and Siobhan looked at each other, paused then burst out laughing. Siobhan stood, pulled her towel off. "Take a good look, Tom, place this body in your spank bank, cos' you're the wrong color for this pussy." Her finger tapping a small tattoo on her knicker line. The ace of spades.

Alex leaned in to look closer, the artwork intricate, the letter 'B' dominated the centre of the tattoo.

"What's the tattoo mean?" Alex asked.

"Means she only loves the BBC," Tom said.

Siobhan's body was glorious, Alex felt herself tighten, her abs rippled, her thigh muscles flexed. So unashamed of her body, and why not? Alex would walk around naked, looking like that.

"BBC?" Alex asked.

"Big black cock," Tom said with a laugh.

Siobhan nodded. "Yep, I only slide for a black man, so I do." She paused. "And you, of course," Siobhan said laughing. Alex felt the urge to pull her, and hold her, Siobhan saw it. "You can touch me, Alex." Nervously, she slid her hands around her tight waist and pulled her in. She felt right, her smell was intoxicating. She had never been sexual with another woman. Fancied them – but then everyone does.

Siobhan kissed Alex's neck, Tom, feeling awkward, moved on to another couple at the bar.

The music playing was a well-known ballad, Alex had heard it before. But not really knowing the tune, they swayed, the warmth of the embrace causing that low current to fizz between them. Alex realized that she didn't listen to music so much anymore. She didn't know what her favorite film was. She didn't know who was number one in the charts today. Alex thought about her children, she didn't know what they were into. Fuck what was Simon into? She thought. Outside of work, Alex thoughts knew nothing. She started to weep, a long inhale told Siobhan that Alex was crying. Instinctively, she held her closer. Her nakedness giving Alex strength, energy and comfort. Alex contoured to the muscular physique of Siobhan. Siobhan swayed, one hand pulling her in close by the small of her back and the other caressing the nape of her neck.

"Hey, baby," Siobhan soothed. It caused Siobhan to stop momentarily, which Alex reacted to, Siobhan glanced it off. She meant what she said. She was falling for Alex big time, in a way she had never anticipated.

"What's up, why are you crying?"

Alex took a long drink, then regaled her with everything. She left nothing out. Down to the unpleasant truth about Broc, what he had done and Devon her daughter. She sobbed through the breaking up of her union with Simon. Siobhan, pulling her towel over, wrapped herself tightly, bringing her supple legs up to the bar stool and resting her chin on her knees.

"None of this is your fault, baby." That word again. Alex liked it. She felt safe when Siobhan said it. It felt as though she was being loved and taken care of for the first time, someone else to look after Alex instead of her looking after the world.

Alex went through her new role within the newly formed B5 Division. Their focus on healthcare-related crimes globally had meant she needed to start taking time for herself. Hence why she was now in the club, finding herself.

Siobhan noted the pentagram ring on Alex's left hand.

"You follow the Craft, Alex?" Siobhan asked.

She pulled her hand away. Alex kicked herself for not removing the ring. She kept her faith to herself. Jenny, the therapist, was the only other person that really knew.

Siobhan took her hand back, ran her thumb over the crown of the ring, feeling the engraved pentagram. "You asked if I was a cup or a plate. I was brought up as a Catholic but found my true calling in my late teens, so I did, me granny came to me one evening, Jesus, it was as though she was in the room. I follow the Craft, Alex, I'm a hedge-witch and I consider myself a pagan."

Alex felt her mouth open. The universe was certainly working in Alex's favor tonight.

"I think our meeting is meant to be Siobhan, I don't think our coming together was by accident."

"I don't believe in coincidences, baby," she said, sliding off the stool and wrapping her arms around Alex.

Alex smiled, kissed her. "I always say that to my guys in the team, there's never a coincidence with anything."

Alex needed to go to the ladies. "I'll be back, need to go to the loo."

"Don't be too long, baby, or I'll come and get you."

Alex laughed and jumped off the stool. She almost skipped to the toilet, her heart racing. She was falling too, she just didn't realize it at this point.

As she approached the bar again, Siobhan was talking to a six foot five black guy. He was enormous. Siobhan knew him, she was familiar to that guy. Alex slowed. She didn't want to intrude, feeling awkward. The disappointment crept through her, the evening was now done, she only goes with BBC, she thought.

She stopped, looked at the bar, watching the reflection of the two in the mirror. Alex felt like a knife had been wedged between her and Siobhan. Am I jealous? Get a grip, she said to herself.

She was miles away in her thoughts when she clocked her name was being called, suddenly Alex felt embarrassed.

"Alex, Earth to Alex, Earth to Alex," said the Irish voice. Alex turned, smiling, "Come, meet one of my boyfriends."

Alex walked over, the guy was wearing just one of the small towels provided by the club. It was barely covering his groin. His chest came to Alex's eye line, the pecs rippled.

"Alex, this is Zaff, remember when I told you about my boyfriends? Zaff is one of them."

"How do you do?" said the booming American voice.

Alex felt dwarfed by the man. "How do you do?" she replied, and shook his enormous hand.

"Zaff and I are going to go have some fun." Alex thought that this was it now, time to go home. Siobhan clocked the look on Alex's face. There was an awkward silence as Siobhan weighed up her options.

"I said to Zaff that I'll only go to one of the rooms if you can come to," Siobhan said. Zaff was smiling down at Alex, two hot women for the price of one, his hopes dashed at the finishing post. "But I don't think I'm ready to share her, Zaff, can we do a rain check?"

Alex smiled. "I'm okay if you guys want to play."

Siobhan shook her head. "Go find some other pussy, Zaff, my evening is all tied up, so it is!"

Zaff shrugged, he bent and kissed Alex on the cheek. "Pleasure to meet you, Ma'am," he turned and grabbed Siobhan by the back of the head, drawing her in and kissing her on the lips. "Later, babes," and then he was gone.

They talked some more, the night drawing in before they knew it. Later, they were hailing a cab together and heading to Vauxhall and Alex's apartment overlooking the Thames.

6

"Alex, wake up." Alex opened her eyes and took a second to get her bearings. She was in her apartment, the window was open, and she could hear the traffic moving along the Albert Embankment. The busy road that ran parallel from Vauxhall Bridge Station to Tommy's roundabout. A stone's throw from the Houses of Parliament and an even smaller throw to her new office in the MI5 building and the newly-formed B5 Division of SIS. Alex thought of the night before. She had never climaxed so many times in one night, her loins tightened at the memory – although they were sore.

She turned and saw Siobhan, but then heard a noise coming from the front room.

Siobhan went to speak, Alex grabbed her mouth with her hand. "Shut up!" Alex hissed, Siobhan furrowed her brow, not used to being spoken to like that. She tried to shake free, Alex just squeezed harder. "Shut up," she repeated.

Her free hand reached behind her, the drawer opened silently. Not by accident, but design. Alex felt the cold steel of her Glock P6 9mm service pistol. She brought it around and Siobhan's face went from indignation to utter panic. Alex squeezed Siobhan's face harder. She raised a thumb and pushed the pistol against the top slide, exposing the chamber. Alex sighed in relief – there was a round up the spout.

"I need you to be quiet, don't move or say a fucking word, do you understand?"

Siobhan nodded, and Alex slowly released her face, leaving red marks behind. Siobhan went to speak, but Alex grabbed her face again. "I said don't say a word, seriously!"

Siobhan nodded again, she muffled an agreement against Alex's hand.

Alex released, slid her lithe body out of the bed, thinking that she could've done without being naked. She clocked her joggers, quickly threw her feet in them, and jumped up. She searched quickly for a top, but she could only find Siobhan's. A bit tight, but it worked. She shunned Siobhan, who pulled the covers over her head, pale with fright.

Alex stood behind the door and crouched. The door flew open and in walked a six-foot-something man. A tee shirt, jeans and a pair of Timberlands, along with a Glock P6 holstered in the back holster. Alex cracked him on the head and kicked the back of the knee out, causing his muscular frame to collapse. Siobhan, thinking quickly, reached for a copy of the complete works of Sherlock Holmes – 2000 page tome of Arthur Conan Doyle's work on the favorite detective – it weighed almost four kilos. She smacked him square in the face with it, knocking him out cold.

Alex looked down. "Shit."

"What do you mean 'shit'? we should be high fiving and calling the police, right?"

"It's Simon Broadstone, my boss."

Siobhan scrambled to the edge of the bed, her naked body exposed. She peered over the end of the bed and saw the man prostrate on the floor. "Shit," she echoed.

"Double shit," Alex said. She positioned him in the recovery position and felt for his pulse. His hand suddenly came from nowhere and grabbed Alex, he then pivoted on the floor, bringing his legs up and trapping Alex in the vice-like grip of his legs. She choked. Siobhan then realized that he had also pulled his Glock out, and she was now staring down the barrel of Broadstone's service revolver.

"You have five seconds to identify yourself, or do I have to shoot you?" Siobhan gripped the gun in utter panic.

Simon felt the submissive wrestler's surrender tap on his sides. He looked down and realized that it was Alex. He released.

Alex pulled away choking, Siobhan sat up on her knees, still naked. Simon stood up, shaking his head.

"What the fuck is going on here?" he demanded.

"Seriously, what the hell are you doing coming into Alex's apartment?" Siobhan demanded in turn.

Simon turned and looked, she was still naked, sat on her knees and her hands on her hips with an accusational face.

Simon turned to Alex, paused and waited. Alex smiled.

"It's my apartment, and a psychopath is on the warpath for one of my employees, and that very employee went off grid for more than twelve hours, and then is late by thirty minutes for work. I think that justifies me entering this apartment thinking that I'm going to find a struggle and a dead body." Simon left his explanation hanging in the air. "And with the greatest of respect, madam, who fuck are you?"

Siobhan shifted uneasily on her knees. Finally remembering that she was still naked. She pulled the quilt up in a pathetic attempt to cover her modesty.

"Oh, don't bother covering yourself on my account, I've already seen all of you." Simon sat on the edge of the bed. He turned and picked up the book that had hit him earlier. "Shit, that hurt!"

Alex got up. "Sorry, Simon." She sat on the bed next to him, Siobhan still kneeling and trying to cover herself up.

"Sorry, Simon!" Siobhan echoed meekly.

He looked at her. "You had us worried, Alex, Ricky is searching every possible scenario on his computer." He patted her. "You really had me worried," he repeated.

"Sorry, boss, I won't do it again."

"I hope you do," said the Irish voice behind them. They both turned.

Simon turned to Alex. "What is this?"

"It's complicated," Alex said.

"Aye, it's complicated, but I'm sure she will fill you in," Siobhan said smiling, letting the quilt drop, exposing her perfect breasts. Simon couldn't fight the hormones and enzymes in his body to catch a quick glimpse at the loveliness of this Irish women sat without a stitch on Alex's bed, he shuddered to think what had gone on.

Alex reached and pulled the quilt back up, Siobhan throwing a cold glance at Alex, Alex returning it.

"I'll put the kettle on," Simon said. He got up and walked out the room.

"He so fuckin' fancies you Alex, oh my freakin' God," Siobhan babbled, jumping up and down on the soft bed.

"Shut up, no way," Alex said.

"Aye he so does, and why not, he's gorgeous, so he is." Siobhan paused to look at Alex, then looked at the door, looked at Alex again and smiled. Alex figured out what she was thinking immediately.

"Er, no chance, forget it, we, as in you and I, are not fucking my boss."

Siobhan pulled a face.

"Not a chance in Hell is that going to happen."

Simon walked in carrying a tray. Three cups, milk, sugar and the coffee pot. The smell of coffee suddenly hit the women's noses.

"Not a chance for what?" Simon said.

"Nothing," Alex said sheepishly.

"She said, not a chance that we three-way you right here and now," Siobhan said.

It hung in the air awkwardly, Alex firing daggers at Siobhan.

Simon cut the silence. "I don't think so, I had a late night, and I'm a little sore, maybe another time."

Both Alex and Siobhan fell about laughing.

On the side table Simon played mum, pouring the coffee. He sat on the bed, crossed his legs, and formally introduced himself to Siobhan. They talked about Derry, the struggles, her experiences and why she was now living in England. He questioned her about her wedding ring and what both her and Alex got up to, Siobhan being happy to share. She stayed lying on the bed face down and naked, chatting to Simon while Alex went about getting showered and dressed.

Alex came out of the bathroom, tight jeans tucked into the calf-length 'door-kicking' boots she loved wearing. Tight tee shirt that read GANGSTA-ish tucked in. She grabbed her leather jacket and slid her holster in the side of her jeans.

She turned and faced both of them. They were watching intently. Simon was inert, while Siobhan was slowly licking her lips, undressing Alex all over again.

Siobhan felt Simon's finger under her chin, and he pushed the chin back up into position, while Siobhan started to chuckle.

"Ready?" Alex asked Simon.

"Yep, let's go, I will fill you in on the way to the SIS." SIS was the name of the secret service building at Vauxhall Bridge, 150 meters down the road from where Alex lived.

In the front room, Siobhan came out, still with no clothes on. She looked good in the cold light of day. Alex's heart skipped a beat every time she saw her. She had wondered when they got home if there would've been an element of regret, trauma, horror when she woke up and got her game face on? But there was nothing. She could feel her presence, it felt nice, warm and enchanting. She needed to speak to Jenny sooner rather than later about it because she couldn't get her head around the last twelve hours.

Simon grabbed his jacket, but then stopped, and again glanced over Alex and Siobhan. They were just looking at each other, the silence becoming crowded for Simon.

"I'll meet you outside, Alex." He paused, his phone ringing. "Broadstone?" he answered.

Simon walked out. "Yeah, I found her, she overslept, we're…" The door closed.

"Will you be here when I get back?"

"Probably not," Siobhan said, walking up to Alex.

Alex pulled a face and Siobhan cupped it. "Call me when you're done at work, I can be here in thirty minutes, I will see you tonight, but something's telling me you might not be free?" Siobhan motioned to the closed door Simon had walked through.

Alex glanced over her shoulder, turned back. She kissed Siobhan, her guts twisting like she was going over a hump-back bridge, heart instantly beating faster. Siobhan felt it.

"I'll text you as soon as I'm free, Siobhan."

"I'll drop everything and come, I feel we have so much to do, I don't want this to end." Siobhan said, her tone soft with a crack of emotion on the inflection – she meant it.

Alex looked around the room. "You don't have to rush out the door, get to know me by rifling through my things?" Smiling, Alex couldn't believe that she had invited her to do such a thing. She had only met her last night.

"I plan to, I saw you having eggs and avocados. I'll make breakfast, search through your things and leave my scent on everything."

Alex smiled, it made her feel warm knowing that.

"Any sex toys? I'm still turned on from last night." Siobhan said.

"Nope, I'm a clean-living girl."

"Oh, we'll have to do something about that, I'll bring some the next time I come, I've got tons, so I have."

"I'd like that," Alex said.

There was a knock at the door.

"Got to go."

The door opened. "Alex, come on." Broadstone's tone and face had changed – she really needed to go!

"Coming."

Alex turned, she walked to the door, and took one final glance over her shoulder before disappearing.

Both Alex and Simon got outside. The cold air nipped at Alex's ears immediately, it was March but there had been a frost.

Simon stopped. "I don't know what the fuck that was in there, but I felt a bit ambushed, Alex, you know you're being protected right now, losing your digital signal and meeting another woman is not cricket."

"Sorry Simon." Alex was still smiling

"She looks good on you."

Alex brushed off the bollocking, looked puzzled. "How so?" Alex asked.

"I don't know, but you both look amazing together, she a feisty one. I don't think you're going to be able to tame her."

Alex watched the barge float by on the Thames, seagulls circling over it. "I hope not."

Simon smiled. "You know with what's going on, I need to address a lack of refinement and ask of her provenance?" Raising his eyebrows, Alex turned to look at him back.

She fished into her pocket. "I spoke to her already. She's put everything about her on this. Alex handed him a note, he pulled his phone, took a photo, found Ricky's number and pushed send.

"She kind of knows what you're doing?"

"Yeah." They started walking.

"She's okay with it?"

Alex shrugged. "I guess, listen, Simon, I don't know what it is, so don't ask."

Simon stopped again. "I would never pry, but your safety and the safety of your family is paramount to me. You're in the crosshairs of Dale Broc, and he's still not found."

Alex shuddered. The memory was still too raw, she teetered on the verge of isolating her emotions every time she thought of the whole event, including the leaving of her husband. A shining light had come into her conscious through Siobhan. Each time her mind wandered, the thought of this, when they had met, and it tethered her to reality and the white light of good.

"We have a job on, by the way."

"Oh?" Alex said, coming back to the job.

"The Yanks have been on the blower. They wanted a meeting at oh-my-God o'clock this morning. They don't really care about the time difference."

"What's up?"

They started walking again with pace in their gait. They were within sight of the SIS building.

"CIA, something about software thing gone missing."

"Software, what's that got to do with B5?"

"Not sure, they said it was above top secret, which is why it's been bounced to us."

Alex's phone went off with a message from Siobhan. She clicked it open, Siobhan was standing in front of the full-length mirror in Alex's bedroom wearing a pair of Alex's panties and bra set. You wear this? Followed by an unhappy emoji face.

Alex snapped her phone closed.

They entered the building – another message. Siobhan, Alex clicked it open, what do you think? A picture of Siobhan naked in a pair of Alex's high heels. Another message dropped in, the shoes that is, babes. Alex smiled, she hit reply. Gorgeous. A heart emoji bounced back.

"Something you want to share?" Simon asked.

"I don't think so," Alex said, smiling into her phone.

7

Jamal was busy tidying up the connections to the array of screen and computers around him. He felt more at home around the hardware than being around people.

He was the first to hear the tires of the BMW crunch up the drive. There were three people in the car, one of who was Mr Veshausen. He was the first to exit the car. He pivoted and opened the rear car door, the suited man got out, tall, slim and very recognizable. Jamal leaned against the window frame of the garage, pulling his phone out and hitting search on Google.

Cabinet ministers, he typed. The top search came up with all the current ministers, and he scrolled with his thumb until he got to the person he thought he recognized. Squinting towards the car while waiting for the screen to render, his memory wasn't working quicker than Google and his android phone.

Jeffrey Brunt, Minister for Health – the picture was unmistakable. What the fuck is the Health Secretary doing here? Jamal thought. The door to the garage opened, and Jongy entered the room, making the pain sear through Jamal's hand and travel up his arm.

"Hey, half-chat, your boss has arrived, time to get yourself in order."

"Don't call me that."

Jongy walked over to where Jamal was standing, he looked out of the window and saw what Jamal could see. "I'll call you what I damn well like you dirty little fucker, eh." He grabbed Jamal by the throat and squeezed. His grip was strong, and his other hand grabbed the bandaged hand, making Jamal gasp.

"You might 'ave convinced the boss about your allegiance, but let me tell you something half-chat, eh, you're the wrong fuckin' color to get into bed with my people. You sub-human."

Jamal started to choke and gasp for air, his voice raspy and quiet, the oxygen fast depleting in his body. Jongy brought his face closer. "Here me now you little fuckin' raghead, when the boss is finished wit' you, you'll be my little whipping boi, verstaan." Jongy threw Jamal against the window frame, Jamal choking for air and rubbing his tender throat. Jamal eyed the South African as he waltzed out of the room. He stopped at the door, turned and pointed his fingers at Jamal, pretending it was a gun, and fired. "Hurry now." He was gone.

Jamal sank to his knees, searching through his mind. He knew that Jongy would be gunning for him at the earliest opportunity, so there was no time to waste.

Minutes later, Jamal heard footsteps. The door burst open and in walked Mr Veshausen, followed by who Jamal believed to be the current Health Minister.

"Jamal, may I have the honor of introducing you to Mr Jeffrey Blunt MP, the Secretary of Health to the current parliament, eh."

Jeffrey Blunt walked in and offered his hand to Jamal.

"I've heard a lot about you, Jamal." Jamal pretended to be surprised.

"Sir, to what do I owe this honour?"

"Please call me Jeffrey, I'm not here on parliamentary business."

"Oh," said Jamal.

"No, I'm here on something completely different."

Blunt looked around the room, saw a chair and pulled it over. The garage was clean and tidy, but it was still a garage. He sat and invited Jamal to sit too.

"Mr Veshausen, would you mind awfully if you could get one of your men to organize some tea?"

Veshausen clicked his heels and walked out of the room.

"Now, I've heard so much about you, Jamal, which isn't your real name, is that correct?"

Jamal sat, he nodded. "Sir, can I…" he was stopped.

"Please, I have to insist that you call my by my first name, Jamal, I must remind you that I'm here as a friend."

Jamal sat back and rubbed his eyes, he didn't really know what to make of this moment. Forcibly removed from his home, the people he paid to look after him murdered in front of him, and now he was sitting in front of the Health Secretary, who was insisting that he not be thought of as the Health Secretary.

"I'm confused." Jamal stated.

"There's no need to be confused, Jamal."

"What do you want from me?" he asked.

"That's very simple, my dear boy" Blunt's public schooling was evident. He sat, flicked fluff from the top of his leg and crossed his legs like a woman.

"Ask me anything you want."

"Can I leave?"

Blunt laughed. "No, you can't."

"Why?" Jamal wasn't laughing.

"Because I need you for something, and when you have done it for me, and you're as complicit in the endeavour as I, then you may leave."

"And what is it that you want me to do?" They were interrupted by Errol coming into the garage, pushing a silver service trolley. A teapot and all the paraphernalia needed for cream tea were loaded on to it, and Errol's shoes scraped along the concrete floor, leaving a trail in the dust.

Blunt looked over, and then waited for Errol to finish. Errol then stood waiting.

"You can leave," Blunt said to the Zulu, and he waited for the door to close.

"What I need you to do is very simple, my dear boy, I need you to use that software you have stolen to help thin out the population."

Jamal stopped, he felt like he really needed to dial in and fully understand what the Health Secretary was talking about.

Blunt laughed, his laugh deep and sinister, which didn't seem to match his appearance at all. Tall, thin, and toad-like in his attitude. The entire health service reviled him, and would think nothing of seeing him swing from a lamp post. Yet, here he was.

"What do you mean?" Jamal asked.

"That software that you stole from the Americans, which I might add has caused a bit of a stir in the White House, I want you to use it against certain demographics in the population to thin it out."

"You want me to kill people with it?"

Blunt nodded. "People that are already dying, it's not so cold blooded, but more lukewarm."

"How many?"

"Around five billion." He poured some tea, paused over the second cup and looked at Jamal. "Would you care for tea, young man?"

Jamal shook his head. He was looking at the floor rubbing his broken arm. Blunt broke the silence.

"Given the uproar the missing software in the US has caused, I suspect that you have indeed got the real deal. After seeing your videos posted on the dark web, I'm convinced that we can make a deal." He took a sip of tea and pulled a face. "This tea is beastly, at least it's wet and warm," he said, smiling at Jamal.

"You're insane," Jamal said.

"I understand where you're coming from Jamal, but trust me, the world is in freefall."

"What do you mean?"

"I represent an organization that crosses the boundaries of many countries. I'm not representing those countries, by the way, merely representing the members of the organization."

"Which organization?" Jamal asked.

"Asclepius, it's remit is to heal the world."

"This is insanity, you would never get away with killing five billion people."

"The numbers speak for themselves." He placed the cup onto the saucer and leaned forward, hands together in a prayer gesture.

"The world's current resources, with the global population, means we are using thirty percent more resources than the world can provide."

Jamal mirrored the Health Secretary and leaned forward.

"If we were to live as the Americans do, we would need four to five other planets just to resource it, the power of the population is greater than the Earth can provide for, and by 2050, the population will have almost doubled, making the current situation even worse." Blunt smiled. "Which is where you come in."

Jamal couldn't quite believe what he was hearing.

"Ninety percent of the fish stock are depleted, the water is drying up the soil and making it too salty. To equalize this balance, the global population ought to be around two billion." He took another sip of tea.

"What about the 'One Planet Living' concept?" Jamal asked.

"Ahh, you're familiar with OPL, the trouble with that is it simply can't be achieved. The technology is just not feasible."

Jamal laughed. "You mean affordable."

Blunt shrugged his shoulders, he picked more fluff on his trouser leg.

"How do you want to play this then?" Jamal asked.

"We obviously don't want to cause panic. Maybe an insidious disease that kills people, we can change the person's cellular make-up, yes?"

Jamal nodded. "The software can make a person jump off a cliff as well as changing their cellular structure."

Blunt drained the last of the tea, picked up the pot to check, smiled and poured more. "Are you sure you won't take tea with me, young man?"

"No thank you." Sharing tea with a person who wanted to commit genocide was a little unsavoury, Jamal thought.

"If we can run the program over, say, ten years, would we be able to kill off five billion people?"

Jamal nodded. "It wouldn't be an issue, although I would have to discover a different way of uploading the software. Only ninety-five million users use fruit smash."

Blunt smiled. "It's a start, old bean."

They looked at each other for a few seconds. Blunt replaced his cup and stood. "We need to talk about the vulgarity of money. What's your fee?"

"My fee?" Jamal asked. "I'm being paid?"

"Of course."

"I thought I was going to be killed?"

Blunt laughed, patted him on the back. "I need you

for approximately ten years, old bean, I don't suppose you would work for free?"

"You suppose right."

"What's your figure?"

"Ten million." Blunt nodded, Jamal pushed the boat out a little further, "per year!"

Blunt stopped, thought about it. "I think we can manage that. Can we select a group of females and adjust their fertility as well?"

"Yeah, I said we can do anything, the program is that powerful."

"Excellent, the board will be extremely happy with this, I shall report to them shortly."

"It's genocide?" Jamal asked.

"I think the term 'genocide' is a bit strong, but you will be well compensated for your efforts."

Jamal said nothing, but his face spoke a thousand words.

"Tell me in layman's term how this all works."

Jamal leaned back in his chair. "From what I understand, the software needs the rapid eye movement that more than three billion people have using this software, along with music in the phones they carry around. If we can have that, then the software can potentially piggyback any other software, including just opening the phone if you're using facial recognition to access it."

Blunt seemed engrossed. "Fascinating, and how long can the software be in the brain for?"

"Its exponential, we can potentially control people's actions indefinitely, likewise, in an instant, we can change people's genome and cellular regeneration."

"But how does the software work in the brain?"

Jamal nodded. "I can explain that." He stopped, looked for his laptop, grabbed it, his damaged hand causing him to wince. He opened it, tapped away then looked up.

"Okay, the origins of pleasure in the brain have been difficult to rationalize, but scientists think they've nailed it. It's no surprised that tech companies use scientists to figure this shit out."

"Go on," Blunt said.

"The mesolimbic system in the midbrain is commonly called the dopamine circuit or the pleasure loop, this is responsible for formulating addictions, we all have them, right? I can feed a separate software code into the brain via the Hypnos software and tap into that."

Blunt was dialled in, spellbound. "What will that do?"

"Well, it'd like having a blowjob for the brain, whoever it taps into, they will quickly become addicted to whatever the phone is doing all the time. The software will tell me via notifications who is playing, their location, every bit of metadata that you could wish for. I can then access the brain and make the person do whatever, including adjusting cellular matter."

Blunt clapped his hands. "By Jove, man, I think I'm excited."

Jamal stared back blankly. "I go back to my original remark, you're insane."

Blunt stood, and walked over to Jamal, he sat back as the thin man towered over him.

"You will do this for me, Jamal, you will also be well compensated for your efforts."

"I don't care, I can't be part of watching billions of people die at my hands to balance the government books."

Blunt grabbed Jamal by the throat and threw him to the floor. Jamal skidded against the workbench, dislodging some tools that clattered over him.

"I won't do it," he spluttered, struggling for breath, massaging his throat with his damaged hand. Blunt walked over and stood on the wounded hand, Jamal cried out in pain.

Jongy heard the commotion as he walked in. "Sir," he said standing to attention.

Blunt spun around. "What is it, Jongy?" he spat.

"You have a phone call, I think it's your private secretary, Ortsgruppenleiter."

"SILENCE YOU IMBECILE!" Blunt screamed.

Jongy looked shocked, he realized what he had said. Blunt looked down at Jamal, who was looking up. It suddenly dawned on him. "Holy fuck, you're a load of Nazis."

"SILENCE you coon fuck!" Blunt spat at Jamal, his face etched with evil. Blunt let Jamal's hand go, he scampered to his feet and pushed his back against the wall, his hand once again silently screaming.

"The final solution comes to the world, you're fucking insane, I won't help you, you can fucking kill me before I help you deranged fucks."

Blunt turned and nodded to Jongy. He closed the door and walked over to Blunt. Standing next to Blunt, Jongy took his jacket off, his white shirt baggy and tucked in far too high to be socially acceptable today. There was a red arm band on his right arm with the black number seven arranged to form a triskelion. He smoothed his greased blond hair back.

"Jongy here is part of the Afrikaner Weerstandsbeweging, the South African neo-Nazi organization, brethren to our greater cause of Asclepius."

Jamal felt sick, it was one thing being the go-to man for the criminal underworld, but helping a fanatic Nazi organization was a step too far.

"I won't do it, you sick fucks."

"Jongy will dole out your punishment Jamal, you will comply, your resistance is pointless."

"Over my dead body will you make me."

"As you wish."

Jongy looked at Blunt, who motioned to Jamal. He didn't need a second opportunity. He strode over to Jamal. Holding his hands up in anticipation for the beating, he closed his eyes so tightly, expecting the first blows. Nothing came. Looking through his hands, his body was rigid with fear. The look of horror swept across Jamal's face when Jongy came into focus, smiling.

"I told you, you fucking coon, I'm gonna sort you right out, eh." His hands moved quickly, before Jamal could fight, a thick clear plastic bag was snapped over his head and a draw string pulled tight, cutting off the air to his mouth. Jamal instantly ran out of any oxygen to breath, the bag stuck fast to his face, moisture instantly fogging the bag. The draw string insured the impending death of the computer genius. He sank to his knees, clawing at the bag, face turning blue, then he felt a swift punch to his solar plexus, driving the last residual oxygen out of the lungs. He started to black out, the blackness vignetting from the corners of his eyes. There was nothing in the bag, stasis, panic rising. Jamal started to flail, his arms grabbing at the air. Suddenly, there was movement in the bag, Jongy had pierced the plastic prison, allowing precious air into the space. Jamal sucked up as much as he could, instantly pinking up.

"What the hell?" he gasped. Jongy reached down and grabbed Jamal by the throat, and lifted him clean off the ground, Jamal's feet dangling.

"Let me kill the coon," Jongy said.

"No, put him down, you've done enough." Jongy turned and stared at his paymaster. "Jawohl, mein Herr." Jongy let him go. He slumped to the floor like a sack of potatoes. Jamal groaned, he wasn't sure how much abuse he could take. They were either going to kill him or he was going to have to play the game. Either way, being Indian, his usefulness had an expiry date. He decided to play.

"Okay, okay," he gasped. "No more," he pleaded.

Jongy walked towards him. "Wait, Jongy," Blunt said.

"What did you say, Jamal?"

"I said no more, I'll do whatever you want me to do, just make the beating stop." He lolled on the floor, eventually rolling onto his back. Jongy looked disappointedly at Blunt.

"Help the man up, Jongy, don't just stand there." Jongy clicked his heels and grabbed his arms.

"Gently, you moronic fool," Blunt scythed. Jongy stopped, considered his attitude, and then gently went about helping Jamal.

Blunt walked over, crouched. "Good, I'm glad you've seen the light, I expect a full demonstration of the software working in, let's say…" he looked at his watch, "three hours?"

The pause was long and heavy. Jamal nodded. "In three hours it should be good to go."

Blunt stood. "Excellent." He turned to Jongy. "Make sure you take care of our guest Jongy, don't hurt him anymore."

"What if he tries to escape, eh?"

Blunt looked down at Jamal, staring at the floor, breathing heavily, blood dripping from either his nose or mouth – he wasn't sure.

"He isn't going to escape, Jongy." Blunt stated.

"But what if he does, Mein Herr?"

"Then shoot him, Jongy, you shoot him."

Jongy looked down and smiled.

8

Both Alex and Simon had made it through the myriad of security checks to get to the newly formed B5 divisional offices for the UK.

The office was a hive, dark recesses bordered with subtly lit glass with maps and screens constantly re-rendering. Drone shots, the NASDAQ ticker updating big Pharma's and health companies' price indexes, mugshots of wanted suspects, CCTV footage of ongoing investigations.

Alex got to the vestry, the inner sanctum of the division. No mobile communication devices, smartwatches, laptops or any tech that could record or transmit were forbidden. Not because someone in the room might do something, but because of external influences. Broadstone had instilled a culture of trusting no one, including the members of the wider division. The reach of these companies and the billions of dollars they had in liquid money meant that anyone and everyone had a price. What that price was, was up to the individual if approached.

A couple of people had already made it into the room. The nearest chair swivelled, where Ricky Lambert, Alex's partner in crime from the Met police and the royal military police was sat. He was running a pencil through his lips from side to side when he spotted his boss. The broadest grin ran across his face.

Alex mouthed, shut up, to Ricky. He followed her into the room by swivelling the chair, and she could feel his gaze on her. They were very close work colleagues from the army, which he had left to be with her in the civilian police force. Ricky had a lot of respect for her. But he was as close to Simon, her husband, and although he was enjoying the banter, he knew he was going to have address the issue of her infidelity.

But she looked good. Better than she had for a long time Ricky thought.

Alex shot him a glance. Using his forefinger, he poked it through the opposing forefinger and thumb that had made a circle. Alex flicked him the bird.

"Right, guys, I have the room," Broadstone said as he walked to the head of the table opposite Ricky.

A man in his sixties was sat to his right, balding and chubby. Alex thought he had just come off a long-haul flight. He had that sweaty, pale disheveled look about him, the kind of look that preceded a heart attack. To Simon's left was a younger more menacing looking individual. Pointy features that gave the unfortunate man a rat-like appearance. He looked like he was born in a suit. Most of the people in the room had seen active service and stared down the wrong end of a gun. This guy epitomized a bean-counter at its worst.

There was still a lot of chatter in the room. "SHUT UP!" Ricky shouted. The room looked at him. His big cross-fitting frame tinged with an air of badassery always gained the attention of the everyone when he spoke.

"Thank you, Ricky," Broadstone said.

"Okay, guys, we have a job on. We've been tasked by the government, that's in cooperation with our American brethren, to investigate something that has gone missing." Simon stopped and looked to the guy on his right. "This is

Channing Stubblebine, CIA technology section," he said, motioning towards him. The man looked around the room for some praise after his name was introduced. Simon took a seat and Stubblebine stood, trying to look nonchalant but failing, his pride was hurt, Alex could see it.

The old man's body audibly creaked as he stood, slow and carefully to not irritate the joints.

"Thank you very much for the introduction, I haven't got much time. I need to get back to the states as soon as I have finished at Grosvenor square."

His voice was gentle, not what you would think from the CIA.

He stopped and surveyed the room. "We have absolute sterility in this room, Simon?" he asked.

"Yes you do, everyone in this room I can vouch for," Broadstone said as he also surveyed the room.

"Has anyone heard of the Human Potential Movement?" There was silence. Eventually the silence was broken.

"The Stargate Project." Alex turned, of course, Ricky would know.

"The TV series?" Another voice asked.

"Yes." He motioned to Ricky. "And er, no," to the other voice, Brad, the data analyzer.

He invited Ricky to tell the room what he knew. Ricky shifted in his seat, feeling a bit vulnerable.

"Well, it's the men that stare at goats project," Ricky said, "the guys in the '50s and '60s who tried to walk through walls."

The man standing at the end nodded and laughed quietly to himself. "I'm impressed, not many people in the US military know, that's not bad coming from a Brit."

"I read the book by Ronson, people thought it was whack, I kind of thought it was cool."

Ricky thought for a moment. "You're not the Stubblebine from the book, are you?"

The man's face lit up, a broad smile showed the yellowed crooked teeth of a person who felt there were more important things in life than dental hygiene. A warmth spread across his face. "That was my father," he said. "Let me begin." He rested his hands on the chair to steady himself.

"The Stargate Project was born out of trying to utilize the paranormal. We know, that scientifically, we have no idea how the brain works. What we do know is based on past experiences and predictable habits." He took a drink.

"We were secret until the book came out, then we became a laughing stock, further mocked when that God-awful movie came out."

The room was captivated, the voice was smooth, soft and almost hypnotic.

"After a successful aviation career, I joined my father's unit in the bowels of Fort Bragg, where I know Simon has been. We reminisced," he said with a chuckle.

Simon nodded with a smile.

"The attention and ridicule that we achieved caught the attention of non-military people that were high up in MIT and Harvard. People that were obsessed with the paranormal and the integration of the digital world in the conscious mind."

He took another drink. The trip was taking its toll on the old man.

"Ten years ago, we achieved the unthinkable. We managed to integrate the digital world with both the conscious mind and the subconscious. Hypnos was born. We ran trial after trial. The achievement was immeasurable, thankfully my father saw the results before he passed."

"We decided, though, that the world wasn't ready for this software. The CIA agreed and so did the president at the time, they thought it should be shelved until the world was ready to receive such incredible progress. It was assigned to the digital vaults of the CIA." He paused, Alex was sat listening, Siobhan creeping into her thought process and causing a slow-growing smile on her face. She shook her out of her mind, but, like an ever-decreasing circle, the thoughts came back, blurring out the voice of the old man.

"Up until last week, the software was unknown to the world, and then it vanished."

Ricky leaned forward, Alex also, suddenly engaged. They were dialled into the old man's story, which immediately took a more sinister turn.

"Stolen?" Alex asked.

"We believe so, yes."

"How can you be sure?" Ricky asked.

"There was a digital maker, the perp cleaned their presence up, but the servers have led us here, to the UK."

Ricky looked at Alex, and Alex frowned. She turned to Stubblebine.

"What are the risks here?"

Stubblebine thought for a moment.

"Think of this, if you could get the population to do whatever you wanted, with criminal intent, what do you think those risks might be?"

Alex thought for a moment. "I'm still not getting it?"

Ricky piped up. "The software can be uploaded to any person's brain, and the brain can then be controlled. Say I tell your brain to go and jump out of the window, or drive your car into a group of pedestrians."

"Exactly," said the old man.

The man thought for a moment, thinking about what to say next, he nodded to himself. "One other thing we know about what the software can do, as well as controlling the affectee, it can also alter the cells at a cellular level. The software can literally kill someone from the inside."

"Is this nonsense or is there a real risk here?" Alex asked, arms folded and leaning back in her chair, kind of not buying it.

The man on the left piped up, he stood. Stubblebine sat, relieved to be off his feet.

"My president has given me the authorization for you guys to handle this by your own means... so..." he said in an East Coast Harvard style, lawyer bullshit.

Alex frowned, and took a glance at Broadstone, he was sat just listening. The last comment wasn't registering. Now for Simon, it had registered. He was good at hiding stuff like that, Alex thought. A stickler for truth, honesty integrity. Hated being spoken down to. She gripped her pencil, which wasn't enough to stop her voice from falling out off her mouth.

"Gee, thanks very much to your President." Alex inverted the 'your' in her fingers. "This is our manor, sunshine, and you're gonna dance to my tune, you feel me. You could have the good grace to introduce yourself. For all we know, you could be the cleaner. In American, I believe the word is janitor."

There was a pause. The man looked at Simon, he waved his hand in a demonstration of, you're on your own, mate.

"My name's Statham, Peter Statham, CIA... so."

There was a pause. "So, what?" Alex said

Mr Stubblebine cleared his throat. He sensed the awkwardness.

"What Peter is alluding to, Miss...?" he waited.

"Alex," she said, filling the pause.

"Alex, what Peter is saying, is that the President has given you access to the files and anything that we can help you with regarding the investigation. We will, of course, be on hand to help you with whatever we can."

Alex nodded. She leaned forward and rested her hands on the table. "Have you got some proof that this software does what it says on the tin?"

"What tin?" Statham asked.

"It's an English term, Alex is saying have you got some proof to show us what Hypnos is capable of?" Broadstone said shooting, a glance at Alex.

Statham nodded. "We sure do, Simon."

He tinkered on a laptop, the screen behind clicked on and there was a video still.

"Is that Abu Ghraib prison? In Iraq?" Ricky asked.

Statham stopped. "Sure is, Sir." Both Ricky and Alex exchanged glances. They knew that prison. As military police officers, they had been to that prison on many occasions. It was mainly run by the US military, but there was a handful of British soldiers there, looking after their own captured prisoners. The prison wasn't a big complex. Alex spotted the date on the screen. Her mental arithmetic said she and Ricky were there at the time.

"This was when the software really broke ground. We used the software on these prisoners to influence their thinking. We made huge ground with them. The CIA being the CIA, they thought of making things a little sinister."

Statham pressed play. The video was sickening. The theme tune for *Barney and Friends* played constantly. Alex remembered the song being played in the prison. She looked at Ricky, they exchanged more glances.

"Why that song?" Ricky asked.

Statham pursed his lips. "Simple, really. The song is repetitive, by playing the song, we could hypnotize the person on the receiving end by impacting subliminal messages in the music. The message would then finally make it into the brain. The neuroplasticity of the brain allows it to retrain the message as influencers. They can even be made to do things that were out of the ordinary, incidentally, none of these guys were under the influence of any psychotropic drugs."

The video was running, Statham moved out of the way so the table could watch.

The man was smashing his own head with a claw hammer, blood gushing out of the hole until he knocked himself unconscious. The video sped up twenty minutes, he was lying on the floor and he stirred, then started smashing his head again. After three goes, the man finally killed himself.

Alex was numb to anything gruesome with what she had seen over the last year, but some of the others were finding it difficult to watch.

The video moved to a group of Iraqi men. Staunch Sunni Muslims. Proud of their faith. All would be married with children, without exception in this group of men. But this group of men were having homosexual sex with each other, openly, while their peers watched, reviled by what they were watching. They ended up throwing stones at the men, stoning them to death. The guards had even provided piles of rocks which dotted the courtyard.

Another man, sat alone. Eyes bloodshot. Red bags under his eyes, and sweating profusely. The Barney song was echoing in the background – the sound of the sycophantic dinosaur and children singing on the background

The man reached for some pliers and, without emotion, or pain, cut his own fingers off. He then ran his good hand through a bandsaw. He stood in front of the camera, as the saccharine sweet song continually echoed over the audio, the man then slowly moved his head towards the bandsaw. The saw sliced through the man's skull, spitting blood and brain all over the room. The man slumped forward, pushing the saw further into his body. The body then slid from the cutting surface, slicing the remaining half of the face off. It audibly hit the floor with a thud before his body followed suit. A figure came into shot, Statham's face became visible as he manipulated the camera.

"I see you were a busy boy, then," Broadstone said. Alex wanted to hug him for it.

"We felt that the software was important." His tone and stance were unrepentant from the sickening video that had just be played.

"How much did this cost the US Government in lawsuits?"

Stubblebine cleared his throat again. "Each detainee that survived the eight weeks, seventy-one in total, received an out-of-court settlement of five million each."

Alex laughed. "This barbaric program cost the government nearly half a billion dollars in lawsuits." The embarrassment finally hit home.

"And you guys are still working?" Alex asked.

"Er no, I retired way before this" Stubblebine said. Statham shifted on his feet. "I was fired but brought back soon after."

Alex took a swig of her coffee. "So, we just need to find the person playing the Barney song and then everything is rosy, right?"

Statham pulled his chair out and sat, he drew in a deep breath. "Not really."

"What do you mean?" Alex said.

"Well, the technology has moved on, so has the program. It's AI-driven so it has learned and adapted. The software is fully customizable. And we feel it can be delivered in a more convenient way, so…"

"What does that mean?" Ricky asked.

"So, it means that there's no need for Barney. The software can be uploaded through eyesight."

"What?" Broadstone said, he followed it with a laugh.

Statham and Stubblebine looked at each other. The old man coughed again.

"Hypnos needs a triad of hypnosis, and the everyday things we carry can provide that precise mode of delivery."

"Like the TV?" Ricky asked. He was very engaged. Alex didn't get it. Seems weird, she thought. She thought back to the previous night. The Swarm, the encounter and instant spark with Siobhan. This, in this room, was weirder and that was way left of field. Alex thought of Siobhan, her tummy tightened, she missed her.

"Alex."

Alex snapped out of it, looked up, and she felt herself smiling. Ricky kicked her under the table.

"Smartphones. The phones have a front-facing camera, with the right music, which can be anything for the code to pass through, the code marries into the conscious mind, and is then filtered into the midbrain. There you can add in free text of whatever you want the person to do or make changes to the cells."

"Woow," Ricky said, louder than he meant to. "That's off the hook," he added.

"When you say changes to the cells, are you talking cancer or something like it, maybe?" Ricky added.

The two men looked at each other, Alex sensed that Stubblebine felt shamed by this revelation.

"Really," Alex said, "we have spent the last 400-odd years trying to eradicate cancer, making real progress in the last fifty years, then the CIA strikes again."

She turned to the gentlemen at the end of the table. "Is that when you decided to shut this horror showdown?"

"Yes," the old man said. "It was decided that the world wasn't ready for this."

"I don't believe you," Alex said, Broadstone swiveled in his chair to maybe catch Alex before she burnt herself at the stake.

"Clarify?" Statham said.

"This software, just in lawsuits, has cost the Fed nearly half a billion dollars, not to mention the cost of making it.

Let's face it, it's a military superpower's weapon of choice. I mean you can make your enemies do everything."

"The previous president locked it up in red tape."

"And the current, how can we be sure that he won't use it? If we help you, then we need an assurance that the software will fall in the trash."

Statham shifted in his chair, he seemed uneasy. "That's under review."

Alex the pragmatist stood, she walked over to the coffee-making table, poured another cup. She could feel the eyes on her, and she felt sexy for the first time in years. What the hell has Siobhan done to me? she thought.

She turned. "What's the game plan, guys? Where do we start?"

Ricky leaned back. "Simple, we keep an ear to the ground, Europe-wide, anything that has happened or might happen that's out of the ordinary. Weird deaths, killings, and suicides, I think we can monitor all the chat sites through the police in Europe. Anything that stands out, we investigate it, if that has legs, we'll chase it up."

"Sounds like a plan," Broadstone said. He stood, thanked the American visitors, and turned.

Stubblebine stood. "Good luck, ladies and gentlemen, God bless you all." He shuffled out.

Alex's gaze settled on Statham, he was staring back at Alex.

A cold chill ran down her spine.

9

Jamal waited at the back of the garage. The raging heat pulsing through his hand was getting worse. His fingers were black and necrotic, the smell of cheese caught his nose now and again, and he turned away as soon as he smelt it. He knew the hand was a goner.

Jongy and Errol were arranging the hardware, connecting the cables and placing the monitors in a way that more than just one person could see them.

"Come on, Errol, you lazy fuck, eh," Jongy snided. Errol, shuffling his ruined snake-skin shoes, was ignoring the abuse from his partner. Jamal watched the exchange. Totally one-sided, it was as though Errol was plotting Jongy's death. Errol's features were unpleasant, his eyes bulged, the white sclera yellowing an insipid shade, disappearing into a myriad of veins. His nose was squat against his chubby cheeks and above his bulbous lips. Most of his teeth missing. Jamal wasn't sure if this was through lack of hygiene or trauma. Errol was unreadable. He stopped and stared at Jamal, feeling his gaze, Jamal tried to hold it but he just couldn't.

"Here, Gandhi. Get your arse over here pronto, eh," Jongy said, dragging a folding metallic chair across the concrete.

Jamal sighed. "Look, Jongy, if we are to have any sort of

relationship, you're gonna have to stop with the racist comments," Jamal said.

Jongy looked at Errol and started laughing. "You're fuckin' joking, right, eh?" he stood with his hands on his hips leering at Jamal. Jamal sat where he was. Partly in defiance and partly because he was in so much pain.

"I said, get your arse over here before I whip you again, you fuckin' Untermensch."

Jamal gritted his teeth. The pain was wracking through him, and he struggled to his feet. "One thing I didn't reckon on, was that you were a Nazi, Jongy." Jamal finally got to his feet. He stood straight and then walked towards the chair where Jongy was standing, still with his hands on his hips. The sun shining behind him – it gave him the sinister silhouetted appearance of Heydrich, the Butcher of Prague. Jongy kicked the chair away from Jamal as he reached it, now having to walk past his tormentor.

Grinning at Jamal, his eyes followed him to the chair. Jamal tried desperately to not give Jongy the gratification that he was in pain. He slumped into the chair, the top rail cold and biting. He winced as he sat.

Jongy grabbed his hair and pulled back, snapping Jamal's head back. Jamal's eyes closed, pain written across his face.

"Don't you judge me, you subhuman cunt. You should address me correctly." He was interrupted by the door and footsteps.

"Jongy, let go of the man," Blunt said as he approached with Veshausen.

Jongy jerked Jamal's head forward and stood to attention.

"Go and do something useful, like count blades of grass, Jongy."

Jongy clicked his heels. "Errol, with me."

"Sorry about that Jamal, he can be a little," Veshausen

was searching for the word, "over-exuberant." He found the word, but Jamal still didn't think it was appropriate.

"So, how does a black man end up serving the Nazis?"

Veshausen and Blunt looked at each other. Blunt took a seat next to Jamal. "Even they have their purposes, your purpose right now is to help us."

"I need more drugs and antibiotics. Your over-exuberant gorilla keeps battering me."

Blunt looked at Veshausen. "I'll take care of it, Sir," he said.

"We will get you the drugs you need. But, first, we need you to get the software up and running. We need to see the software working. Jongy tells me that you can piggyback a gaming app, is that right?"

Jamal nodded.

"Can we see it running, Jamal?" Blunt asked. His voice was soft and patient, but Jamal was no idiot. The orchestrator to everything that was going on here was firmly at the door of the Health Secretary.

Jamal dragged himself into the desk space, holding his bad hand. The computers were already fired up. Four monitors blinked simultaneously, each one welcoming the Sith Lord, Jamal. Blunt saw it but saw no relevance.

Jamal moved the mouse, it seemed awkward. "Is there a problem, Jamal?"

"Well, sort of, you see I'm right-handed, so you're going to have to bear with me."

The screen asked for authentication, Jamal typed it in. He then placed a headset on. A second authentication panel came up. "This is Jamal, may the force be with you." He quickly glanced at Blunt, who was still not picking up on the Star Wars theme.

"Can you?" Jamal nodded to the chest harness resting on the end of the table. "Of course," Blunt reached and passed it to him. Jamal held up his bad hand. "You're gonna have to help me out, I'm afraid, but it's okay, you won't catch it."

"Catch what?" Blunt asked.

"My colour!" Blunt stopped, looked at Jamal. A smile crept up one side of his mouth. It was a tell. He was as racist as the other assholes.

"Of course I won't."

Jamal pulled his shirt up. It took Blunt a few seconds to figure the tangle of wires out, then quickly slid it around the bruised throat of the young man.

"This is for the fifth authentication, my EKG."

"What's the fourth?" Blunt asked.

Jamal held up his good hand and wriggled his fingers. "The fingerprints, coupled with my constant temperature, are required for the fourth authentication. Basically, you can't kill me. And now, I'm plumbed into the system and my location will transmit if I don't exit the program properly."

Blunt smiled. "It's good that you ensure your usefulness to me, Jamal, do a good job and you will be rewarded."

Jamal nodded.

"Okay, let's get this ship going." Even with one hand, Jamal moved around the dark web like it was nothing. His fingers tapping away, Blunt couldn't keep up. Veshausen joined them and sat on the other side of Jamal. Being sandwiched between two racist neo-Nazi's had never been a life goal of Jamal's, but here he was.

"Right, the software is live, and it's shadowing the game, so let's look for users."

A nanosecond later, a list of users totalling over one million in the UK appeared, two-hundred thousand in London alone. Of this number, one hundred and sixty thousand were listening to music. This would complete the triad of hypnosis. Jamal explained away, and the two men sat

80

fixated on the numbers, scrolling and listening to parts of what Jamal was saying.

"Gosh, that's incredible," Blunt said. "So, can we dip in?"

Jamal ran some code and located a bus driver. The nearest CCTV camera picked him up. Jamal ran a bit more code and the camera above the driver's head was now on.

He was a middle-aged man, white and balding. He was sat at the bus terminus at Arnos Grove Tube station in the single decker 251 bus, engrossed in Fruit Smash, Jamal even had the music streaming through his speakers. The smooth Caribbean notes of Eddie Grant's 'Electric Avenue' were playing. Jamal brought up the driver's details from the name badge. He had his address, bank details, his bank account balance as well as access to the entire family.

"If the children or a spouse are wearing headphones, and on the same sharing network such as Spotify or Apple music, I can cross-pollinate and upload Hypnos into them as well. But I haven't quite figured that one out yet."

Blunt's left leg was shaking, Jamal stopped and looked down at the leg, then looked back up to Blunt, he stopped.

"Sorry, old bean, I get this restless leg syndrome when I get excited."

"Okay, see the guy resting against the wall looking at his phone? The software identified him as playing the game with his headphones and he's a prime candidate too."

"Time to infect, watch what they do, it's a classic tell."

Jamal hit return on the keyboard, watching the guy resting against the wall on his phone, and, on the next screen, the bus driver still engrossed in the game. Suddenly, both heads snapped upwards, then levelled back out. The heads shook twice. They then returned to the game.

"Did you see that?"

"Bugger me," Blunt said. "So, I presume they're infected?"

"That's right. What do you want to do?"

Veshausen coughed. "Make the guy leaning against the wall take the purse of the woman next to him. Get him to empty it out on the floor, leaving the contents there, and return back to the game."

"Our friend here is cynical of the software, prove him wrong," Blunt said.

Jamal returned to the texted screen, typed the instruction into the panel, then hit return.

The man playing the game stood and pocketed the phone. He calmly reached for the purse, she was busy on her phone chatting. Astonished, she smiled at first, then the look of horror as the man suddenly tried to take the purse. He smashed her in the face, and she let go. He unzipped the bag and tipped the contents onto the floor. Leaning back against the wall, he pulled his phone out and carried on playing the game.

The woman was gesticulating wildly and angrily screaming at another woman who came to her aid.

"Bring the bus driver in, pull her skirt up over her head and kick her to the gutter."

Jamal swallowed, made a noise, feeling uneasy, but knowing that this was where the software was always going to go. He couldn't afford to be temporary in his compassion.

He rubbed his eyes first, then typed in the instruction.

The bus driver placed his phone in the top pocket of his blue shirt, then stood and climbed out of the bus. He walked over to the woman, crouched behind her while she was still screaming at the man that had just emptied her purse all over the floor. He grabbed the hem of her skirt and pulled it up. The lady was almost yanked off her feet. Inadvertently, her blouse had come off in the process. The driver tossed the skirt and paused. She was stood half naked, speechless. The two men either side of Jamal were sniggering like schoolboys.

The bus driver walked around her, rested his hand against the wall, and then kicked the women violently onto the road. She didn't quite make it, so the driver took a few steps closer, he kicked her very hard in the solar plexus. Unconscious, the women lay in the bus lane in her bra and knickers. Bystanders just stood by and didn't do anything, other than film it on their phones.

"Send the bus driver down the tube station, make him do something like jump onto the electric line."

Jamal darted a look at Blunt. "Do it Jamal, or I'll get Jongy in here."

Just buy your time, he thought to himself. He typed the instruction into the panel.

The driver turned, ignoring the bystanders vocalizing their indifference. He walked into the station, down the steps, jumped over the security barriers and descended the stairs to the platform. The tube staff was in hot pursuit, shouting. The driver ignored them too. He made it to the westbound platform, smiled at the passengers and nonchalantly jumped down onto the track. People began shouting at the man, they tried grabbing him, and he turned to face the passengers on the platform who were screaming for him to come back. But it was too late. The husband, father of three beautiful children, stepped onto the track. The high voltage ran through the driver's body like a bolt of lightning. Sparks burst above him like mini fireworks, his body violently shaking as the water in the driver's body super-heated and turned to steam, splitting the skin and bursting into the air, instantly precipitating into fat and blood globules on the platform surface and the bystanders who were now recoiling in horror, a few throwing up their lunch. The driver finally slumped off the track, his contorted face visible on Jamal's screen. Both his eyes had ruptured. He moved, one arm came purposely to his mouth. "He's still alive," said Blunt.

The three of them looked closer, then in an instant, the westbound train from Bounds Green obliterated what was left of the driver as it screeched to a halt.

"Wow, did you fuckin' see that?" Veshausen said. Blunt felt he hadn't breathed through the whole episode. "What else can you show, eh?"

Jamal typed and pinged a couple of phones in Trafalgar Square, central London. He knew he needed to give these guys something spectacular. He needed more time to think.

"What about this?" Jamal asked. The two Nazis leaned in, Blunt grinning.

"What are you going to do?" Blunt asked.

"See the policeman by the steps leading up to the National Gallery?" Jamal said.

Jamal uploaded to seven of the ten phones being used within one hundred meters of the policeman. The simultaneous snap of the head and the three shakes left and right. The group approached the policeman, from different directions. Each person minding their own business. Waiting for a loved one, friend, colleague, or just enjoying the spring sunshine. The seven circled the policeman, arms width from him. The three in the garage watched as they all stayed at that specific arm length, staring down. The policeman reached for his radio, and he started to walk. They carried on encircling him, walking with him. Panic could be seen shooting across his face.

"Kill him?" Veshausen said, breaking the silence in the garage. Blunt looked over Jamal at Veshausen, Blunt smiled and looked at Jamal. Jamal stared back at Blunt, please don't say it, he thought.

"Do it!" Blunt said. Jamal closed his eyes, his head sagged, Veshausen pushed Jamal, "Do it, eh, kill the policeman, have him beaten to death."

Jamal reached for the keyboard, highlighted all seven,

typed beat the policeman to death, show no mercy. Jamal felt sick, his finger hovered over the return key. Blunt's hand came over the top and pushed Jamal's finger onto the key. The screen blipped.

Jamal couldn't watch. The seven people, three men, and four women started punching, kicking. It took seconds for the copper to be subdued and wrestled to the floor. Then the kicks started, blow after blow to the head and neck. Bystanders were pulling their phones out and filming, thinking it was part of a street act, as these were frequently performed in that part of the square. A crowd gathered, some looking on in fascination while most struggled to see the performance. It seemed so real.

The policeman was unconscious, his features spread across his face, blood pumping out. The shortest woman stepped forward, stamped hard on the policeman's neck. The neck visibly broke, making the head of the policeman look unnatural.

"Dear Lord," Blunt said. Jamal opened his eyes, the policeman's body was left. The perpetrators disappeared to carry on with their daily routines. He felt sick to his stomach.

"The people that have walked off…" Vesheasuen said.

"What about them?" Jamal said, looking blankly at the screen, feeling numb to what he was now part of.

"What happens to them now, how long will Hypnos be in their system?"

Jamal slowly shrugged. "No idea, the program isn't proven to remain in the system. I told you yesterday. But we still have control over them while the program remains active."

"How does that work? They're not like a phone, they don't have batteries," Blunt asked.

"It's pretty simple, really. If you look at the paranormal world, they have been doing this for centuries."

"I don't think I understand, Jamal," Blunt added.

Jamal took a swig of water, dropped some pills in and chased it with some more. "We are energy, our bodies produce energy. Like a battery. The software links the brain to the phone, the phone acting like a Wi-Fi connection for the brain. While the game is still active on the phone, the subject will still potentially be affected and influenced by Hypnos."

"Jesus fuckin' Christ, eh," Veshausen said. "I've witnessed it, but if you told me what this software could do, I just wouldn't believe you."

"Okay, tomorrow, we start in earnest. I will have the NHS codes for you for all the patients' notes and lifestyle disease demographics for us to upload the information."

Blunt stood. "Mr Veshausen, would you mind escorting me to the office? We must remember to use your drug as well"

"Jawohl, Mein Herr, the company will appreciate the sale of the drug." Veshausen stood, clicked his heels with a curt nod to Jamal and left, Blunt following. He stopped and turned to Jamal. "Get some rest, you're going to need it. I know Jongy has something planned for you. Enjoy," he said turning and leaving.

Jamal sat, still looking at the screen. The police had arrived en masse. The seven people rounded up and paramedics working on the victim.

It must've been a few minutes. Jamal heard the door go, he turned and Jongy was stood, his trademark stance – hands on the hips. He smiled in the corner of his mouth, eyes full of mischief.

He walked towards Jamal, unbuttoning his shirt. When he got to Jamal, his shirt was off. His chest was barrel-like, muscular and powerful. No hair. A large swastika adorned his left breast, on the right in English, the SS oath of allegiance.

I swear by God this holy oath, that I will render to Adolf Hitler, Führer of the German Reich and People, Supreme Commander of the Armed Forces, unconditional obedience, and that I am ready, as a brave soldier, to risk my life at any time for this oath.

He stood next to Jamal, looked at the screen and smiled. He looked down at Jamal.

He was feeling awkward with Jongy standing there, was he in for another beating? Jamal heard the unmistakable sound of a zipper being pulled down. He turned and Jongy had removed his penis, still looking down, he pulled his foreskin back. "Now you get to feel how a real man feels, Untermensch."

10

Alex left the room. The air was stuffy and thick with the air of stupidity. She went to the tray that contained all their phones and grabbed hers.

There were fifteen text messages, one from Frank, her old boss from the Mile End nick, and the other fourteen were from Siobhan. Alex smiled, and brought the corner of the phone up to her lips and tapped, thoughts smoldering into her mind and causing a tightness in her chest. There were people milling around her, she realized she was in the way.

"Sorry." She moved.

"Yo, Alex, shall we run some searches?" Ricky said from across the room.

"Yeah, in a tick, Ricky, give me a second!"

She clicked through her phone, ignored the messages, as she didn't want to get sidetracked. She found Jenny's number and hit message. Jenny, are you free to talk right now?

Dots, she was reading it. Call me now, I have a client in five minutes if you can be quick?

Alex pursed her lips, sighed and hit dial.

"Hi Alex, nice of you to call, how are you?" Jenny asked. Her voice was soft and perfectly pitched, the calming music wafted through the phone, and Alex could almost smell the essential oils coming through.

"I'm very good Jenny, I mean, I'm really good." She paused.

"I met someone."

"Oh, who, where, tell me more."

Alex checked her surroundings, making sure that she was on her own. Three minutes later, Alex had given a brief account of the previous night to Jenny, when she stopped, Jenny didn't say anything immediately.

"How does she make you feel, Alex?"

Alex thought for a moment. "Whole, she makes me feel complete and whole. I have never felt this before, Jenny."

Alex heard Jenny close a door. "Have you got to go?"

"I do, Alex, but this can wait, I need to tell you something, are you aware of the twin flame?"

Alex checked her memory banks, looking out of the window. "No, I don't think I have."

"Plato talks about the twin flame in his Symposium."

"As in Plato, the ancient Greek?"

"Yes, that's right, he talks about humans having four arms, four legs, and two heads. The ancient Gods worried that they would be overpowered by the humans. Zeus split them in two, making two people. They embody you, they are your yin to your yang, you feel a very intense connection from the get-go. Sex often happens immediately, as you feel a burning desire to connect, get inside each other. Like you have found a home – time stands still."

Alex began to well up, the information from Jenny resonated, and there was another pause.

"Are you okay with me saying these things, Alex?" Jenny said with a loving tone.

Alex wiped her nose. "Yes."

"It sounds as though your angels have worked for you and placed you in the company of your twin flame, I don't think this is a coincidence, Alex, meeting this woman is by design. The fabric of your life, Siobhan has been sent to you to heal you, so let her."

Alex nodded. "I will."

"What do you want to ask me, Alex?"

"Does this make me a lesbian?"

Jenny laughed. "No, sweet child, no it doesn't. It means that the physical presence is irrelevant. You are connected beyond the physical world, she is not a replacement for Simon. Let her heal you, let her love you and Alex, love her back. The love that you share will heal both of you."

Alex smiled. "Thank you."

There was a pause, and Alex heard the door open, hushed voices. "Alex, just a word of warning, though."

"Okay, I'm listening," she said.

"The relationship can escalate to infatuation, remember you both have lives out of your union, don't compromise that, okay?"

Alex dialed in and nodded. "Also, twin flames are connected so heavily that you will read her mind and she to you. You will know what mood she is in before you even see her."

"I feel her right now."

"How does that make you feel, Alex?"

She thought for a moment. "Amazing, I don't feel cold. I feel alive, buzzing. I can't wait to see her."

"Can you go see her now?"

"No, there's no chance right now, something's come up with work."

"Okay, you tread carefully, Alex," Jenny said. "And, please, if you need anything, call me, be well, Alex!"

The line went dead. She stood and thought for a moment, her tummy was doing somersaults every time she thought of Siobhan. She clicked the messages on her phone. Picture after picture, Alex checked her G-Shock, it was nearly lunch. She hit message.

You still at my place? Alex hit send. Dots…

Yeah, trying all your panties and bras on. The message followed a picture message of everything out of the closet, another picture message of Siobhan in the full-length mirror again, naked.

Have you actually got dressed? Alex typed with a smile spreading across her face.

Nope, I'm too wet to wear any clothes, was the reply.

I have to go, Alex said

An unhappy emoji, love hearts and a sad face. *Go save the world!* was the reply.

Alex closed the phone, shoved it in her back pocket. She looked up and saw a group of people around Ricky, she frowned.

Alex went up to Ricky's desk.

Ricky clocked her, he nodded.

"What's up?" Alex said, the team turning and watching.

"I think we might have our lead already," Broadstone said, he stood. "You need to check the footage on the screen, it's not pretty."

The incident at Arnos Grove, fifteen minutes of footage followed by the incident at Trafalgar Square.

Alex stood. "The incident at Arnos Grove, weird for sure, but the incident at Trafalgar." Alex had to think. "It looked choreographed, the finality of it was pretty sick."

Broadstone mused, "There's no other chat on the net of other incidents."

"That's correct, I've been on the nationwide crucible, there's nothing out of the ordinary, just this," Ricky said.

"What's plod said?" Alex asked.

"They have interviewed the perps, they have no knowledge of the incident. The people at Trafalgar Square are not connected, or they didn't realize what they were doing."

"Where are they now?" Alex asked.

"Paddington Green," Ricky said. "They've placed them in separate cells so they can't communicate."

"Wise," Broadstone said.

"Can I see the footage?" A voice said from behind.

Ricky eyed Alex, she nodded. Stubblebine gently forced his way through the melee of onlookers crowded around Ricky's computer screens. Ricky dialled the video back and hit play.

"Can you isolate each of the people involved?"

Ricky did in seconds, they appeared in their own panels on a huge screen in front of them. Ricky hit play.

"Did you see that?" Stubblebine said.

"Play it again," Broadstone said, hands on his hips, a frown that would start a storm.

"I'm not getting it?" he said.

Stubblebine walked to the big screen. "Play it again, one more time, watch the heads of each individual person in the group."

Ricky hit play. Three seconds into the footage, at the same time, the seven members snapped their head back and shook twice from side to side.

"What was that?" Alex said, skirting around Ricky's desk, pulling up alongside Stubblebine.

"That, my dear, is Hypnos."

Alex's blood ran cold. "What does the shaking of the head and the nod mean?"

"It means we're in trouble, Alex." He glanced away from the screen to look at Alex. "It means we're in trouble."

"Grab your coat, Alex, we're off to Trafalgar, Ricky speak to whoever the incident controller is. We should be there in fifteen minutes."

"Roger that, boss," Ricky said, reaching for the phone.

It took Alex and Broadstone less than fifteen minutes to make it to Trafalgar Square. The blacked-out Range Rover Velar with blue lights cut a menacing presence speeding past the Houses of Parliament and the Cenotaph. Eyes darted to glimpse inside, but to no avail, the windows hid the occupants. Broadstone, tasty at the wheel of the monster 4X4, weaved through the busy traffic. As they sped past Horse Guards, Broadstone still had time for a nod to the poor blighter sat on his horse outside the Horse Guards Parade.

The car screeched to a halt at the now closed off road that circled Nelson's Column, at the junction of Cockspur Street.

Broadstone got out first, strode over to the bobby manning the tape. He showed his card, the bobby looking carefully at it. Alex noted that the officer hadn't the foggiest who Broadstone was, but his very presence spoke a thousand words. He lifted the tape and nodded the two officers through.

"Who's in charge?" Broadstone asked, Alex was playing the game too. Hands on her hips, a show of force, the P9 Glock standing out like a sore thumb. Coppers were looking and nudging.

"You must be Broadstone from B5?" A fresh-faced young senior police officer said, breaking rank with the gaggle of officers comparing notes.

"Yes, I am," he said, offering his hand. The handshake was weak and fetid, the kind of shake you get from an undertaker.

"Glenton, Mark Glenton, incident commander from the Met, erm, not sure that I've heard of you guys before. I confess, I made a call, and was told unequivocally that I am to help you with whatever you need."

"Excellent," was all Broadstone said. He paused and surveyed the scene, realized that the officer was still waiting for an explanation of who B5 was. None came.

"First things first, switch every camera off around this location immediately. I don't care who you have to phone, this place goes dark until I say otherwise." Glenton nodded to one of his officers.

"I hear that you've taken the offenders to Paddington Green, have they been charged?"

"Yes, they have had their rights, but they've not been formally charged," Glenton said, he looked around and then stepped closer. "What's going on?"

"I can't tell you that right now, I need you to do something else – it's going to sound a bit weird."

"Go on?" Glenton said.

"Their phones, locate them and switch them off, and take the SIM cards out too."

Glenton eyed Broadstone, he bit his bottom lip. He looked at Alex, but she wasn't offering any explanation either.

"Okay." Glenton nodded to another officer, and the officer went to speak on the radio.

"Stop." Alex said. The officer stopped, looked at Glenton.

"Nothing over the net. Get an officer to wherever the phones are, and switch them off. Don't utter a word over the telephone, radio or text."

"Okay," Glenton said, he turned and nodded to the officer.

"Have you managed to interview them yet?"

Glenton pulled his notebook out. "Not really, they say they don't know each other but I simply don't believe that."

"How so?" Alex asked.

"You've seen the video footage, right?" Glenton said.

"We have, but something is at play we can't talk to you about right now. Was there anything the people that were arrested said?"

Glenton pulled a face. "The woman that delivered what we believe to be the fatal blow was a tiny woman, a Bristolian called..." he checked his notes "...Edwards, Claire Edwards. She had a mouth on her, full of sass and attitude but nothing that would make us suspect anything."

"Was she aware of what she'd done?" Alex asked.

"Well, that's the thing. She...actually, none of them ran away from us. They all seemed really surprised that they were being arrested. The arrests happened within ten minutes of the incident. It was witnessed across the square by some other officers just outside the South African High Commission. They called it in and started rounding them up."

"Was there anything else said by the group?" Broadstone asked.

"Nothing, they're being interviewed later today. Maybe you guys should make your way to Paddington?" Glenton said.

Broadstone walked a few paces and looked around.

Ricky was getting the footage from Broadstone and Alex's button cameras.

"You getting this, Ricky?" Broadstone asked.

"Yeah, loud and clear."

"Okay, what is the quality of the cameras being used around the square?"

"I've checked that out. After the bombings and shootings in mainland Europe, and the lunatics driving vans into people, the police updated all the cameras around the iconic locations," Ricky said.

"Okay, what are the cameras?" Broadstone asked.

"They are off-the-hook, top drawer, linked to all the law enforcement and specialist agencies."

"Like the secret service?"

"Yeah."

"Is there any way the cameras can be hacked?" Broadstone asked, looking at Alex. She was fifteen feet away, but could still hear everything.

"No matter how secure, if it has a connection to the

internet, nothing is safe. The only way to make things like this safe is to run them from their own network."

"And these cameras?" Alex asked.

"I hack into these cameras all the time. It would take a mediocre computer geek to access the mainframes and control the cameras, what are you thinking?" Ricky asked.

"We're dealing with someone who stole this from the digital vaults of the CIA, how easy would that be, Ricky?"

There was a pause. "It would take real skill."

"But they left a digital marker?" Alex said.

"You can't avoid that. They got away scot-free, to do that takes real genius."

"Okay, what happened here today was orchestrated from the comfort of some control room, there was no one here running things. The whole thing was remotely run." Broadstone said.

"That's how I would do it," Ricky said.

"Ricky, how many people would you know that could break into the CIA vaults?" Alex asked.

"Not many."

"I think if we find that person, it's going to be Ockham's Razor," Alex said.

"Oooh, check you out," Broadstone said.

"Never heard of her," Ricky said.

Broadstone and Alex laughed. "What Alex was alluding to was the William of Ockham's writings, a scholastic friar and philosopher. He said that when problem-solving, always look for the line of the least assumptions, in this case, my friend, we find the hacker, we find the person responsible for this crime."

Broadstone's comments brought a silence over the radio earpieces. "This will be the first of many, so time is of the essence," Broadstone said.

"Find the hacker!"

11

"Where is he?" Alex asked as the Range Rover sped through the center of the city. Cars were darting out of the way and cyclists were gesticulating as the massive SUV roared past.

"He's in the Blackfriars, watching him flick through the paper, probably on his third pint," Ricky said over the hands-free.

Alex looked at Broadstone, he knew what she was thinking.

"Yes, I know it, behind Blackfriars Station, near the Old Bailey."

Alex nodded. "We're about ten minutes out, Rick, I'll call as soon as."

"Roger, boss." The line went dead.

Alex scrolled through her phone, found Siobhan's message thread, another photo – more explicit. She scrolled up to hide the message so Simon wouldn't see it. Alex was trying to sit still, she felt like the car was a fairground attraction, her frame rattling around in the seat.

Need to rain check tonight, probably gonna be mega late, she typed.

Dots…

Ok, babes, no problem, been chatting to this dude on threesome.com, wants a meet, him and his wife.

Alex frowned. Things have really changed, she thought, 'she called me *babes*, she liked it.

Okay, call me when you're done, doesn't matter how late, will probably be up anyway. Alex ended the text with some emojis. She felt silly, and she looked at the floor thinking about what she was feeling, trying to understand.

"You okay, Alex?" Simon asked.

"Yeah, course." She waved the phone. "Stuff, you know."

"It looks good on you," he said.

"What do you mean?" Alex said with a small smile.

"You've softened around the edges that is, whatever that *stuff* is, it looks good on you."

"Thank you," she said and looked at her phone. *I need to tell you something amazing, my therapist told me something. It's very cool.*

Dots...

Ok, I'll look forward to that. If you're at home tomorrow morning, I'll swing by with some breakfast and a feel, lol blushing emoji.

Alex laughed, pocketing her phone.

The car pulled up outside. Dust and road debris carried on past the car. The people sat outside stood, looked and walked away.

Alex got out. "Simon, I'll lead this, just nod and be a good boy."

Simon knitted his eyebrows together, he stood and looked at the pub – incongruous to the rest of modern London sprawling up over it. The building actually looked like a cake wedge, stuck in a moment of time. Simon had always wanted to go into the pub, it was quintessentially a London pub, but odd. The pub was known for wrong'uns, close to the Old Bailey, the infamous courthouse, but just out of reach from the law that resided in said courthouse.

They stepped in. A cloud of smoke hung in the air like spirits would in the afterworld. Everyone was smoking. The pub had such a reputation, even Trading Standards avoided the place to enforce the no-smoking law.

Eyes twitched, papers covered faces, heads turned to avoid the look from Alex – she was used to cruising pubs like this in the Met. They didn't bother her, nor scare her. They were always more afraid of the law and hid themselves away when faced with it.

"I THOUGHT I COULD SMELL SOMETHING 'ORRIBLE!" A voice boomed from the corner of the pub.

Alex clocked him and walked over. A fat, big ruddy-cheeked man sat there reading a copy of the *Sun*, two empty pints sat next to a half drunk one. An empty plate with two bags of chips sat on it. He couldn't be more stereotypical. White tennis shoes, jeans that were too tight, tucked in Sergio Tacchini shirt, dripping in gold. A large Arsenal tattoo on the inside of his left arm.

"Watch out, fellas, 'eres the fuckin' filth, and by the looks of it, she's brought some Gucci filth too." He indicated to Broadstone. Broadstone fingered the butt of his Glock, checking his archs, working out his exit if it went pear-shaped, Alex sensed it, and she touched his hand. Some of the clientele were snorting like pigs, some leaving urgently, the music stopping. The air was already thick with cigarette and cigar smoke, and it became even thicker with the arrival of Alex and Simon.

"I've got nothing to say to you pigs, halfway through my lunch and you 'ave the front to disturb me, it's harassment if you want a drink you're too late. I've bin for a gypsies already, you can find it in the bogs."

"Problem, Pork-Pie?" Said a seven-foot mutt head, clenching his fists.

"Nah mate, they've taken a wrong turn, McDonald's is

a bit further up the street, go 'ave your 'happy meal' and fuck off."

"We're looking for Alfie," Alex said, walking up to the table.

"What do you want?" A voice came from the back.

Alex and Simon turned. The landlady, Vanessa, stood there holding two plates of fish and chips.

"Well, bugger me with a cricket bat, if it isn't the slag herself, you were warned last time you stepped your muddy trotters over my doorway to *bell me*." She looked her up and down through the steam of the food. "Nothing but trouble," she sneered.

"Vanessa, been a while," Alex said.

"Not long enough, Sergeant Brown, "'ave you got some paperwork to be in 'ere?"

Alex shook her head.

"Well then, me old china, best you make like a sheep and get the flock out of my boozer, then."

Alex nodded.

"Yeah, fuck off, slag." The fat guy Alex had walked up to said.

Alex turned to Simon and nodded to the door, he frowned. "We'll go to the magistrate and get a search warrant." Simon nodded.

"Alex?" Vanessa said as she walking out.

"'Erd about your little one, Devon." She nodded with a grimace. Alex knew what she meant, she nodded back, appreciated the sentiment from mother to mother and walked out.

"What the fuck was that about?" Simon said.

"Shut up, get in the car, and say nothing."

They got in the car. Alex directed Simon across the Thames over Blackfriars Bridge, then they turned left onto Hopton Street, driving to the end. He parked and got out, walked the short distance to the Founders Arms. The only pub in the UK where you could also buy stamps and post letters. They still had the license from five hundred years previously, when the explorers left the UK to explore the New World. The pub still stood where it had been when Sir Francis Drake sailed down the River Thames.

Alex and Simon got some drinks, then took seats at the window.

"What's going on?" Simon said. Alex winked and took a sip of her drink. They didn't have to wait for long.

"OI OI SAVELOY!" Simon looked up and saw the fat man from the Blackfriars pub approaching. Alex stood, Simon instinctively reached for his pistol. "Stand down!" Alex said.

The man wrapped his hands around Alex. "It's been too long darlin', let me look at you." He held her at arm's length, took a good look up and down. "Jesus look at you, OFF the HOOK, Alex." He wrapped her up again, for about four seconds, and the man looked at Simon through Alex's hair.

"Watcha mate?" Simon looked, a little puzzled.

Alex laughed, she broke away. "Simon, meet Pork-Pie, a very dear friend."

Pork-Pie held out his hand, his fingers horribly swollen from the four massive sovereign rings garrotting the flesh on them. He had the biggest gold bracelet Simon had ever seen. Simon took his hand, it was almost a hand crush trying hard to not wince.

"How do you do?" Simon said.

"Gosh, he's a posh one, ain't he?"

Simon joined them at the table. "What was that charade all about then?"

Alex tapped Pork-Pie's hand.

"Simple, mate, I don't answer my phone, only to the missus and me *brief.* The only way you're gonna get me is either in the Black," he thumbed over his shoulder to the pub across the water, "or down the dogs at Harlow."

Simon was still puzzled.

"The pub is six hundred meters across the Thames, if you wanted to be clandestine, then maybe Chiswick or Fulham."

Alex and Pork-Pie looked at each other and stifled a laugh.

"For a spook, you don't know much do ya, mate?"

Simon still looked puzzled.

"The Thames is a natural barrier, the hoods in that pub wouldn't be seen dead this side of the water, we're safe to meet here."

"So, as much as this should be a social call, I know you're a busy lady and all, what's up?" he turned to the barmaid. "Yo, gorgeous, pint of your smooth stuff, and 'ave yourself a little snifter yourself." Winking, he turned. "Drinks?" Circling both index fingers over their glasses.

"I'm good, thanks," Simon said.

"I'm good too, still on this one."

"Spill, what do you need?"

"Something very important was taken from our American brothers, like some software. We need to find it, who would have the skill to nick something like that?" Alex said.

"Software, we're not talking about Tetris or Donkey Kong, we're talking proper spook shit, right? The sort of shit that would wind up with you floating down the Thames; brown bread?"

"Yes, we're talking about that kind of thing."

The barmaid came up and put the pint down. "'Ere you go, love, a cock n hen, keep the change."

He took a large gulp of the beer, one-third already sunk.

"I only know two geezers that could do anything remotely like that, one is a dude called Jamal. Now, your boy Ricky will prolly know about him. He's your geezer that works on the dark web. Gets you in and out of trouble fast if you see what I mean. I've used 'im a few times when selling on the *silk road*."

"And the other?" Simon said.

"Well, he's a bit of a toad, you know, the sort of cunt that would sell your mum's kidney for a Commodore."

"Commodore?"

Alex took a sip, Pork-Pie looking at her in disbelief. "Three fivers, you know, three times a lady and all that."

"Anyway, he's done a bit of Captain Kirk for me, but I don't think he has the minerals." Took another swig, two-thirds gone.

Pork-Pie whistled and held up the glass, the barmaid nodded. He downed the rest of it.

"He's a little Irish fucker called Mickey the Modem, lives over Putney way."

"Let me bell Jamal, see what he says?"

He scrolled through his phone and found the number. "You guys can get the drinks in, my throats been cut, you know what I mean," he said holding the phone to his ear and massaging his dry throat.

Nothing, he rang again, put it on speaker phone. The barmaid came with the second. "Ere's another cock n hen, and keep the change, they want to order a drink as well, so you might as well bring me another, sweet cheeks, this time they're payin'." The barmaid smiled.

"That's odd, I have Jamal's go-to phone, he answers even if he's on the nest."

He scrolled again. "Let me call the Fenian shit bag Mickey."

The phone rang and was picked up immediately.

"Well look here, the fat godshite finally calls me, to what do I owe the honour, you horrible bastard?" The Irish accent was strong.

"Looking for Jamal, Mickey, have you seen him?"

"Have aye fook, and why would I? Been sellin' that stuff he nabbed from the Yanks, gone to ground, hasn't been off the grid for a few days now. Bin cleaning up cos that fecker isn't about."

Alex knitted her brow, looked at Simon.

"What do you mean gone to ground?" Pork-Pie said.

"Well, he was peddlin' something on bBay, had a couple of watchers. I asked him about it and he told me to mind my own business."

"What was he sellin', Mickey?"

"I dunno, he wouldn't say and I wasn't that bothered, now fook off and leave me alone, you fat bastard."

The line went dead.

Pork-Pie necked the second beer and the barmaid brought two cokes and another pint. Pork-Pie gave her something – she looked at it, smiled and flushed, made the phone sign to her ear and nodded.

"There you go."

"What's bBay?" Simon asked.

Pork-Pie took a heavy sip form the third beer. "It's like eBay, but on the dark web, took over when the Yanks pulled Silk Road, all a bit beyond me if I'm honest. I just nick the stuff." He stopped, looked about. "I mean, I *acquire* the stuff, these guys fence it off to whoever."

He drained some more of the beer. "You can buy anything on it, booze, girls, drugs, kids, guns, ammo you name it. The listing stays on it for twenty-four hours. If it's not sold, it can be re-listed seven days later. There's also a section called 'wish-list.' So, if you wanted a Porsche, someone will steal one and sell it to you on there."

"Can we see it?"

"No, I can't access it, you have to be cleared, and how that's done is not my cup of tea, mate. This digital world, as good as it might be in your world, in mine, it's a fuckin' pest."

Another sip. "This is odd, though. He always answered his phone."

"Should we be worried?" Alex said.

"Jamal knows how to look after himself. If there was a problem, there is an army of wrong'uns that would bail him out, so I think I would be a bit worried that he isn't answering." Pork-Pie tried again, the phone rang out.

"What's the number?" Simon said. He looked at Simon and eyed him suspiciously.

"We'll send it to Ricky, ping the number, the phone is ringing and not going straight to voicemail."

"That's a good shout," Alex said.

"Okay." He scrolled and pushed it to Alex's phone. Alex pulled it up, then pushed it onto Ricky.

This number belongs to a guy called Jamal, dark web fencer, hacker. We need to speak to him. Might be involved with the software theft. She texted.

Dots…

No sweat, give Pork-Pie my regards.

Alex nodded. "Ricky has it, sends his regards."

"I think my work 'ere is done, just gonna see if that barmaid is free for a bit of a *tumble*."

"Thanks, mate," Alex said.

"No dramas, Alex." He drained the last of his beer.

"I heard about Devon, how you holding up?"

"Well, it's been a struggle, but I'm sure we'll get her back, we're working on it." Alex looked at Simon, he smiled.

"If there's anything, call me. You can get me on the Facebook thing now, just send me a message."

"You on Facebook?" Alex said in disbelief.

"I know, right, Marlene got me set up on it, I don't really go on it, though."

"We have to go," Simon said, breaking the connection. Alex resented it, it was fleeting.

Got a ping on the phone, here's the address.

"Ricky's on the ball, he's just pinged me the location where the phone is," Alex said.

"Let's go, been a pleasure, and thanks for your help, Pork-Pie." Simon was struggling to use that name and shook his hand.

"Yeah, cheers mucker, you look after this one. She's a bit special in our lives." He gave her a hug. He turned and walked to the bar, the barmaid was waiting for him with the broadest of smiles.

Both Alex and Simon walked. "What have we got?" Simon said.

"An address."

She typed as they walked, *bBay, have you heard of it???* to Ricky.

Yeah, dark web auction site, been on it a few times, he typed.

They got to the car, Simon got in. Alex was still typing and stood by the door of the car. *Go on it, find Jamal's profile, I know that the listing disappeared after twenty-four hours, do whatever you can to find what he had listed, we are off to the address!*

Alex got in, clicked her seat belt on and Simon revved the engine.

Stay frosty, Ricky said.

12

Siobhan cleaned herself up and got dressed. After showering and laying on Alex's bed for most of the morning, Siobhan felt confused. She had lived an alternate lifestyle for so long. Being attracted to another woman wasn't anything new to her, she had had relations with women in clubs and parties, but Alex was something different.

'What had she to say to me?' She thought. She pulled Alex's pillow from her side of the bed, and inhaled deeply, the smell of Alex causing Siobhan's heart to ache. She felt lost and empty that she wasn't there. 'Was it the sex?' she thought. She breathed in again, her eyes glistened and she missed her. She didn't even miss Ray when he buggered off on business for the week. She had only just met this woman, who was full of secrets, 'What the hell happened that morning with that dude coming into the house?' Siobhan was inexplicably attracted to her, she couldn't rationalize it.

Her phone beeped. A push notification came up from VXN.com, the hookup sex dating app.

She clicked open, there was a raft of waiting messages. All time wasters, but a fresh message caught her eye. In town for the night only, threesome with my secretary at a swanky hotel?

Siobhan, a sucker for a three-way, clicked open. The

email was brief, the pictures of the guy was too good to be true. But he had taken the time to message her, *here's my mobile, send me a selfie in five minutes then I'm interested, pass that we are done.*

Thirty seconds later, Siobhan's phone beeped, a message. She clicked it open, the selfie was of the guy in the dating app. Siobhan smiled. *You've got me, where and when.*

Dots…

Crown piazza, Albert Embankment. The hotel just up from Tommies, the hospital.

Siobhan thought for a moment. That was literally four doors down from where she was.

The phone vibrated. *What time would suit you?*

She was carefree. She had the day, and now Alex had blown her out, she most likely had the evening too. She decided that she would stay at Alex's apartment for the night in the hope that Alex would come home, even if she came home at 4 am, seeing her for a few hours was better than nothing. She inhaled into Alex's pillow again.

How about now, stud? I have been blown out, so I'm pretty free if you are.

Dots…

Sure, just go to the concierge, ask for Room 37, they'll know where to send you.

Siobhan swung her legs off the bed and thought, who might you be? She walked up to the long mirror and checked herself. She looked good, even though she had had hardly any sleep, and was sore form an evening of fun and only had light makeup on.

She made sure the bed was made, and everything was shipshape. She left the apartment and walked the short distance to the Crown Plaza. The hotel was almost entirely made of glass.

The doorman nodded and opened the door, his eyes

following her slim figure over the threshold, Siobhan giving him a wink as she passed. Turning heads was a pastime for her, everyman turned, even the gays.

She stopped, surveyed the room, and saw a chap stood watching her at a desk. Looked like the concierge.

Striding up, the guy smiled from one side of his mouth, not cleanly shaven, but buff, his Slovak features giving his provenance away even before he spoke. Siobhan liked him.

"Room 37, please?" she asked.

"I thought so," he said, his voice gruff and harsh. He picked the phone up. "Your friend has arrived, sir." Watching her, she was listening to the talking on the other end, "Of course, right away."

He replaced the receiver. "Come with me, please, your friend is waiting."

He skirted around the desk and walked, extending his hand out, his strong hand pressing the small of Siobhan's back. She flushed between her legs, a warmth spreading through her like the warm glow of the summer sun. Gone was the rawness of the previous night's escapades, this was intriguing.

They entered the elevator, he reached across her, not really paying any attention to personal space, she didn't mind. His smell was alluring. Is he in the tryst with the couple in room 37?

She pushed the hair over her ear and smiled at him.

"You know who I'm seeing?" she asked, he ignored her, just looked and smiled.

The doors opened, they turned right and walked the short distance to Room 37. The concierge swiped the card through the lock, he knocked as he entered. "COME," Siobhan heard.

The man ushered Siobhan in, he followed, and she felt a tinge of nervousness. Her guts tightened, this wasn't unusual. Every new encounter brought this same feeling, she was always nervous, especially if there was another woman involved.

She walked in – the suite was enormous. The view of the Thames, identical to the view Alex's apartment had one hundred meters up the road, just a bit further down. As she entered, a well-dressed man stood there, the clink of fine-cut crystal glass tapped the coffee table. He buttoned the single-breasted suit up and approached. His Germanic features were striking, shit, he's a good looker, she thought. Jackpot.

Offering his hand, veiny and strong, Siobhan took it. She thought that was odd, because in her experience of meeting guys on VXN.com, she would be naked and having sex in about five minutes, she felt giddy.

His grip tight, strong, but taking care not to hurt. "Siobhan," she said.

"I know," he said, she canted her head and knitted her brow. How did he know? She thought.

She felt someone behind her, suddenly something was slipped over her head and around her neck, with the sound of ratcheting of electrical cable tie, her throat closed. Siobhan instantly struggled to breathe, the air suddenly thinning out, she went to grab at it, but it was too tight to get her fingers in, she dropped to one knee, the sound of her breathing getting raspier, like tearing cardboard, all of Siobhan's accessory muscles kicked in, the platysma muscle on her chest tugged violently as her body was trying to draw as much air into the lungs as possible. Her other knee hit the floor, she started becoming weaker, a blue tinge faded across her lips, replacing the red. The man took a knee next to her smiling.

"Stop panicking, Siobhan, you're not dying." He smiled. His aftershave was intoxicating, almost replacing the precious oxygen that Siobhan so desperately needed.

She tried to speak, the faded colour now spreading across her whole face and neck. "Help me." She breathed out. "Help me."

Siobhan fell face down and started crawling towards the balcony door, the air fresh and ubiquitous. Siobhan's natural instinct was just to get outside. Confused, she had no idea what was happening. Using the patio door, she tried to climb up, trying to drag more air into her.

The man followed her out onto the balcony and took a seat, crossing his legs. He motioned to the concierge. He strode over and pulled out a tactical knife, exposing the blade. He grabbed her by the hair and threw her onto the balcony, Siobhan screamed. He grabbed the hem of her dress, the knife, and like sharp scissors on Christmas paper, sliced through the dress. Siobhan, unable to fight, turned to her side, drew her knees up to her chest, tears tumbling down her face.

She felt the man tug at her feet, with no energy, she let him pull her panties off, he flicked her over to her back like she was a piece of meat, the knife bust through the central bridge, and her bra bust open. Her breasts were pert and full, hardly moving. The man looked down. Siobhan's eyes were trying to roll back, she didn't know if she was dying. She wanted to die, she had never felt so powerless. Naked, choking on some random man's hotel balcony while he sat and watched with an empty smile, his eyes like empty wells of evil. His features looked less attractive by the second.

She felt the movement above her, legs. She tried to focus, the legs were long and slender, a pretty short dress, a young girl, pretty. She looked familiar to Siobhan, but she knew she had never met her. The girl sat on the man's knee, and he curled his hand around her, his hand on her thigh. She was smiling, looking down.

Siobhan lay still, eyes darting around, trying to take her environment in.

"Have you settled down now, Siobhan?" The man said. Siobhan could feel her lips, swollen, her own blood trying to leave her body to find oxygen. She said and did nothing, she realized that if she took shallow breaths some air could get to the lungs through the ligature.

You can take the girl out of Northern Ireland, but you can't take the Irish out of her. Fuck you, she thought.

"Your stillness tells me you're finally settling into your predicament. Let me introduce myself, my name is Broc, Dale Broc." Nothing, Siobhan still had no idea who this prick was.

"And this lovely little filly is Devon, you know, Alex's missing daughter?" The girl blushed and giggled on Broc's lap, burying her face into his neck. "Daddy, please," she said.

"It's okay, baby, she can't hurt you," Broc said.

Instantly, the recognition shot across Siobhan's face. The long chat that Alex and Siobhan had had. Siobhan now recognized the features of the girl. Alex had gone into great detail about her daughter, and how she went missing. She didn't mention Broc though, Siobhan thought, but seriously, a bad case of Stockholm Syndrome here.

Siobhan, a strong woman, kept her breathing under control, but she couldn't speak. All she could do was control the air slowly, making its way into the back of the throat. The tears had stopped but the sweat came. She was soaked in it – the body's stress response.

"I think Devon is a little upset that you had sex with her mother last night," Broc said.

How did he know? She thought,

"You see, that woman, sorry, baby–" he stopped, looked at the girl on his lap. "I know that I shouldn't disrespect your mother so openly."

The girl was looking down at Siobhan, both staring at each other, eyes fixed. "It's okay, daddy," she said.

Fucking daddy, Siobhan thought.

"Are we going to kill her?" Devon asked.

Broc pulled a face. "God, no petal, we won't be doing that, maybe sell her or cut her up, what would you want to do?" he said.

"I want to watch you cut her up, daddy, maybe while she's still alive?"

He laughed. "Gosh, you are full of surprises."

He motioned to the concierge, and Broc stood, the girl sitting on the other chair.

Siobhan's eyes were trying desperately to see what Broc was doing.

"I have a plan for you, young lady. Firstly, though, you're going to sleep."

With his fore and index finger, Broc felt along Siobhan's neck line, and she screamed. "Thank you," Broc said.

Her screaming caused a vasodilation of the major neck veins, without hesitation Broc plunged a long needle into the jugular vein. He went to press the plunger down but stopped. He looked up at the young girl who was sitting and watching with the broadest of smiles. "Do you want to do this?" he asked.

She nodded excitedly, got up out of the chair and slid over to Siobhan. She took hold of the syringe and inserted it into the vein. "Steady, babygirl, just push that plunger down."

She did, Siobhan powerless to stop her. She could feel the viscous white propofol sear though her large bored vein, gritting her teeth, a shroud of darkness creeping up her like a mist, her head swimming and spinning out of control into total darkness. Her body became limp, almost instantly cold and clammy. He nodded.

The concierge, and two other Slovak-looking men entered the space dressed as paramedics, put an oxygen mask onto her and bungled her onto a trolley.

Both Devon and Broc stood by. "We're going to kill her, right?" she asked, Broc draped his arm around her, and spun her around to look at the view.

"Patience, baby, we have plans for her, don't you worry. Just take that view in, London in spring is just so gorgeous, don't you think?"

"Only when I'm with you, you make me so complete." Devon said, turning to her man.

13

Alex and Broadstone careered up the Haverstock Hill near Belsize Park, blues and twos wailing. They turned into the Belsize lane, and parked outside the fruit and vegetable store. Alex got out of the car, checking her Glock, she orientated herself and saw the back of Jamal's house, the black gate ajar.

She motioned to the gate.

"Whatcha, mate," said the fruit seller, Broadstone nodded, and, with his hand, pushed back, telling the guy not to get involved, and for good measure he pulled his pistol, and checked the chamber. The fruit seller instantly retreated back into the store.

"Let's go," he said. They crossed the road and got to the gate. The village of Belsize was busy, post-lunch hangout with the yummy mummies waiting for their little ones to exit their perfect little schools.

They entered the garden, Alex whistled. "Posh pad."

"Who is this Jamal then? This property has got to be worth a couple of million."

"Ricky said the deeds are in his parents' names, with him as the sole benefactor, late twenties. Bit of genius, turned to the darker side of life." Alex checked the outhouse at the end of the garden. Unlocked and neat. It was Belsize park and not a part of London Alex was used to.

"Crime does pay," Broadstone said as he approached the house, his back to the garden wall.

"Well, ask your mate Tao Ng about that!"

Simon smiled, ruefully. "You will get your day Alex, I'll make sure of it."

They got to the house. From the garage next to it, Simon peered into the window, seeing no one. He tried the door and it clicked open.

"Outhouse open, I can't understand that, the back door to a million-pound property, not so sure."

Alex went in first. "POLICE, we are armed, CALL OUT!" Pulling her gun, she took the safety off and ran her finger along the body of the pistol, arm outstretched. Broadstone held his pistol closer, the difference between law enforcement and special forces-cum-spook. He certainly had the training and had put it into practice more times than she would dare to ask.

Alex had an unsettling feeling, it wasn't a normal anxiousness that she felt. The house didn't feel right, but deep down she felt wretched.

"Wow, shit!" Broadstone cried out, standing back.

Alex peered around him, in the sink remained the head of the lady Errol had decapitated.

"What the hell?" Broadstone exclaimed.

They both looked around the kitchen, Simon spun and walked into the hallway, using the wall as cover. Alex followed. The house was empty – the front of it was secure, with no sign of forced entry. They went back to the kitchen.

"Okay, as a police officer, it's an easy call. We're supposed to be dealing with health-related crime, this is a bit of a sidestep," Alex said.

"We can't process this scene, Alex, chatter on the net about this location could compromise our investigation." Broadstone peered closer at the head.

"Don't touch it, I have an idea." Alex pulled out her phone and flicked through the screen with her finger. She found what she was looking for, hit dial.

The phone on speaker answered immediately. "Hey Alex, long time, we were talking about you this morning," the voice said.

"James, how are you doing? I hope it was all good, right?"

James laughed. He was Alex's favorite pathologist, a man of detail yet absurdly melancholic in his approach. The weirder the better, there was nothing he hadn't seen or done as a scientist. He had a bit of a soft spot for Alex that was purely professional. Grim crime scenes were his thing. "This isn't a social call, I need a massive solid, can you help me?"

There was a pause. "Give me a second, Alex." They heard footsteps, a door, then a car door slamming.

"Shoot."

"How averse are you to processing a crime scene without reporting it until we give you the green light?"

"Erm, if you're involved, Alex, I'm pretty sure I'll be okay with it, why?"

"Can you get to Belsize Park? The back of Belsize Terrace, we'll meet you?"

"I'm all done here, so I can be with you in about forty-five minutes, how's that?"

"Perfect, and James?"

"Yes?"

"Please don't tell anyone where you're going or what you're doing," Alex said.

"That's okay with me, see you in a tick, wherever you are in the property, leave it now and don't enter it again until I get there."

Both Simon and Alex nodded at each other. They left the property and hung around the back of the garden. It was only twenty-five minutes before James texted.

Alex opened the gate slightly, and James was waiting with a couple of hard boxes and a big rucksack, he squeezed through.

"James, this is Simon Broadstone, my boss."

"Ahh, the spook that stole the golden child, pleased to meet you, James Duggal, what have we got?"

Broadstone nodded, went through the story, and then told him that the only thing in the house was the head of a middle-aged women.

"Okay, first thing first, chaps, put these on." He handed out two paper jump suits and shoe covers.

They entered the kitchen, the jumpsuits swishing as they walked. James stopped them from following him in. "Would you mind awfully if you guys just waited outside until I have done a preliminary pass?" Both Alex and Simon stopped dead, like a pair of naughty children caught by their mother.

He pulled out a spray bottle, and sprayed the room, all over the floors and surfaces. He pulled out a light and switched it on. The kitchen was bathed in a green light, blood spatter everywhere. The outline of the body showed where it had fallen, and the footsteps too.

"Shit, I'm impressed!" Broadstone said.

James looked up. "Pretty impressive, right? They were killed here." He was pointing exactly where he stood. "And I know how," he continued, walking up to the head in the sink.

"Well, I have a clear indication of death, her head was removed from the body," Alex said, trying to add some humour.

"Very good, Alex, come?" They walked over to the sink. "Look at the incision, it's a classic cut."

"From what?" Simon said.

"This is with a Zulu or Tutsi, classic machete kill."

"How would you know that, James?" Alex said peering closer.

"Look at the angle of the cut, it's clean too, no fuss, no ragged edges. Even ISIS aren't this good. This was the same in Rwanda." The three of them stood by staring.

"If I was a betting man, this was done by a Zulu, or a Bulawayo tribal member."

Simon looked at James. "Why do you say that?"

"Have you been to Rwanda, Mr Broadstone?"

Simon pulled a face. "No, I must confess, I haven't."

"Apart from the blight on the country in the mid 90s, it's very beautiful. Wealthy as well. Worth a holiday. The Virunga Mountain Range is just unspeakably stunning." He was staring out of the window, his mind being whisked elsewhere.

"Your point, James?" Alex said.

"The people of Rwanda do not leave Rwanda, Alex, but a South African, especially a Zulu with a talent for killing, that's where I would back my money, guys."

Both Alex and Simon looked at each other.

"The rest of the house is clear, not sure where Jamal's computers were kept. House seems untouched," Broadstone said, and he walked across the kitchen towards the garage door.

"We haven't checked in the garage, though." He turned and pulled his Glock, smiled.

"This isn't like Sweets Way with the girl in the bath Alex, please, you know with my boiled victim?" James said.

"I think we'll be fine, James, sit tight and wait."

It took another three minutes for Alex to emerge from the garage, James had timed it.

"Come," she said.

They entered the garage, the concrete floor scraped, the dust disturbed. A bank of twenty plug sockets could be seen, a socket for a wide bore ethernet cable.

"There was some hardware in here," Broadstone said.

James nodded, scanned the room. His eyes saw different things that the other two wouldn't be able to see until he had pointed them out.

He reached into one of the bags and pulled the fluorescein, and started spraying the room. "Do you mind just waiting by the door?" he said.

When James had done the room, he replaced the bottle and switched the black light on. There was nothing by the garage doors. The people out on the street could be heard in the cafe. He turned, the faces of Broadstone and Alex turning an eerie purple, looking back at the scientist.

"Wow, we have a second crime scene, ladies and gentlemen." Both Alex and Simon walked in spinning around, the blood spatter from the head shot, and the blood from the workbench.

"They've been busy here, but not so careful about cleaning up by the looks of things."

"This will take me too much time to process, I need a good few hours, Alex," James said, opening the other boxes that he'd brought.

"What's the deal, you don't want me here officially, but this crime scene has witnessed two murders, and by the looks of things, torture too." He jerked his thumb towards the vice on the workbench.

"Given the nature and that there have been fatalities, I can only give you three days, then I have to open this as a murder investigation or you're going to compromise me."

"Why three days?" Alex asked.

"Forensics will become too degraded to follow up on, and let's face it, we need to process this scene urgently. Two people have died here."

"Okay, what are we going to do with the house in the interim? What if people come?" Alex said. "You know, like a neighbour, or a family member? This house is cared for, there will be visitors."

"Good point," James said. "The property needs to be secured."

"I can stick a team in here. They can front it as an Airbnb rental. The family has gone away. If we can get some clear intel on their family connections, maybe abroad. The house has been rented to a couple, and they will stay in here until we either have more news or the three-day embargo ends." Broadstone looked at James and Alex.

"That works for me," James said. "I will be turning up here in exactly three days' time, if I don't hear from you, with my cavalry, I won't be calling you to let you know, understand that?" James said.

"Okay. How soon can you get a team in here, Simon?" Alex said.

"I'll make a call." He walked to the corner, pulling his phone out.

"Frank misses you Alex," James said. Alex found the conversation odd – standing in a crime scene, the black light still on, talking about her old life. An old life that seemed so long ago, but in reality only six months had passed. Where did that go? Alex thought.

"I must catch up with the gang soon."

"I heard about you and Simon too, I'm truly sorry Alex."

She shook her head. "We'll work it out, James, I'm sure of it." They both turned, hearing Simon returning.

"There's a team on the way. We can stick some surveillance teams at the front and rear aspect of the house upstairs. And a millennial couple for front of house, given the nature of this location, they will be bombed up."

"Bombed up?" James asked.

"Armed, I'm not taking chances with some lunatic group of criminals."

"Agreed," Alex said. She was stopped by Simon, holding his finger up to his face, gently saying, "shush".

Both James and Alex exchanged glances. Simon extended his arm, and steered James behind him. "Get over in the corner, James, Alex, bomb up. Time to make some grass grow."

Alex turned to the door – then she heard it, voices. The voices of men. They weren't quiet.

Simon and Alex, weapons drawn, sprinted to the wall by the door connecting the kitchen. Alex glanced at James, crouching under the workstation, looking pale, she winked at him, and he nodded back. Her winking reassurance was doing nothing for his nerves right now.

The voices were still loud as Simon pulled his phone out, flicking through it while staring through the door, facing the kitchen, he found the app he was looking for. He opened it, and hit record, placed the phone on the shiny tiled floor, and pushed the phone into the kitchen.

"Hey, that twat Jongy thinks he owns the store, I can't stand him, eh." The South African accent was strong, menacing.

"Jongy is okay, that fucking coon who follows him around like a lost dog, though, who doesn't speak, I'd slot him in a heartbeat."

"I think Jongy fucks him eh?"

"You think Jongy is a gayboy?"

"All those fuckin' Afrikaans Nazis are fucking each other, eh."

Then men came into view, seeing the head in the sink. "Holy shit man, eh, what the hell is this?"

"Jongy said there's a head in the sink, come on. Mr Veshausen needs this place spick and span, no loose ends or we'll become loose ends if you see what I mean?"

"The work surface is wet, eh, why would it be wet?" The

hooded one slid his fingers along the surface and held them up to his nose.

"Smells funny, why would the room be wet eh? It's fuckin everywhere."

"Who cares man, let's get on, finish early and we can go for a beer, eh?"

Simon slid down the wall and half-turned his head to Alex. "Two pax, big, can't see any weapons, they will come in here any second, you up for this, Alex?"

She nodded, her heart beating in her chest like the dropped base in a club. She flicked the safety off. "Rock and roll," she said. Simon smiled and glanced at James, trying not to shake. She nodded; James nodded back.

"On three, one, two–" Simon opened the door further and stood, Alex followed suit. "Three."

They burst into the room. "STAND STILL, ARMED POLICE!" Simon shouted, the two men turned, blood draining from their faces, and the hooded one reached into his pocket. That was his last memory, Simon fired three times, two centre mass, as the man buckled under the power of the bullets smashing into his bullet proof vest, instantly the man smiled, which was vapourized as Simon spotted the vest and pumped another round into the man's head. Dropping like liquid at the feet of the other, Alex was training her pistol on him. "HANDS, MAKE 'EM CLEAR OR YOU'RE DROPPING TOO!" she shouted.

The man held up his hands, looking frightened, two more rounds snapped to the left of Alex, one of the empty cases bouncing off her forearm. Alex turned and then looked back to the man surrendering, watching him fall to the floor, both knees blown out.

"Jesus, Simon, what did you do that for?"

"He's bombed up too, I'm not taking any chances with him, took his caps out, we can get some intel," Simon said.

He quickly skirted over to the dead man, his pistol slipping out of his hand, Simon kicked it across the room, feeling the neck – no pulse.

Turning to the man shifting on the floor, Alex was already rifling through his clothes. A machete and a Browning 9mm pistol – so worn the black metal had become like a shiny nickel and a round chambered. Alex pulled the top-slide back and ejected the round. The man tried to crawl away, blood oozing out of both legs, oddly not making any sound.

Broadstone walked up to him and placed the warm barrel of his Glock in the nape of his neck. "Where the fuck do you think you're going, sunshine?"

The man stopped. "Please, please I'm not important, please let me go," he pleaded.

"That's not gonna happen, at best you'll be trundling around a British prison for life, at worse, if armed response don't turn up, I'm gonna kill you myself," Simon said, pressing the pistol in further. He turned and looked at Simon quizzically. "That's right, my friend, we're British Intelligence, we don't conform to the rules, not a good day for you, is it?" It was the first time Alex had heard Simon say 'British Intelligence,' the guise was Interpol, and she had mixed feelings about it.

The man gasped. "Please, I don't know anything."

"Say who sent you and I will speed dial a paramedic," Broadstone said.

"I don't know, we were just sent, I don't know any names." Simon indicated to Alex for his phone lying on the floor by the door. She quickly stepped over to it and grabbed it, switched it off. She knew that anything they said could be used against them by the lawyers. She handed the phone to Simon.

He dialled it back to the beginning.

Hey, that twat Jongy thinks he owns the store, I can't stand him, eh.

Jongy is okay, that fucking coon who follows him around like a lost dog though, who doesn't speak, I'd slot him in a heartbeat.

I think Jongy fucks, eh.

You think Jongy is a gayboy.

All those fuckin' Afrikaans Nazis are fucking each other, eh.

A couple of seconds passed, the man lying on the floor trying to dig a hole with his eyelids to get away from the audio. Alex was impressed with Broadstone.

Holy shit man, eh, what the hell is this? The recording went on.

Jongy said that there's a head in the sink, come on. Mr Veshausen needs this place spick and span, no loose ends or we'll become loose ends if you see what I mean.

The work surface is wet, eh, why would it be wet…?

Simon switched the recording off. "So, the obvious question is, who's Jongy and the, what I like to call, the black man who follows him around, as well as this person Mr Veshausen?"

"I can't tell you, please, please you have no idea what you're uncovering here."

Broadstone crouched. "Then enlighten me, and you'll have a bargaining chip, by saying nothing." Simon looked at Alex, then looked back down. "Have nothing." Replacing the gun back on his neck

"Mr Broadstone," Simon looked up. James was standing in the doorway.

"You okay?" Alex asked.

James smiled. "I realized the full function of what the sphincter of the anus is for."

Alex smiled. "You never get used to it."

James held his phone. "I've called it in, armed police are on their way."

"Shit," Alex said, she pulled her phone out.

"Sorry Alex…" Alex held up her hand to James. "Ricky?" she said.

"We've had a moment at the target house, armed response has been dispatched to this location, get the officers on the blower immediately and make sure they're waving a white flag, the house is secure, I repeat, the house is secure. I will leave the front door open."

She hung up, James looking nervous. "Have I done something wrong? I can't leave this scene any longer, things have escalated."

"James, don't worry, you did the right thing," Alex said.

Two police officers were suddenly walking down the hallway tactically.

"Friendlies!" Simon shouted. "Everything is under control.

The officers softened, stopped, look at each other and walked into the kitchen.

14

"Why is he withdrawn Jongy, what have you done?" Veshausen said, as he tried to role the Indian.

"Nothing boss, he's a lazy fucker, eh."

"These bruises are new, did you fuck him, Jongy?"

Jongy stood back. "What do you take me for, boss?"

"You're a psychopathic neo-Nazi that likes bumming young men, of course I know what you're like, you buffoon."

They helped him. "Jamal, get up man." They put him in the chair, Veshausen stopped to look at him. "Jamal, wake up." He tapped around his face.

He roused, eyes heavy, the Adam's apple bobbing. His eyes looked up, saw Jongy and Veshausen. "He raped me," Jamal muttered, still half dazed.

Veshausen punched Jongy in the, chest mouthing, "I fucking knew it."

"I need something for my arm," Jamal said, his face screwing up.

Veshausen looked down at the arm. The infection was getting worse, he lifted one of the dressings, the wound looking purulent and angry. He looked up at Jongy, who tried to look at it, but when his eyes clapped on it, he averted immediately.

Blunt walked in. "I've just had a report that armed

response is required at Jamal's house, please tell me that's not connected to our operation, De Jong?"

Jongy turned to the computer screens and radios, dialled into the Met's radio net. The net was awash with chatter about a shooting in Belsize Park.

"Get your network online, Jamal, and we'll get you analgesia for your arm, we need to use assets in and around that house."

Begrudgingly, Jamal fired the computers up and had them up and running in seconds. He accessed the Met's computer systems, whizzing around the CCTV cameras. He accessed the ambulance service as an ambulance had been dispatched, he then accessed the cameras inside the house that Jamal had set up, as well as the CCTV on the street.

The three captors stood back and watched.

"Right, there's a fatality, I guess this is your guy, the injured person is the second of your guys, what do you want me to do? I have options."

The three men looked at each other, Blunt spoke. "He can't get into the hands of the authorities. I don't know what he knows but he cannot be taken away."

"He knows nothing, eh," Jongy said

"Let's not take any chances," Blunt said, he leaned into Jamal's ear. "Dispose of him."

Jamal nodded and launched Hypnos.

Across the street, adjacent to the house, was Greenfields. A trendy brassiere that served fresh coffee pastries and smoothies. It was the perfect location for the mummies to congregate between dropping the kids off, yoga, gym and pretending to give a shit about the person next to them, chatting idly about who had the most money or the biggest house. In yummy mummy terms, it was similar to men metaphorically measuring their penises at the pub.

Caitlin, the 36-year-old wife of a successful hedge fund manager, was sat with her friends, pretending to listen but playing a game of Fruit Smash. One earphone in her ear listening to 'Careless Whisper' by George Michael. Level 122 was beckoning, maybe today she would do it!

Caitlin never felt the upload. The binary digit converting to proteins and enzymes absorbed into the cortex. Her head snapped back, and shook side to side twice.

Her head turned to the unmarked police car parked outside the house on Belsize Terrace, she stood. "You off, Caitlin?" one of the friends said while in mid-sentence about how cool the nanny was.

"I'll be back in a sec," she said.

She strode over to the police car, opened the boot. Her friends watched in bewilderment as she reached in, pulling out an MP5 Carbine. She inserted the magazine, pulled the cocking lever back and forward assisted the action, chambering the round.

"Caitlin, what the hell are you doing?" Another friend shouted.

She smiled at them. Walked to the house, stepped inside, the first policeman walked up to challenge, from the hip, three rounds into the groin, he dropped. The next copper drew his Glock, Caitlin shouldering the carbine, three rounds, two to the chest one to the head.

She entered the kitchen, saw Broadstone and Alex, they didn't have time to draw, she saw the man lying on the floor, flicked the carbine to fully automatic and operated the trigger. Alex saw the stream of 9mm empty case eject from the gun as the rounds slammed into the injured guy on the floor, his body jerking violently. The gun emptied pretty quick, she threw it, reached across the work surface and pulled the butcher's knife from the block, she stood and looked at the three of them, aghast in the corner of the kitchen.

"Put the knife down?" Broadstone said, as he stepped slowly towards her, Glock drawn, staring down the sights of the pistol. "I won't say it again, put the knife down." The room was thick with the smell of spent bullets and carbon, a light haze of smoke hung in the air, taking Alex back to the ranges as a young soldier.

Caitlin smiled at him, looked at Alex, Alex unable to move. The demeanour of the woman was unnerving, distant yet present, Alex couldn't understand what she was doing.

Caitlin brought the knife to the side of her throat and pushed the sharp end of the blade horizontal, slowly, deliberately pushing the knife into her throat. Blood jetted from the side of her neck as she pushed the blade in, still smiling. Alex wanted to stop her, but she felt powerless. Simon lowered the pistol, confused, he turned to Alex.

Caitlin reached the hilt of the blade, and in a twisting action, like throttling the accelerator of a bike, she twisted the knife, and in a pushing action, ripped the front of her throat out. Blood and tissue fell to the floor like a wet dish-cloth. The sucking sound came, as the body tried desperately to draw in air. Even in a traumatic episode like this, the body still stuck to its remit of drawing air in, the amygdala still defaulting to survival mode. Caitlin fell to floor, one knee at a time, still smiling, her chest heaving desperately to reoxygenate her dying body, the sound like a fish out of water made Alex recoil in horror. She ran over to her, in a vain attempt to help, but there was nothing that she could do. Blood spurted everywhere as the heart still pumped the blood that was left in her body. The breathing increased to a shallow rapid breath rate.

Simon grabbed Alex. "You can't do anything." He pulled her back to the corner, blood all over Alex's hands. Crumpled together, they watched for what seemed like minutes. But in real terms, it was only seconds, her chest rapidly going up and down, the sucking sound getting quieter and quieter, then suddenly it stopped. For a second, she knelt still, smiling at Alex. Alex watched as the pupils dilated and the spirit of the woman fluttered away, her face changing to nothing but a stony thousand-yard stare. She was gone.

"What the fuck?" Alex said, "what the fuck?"

James stumbled in. "I don't know what I've just seen," he said, pale and shocked.

"The officers," Alex said, she scrambled to her feet, slipping on the blood spreading across the floor and, banging her knee on the floor, she gathered herself against the work surface and ran into the hallway. The first officer she came to was dead, most of the back of his head was missing. The second officer nearer the front door was groaning, lying in a pool of his own blood, barely conscious. Her previous medical life as an ODP knew that all three rounds in the pelvis would hit three or four major vessels, he needed surgery urgently.

She grabbed the radio, the control room had to know to get the right team to him.

"Officer down, officer down, multiple shootings Belsize Terrace, urgent medical assistance, HEMS required, over." She said down the radio. Alex made sure her voice was slow, clear and succinct. The last thing the other person on the other end needed was to hear how Alex really felt, wanting to scream down the radio.

"Roger, send constable collar numbers over."

She checked the epaulettes of the injured officer, she pressed the presses of the radio. "Charlie Oscar 56982 roger so far, over."

"Roger," came the reply.

"The fatality is Charlie Oscar 56782, and the suspect, over."

There was a pause. Alex could imagine about eight people crowding around the operator at the other end.

"Your ID? Over."

Alex glanced over her shoulder, Broadstone was standing behind her, pistol drawn, covering her, eyes fixed on the front door. Anyone not wearing a uniform would be dealt with, Simon had the look of the devil in his eyes.

"What the fuck do I say, Simon?" she said, gritting her teeth.

He looked down. "B5 intelligence, just tell them that."

She pressed the *pressel* switch again. "Bravo 5 Intelligence, over."

"Roger, standby, out."

The officer's breathing was shallow and rapid.

"He hasn't got long left, he needs an anaesthetist and an ODP as well as a barrel of blood."

"He's not your problem, Alex, this isn't our fight, we have to move as soon as those overt agencies are on task."

Alex threw a look at Simon, eyes fixed on the access points where she knelt. James came into the hallway.

"I just heard on my radio that most of the Met will be here in about three minutes, in two minutes the HEMS will land on the crossroads, I have to go and meet the docs getting off it."

Alex heard the distinctive rotors of the HEMS, it was looking for somewhere to land, buzzing about, the engine pitching to and forth, any second the engines would power down and they would be here.

She looked down, the officers breathing had become very shallow. She checked the carotid, thready and weak. "Fuck, he's about to arrest, help me!" she screamed.

Broadstone grabbed his feet and pulled his slumped frame away from the wall, the body heavy, blood loss more apparent as they moved him.

Alex opened the chest rig, pulled the officer's trauma scissors out, and cut up the tee shirt. He was fit, which meant that he had a good chance of surviving this.

With the heel of her hand, she felt the xiphisternum a couple of centimetres up, between the nipples, she started pumping, a rib cracked, then another.

"Check his chest rig, he may have a pocket mask, give him rescue breaths."

She pumped, the song 'Nelly the Elephant' ringing in her ears. Medical professionals are now taught to compress to 'Staying Alive' by the Bee Gees. Nelly sounded better. Then she heard them, the sound of boots, suddenly on them.

"What's happening?" Asked the voice, she looked up. Alex felt the sting of tears, overwhelmed, she struggled to control them.

A paramedic pushed her out of the way, Alex half crawled to the first step of the stairs, blood all over her hands, on her face and down her trousers, the knees soaked. Sweat was pouring out of her forehead, armed police turning up en-masse.

"He's got three rounds in his pelvis, he bled out about ten minutes ago, he went peri-arrest about a minute ago." Alex suddenly remembered the woman. "Shit."

The doctor turned. "You okay?" he asked, eyeing her up and down.

"Yeah, I made a mistake, there are three fatalities, not two."

"Where are they?" he asked.

"The officer there, our suspect, and a woman. Weird, she just appeared in the hallway, shot the officers and then came into the kitchen, killed our suspect and then cut her own throat."

He furrowed his brow, looked up the hallway, another doctor came through and confirmed the dead bodies in the kitchen.

Veshausen, Blunt and Jongy were watching, speechless, staring at the carnage created by Jamal. Still typing single-handedly, ferociously.

"Who are these people?" Blunt said, peering at Broadstone and Alex.

Jamal ran facial recognition software, Alex came up but Broadstone didn't.

"I know this woman, I had dealings with her not so long back, she doesn't know me but some of my ex-clients have had run-ins with her."

"What do you mean ex-clients?" Veshausen said, pushing his shoulder .

"She had them arrested or killed, her name is Alex Brown, but she isn't police anymore. The no-show of the guy means that he's off the grid."

"Meaning?" Blunt said.

"Meaning that he's intelligence, the fact that they're at my house means that they are onto you," Jamal said, pulling his tee shirt up over his nose, the waft of body odour singing his nose.

"Can you dig further, and glean me some more information?"

"I can, but I'm going to need assurances," Jamal said, looking up over his shoulder.

Jongy clouted him around the head. "Shut your mouth coon, eh."

"Jongy," Veshausen snapped.

"I'm either working for you or I'm not, you have to make me part of your team." He tapped the screen. "I did this for you, you have to stop this monster from getting anywhere near me," Jamal said, gesturing in Jongy's direction.

"Okay, we can accommodate that," Blunt said.

"Sir!" Jongy protested.

"ENOUGH, DE JONG, GO AND DO SOMETHING

ELSE!" Veshausen spat, Jongy paused, looked at the two men standing behind Jamal, he screwed his face up, turned and left.

Jamal was already typing, the legend of the man came up.

"His name is Simon Broadstone, he's your regular special forces badass."

Vensausen looked at Blunt.

"Can you influence the intelligence service at the cabinet level, and call these clowns off?"

Blunt shrugged. "I can try, I can speak to my contact in the intelligence service, see what she has to say."

"Make it happen, we don't need a pair of sniffer dogs around the cause!" Veshausen said.

"Indeed," said Blunt.

"Okay, I've uploaded everything to Ricky, we need to bounce, let these guys sort out the crime scene, we're literally treading on toes here," Broadstone said.

Alex looked around the room, she saw James and called him over. He made his way through the melee of people, trying to look more important than the next person.

"You okay?" Alex asked.

"I should be asking you that, I was very brave sitting under that workbench."

Alex smiled. "Simon and I are heading back to SIS on Vauxhall. Can you feed me everything you find?"

James looked over his shoulder. "Yeah, my boss is here, so it might be difficult. I know he won't want to share, but I promise I'll keep you in the loop."

Broadstone tapped his shoulder, James nodded.

"Catch these people won't you?" James said.

Alex nodded. Both Alex and Simon left. They got to the car. It seemed like weeks since they were last in the car, but less than three hours had gone by. Alex felt exhausted.

She pulled her phone, a missing call from Simon, her husband. She pushed him to the back of her mind, the pang of anxiousness was still in the pit of her stomach. She found Ricky's number, hit dial.

It rang once. "Boss, talk to me."

"We're on our way back, get that coffee on and assemble the troops, we need to consolidate."

"Roger that."

"Anything on the media that Simon sent to you?" she said, getting in the Range Rover.

"Yeah, I got something, something that you and Simon are gonna need to see pronto."

"Okay, make sure that those Americans are there too, we need their opinion."

"Sure, they haven't left. And keeping them away from the control room has been a challenge."

Alex was about to hang up.

"Oh, one more thing, Simon's been in touch."

"Oh," Alex said.

"Yeah, I think you ought to know. Really, he's not happy Alex, he knows about you and… is it Siobhan? He mentioned her name. I'm guessing that's who you were with last night?"

"Are you fucking kidding me?" Alex said, Broadstone glanced at her as he accelerated onto the high street.

She hung up the phone.

"What's up?" he said.

"It doesn't just rain, does it? It generally shits it down."

15

Alex and Broadstone made it back to SIS at Vauxhall. Alex beelined for the showers, a change of clothes always in the locker, while Simon went to the vestry. Working the beat undercover or on stakeouts required something to be thrown on when returning back to base.

Under the hot showers, Alex looked at the floor, the blood from earlier swirling around the drain like a tornado, disappearing after.

What was all that about? Alex thought, soaping herself down. She was startled.

"ALEX, LETS GO! YOU HAVE A VISITOR!" It was Broadstone. Alex stared at Simon through the thin nylon curtain, the bottom of it stuck to Alex's leg as the draft came in from the door closing. Who could this be? she thought.

She got out, and dried herself quickly. She was throwing her clothes on when the door opened again.

"I'm coming," she said, lacing her Converses up. She noticed that the door hadn't closed. Ricky was stood at the door.

"What's up?" Alex said, raising her other foot to tie the laces.

"Si is here, Alex, he's in a bit of a state."

Alex stopped, then quickly finished the job, and stood up. "What do you mean Simon? My Si?" she asked.

"Yeah."

"Okay, a bit weird," she said. Alex was thinking, playing the jealous type at this juncture was a bit odd.

"You need to come quickly?"

"Okay, let's go," she said, ushering him away from the door.

Alex walked in, determined to show Simon that she was strong. She was feeling nervous, she still loved him deeply. As she walked in, her world was pulled out from under her feet.

Broadstone and Simon were stood under the big screen in the vestry, the unmistakable face of Dale Broc filled the screen. She stopped, looked at the screen, her heart skipping a beat. Nausea washed over her. She reached for the back of a chair for support, unable to take her eyes off the screen. Alex was unaware of the eyes from the rest of the room, watching her.

"What is he doing up there?" Alex demanded.

"Alex, please sit down," Broadstone said.

She looked at the two of them, Ricky joined them. Even with his dark complexion, he looked washed out.

"Yes or no – is it Devon?" she asked, her voice cracking, giving away the emotion of her true feelings.

"Not exactly," Broadstone said.

"Alex, please sit down." Si skirted the large board-room-like table. Alex stepped back into the chair, she held out her hands as Si got to her.

"I know about Siobhan, Alex."

Alex was confused, she knitted her brows and looked at him. What has Siobhan, Si and Broc got to do with this? She thought.

"I'm okay with this, Alex," he said softly.

"Can someone please tell me what's going on?" she looked at Si. "What about Siobhan, how do you know about Siobhan?"

"I got an email today, the attachment was from him." Si indicated to the glaring image of a monster on the big screen. He nodded to Broadstone, reluctantly he reached down and pressed the spacebar, which started the video.

Broc instantly came to life. "Hello, Alex, Dale here, not that I need any introductions to you. I thought I would share with you a clip of your daughter, Devon."

The camera panned around to Devon, sat in a chair, reading a magazine. "Devon, say hi to mummy." Devon looked up. "Hey, mummy."

Alex was struggling to understand, Si squeezed her hand, his back to the screen.

"Come and sit on daddy's knee, Devon, be a good girl."

Devon jumped up, almost skipped over to Broc's knee, and took a seat, sitting with her back to Broc, him peering over her shoulder. "Thought we would send you a quick video. Devon's been a smashing girl, haven't you, babygirl?"

Alex was feeling cold, sweaty and drained of any life she had in her.

"Her bimbofication took less time than I thought. She was bratty and feisty at first, but always very wet, but now she's a very good girl and still very wet. She has an affinity for discipline." He kissed her cheek, she giggled.

Alex shuddered.

"What have you fucking done to her, you bastard?" she hissed.

"She is regularly taught the ways of a submissive slut, only having to resort to the cane once or twice, but forgive me, would you mind getting off, petal?"

"Sure, daddy," she said. Devon slid off Broc's knee.

"You should be very proud of her, Alex." Broc wiped himself down, paying attention to his legs.

"The real reason for my message is that I want to introduce someone to you."

The video cut to Alex and Siobhan at the bar at the sex club the previous night, then the video cut to Alex's flat, her bedroom. Alex felt the rising panic in her gut. Goose pimples bounced up, causing an instant chill. Alex and Siobhan were entwined on the bed.

There were so many questions that Alex was asking in her head. Broc is in my apartment? Is Siobhan working with Broc? How long has he been bugging my apartment?

The video cut back to Broc, his angular Germanic features striking. Looking impeccably smart in his tweed suit, to the back of him was the Thames. Almost the same view as her apartment, she got up and walked to the screen. "Alex, the worst is yet to come," Si said.

Alex didn't hear it, she kept walking, as though Broc heard her, and he looked over his shoulder.

"That's the Thames, I know you're looking, you don't miss a trick, but I want you to see this first." The camera moved as he picked it up. The image was juddery as he walked from the room he was in. The camera was then posted to the floor, in the narrow hallway. He was in a hotel, the camera image focused automatically on the naked figure on the floor, he zoomed in. "Show Alex her face," Broc said behind the camera. A pair of hands came into shot, yanked the hair up, exposing the face. Siobhan, her neck choked in by the cable tie, her breathing laboured and raspy. Her eyes were heavy, bloodshot but still filled with fear. The cable tie was biting into the neck line, with different hues of black and blue, her lips were a dusky shade of blue.

Alex sank to the floor, still looking at the screen.

Broadstone was the first to her, he crouched down, Si came, crouched on the other side.

"He was in my house and now he's taken Siobhan, what else does he want? There's nothing else I can give." She sobbed forward, Si grabbing her, hugging her. His eyes glistened as he was struggling with the information over-load that he had received.

Alex looked up at the screen, her face wet. She bit her bottom lip, her brain working at a million miles an hour.

She stood, both the men still crouching. "What is it?" Broadstone asked.

"I know where this is," Alex said.

Broadstone stood. "Where?"

She turned and dialled the video back to when Broc was sat, after Devon left his knee. "That view, it's the same view I have from my apartment, that's the fucking hotel just down from my apartment block."

Broadstone studied it carefully. "Bloody hell," he said. "I think you're right."

Broadstone sprung into action. "Ricky, isolate the floor, pinpoint the room." He picked up the phone, pressed a speed dial button. "I need a gun team, Crown Plaza on the Victoria Embankment front and back to be restricted now." Broadstone didn't have to repeat himself, the line just went dead, which was acknowledgment enough.

"Get on the blower, get plod around there urgently and seal off that building as well."

"Roger," Ricky said.

"Alex with me." It took a few seconds for it to sink in, she turned, clocked Si. Still on the floor, she stopped and looked. "I'll sort him out, Alex, go!" Ricky said.

Alex nodded and left the room.

It took Broadstone, Alex and Ricky eight minutes to exit the SIS, run down the street, Alex's gun drawn, arms pumping like pistons. She didn't even feel the build-up of lactic acid in her muscles. Down the middle of the Albert Embankment, cars were slowing and honking their horns. It was deliberate, Broc was no fool, any one of these cars could have him, Devon and Siobhan in. Anyone else would just be collateral damage, she quickly pushed the top slide of the Glock back one-handed, the reassuring glisten of the brass jacketed round in the chamber made Alex's heart swell, she got faster.

They got to the front of the Crown Plaza, the gun team already jumping out of their van, milling around the front. Tourists for the hotel were pointing their camera phones at them.

Alex, followed by Simon, crashed through the front doors, breaking into a walk to the main reception, gun down one side.

Alex, the devil in her eyes, was holding up a picture of Broc. "This man is in this hotel, where is he?" When she got to the desk, the reception staff looked petrified, and Alex slammed the photo onto the surface. "WHERE IS HE?" she screamed.

They looked, shrugged at each other. A young fresh-faced lad came out of the back, wondering what the commotion was. Confused, he peered over one of his colleague's shoulders. "Room 37." Looking up at Alex. "He's in Room 37, third floor."

He didn't get to finish the sentence when Alex took off, Broadstone following. "Alex stop, let the cannons in first." He grabbed her hand.

Alex stopped, clenching her fists, the busy lobby, people watching, Alex screamed and looked up to the ceiling.

Broadstone clicked the pressel on his radio. "All callsigns, split your teams, a five-man gun team with me to the third floor, the room is number 37, weapons tight, out."

Simon grabbed her shoulders, looking her in the eyes. "Alex, I know you're hurting, we are all with you, get a grip, let's go, yeah?"

She nodded, the team was already assembled at the door to the stairwell.

The radio clicked. "Only one staircase to the third, the elevators are covered, as are all exits, ready to go?"

"Roger out," Broadstone said, nodding to the guys at the doorway to the stairs. The weapons were shouldered as they entered the stairwell, the radio clicking clear as they proceeded. Alex and Broadstone followed. Ricky was holding back, using the reception desk as his temporary base, firing up his hardware.

They reached the third floor. The stairwell space was airy, the air cool, almost damp. The smell of concrete took Alex back to her childhood, playing on building sites in West Germany as an army child.

The third floor was in contrast to the grey, smooth concrete stairwell. Dark, almost gloomy, but plush. The walls were adorned with frescos of the London skyline and famous landmarks in the capital. The carpet was soft under foot, crazy pattern disappearing to the forties and fifties. Room 37 came quickly, the gun team lined up each side of the door.

Broadstone and Alex waited back, Alex kneeling, looking down the corridor. It would be typical of Broc to either make an escape as soon as the room was breached or send someone down, like the crazy Korean. She heard in her ear piece, "Standby, GO GO GO!"

The door burst open, it took another twenty seconds before the clear came over the radio.

Alex stood and filed into the room. Nothing. The room was clean, no one had even slept in the bed. There was some dried blood on the balcony, Alex walked out, looking across the Thames. From the right she could see her apartment block, to the left, she could see the SIS. She scanned the pathway below, traced the steps she and Broadstone had walked that morning after disturbing Siobhan and herself so rudely. Siobhan, she thought. Broadstone joined her.

"If I knew what he was playing at, I would have a rational explanation for you, Alex, but I just don't."

"Seems weird, Simon, we walked that path this morning, he must've been watching us." She turned to look at Simon. "How long has he been here?"

"We'll find out in a second." Broadstone motioned to the hotel manager and the young lad from the reception walking into the room.

They walked onto the balcony.

"The hotel will be whatever help you require, sir." He addressed Broadstone. Misogyny alive and well in this hotel, Alex thought, Simon introduced her.

"The room was rented late last night, a couple. The man in the picture and a woman who he introduced as his wife."

"Was she oriental looking?" Alex asked. The manager obviously wasn't sure, he was here as the voice of the hotel. Most likely at the time Broc booked in, he was tucked up in his bed. He turned to the young man with him.

"Yes ma'am, she was." Alex fished in her pocket, pulled her phone out, opened the photos app, scrolled and found what she was looking for. She clicked it and the image of Ji-Yeon, the North Korean transgender assassin, and Tao Ng's right-hand killer, appeared.

"Yeah, that's her," he said.

Alex looked at Broadstone. "Boss?" One of the gunners was standing at the balcony door. "We've found something."

Broadstone walked past the manager and his minion, stepped into the room, in the bedside table was a flash drive with Alex written on the side.

"Anyone open it?" Broadstone asked.

"No, we just found it."

"Okay, I don't want anyone opening it until we can guarantee it doesn't do anything like blow up the Houses of Parliament."

"Roger that, boss."

Broadstone spoke into his mic. "You getting this, Ricky?"

"Loud and clear, Simon, and the video."

"Any thoughts?"

"I've just run some diagnostics, there doesn't seem to be anything digital linked to the device, get it back so I can take a good look."

Alex came into the room. "The manager has said that the guy on concierge has disappeared. He's a new member of staff, took the job about two months ago."

"Can we get his details, Ricky?"

"On it already, accessing the staff database now, have we got a name?"

"What was the chap's name that was on the concierge?" Alex asked.

"Don't worry, if the guy was working here under Broc, the name will be false. I have him on CCTV, just wait. Running facials now."

"Broc's been tailing you, and we missed it, Alex!"

"It's okay, he's not stupid and even I was complacent. I didn't think that he would do something like this."

"We need to bring Siobhan's husband in," Broadstone said.

Alex stopped and looked in astonishment. "How did you know he was…" she stopped, he raised an eyebrow.

"GET IN!" Ricky said on the radio.

"Speak to me, Tonto?" Alex said.

"Your man is Goran Vuk, works for a Serbian trafficking organization run by what looks like the shell-suit brigade, pinging you the details. The ring leader is a chap called Aleksander Dragoslav."

"I've heard that name," Broadstone said. "Check out some sex worker cases we busted about five years ago." This group was bringing heroin from Afghanistan along with an army of prostitutes. The ring was busted open, the gang imprisoned or deported. But it's a name you don't forget."

Alex opened her phone, waiting for the message. It came, she opened it, the image of the gang indeed looked like a male catalogue picture from 1990.

"You're right, Simon, Dragoslav is on an international arrest warrant, you're not going to like this. The guy runs an operation out of Slovenia. Drugs, sex trafficking, child porn, slavery you name it. Including the main supplier of live snuff videos on the dark web."

"What do you mean?" Alex said. There was a pause. "Rick, I'm a big girl, talk to me."

"Okay, it's pretty bad, you pay on the dark web and you watch people get murdered, you can pay extra if you want to watch them being raped afterward."

Alex listened and looked at the floor, Simon shook his head. "Nice."

"Okay, let's get out, I want every man on this outside of the Hypnos case. They are still in the capital. Find them. Get plod on it, all the available assets. Someone will talk."

"Let's get back to SIS." Broadstone turned to the manager. "This floor is off limits for the next three days, understand?"

He went to protest but knew it was fruitless.

16

The following morning, Blunt met with Jamal in the garage. Their relationship was still not warming, Jamal now accepting and even suggesting. He was waiting as Blunt entered the garage.

"Good morning, Jamal."

"Morning," he said, tapping away at the computer screen. Jongy sat on a stool in the corner, looking bored.

"Not so sure about him," Jamal said, rubbing his bandaged arm.

Blunt glanced over his shoulder. "De Jong, go do something more constructive with your time."

Jongy looked at the two of them, scraped his feet across the concrete and stood, sucking his teeth. The door slammed.

"Brut," Blunt said, standing behind Jamal.

"You going to stand there all day?" Jamal said, pulling a chair out. He looked up. "I won't bite."

"Of course, we're going to take some time this morning." He paused. "I guess it will only take the morning as I'm due in London this afternoon, parliamentary work you see."

"We should be done in a jiffy."

"I've spoken with the board, here is the thumb drive of the numbers that you need, that should be all you will need."

Jamal took it and plugged it into the USB port on the main drive. The files shot up with a vibration and a whirling of the hard drives, he double clicked one, a plethora of names, contact details, and medical history notes on a very complex spreadsheet appeared.

"These are medical gold, outside of what we're doing, the data on here alone is worth the best part of twenty million pounds."

Jamal shook his head, the importance of the data not lost on him.

He began the task of separating the demographics. Obese, smokers, elderly, drinkers, registered disabled. The data drilled down to sexual orientation, gays, bisexual, non-binary, transgender also targeted, the unemployed and long-term sick. Foreigners that are not naturalised in the UK.

"How long will this take?" Blunt said.

Without looking up, Jamal typed furiously with one arm. "Shouldn't take too long, the software will do the hard work, and the algorithms I have coded will target the right people."

Blunt watched on, fascinated.

"The long-term sick, the software needs to know at what point you want them exterminated?"

Blunt looked at him, confused. "That's a strong word, Jamal."

He looked him blankly, like a bank teller waiting for more information.

"Six months, can we start with that?"

Jamal looked back to the screen and carried on typing. "Six months," he said.

A few minutes later, Jamal was coming to the end of the data gathering process.

"Mr Blunt?"

"Geoffrey, please."

"I'd rather not, Mr Blunt"

"Okay, if you insist," Blunt said. "What do you need?"

"The data is in, and the software is ready to collate into the right processes, how do you want that to proceed?"

"Right, the board have said that all cancer sufferers, their tumour markers are to become more aggressive, in order to do this, you need the information in file twelve."

Jamal searched for it, found it, tapped it open, converted the text into code and added it into the software.

"Next?"

Blunt was taken aback. "That was quick."

Jamal nodded, took a swig from an energy drink, the smell of taurine heavy on his breath.

"The haematologist within the organization wants the information in file nine to be coded."

Jamal found it, repeated the same.

They went through the list, not missing anyone. The whole process took a little over an hour. The speed of the computations was impressive, as was Jamal's one-handed typing.

"Ready?"

"Is it ready to go?" Blunt asked.

"Yup, the software will be loaded into a push-notification on the game, so the users will all be notified. The hardcore addicted players will be infected within minutes, no doubt. Of all the people," he checked another screen, "just over one million are active on the game right now. So, they will be the first."

"Okay, press the button."

"Do you want to press the button, Mr Blunt?"

Blunt was surprised by the request. "Err, yes, it would be my honour."

Jamal pushed the keyboard towards him. "Hit return."

Jamal couldn't bring himself to press the button that would kill thousands of people, his conscience was screaming in his head.

Blunt leaned and studied the keyboard. "I feel like I need to give a speech."

"It's a big moment, why don't you?"

He thought for moment, Jamal was thinking he was a bit of a twit, he clicked the webcam on to capture the event.

He began by standing. "Today, a new breed is born. The movement of Asclepius, I believe, will achieve its goals. We will not lie, we will not cheat. I will not give promises, the destiny of the white supreme. Through their own labour and achievement. In four years, Asclepius will create the perfect world, free from inbreeding, poor lineage and free from disablement. One nation, one people, living in harmony." He leaned down and pressed the return button.

The screen beeped, went dark – and then the hour glass. Three seconds later, the software was heading the phones on the list.

"Is that it?" Blunt said.

"Yep, we just have to wait, the system will tell me who is now active with the upload, oh," Jamal leaned, "three, ten, twenty, one hundred."

Blunt sat, elbows on the table, hands resting on his chin, watching the numbers.

"Can we see them?"

"Sure, hold on," Jamal said.

He tapped away, the screens to the left and right of Jamal sprung to life. The screen sectioned, different people on their phones. Some images from the actual phones, others from CCTV, internal security cameras connected to the grid.

Tommy, a middle-aged builder, drinker, early stages of cirrhosis. He was sat in the pub in Darlington, North

Yorkshire, watching the horse racing on the TV. It was early in the morning, but Tommy hadn't been working for a couple of months now. His drinking was becoming out of control. The money he got from the welfare went straight down his throat or in the fruit machine next to the bar in the Ferret and Sprout pub. A pub that Tommy had drank in since he first sneaked in there in is mid-teens.

"You okay, Tommy? You're looking a bit pale there, sunshine."

"I'm okay, Bill, just a bit of heartburn." He buried his head into the *Racing Post*, checking the nags he could back today, so he could buy more beer. He felt excited about the fiver he was going to put on Black Betty running at Sandown Park at two o'clock. The reality was, the fiver might as well have been set on fire with the luck that Tommy had.

The heartburn was getting worse. "Oooh, Bill have you got any Andrews? It's getting worse, mate."

"Sorry, Tommy, this is a pub, not a pharmacy. Boots is just down the road, mate," Bill said as he clinked the glasses out of the dishwasher under the bar.

Hypnos uploaded into Tommy's brain as he played the game regularly, addicted to the melon running about the screen controlled by his eyes. He got fed up with the game within five minutes of playing. But Hypnos didn't care, as soon as the code was piggybacked via the game app, Tommy didn't stand a chance. Already with cirrhosis of the liver, the disease was causing a backflow of blood to the liver, backing up through the major vessels that fed the oesophagus. These vessels were dilating and becoming weak. Hypnos changed the Ph of the blood running through Tommy's body, irritating the intimal coating the portal vein. The vein becoming excited and twitched, giving Tommy the sensation of heartburn. Bill didn't see Tommy slide off the bar stool, as the oesophagus split because of the weakness in the vessels.

The heart pumped faster to compensate for the sudden loss of pressure in the vascular system. Blood spewed from Tommy's mouth, and, within thirty seconds, Tommy had dumped the entire circulating volume on to the wooden floor of the Ferret and Sprout.

Bill, noticing a horrible smell, looked around. Tommy had disappeared – gone to the bog to puke, he thought. Tommy puked at least three times a day in the pub. Bill felt sorry for him, but still served him his beer. The smell got worse. "What's that smell?" Bill said.

Sally, Bill's busty barmaid and who sometimes doubled as his wife, he always joked to his punters, came in. "What's that smell?" Sally said. She walked around the bar and screamed.

"TOMMY!" Sally screamed. Bill looked over the bar, Tommy, his body lifeless, was in the foetal position, a huge lake of blood, still oozing further away from his dead body, the smell was the liquefied shit that had jetted out of his anus as he fell to the floor. What set Bill off, making him spew into the bar sink, was the shit that was pumping out of Tommy's mouth, mixing with the blood.

"Call 999!" Sally screamed.

Tina had been a troubled child. She had struggled through school, although she was bright. She was bullied by her peers and emotionally abused by her parents. This was the reason that she'd become a big girl. The chiding, narcissistic parenting and a lack of understanding of the addiction cycle – she carried on eating.

Now in her late twenties, morbidly obese and finding the most mundane tasks difficult as the additive cycle had separated her, isolated her and now was in the process of destroying her. The type-2 diabetes she was diagnosed with two years earlier had made a statistic.

She was hidden away in the bed sit above Rapresh Indian tandoori on the lower Bristol Road. The tandoori always gave her leftovers, and she gladly took them too. "She's a big girl, she eats anything," she heard them say. "Better to give it to her so the rats don't come when we chuck it out, the rats can come later and feed off her body when she karks it," she once heard another time.

Her days were spent mainly playing Fruit Smash and watching those hateful chat shows, where the ugliest dude on the planet had impregnated all the females in one family. It took her mind off her own isolation. Ben and Jerry's in the fridge that she bought on offer down the Co-op.

Hypnos took only three seconds to infect Tina's brain. Her head snapped back, nodded twice and carried on playing the game, one eye on the telly while she watched her melon zoom around the screen, the silly soundtrack she was listening to seemed pointless, yet you couldn't turn it off.

The messages to Tina's physiology was simple – create markers in the digestive system to elevate the pancreatic recreations. Type-2 diabetics always have an immunocompromised digestive system. The first thing to fail would the pancreas, secreting enzymes that would start to eat itself. Acute pancreatitis causes so much pain that it can't be abated by drugs. Within three hours, Tina would be an acute admission to her local hospital. The pain would be so unbearable that she may even be unable to raise the alarm. The fix is simple. Antibiotics, a small procedure, a nasal tube fed into the stomach to stave off the digestive enzymes from the stomach. In Tina's case, like with four hundred and fifty thousand of the three million sufferers of the disease, she would die in the next twenty-four hours, choking the health service beyond breaking point. With a code that adjusted the antibiotic resistance as well, even if she made it to the hospital, any antibiotics would be impotent, leaving her to die horribly from sepsis.

Kenneth, a WWII veteran, had mild dementia. His daughter, Penny, bought Kenneth a smartphone, and the games on the app store were geared to people like Kenneth with this common disease. Fruit Smash was marketed as a means to prevent and slow down dementia. Kenneth set his alarm on the phone five times a day, he played Fruit Smash for the prescriptive time that Penny had said, fifteen minutes. He didn't see the point. But Kenneth had lost his wife to dementia, finally going bonkers, walking off a balcony and falling to her death. He still missed her, desperately.

Playing the game when Jamal uploaded, his head snapped back, then nodded. "You okay, daddy?" Penny asked, seeing it happen over her morning read of the paper.

"Yes, darling."

"What did you do that for?" she said.

"Do what?"

"With your head, looked a bit weird."

"I didn't do anything, darling, just playing this infernal game and counting the clock."

She smiled. She and her father were unaware of the coding happening in Kenneth's brain.

Elderly people like Kenneth can become very dehydrated quickly, and the natural inbuilt thirst mechanism makes you drink. Even people with dementia, brain injuries and those who are under the influence of drink or drugs rely on this mechanism. The liver secretes angiotensin and the adrenal glands that live on top of the kidneys secrete renin when it detects a drop in fluidity in the blood running through it. The angiotensin is then converted into angiotensin I, which travels through the bloodstream to the lungs, where the lungs then secrete angiotensin-converting enzymes, changing the molecular make-up of the enzyme to angiotensin II. This change causes a vasoconstriction in the arteries and veins, raising blood pressure. This compensates for the drop of fluid volume in the veins. Part of this mechanism is a constriction of the salivary glands, making the mouth dry – this makes people reach for a glass of water. Kenneth, as with seven hundred and twenty thousand people in the same situation, will have drunk their last glass of water ever. Acute dehydration would kick in. Firstly causing a further drop in blood pressure, thereby causing the inside of the kidneys to stick together, rendering them useless. Uncontrolled diarrhoea and vomiting will deplete Kenneth of the vital fluids left in his body. Toxicity will build rapidly, causing respiratory failure and the electrolyte imbalance will then cause an irreversible cardiac arrest within five hours. Kenneth's clock was ticking – he and Penny had no idea.

Daniel was a fifty-year-old smoker. With a family of four, and working as a truck driver, Dan had already seen his doctor about quitting. His lungs were damaged, but not bad enough to be disabled. His only crime here within the statistics, was that he had seen his GP regarding quitting smoking. Hypnos and the other software parameters weren't that dynamic to take more into consideration. He smoked, end of story!

Driving his 44-ton articulated lorry down the N175 south of Rennes heading towards Nantes in Central France, his truck stop finished, he needed to get to Nantes so he could get south and head to Toulouse where his day would be over, after a quick stop for a pee and a five minute go on Fruit Smash, Daniel hit the road. The tightening in his chest was a concern, although the pesky cough started without warning as he drove onto the slipway then onto the carriage way. The traffic was heavy as always, but fast moving. The tightness got tighter and tighter. The cough more raspy. Some mucus came up, and Dan wiped it with the back of his hand, and blood caught his eye. The mucous that lives in the base of all smoker's lungs is fairly harmless. Hypnos changed this by changing the Ph of the water content, making it more acidic. The acidity burning the alveolar, making the gas exchange impossible. Carbon dioxide was building up in Dan's body, the oxygen unable to perfuse into the system. His body was dying at an alarming rate.

Light-headedness followed. The truck was traveling at sixty miles an hour, and on board was sulphuric acid. Suddenly, out of breath, Dan passed out. Mercifully, he didn't feel the head-on collision on the other side of the carriageway with a coach full of retired pensioners returning to England after a coat trip to Bordeaux.

The truck slammed into the coach, the occupants were ripped from their seats, thrown around, still strapped to their seats like food in a blender. The mass of metal, glass and people flying around minced the pensioners to pieces. Arms and legs traumatically amputated from the host added further complication to the carnage. The tank of sulphuric acid ruptured and sprayed the contents of the wrecked coach. The people that had miraculously survived the impact were now showered with acid. It burned them on contact, and they were unable to get away from the raining fluid. The dead just lay there, fizzing horribly and smoking. The smoke further hampered the living, now dying from acid burns, the noxious fumes stripped the lungs of anything vital.

Cars slammed into the back of coach. One car, two cars, five, until the cars up ahead could react, the cars kept coming. People were screaming. The acid spread down the carriageway, people lying in it, walking in bare feet, the smell drifting down the road. The people that had stopped and survived the accident stood by, the noxious drifting cloud enveloping them, suddenly becoming casualties themselves. Dan's upload of Hypnos had done wonders for Asclepius. If his demise was scored the same way as a good streak on Fruit Smash, he would have scored a bunch of cherries and an extra life. His life was extinguished, along with thirty others from the collision, and a further one hundred from noxious poisoning. Asclepius was going to have a good day. Along with Dan and his impressive collection of kills, another six hundred and twenty will have died around the same time in the UK. The health service was already ringing alarm bells, Blunt's phone ringing incessantly.

"I need to stop for a minute," Jamal said. He pushed his chair back. "And you need to answer that." He looked to the phone on the table top.

"I'm no expert, Mr Blunt, but I guess that you're going to have a busy day, the best part of two million people will die today, more than normal I would say, like I said, I'm no expert."

Blunt picked up the phone while Jamal put the BBC news live streaming channel on.

Unprecedented emergency calls, hospitals gripped with an unprecedented level of admissions. The Department of Health has stated that people should only attend if their condition is life-threatening. Still no sign of the Health Secretary, Mr Blunt. Back to the studio.

"Oops," Jamal said.

"I expected this, get on with the rest of the uploads, I will be back later today," he said, getting up from his chair and walking out of the garage. Jongy walked in.

"Golden bollocks, eh?" he walked up to Jamal, and looked at the screen.

"Not many things impress me, but this is pretty cool, eh." He patted Jamal on the shoulder, Jamal trying to not show any emotion.

17

Ricky had spent time listening to the voice recording Broadstone had made at Jamal's house. He had found De Jong on the NCIC database, on a watch list for his views on white supremacy, links to the Afrikaner Weerstandsbeweging, and just for being your average white African gun-toting lunatic that sees life a cheap commodity.

The vestry had the usual suspects sat pouring over the data. Ricky came up to Broadstone. "I've got a hit with De Jong, or Jongy, as he's known."

"Oh," Broadstone said, not looking up, the team focused not only on the Hypnos investigation but now the disappearance of Siobhan, which was linked to a warm case involving Dale Broc.

"He's got form, and links to a neo-Nazi outfit from South Africa, there was contact in the SA High Commission, he can get you more information."

"Can't you just call him and get the details?"

"I can, but I think we ought to attend, boss." Broadstone looked at Ricky, his facial expressions and demeanour could cut armour plate in two. He wasn't getting it, Ricky persisted, immune to stern looks and stroppy officers, he'd been Alex's partner for years.

"The consulate is in Trafalgar Square."

Broadstone raised his eyebrows. "Still not with you."

"The incident yesterday with Hypnos and the police officer, and now this De Jong, comes up on our radar, the consulate must be a hive of activity. I'm not suggesting that the consulate was involved, but I've done some investigating."

Broadstone turned and leaned against the table, folding his arms, still holding the plethora of pages.

Ricky fired up the iPad and flicked the screen to the left to find the app he was using.

"The consulate has a total UK staffing of three thousand, two hundred. There's hardly any women in the building and the amount of blacks is less than four hundred. Most of the employees of the consulate work outside of the building."

"Meaning?"

"Don't you think that's a bit odd?"

Broadstone shrugged.

"The WA has a membership in the thousands, not hundreds."

"The WA?" Broadstone asked.

"Erm, the Afrikaner Weerstandsbeweging, it's a white supremacist organisation that wants apartheid back, all that kind of stuff. The grassroots of the organization is fairly tepid at best. But the hardliners are on watch lists all over the world, including ours."

"Really?" Broadstone asked.

"My thinking is, you walk through there, check it out, have a chat. Go mic'ed up and with the cameras. I can run facials on everyone you encounter. Gives us cause to tail if there's anything going on."

"Okay, set it up."

"Done. You're meeting Joost Van Der Meld, the secretary under the High Commissioner in the next few hours."

Ricky went to leave. "I checked the memory drive we brought back from the hotel, I couldn't view it."

160

"Why?" Broadstone said.

"Devon is like my own daughter, and he did things to her that I can never unsee, I had to turn it off. It has been professionally edited and he called it *The Bimbofication of Devon*."

Broadstone brought back his killer stare again. "Where's Alex now?"

"She's over at the control base looking at other footage."

"Has she badgered to look at it?"

Ricky walked back to Simon. "Not really, I think she can only guess what's on the drive."

"I'll get a contact from the vulnerable children unit to look at it and run a report, I need one of our guys to watch it too, we need to gear Int from the footage no matter how bad," Broadstone said, tapping Ricky on the chest with the rolled up papers.

"I think Alex and I better pop-smoke and get over to Trafalgar Square again."

Ricky checked his watch and nodded. "I'll make sure you're wired up to the grid so we can record everything, got some other things that I need you to do while there, boss."

"Roger that." He looked at Ricky, smiling.

The car pulled up outside the High Commission. Alex stepped out of the car and looked to where the officer was killed the previous day. It was as though nothing had happened. The tourists meandered around the square taking photos, climbing the lions – although that was banned now. The police turned a blind eye.

"How much a day goes by," Alex said.

Simon stopped and looked over the car's roof, he clocked what she was staring at.

"Let's go," he said.

They entered the foyer of the High Commission, oddly,

an East Ender was at the desk. Six or seven different swipe cards hung from his neck, along with a large bunch of keys.

"That must hurt," Broadstone said, pointing to the lanyard.

"Sign in," was all he said.

As Alex was signing in after Simon, the man was printing out some visitor cards. "Who're you seeing?" he barked.

"A Mr Van Der Meld."

"Second floor, turn left, his office is at the end of the corridor on the left."

"Thank you," Broadstone said.

They took the ornate stairs. "Happy in his job," Broadstone said.

Alex smiled. "I thought it odd there's a Cockney on the front desk?"

"I didn't think of that," Broadstone said, laughing.

They turned left and walked down the corridor. Paintings of the African Veldt, tribal images. Images of Mandela, Mbeki, and other notable South African statesmen.

"When you say how different a day makes, looking at these images, can you remember the apartheid government?"

Alex nodded. "The world's come a long way since."

They got to the door. "We still have a long way to go."

Broadstone didn't knock, he just entered.

"Excuse me, sir," said an officious white South African female. "Have you not heard of knocking?" she stood up in protest.

"We're expected," Broadstone said. Alex loved his belligerent English asshole attitude. He was expected, so why knock? She could see where he was coming from.

The secretary looked down at her schedule. "I don't think you're expected, Mr…"

"Mr Broadstone, British Intelligence, with my partner, Alex Brown."

Alex nodded and smiled. He used British Intelligence again.

She paused, using the Intelligence trump card in the capital always opened doors. Whether they were expected or not, she had to get them in front of Van Der Meld.

"Could you wait a moment, sir?" she said, a little more reticent and guarded.

"No need, through here, madam," Simon said, striding to the door.

"Mr Broadstone, please," she begged, but it was too late, he was already through with Alex buffering her attempt to stop him. They filed into the office, Alex closing the door in her reddened face.

Van Der Meld looked up from his desk and put his pen down, his forehead creased in confusion.

"Sorry, Mr Van Der Meld, Mr Broadstone from British Intelligence and his associate Ms. Brown," the woman barked through the intercom.

He held up his hand. "From British Intelligence, yes, I have been expecting you, eh." Standing and offering his hand, Broadstone took it, then he shook Alex's hand.

"It's customary to knock and be escorted into a diplomat's chambers, eh."

The man was a number eight in his youth, tall and well built. A beast of a man, chiselled good looks, thick blond hair with piercing blue eyes. He was so well toned that even his jugular veins were obvious under the thin layer of tanned skin. He looked formidable.

"Sit, please sit, Lucy get me coffee, eh."

Alex heard the door click behind her.

"How can I help her majesty's government?" he held his hands open, sitting in his enormous chair.

"We need some information on a Mr De Jong, anything you have."

"That won't be possible I'm afraid, Mr Broadstone, I have taken advice from our council, unless there is a warrant for his arrest with a clear explanation to why you need to speak with him, then the consulate cannot help you." His accent was thick, almost difficult to follow. The arrogance was palpable.

"So, he works for the High Commission?" Alex said.

"I didn't say that I said that we won't fetch the man for your Intelligence service to interrogate a South African subject without proper due process, eh."

"We don't want to arrest him, we just want to talk to him," Alex added.

"My hands are tied, eh." He held out his hands.

Lucy entered carrying a tray. Van Der Meld looked up. "Coffee only for one, our guests are leaving, Lucy, eh. What has De Jong done to attract the attention of your agency?"

"What are you worried about Mr Van Der Meld?" Broadstone asked.

Van Der Meld shrugged.

Broadstone smiled sardonically, he upped the ante. "I can tell you but that would require an ounce of cooperation."

Alex's ear crackled, Ricky came on. "Van Der Meld is a part of the High Commission in the UK, pretty much banished from South Africa. He has far right views and, although not a racist, his opinions about immigration, and liberalism were considered, even by South African standards, to be to subversive. Hence why he's in London and not Johannesburg."

Alex pulled her phone out while Simon and Van Der Meld exchanged questions like a tennis match at Wimbledon.

How do you know he isn't a racist? Alex typed.

Dots…

His wife is a Zulu, unusual for a white man to marry a Zulu, let alone a racist.

Alex looked up, saw a picture of Van Der Meld with a beautiful black woman and three teenage children.

"Your wife?" she said.

Van Der Meld swivelled in his seat, saw the picture, he turned back. "Yes, my wife. Not what you expect, eh?"

"What do you mean?" Broadstone said.

"I am of Aryan descent, you must think that I'm a racist bigot, eh?"

Broadstone pulled a face. "I didn't think that at all."

Ricky crackled into life again. *Military background, officer training in the late eighties, left to join the police after apartheid and then took a governmental position in the mid-noughties. The guy is pretty badass, guys, been married for twenty years.*

Anything else? Alex typed.

Yeah, he's got a temper, been known for it.

"What's your opinion of the WA?" Alex purposely provoked.

He looked at Alex, the look of scorn written across his face, Alex felt his piercing eyes bore right through her, Broadstone noticed it.

"What's that got to do with anything? Actually, I think you ought to leave, eh?" he stood, looking irritated.

Alex stood, the office overlooked the Square, Nelson's Column obscured by a mature tree, the leaves already out, but the route went through to the opposite corner where the officer was killed by the affected group.

"Great view of the Square, you must see all sorts from here."

"What does that mean, Mrs. Brown?" Van Der Meld said.

"Did you witness the killing of the officer yesterday?"

He looked out of the window. "I wasn't here yesterday."

"And your schedule will attest to that, sir?" Broadstone said.

"Mr Van Der Meld was away on business, I saw what happened yesterday, please"

Both Alex and Simon turned, Lucy's arm extended, indicating to the open door.

"Thank you for your time, Mr Van Der Meld, I would say that you have been very helpful to Her Majesty's Intelligence Service here in the capital of the United Kingdom, and as a guest of Her Majesty, with all your diplomatic perks, I shall make sure that this is annotated in my report," Broadstone said. It cut like a knife through the South African, Van Der Meld wanted to reach across and rip Simon's head off, Simon would have welcomed it.

"As you wish, Mr Broadstone, I shall also be submitting a report to the High Commissioner myself."

There was a pause, a stalemate between the two men, the testosterone seeping out of their pores.

"Let's go, Simon," Alex said, breaking the man off and walking towards the door. Simon filed in behind her.

"Lucy, escort these two to the main entrance, please, I don't want them getting lost." Lucy nodded.

"Follow me?" she said. Her curt officious manner was grinding Alex's gears.

"You getting all this, Ricky?" Alex whispered in the mic.

"Yeah, loud and clear, you guys got some great footage, get back to the Vestry now, urgent."

Alex and Simon looked at each other.

"What's up?" Alex said.

"We have a problem, there's a massive influx of acute patients at all the hospitals all over the country, I mean, it's fucking chaos. Two-thirds of the ED departments have closed their doors. Patients are turning up at GP surgeries with no chance of being treated. The news is awash with it."

They descended the stairs, Lucy looked around to see who Alex was talking to, she had the forethought to pull her phone out, pretending to speak. "Hand in your badges please?"

"Thank you for your time, Lucy, it's been a pleasure." Simon walked out, Alex following, she didn't say goodbye.

Outside Simon was stood waiting, Alex caught up with him, and the car was waiting on the curb, the back door open.

"What have we got?" Broadstone said.

Ricky crackled into life. "Mr Stubblebine thinks it's started."

Simon stared at Alex. "The clock is ticking, guys, you need to get your asses back to the Vestry NOW."

They both climbed in the car. "Stick Radio 4 on," Broadstone said.

"Sure, back to SIS boss?" Said the driver.

"...*service is in crisis. With so many unexplained patients arriving in droves to hospitals up and down the country. People with diabetes that would normally be managing their symptoms themselves at home are now too sick to leave hospital. The worrying trend of smokers. There's been an unprecedented number of deaths relating to smoking. One emergency consultant told me that it's as though a switch has been flicked and that certain groups of patients are now dying as a result.*"

"Switch it off," Broadstone said. He looked at Alex. "I think it's going to get a tad bumpy from here on in," he said.

The line rang for the third time. Van Der Meld was getting impatient. Lucy came in with a tray. "GET OUT..." he screamed.

Fourth time lucky, the line answered. "Hello?"

"You fucking lunatic, Jongy, get your fucking arse back to headquarters, and bring the kaffir with you, I've just had British Intelligence barge into the High Commission because of you."

"But sir?" Jongy said.

"There's no 'but sir,' you have compromised the mission, get your arse out of there and back to headquarters, pronto, eh."

"Jawohl Mein Herr, Heil…"

"Not on the fucking phone, Jongy, you fucking idiot."

The line went dead.

Van Der Meld looked out of the window, sucking at the back of his hand. A childhood habit when he was thinking. He wasn't there the previous day but after a conversation with Mr Blunt, he wished he had been. He could see the link the Intelligence Service were making, and making assumptions. He needed a better source of advice.

He opened his desk drawer directly under the table. A long thin drawer was hidden from sight. There was an array of mobiles, a picture of Hitler and Donald Trump and a swastika armband. He pulled a phone out.

Once powered up, he hit the only number in the phone.

"This better be good?" The American accent said.

"We have a problem, sir."

"I'm staring right at your problem, put that idiot on a leash, I'll decide what to do with him after I've spoken to the chairman.

The line went dead. A cold sweat bobbled across his forehead, things were getting a little hot for his liking.

Sat outside the Vestry, Ricky saw Alex and Broadstone arrive. He edited the video, and uploaded it to the Vestry projector, the team assembled. The impending catastrophe was splashed across all the world media: BRITAIN SHUT, HEALTH SERVICE IN MELTDOWN.

18

Alex was stood at the water cooler, her head a mindfuck of confusion and loss. Si had been taken back home after they left for the Crown Plaza Hotel. She knew she had to deal with that as soon as humanly possible. Ray, she thought, Siobhan's husband.

"Penny for your thoughts, Alex?"

Ricky had spotted her, walked over. He pulled a plastic cup from the dispenser and pressed, filling only a quarter of the cup, the upside-down container bubbling as it emptied.

"I have to tell Siobhan's husband, Ray," Alex said.

"We can do it together, I'll have him brought in?"

"I don't know where she even lives, Ricky," Alex said, her voice still strong. "What a fucking mess."

"You can't blame yourself, boss, Broc has you in his head, don't play his game. There's always a silver lining."

"Which is?" she turned to look at Ricky, narrowing her gaze, not seeing it.

"Devon's alive and well."

"Have you seen the thumb drive from the hotel room?" Alex probed.

Ricky paused, took a drink, finding the words he needed to say, but he couldn't, Alex was too astute, he knew it.

"I couldn't watch it, Alex."

"What's on there?" Alex asked.

"You know what's going to be on there, Simon's brought some guys in that he knows from a vulnerable children's unit to watch it along with some of the guys from the team to glean any info."

People passing, Alex nodded. "I don't want to know what's happened to my daughter, Ricky, I just want her home," she said in a hushed voice, leaning into Rick.

He put his arm around her. "Me too, babes, I miss her, you know."

"She says that you guys always text."

"Come on, we need to focus, I know it's not a good time, but we really need to grip the shit that's going down out there right now." He thumbed to the Vestry, the room filling up.

Alex walked in, Broadstone smiled, he waved her over, as a chair next to him was vacant. He indicated that the chair was for her.

The door closed, and an eerie silence filled the room. The acoustics were monitored and controlled, so the sound stayed in the room when it became sterile, playing with the atmosphere of the room. It almost gave you a queasy feeling, like your ears were popping, but not actually popping.

Broadstone stood. "Okay, guys, Ricky has the floor."

Ricky walked to the front, and opened his laptop. The mouse skirted expertly around the big screen that everyone was looking at. There was a picture of Si and Alex sitting at a canal side enjoying beer on a late summer's day. Alex smiled. She remembered that day, a canal holiday after the case before Broc on Daventry canal. The kids were with them, it was five days of non-stop laughter. It warmed her heart to remember better times. She made a mental note to text Si.

"You're all aware of the clusterfuck happening with the

health service. Our American friends have advised us that Hypnos has been activated."

The eyes of the room travelled to where they were sitting.

"We have a lead." Alex leaned forward, glancing at Broadstone, eyes back to him.

The screen came to life, Alex recognized it instantly. The video was the inside of the South African High Commission.

"There was nothing untoward in the building or in Mr Van Der Meld's office." On another screen, there were images of Van Der Meld. Some were him walking his dog, another with his wife. Then some public engagement images, even one with Nelson Mandela.

"I gave Simon a button camera with a microphone in it." Ricky held up the button, just a bit smaller than the head of a drawing pin, and he passed it around. Alex looked at Simon, he smiled and winked.

"The magic happened after both Simon and Alex were asked to leave. Van Der Meld pulled a phone out, of which I can't access the numbers as the phone was set to silent, so transducing the tones as they were pressed just was a no-go. However, enjoy." Ricky stood back.

The footage was clear, Broadstone had placed the button in a prominent position where the camera optimized a clear view of most of the room. Van Der Meld was sat at his desk, looking pensive. Both Alex and Broadstone had just left. He opened a drawer under the desk and pulled out a phone.

"GET OUT!" he screamed, the door clicked shut. Must've been Lucy, Alex mused.

After a couple of times trying to ring the number, the person on the other end finally picked up.

"You fucking lunatic, Jongy, get your fucking arse back to headquarters, and bring the kaffir with you, I've just had British Intelligence barge into the High Commission because of you."

Van Der Meld leaned back in his chair and rubbed his face with his free hand.

"There's no 'but sir,' you have compromised the mission eh, get your arse out of there and back to headquarters, pronto eh."

He leaned forward, the chair protesting.

"Not on the fucking phone, Jongy."

The line went dead.

Van Der Meld was looking out of the window, sucking at the back of his hand.

He opened his desk drawer directly under the table. Once powered up, he hit the only number in the phone.

"We have a problem, sir."

The video ended.

"We need to know who that was, who did he call? This chap is suspect two, the first is this pleasant man."

De Jong's life flashed up. His criminal record, abusive behaviour, member of the WA South African neo-Nazis. His military career that ended abruptly for abusing black recruits and encouraging the white recruits to go after their black peers. The language used in the military Court Marshall wasn't fit to be read out. The words that everyone knew had been used by De Jong were redacted by a black stripe.

"Nice chap," Broadstone said.

"He's not your common-garden racist, this guy genuinely believes in the Fourth Reich. He's convinced Nazism will prevail and take over the world, a sadist and homosexual to boot. He has a very cruel streak by all accounts."

"What's that got to do with it, him being gay?" Alex said, she resented the comment.

"Nothing, but Nazis think homosexuality is unnatural, so how can a Nazi be gay?" Ricky said.

Alex cocked an eyebrow. "How many of Hitler's closest friends were gay? I can't believe that they were all straight."

Ricky shrugged.

"How long has he been in the UK?" A voice asked from the other side of the table. One of the analysts was writing in her notebook, face flushing as all eyes gazed on her.

"A few years by our records, I have no reason to believe that that isn't true, why?" Ricky said.

"If he's gay, then he either has a boyfriend, or he's got himself a beard and cruises the gay sex scene. Given his interests in life, I suspect that the latter is the truth."

The room was still looking at her, she felt the need to explain.

"My dad's gay, he's been married to my mum for thirty years nearly, thinks we don't know." She looked around the room. "It's complicated. Anyway, the white alpha male apex predator has to exercise his dominance sexually. If this guy is as unsavoury as they come, he will have a trail."

"I think that's a great point and we need to follow that up, we can assign someone to that. But the first thing we need to do is tail the High Commission. Either wait for this Jongy to turn up or follow Van Der Meld to wherever he considers the HQ."

"Another thing, guys," Ricky added. "He's a monkey here, he's pretty stupid by all accounts. His only saving grace is that he will kill you for free, and enjoy it. He's muscle and he's dancing to someone else's tune. Find him then we find the organ grinder."

"This is all very interesting," the voice came from the end of the table where Stubblebine and Statham were sat.

Broadstone craned his head.

"You have a public health emergency occurring outside your four walls, we need to get to the bottom of it, find the perps and shut Hypnos down," Statham said

Broadstone thought for a second. "But we believe that this De Jong is involved as well as Van Der Meld. I think this line of enquiry has legs, don't you think?"

"Currently," Ricky said, "we are looking at a death toll of around forty thousand so far, and that figure is climbing each hour. There is a trend."

"Go on?" Alex said.

"Smokers, unemployed, addicts, and alcoholics are the main demographics so far. The road agency has issued a travel warning as there are road traffic accidents everywhere, which is also hampering the emergency services."

"This sounds like some form of cleansing to me!" Broadstone said.

"What do you mean, Simon?" Ricky said.

Broadstone stood, walked to the screen. The colourful pie chart knocked up by Ricky, the shadow of Broadstone growing larger, then disappearing as he turned to face the group.

"Look at the groups – smokers, gays, drinkers, eaters, unemployed, Jesus, there's disabled people here. With the power of what this software can do, the less fortunate, addicted and non-straight people are being targeted."

"Indeed, they have been targeted," Ricky said.

"Rest assured that they have, ladies and gentlemen." The creaking frame of Stubblebine got to his feet again. He doddered around the large conference table. "And getting the public to just simply switch their devices off to break the cycle will not do."

"How have you come to this assumption?" Alex asked, looking curious.

"The developed world is addicted to the feedback loop of social media, immediacy of data and information. Who here has their favourite newsfeed send push notifications to their phones?" he coughed, and pulled out a bright red polka-dotted handkerchief. He blew his nose in a way that would have woken the dead. Alex loved that attitude, she smiled.

"Ten years ago, we had to wait to go home to watch the news. Daddy would walk in, put his feet up, the news at six would be on and the broadsheet opened. Children had to respect their father's time, now, we get our sports results delivered immediately as they happen. We can even watch that game live on our phones. Telling the public to switch them off just isn't feasible."

"How do we overcome this then?" Broadstone asked.

Stubblebine shrugged. "That's simple." He pulled out a chair nearer the front, and sat down, making a heavy sigh. He caught Broadstone looking at him. "I can't see the screen way back there." Broadstone smiled at the old man.

"The software is far too advanced for us to meddle with it. It hits the amygdala, the almond-shaped part of the brain connected to the temporal lobe. This part of the brain deals with emotions, inhibitions and our inbuilt survival instinct. By the looks of things, they have successfully integrated cellular decoding, your issue isn't with the software."

"Why is that?" Broadstone asked, gripped.

"They can use any medium they like. The holy grail of Hypnos is that is doesn't need anything other than a means to access the amygdala. Once its achieved that, the person has either a victim or soldier at their disposal."

"Then what do you propose?"

"You have to cut the head of the snake off, find the controller and remove them from the equation. People don't know that they're infected. What have the interviews of the people that killed that poor officer said?"

The eyes of the room shifted to Ricky, he flipped through his pages. "Nothing, they're not connected, they don't know each other. The rationale police inquiry puts them at the scene as a gang. We're going to have to tell them at some point that the people were not of sound mind."

"This is your mistake, people, using vocabulary that fits your social norms. These people were of sound mind, they were just not in control of their actions, critically, do they remember the incident?" Stubblebine asked, swivelling in his chair.

"They do," Ricky said.

"Of sound mind then?" Alex said.

"Indeed." He stole a glance at Alex. "You shut the software off, people will go about their business as normal and subject themselves to the social media feedback loop, they won't even notice."

"So, our principal target is De Jong?" Broadstone said, swivelling his chair to face the screen. Jongy's face was big and imposing in the room. "Then we find the snake and cut his head off," he added.

Broc knew that Alex would figure out the location when she saw the message. They had bailed as soon as Siobhan was secured.

She had come as a gift from God. Alex's flat was bugged with cameras, and always had a tail, especially as she went out at night. The plans for Alex were a long-term goal for Broc. His life was in tatters after being discovered removing the organs of live patients for the Triads. He blamed Alex for it. Taking her daughter, Devon, he had brainwashed her through the bimbofication process, only taking a matter of weeks. In a weird form of Stockholm Syndrome, Devon had become totally besotted with her master, Broc. He hadn't even touched her in that way.

Now, Alex had strayed from the marital bed by finding love with another women. It was an opportunity that he couldn't resist.

He had quickly mobilized his contacts and took her. His plan was simple, to draw Alex out. Not to kill her. That would come at another time. For now, he was going to play with her.

Siobhan was going to be handed over to Aleksander Dragoslav, simply known as The Tamer. An ex-Serbian military officer from the Balkan war, now an international haulage contractor working out of Maribor in Slovenia. The man was still on an international arrest warrant, but he managed to evade capture each time the authorities turned up to arrest him. Interpol thought this was a coincidence, but the haulage firm was a front to a much seedier, unpleasant business action. He had turned a trade in trafficking sex workers right across the European continent as well as the USA. This didn't stop at vulnerable women. His trade was children, slave workers, drugs, weapons, immigrants and jihadis from the Middle East, hell bent on killing large groups of people. If someone was paying, then he did business. His mode of business was simple – pay and accept his terms, which were always in his favour, or face the consequences. Many suffered the latter. Once in the bed of The Tamer you were marked for life.

Another of his unsavoury side-lines was his live rape and torture videos. It was pay per view and based in the dark web. Women were subjected to horrendous physical and mental abuse, gang raped, and the select few that paid more than one thousand euros could watch the poor girl be killed. This was conducted as a roulette, like a game show. Then studio quality production made the show high class, like *Family Fortunes*, streaming to thousands of people. The viewers could auction off the method of death – fire, gun, electrocution, acid bath. The modes changed as the weeks went on, always keeping the production fresh, as well as massaging the figures even higher by allowing the auction.

Dragoslav had made tens of millions this way. The thirst for female cruelty by the fat middle class white man in Europe and the USA even disgusted Dragoslav, but business was business.

Siobhan was to be handed over to Dragoslav's organization. The concierge was a key member of the team. They escaped through the service exit at the back of the hotel, and bungled Siobhan into a van, the engine rattling away.

"Make sure that Dragoslav keeps her alive, he can do what he likes apart from kill the bitch," Broc said.

The man nodded, Broc gave them the papers for the Channel crossing. It would take at least fifteen hours to travel to the heart of Europe. There were three of them, so the van wouldn't stop. As long as they made it to southern Austria, they would be able to make it into Slovenia.

"Let's go," Broc, Devon and Ji-Yeon got into the old Ford Mondeo. The car left under the Waterloo Expressway, and headed out of London towards the South Coast

19

Jongy was confused, he couldn't understand why there was an issue. The loose ends had been tied up, he had got Jamal to access the police chat nets. His name was mentioned and it led them to the B5 intelligence agency.

"Where are they based, eh?"

Jamal clicked one-handedly. "Hurry, man," Jongy chided. It took Jamal less than a minute to scan the faces at his house. The two people that were of prominence were the man and the women, who seemed to be partners. There was another man, a blond-haired studious type who came into the shot after the woman had killed herself.

Simon Broadstone and Alex Brown, both of Interpol and B5 Intelligence.

Jongy was looking over Jamal's shoulder.

"What's B5 Intelligence?" he asked.

"Hold on." Jamal typed, the screen rendered, then rendered again. He was on a government assist website that listed all the intelligence services in the United Kingdom.

"B5 Intelligence is a group working out of SIS, in the secret service building on Vauxhall."

"What's their function?" Jongy asked.

He typed again. "Their function is to support Interpol, dealing with mainly healthcare-related crimes."

"You're fuckin' kidding me, eh?" Jongy said. He pulled his phone out and dialled. "Hey, Jongy here, what's the British Spooks sniffing around our operation, eh, you said there'd be no involvement?"

He was listening, Jamal tapped into it, located the cellphone signal. Jongy was too busy looking at the floor talking to notice. The signal came from inside the Houses of Parliament – he assumed it was Blunt, but there was no signal from his phone. He ran a quick diagnostic, and located the health secretary giving an interview to Sky News.

He digitally painted the phone, triangulated it as soon as it left the parliament building and it was picked up by a CCTV camera on the street. His phone would tell him when that happened.

"Hey, coon, get me the details on those two, they're to be eliminated, pronto, eh?"

"Can you please stop calling me that word?"

Jongy stopped looking at his phone, scrolling. "Shut the fuck up, kaffir, and do as the white boy says or you will be sucking my dick again, eh." He patted Jamal on the head.

Errol came in, shuffling, his snake-skin shoes looking a little battered.

"Get the car, we're going for a drive, eh."

He nodded and shuffled back out.

"Send me all the details of these two. I need to know where they live, and I want Hypnos helping me when I ask, understand?" he stopped to stare at Jamal. "I said, understand, boy?"

Jamal nodded, and carried on tapping away. "I'll text you the locations."

Jongy saw the car pull up outside the garage, he opened the door, before stepping out he looked back at Jamal. "Don't do anything to stupid will you kaffir, I have text Mt

Veshausen he will down shortly to keep an eye on you?"

The door closed, the silence overwhelming for Jamal. The energy that Jongy brought to a room was thick with untrustworthiness. He sat for a moment and considered what he could do.

He opened the newsfeed from Sky, the health service was in meltdown. It hadn't seen a situation like this ever before. He felt responsible, his life was based around providing currency and alibis for his criminal network. He had no idea that he would have a hand in the culling of the national population.

The screen still of Alex was on the left-hand screen. He searched the database, and hacked into some networks. Seconds later, he had access to Alex's phone. The secure phone was provided by the intelligence service. He considered what to write, but quickly heard the footsteps of Veshausen.

He typed, *I need your help, I know what's happening. You raided my house this morning, I'm Jamal. Don't reply, I'm being held against my will. I will find a way of contacting you.* He hit send, and closed the screen.

"What's happening?" said the posh South African as he sidled up to Jamal.

"Ah, you know, bit of genocide here and a bit of mass murder there."

Siobhan came to. It was dark and damp, the air was moist and had a taste to it. She was naked, suddenly releasing that she was freezing. She started to shake, her bones rattling inside. She felt violated, bruised and sore everywhere. Her vagina felt as though it had been ripped inside, she daren't touch herself. The pain made her breathing shallow and laboured.

Gripping herself, she stole her right hand and felt the

around her, she couldn't see her own hand in front of her face. There was a movement in the environment she was in.

"Hello," she said through gritted teeth. There was a scraping, like a foot moving on gravel. The floor was dirty, it was hard, like concrete, uneven too, with bigger stones jutting out of the surface.

She called again, there was nothing. She felt around where she thought the movement and sound had come from. She reached in the dark like she was trying to grab a wad of £50 notes. Stretching, she felt the cold heel of someone. It retracted quickly. "Hey, who is that?" she said. Her body ached beyond anything that she had felt before, her left shoulder was deformed, she knew it was dislocated. It had dislocated a few times before as a teenager, something that she planned to sort out but never got around to it. Using her bare feet, and ignoring the pain, she pushed herself in the direction of the foot.

The person on the other end of the foot whimpered, "Please, don't come any closer." Siobhan stopped. The accent was European, maybe German, she couldn't be sure.

"Who are you?" she said. "My name's Siobhan."

"It doesn't matter who you are, or who I am."

Siobhan was confused. "Look, I know you don't want to talk, but we're both freezing, if we hug we can generate warmth between us, make ourselves more comfortable."

"Don't come any closer…" the voice said, trailing off as her emotion scratched away, Siobhan heard the feet recoil even further away.

"Where are we?" Siobhan asked.

"What day is it?" the voice said.

"The day I remember was the 20th March."

The person whimpered again.

"Why's that?"

"I was taken on the 12th June, 2015."

Siobhan ignored the pain, she sat up, her mind calculating – that was three years ago. "Are you sure?" she said.

"I was on holiday in Spain when I was taken."

"By who?"

"I don't know," the woman's voice became more lucid and coherent as she spoke.

"There was more of us when I arrived."

"Where are they now?"

"Dead!"

A cold chill fired through Siobhan like a bolt of icy lightening, her blood running even colder.

"We are used for their pleasure and they film it."

"Who are they?" Siobhan asked again, her mind trying to figure out what had happened. She remembered the chat on the dating site, going to the hotel, and the man. The next thing she remembered was the cable tie around her neck, she touched the area tentatively, it was still sore. She pushed closer.

"What do you mean for their pleasure?"

"They rape us, they keep raping us, and when they're finished, they kill us."

She moved again. "Now you're here, I might finally be killed."

"What do you mean 'finally'?" Siobhan asked.

"I can't do this any more, I just want to die. They're so cruel." She started to sob.

"You've been here for nearly three years, honey," Siobhan said. "It's March, 2018."

She stopped sobbing, Siobhan could hear the cogs turning in the mind of the woman who was so physically and mentally isolated.

"I was taken on the 20th, if we're anywhere near that date. My neck still feels sore, so I'm guessing that's the case. I was in London when I was taken."

The woman moved again, and Siobhan felt her hand

touch her fingers. Siobhan grabbed her, and used the energy she had to cling up to the women. She winced.

"We are in Slovenia," the women said, grabbing Siobhan like her life depended on it.

"Slovenia?" Siobhan said.

Suddenly the ceiling of wherever they were was flooded in brilliant white light. Voices came, men angry and abusive. Siobhan felt a noose slip around her throat, and it pulled, and she started to choke. The noose yanked at her, and she submissively complied. She was dragged out of the hole, on her knees, crying in pain. Watching the hole, she saw the woman being dragged out in the same way, Siobhan trying to fight the noose. She felt a blow to her right side, winding her. The voice above her was deep and threatening, the breath horrible, moist and fetid. The woman coming out of the hole said nothing, she was used to it. Three years of this meant she knew how to behave, as

this had been happening to her regularly. Siobhan looked about the room – men sat in chairs drinking beer. She counted four cameras, with lighting, this was a show.

The women in the hole next to Siobhan was placed on a wooden dining table. Her head to one side, Siobhan caught the girl praying, the Lord's Prayer was easy to spot.

The girl was then stretched out among a group of men, naked form the waist down, who were stood in line masturbating, patiently waiting their turn on the girl. Siobhan struggled to watch, she kept looking at the girl's face, pain etched. Siobhan then realized why she was in so much pain in her genitals, she felt between her legs and felt the unmistakable moisture of a man's deposit. There were fifteen men that she counted. It wouldn't have taken them long to get through her.

Siobhan's senses were in overdrive, she had never felt so terrified. The men had just finished on the woman, and they looked down at her smiling.

The table was then upended, the woman's battered body in the cold light of day was ruined. Siobhan felt nausea wash over her like a wave.

A man came out wearing a dinner suit, the tuxedo cutting a fine figure. The man was tall, athletic, his face obscured by a gas mask. Carrying a microphone, he spoke in what she thought was Russian. Every man in the room appeared to be Slavic, or Russian. The cube-like features of their heads and the air of arrogance were uncomfortable.

He started speaking, and the men in the room laughed. He was speaking into a camera that followed him around on a boom. He walked over to Siobhan, and grabbed her hair. She tried to fight him, but the bolt of pain that came from the rear as she was cattle prodded stopped her. The unmistakable crackle was still buzzing behind her ear – immediate reaction. He pulled her hair back again, scream-ing into the microphone. Again the men laughed. He stood behind her, still talking, and then the sharp pain of his boot smashed squarely in her back, forcing her to fall forward, smashing her face on the concrete floor.

Siobhan was utterly terrified. What seemed like just an hour ago, she had been in Alex's flat, messing about. She thought she had found the one. Even Ray would let them be together. Ray? She thought

She felt hands grab her under each armpit. She looked up, the man was counting something on a large flat screen. Numbers that looked like money, like an auction.

The man spun the wheel, Siobhan couldn't see what was written on it, and her knees were still wincing in pain.

She watched a large oil drum be sack-trucked into the studio, the lid removed. The girl from the pit was hoisted into it. Siobhan could smell the fumes, causing a haze out of the top, like the rear of a fast jet taking off. She didn't know what 'chlorosulfonic acid' was, those were the words written on the drum. The girl was lowered in the barrel, first her feet. Her face was taped with grey gaffer tape, two small holes had been made to allow for some breathing. She screamed as her toes entered the fluid. They held her there for what seemed like hours, although the time was only two minutes as there was a clock counting it down. They pulled her out, the skin, muscle and fascia stripped form the foot, exposing just bare bones. The bones were still held together with the ligaments, Siobhan wanted to throw up, her throat raspy and sore, belched out with vomit.

This time, they dunked the poor wretched girl up to the waist. She bucked and screamed through the tape, veins almost popping in her throat as the skin sizzled in the fluid, making the room stink. A smell like no other, Siobhan couldn't hold it any further, she threw up, with her bladder also voiding the dehydrated urine out of her.

The men in the room were jeering and laughing, drinking cans of beer. The girl appeared to have passed out, and they hoisted her out. Siobhan couldn't fathom what she saw. The girl was stripped to the bones all the way up to the waist. She hung unconscious from the hoist – from the waist down, she resembled a character skeleton you would see at Halloween. The masked man poked her, prodding her with a stick. She roused. She was still alive.

"LEAVE HER ALONE…" the crackling again, the bolt right through the nape of Siobhan's neck as she held herself up. "FUCK YOU!" she screamed, another bolt.

The compere came over, he crouched. He removed the gas mask, underneath he was only wearing a latex hood, his lips bulging horribly from it, his eyes cold and piercing, he held his finger to his mouth and said, "Shush." He walked back to the poor girl.

She was whispering like she was in the cellar they were in. She was hoisted again, and then lowered into the drum right up to the neck. The camera on the boom closed in for the money shot. Her shackles burning away with the acid, she became free, her arms desperately trying to escape the constant burning, the man in the hood laughing. He handed his mic to another hooded person, and picked up the lid. For Siobhan, this was the worst. While the girl was still alive, he placed the lid on the top of the drum and secured it. The banging on the side became fainter and fainter, and then it stopped. The man was crouching, holding his ear to the drum, smiling at the camera. "Mrtav," he said. Then there was a cheer form the room. The oil drum was picked up by the sack truck and taken out of the studio.

The man turned to Siobhan, and walked over, saying something. The camera followed him, taking a close look at her, and she suddenly felt hands on her. She thought she was going to suffer the same fate. She was dragged across the floor, her feet scraping, and Siobhan wincing. Then nothing. She was falling. She hit the stony uneven surface with a thump, knocking the wind out of her. She cried out, looking up to the aperture above the ground, the man stood there, and he took his mask off.

His face was scarred, the skin pockmarked, thick lips, and a thick head of hair.

"My employer wants me to keep you alive." His accent was heavily Eastern European. "Let's see how long you last, kurva." He pulled his penis out, and started urinating on her. She tried to escape the torrent musky urine as it splashed all over the place. His laugh was shrilling and incongruous to the physique of the man. She stole a glance of her surroundings while there was light, there wasn't much room. The splashing stopped, and suddenly, Siobhan was plunged yet again into darkness.

20

Alex was viewing the CCTV footage of Broc leaving the hotel. The hotel reservation had them at the property for twelve hours, yet Broc seemed to know more than was feasibly possible. The reason why she was on the Albert Embankment, next to SIS, was to provide close protection and to shorten her commute. A ball had definitely been dropped, and she was also worried about Si. A team had gone to the family home to give the whole picture to him. Alex couldn't face it. It was the wrong decision, but there were now two cases burning like an out of control arson attack. Alex's phone beeped.

She opened it instantly, snapping forward, the text read: *I need your help, I know what's happening. You raided my house this morning, I'm Jamal. Don't reply, I'm being held against my will. I will find a way of contacting you.*

Alex clicked her fingers to Ricky, who was busy on the phone. He cut the conversation short. He walked over and Alex handed him the phone.

"How did he get my number?" Alex asked.

Ricky shrugged, Broadstone saw them in deep conversation from the other side of the room, and he came over too.

"What's going on?" he asked. Ricky gave him the phone, Broadstone read it and read it again.

"Is this legit?"

Ricky pursed his lips. "There's no reason for it not to be legit, boss."

"How did he get the number?"

"That's pretty easy." Both Alex and Simon pulled a face. "Easy for Jamal that is, I think I would struggle. He had obviously clocked you and ran you through the facial network. He pinpointed you through whatever systems you're on, outside of the secure network. And then just probed whatever secure servers there were, simple."

"Is this your sterile phone?" Broadstone asked, like a child about to start a puzzle.

"Yeah," Alex said, pulling her non-sterile phone out.

"Text him back?" Broadstone said.

They stood in silence for a second. "Text what?"

"What do you want? Why have you been kidnapped? What's going on? You know..." he said with a shrug. "What would you normally text a dude that's committing genocide?"

Alex typed, Broadstone peered on the phone as Alex typed. "Leave the genocide bit out, right?" A smile crept up the side of Alex's mouth as she paused, looked up at Broadstone and hit send.

Dots...

I'll be in touch when I can, in need some conditions before I agree to anything with you. But look up Asclepius.

Alex repeated the message to the guys.

"Could be a come on?" Ricky said.

"Maybe," Broadstone said. "But he's got everything to lose. He has to explain what's gone on in his house before we even deal with the rest of the shit he's connected to and he knows it."

"*Asclepius*?" Alex asked. "What's that?"

"It's from Greek mythology, it means 'healing', I think,"

Broadstone said, he shrugged. "Private schooling, the shit they teach!"

Ricky was already on his iPad, googling the name. "The Roman God of medicine. Brought up by a goat and dog, according to Google."

Broadstone nodded. "Is this connected? What's this mythical God got to do with Jamal and the woes of what's happening in the healthcare system?"

"Those woes have a death toll of over one hundred thousand people. The Health Secretary is trying to put fires out in the Houses of Parliament, I don't envy him," Ricky said.

"My memory is coming back, Asclepius is the symbol for medicine, or healthcare, you know the two-headed snake that you see all over the world? Isn't that Asclepius?" Broadstone asked.

"It's called the rod or staff of Asclepius, you're right, it's symbolic for healing."

"I don't get the link!" Alex exclaimed.

"We need to look at this, are there any markers that tell us where this chap is?" Broadstone asked.

Ricky was already running the software. "Nope, he covered his tracks pretty well."

"We don't know exactly what's happened here just yet, I mean, we have the words of a sadist and a guy that really shouldn't fly long-haul anymore. I'm still not convinced that we're dealing with a software upload into the brain."

"You were at the house, Simon," Alex said, glaring at him. "That wasn't normal in any way. That woman was a mid-thirties yummy mummy out enjoying a drink with her friends before picking her kids up." Both Simon and Ricky nodded. "What she did was so left of field, and to kill herself in that manner, what was all that about?"

"Agreed, that was an extraordinary situation we

witnessed, but even so, does that constitute evidence?" Broadstone asked.

"Let's see."

Alex pulled her phone out, clicked messages, found Jamal's thread. *Before we do anything, confirm the incident in your house with the woman, the police officers and our suspect.*

A few seconds passed.

Dots…

Yes, I controlled her through Hypnos.

Alex's blood ran cold, she shivered as it rattled up her spine. She blew air out of her cheeks and gave the phone to Broadstone and Ricky.

"So, that confirms that the software is in use, we have to rely on that because right now, this is all we have," Broadstone said.

"Should we call a meeting?" Ricky said. Broadstone was going to answer, but was interrupted.

"No." They both turned to look at Alex. "Let's keep this between ourselves."

Broadstone frowned. "Why?"

"Who can we trust? We're all connected, we, as in the three of us need to disconnect from the grid, go back to old school *comms*. Have we got any old Nokias that don't connect to the WIFI? You know, the phones that you could literally set fire to and they would still work?"

"I can source some!" Ricky said.

Simon was still looking a little perplexed. Alex held her phone up. "The network is the source for Hypnos to hit the target audience, correct? Then what's stopping this organization from turning even our closest colleagues against us? Seriously, we have to ditch the tech and go to good old-fashioned policing!"

Simon stood, thinking about it for a moment. "I think that's a plan, Alex, good job" Broadstone said.

"Gimme your phones and stay away from any computers that are connected to the grid, the only computers we can trust at this moment are in the Vestry, other than that, we are totally blind to what's going on out there," Ricky said. The two of them gave their phones to Ricky. "Give me ten minutes, and I will have the old-style phones for you."

"This is freaking me out, Simon," Alex said.

"I know, not being able to trust even the people in this division is unsettling to me." Both Alex and Simon watched the room, people going about their business as though nothing was happening.

"Is there any way that we can place a measure in the system to recognize if someone has been affected?"

Ricky thought for a moment. "I'll check it out, I'll see if I can push that relationship with Jamal."

"He's not our friend. Let's remember that he always had a choice, by the looks of things, he's decided to bat for the other team after realizing what a dick he's become," Alex said.

"We're not sure that he's been totally complicit, they might have something over him," Ricky said, scrolling through the iPad.

"Shit," Ricky said, both Simon and Alex looked at him, they waited… and waited… he was still transfixed to the screen. "Shit!"

"What is it?" Alex said, breaking the silence.

"Simon, can we go and talk? I need you to see something."

"It's about Devon, isn't it?" Alex said, concern shooting across her face. "Simon, please?"

"Alex, stand down," Broadstone said. "In here," he ushered Ricky into the side room.

It was a spare office, glass encompassed it, and they shut the door on Alex, who was watching helplessly through the glass. Broadstone stood staring at the screen, slowly shaking his head. His hand came up to his mouth and he turned pale. The minutes ticked by, Alex watched the big hand turn ever so slowly with her forehead pressed against the glass.

Broadstone nodded, and Ricky came to the door.

"Come in," he said.

Alex sheepishly followed Ricky into the room. She felt sick, her life for the last twelve months had been in such turmoil, she didn't know how much more she could take. First, that case with the *Troll* that nearly broke her. Then following that and a period of sick leave, the Broc debacle.

"It's not Devon!" Ricky said, Alex cried out, relief shooting across her face. "It's Siobhan."

"What do you mean?" Alex said, wanting to look at Ricky's iPad.

"I think you should see it," Broadstone said.

He nodded to Ricky, reluctantly, Ricky opened the tablet and hit run.

"Sweet Jesus," Alex said as she saw Siobhan. She looked battered, ruined and terrified. The poor girl being gangraped was just as shocking, and Alex struggled to watch as the queue of men went through her. The final act of the auction on the video – the money being transacted was to determine her fate.

"What the actual fuck is this?" Alex asked.

"I've been surfing the dark web. This site has a massive following, the hooded guy is almost certainly Dragoslav, the lunatic Serbian, got his voice on recognition software. He fits the digital composition on the international arrest warrant. There's at least twenty-one thousand people watching this, actively paying, it's in the thousands. My software has predicted that over three million dollars was wagered on the broadcast."

"Can we trace it?" Broadstone asked.

"Acid bath," Ricky said.

They looked as the girl was hoisted above the drum, and lowered, when her feet came out, all Alex could see was Siobhan. The look in her eyes was pure terror. The screaming of the girl suspended over the barrel through the gag was gut-wrenching. Alex had to look away. "How can anyone be so cruel?" she said.

At the end of the video, when the girl was sealed in the drum, the three of them heard the banging on the inside fade to nothing. The camera panning to the host, he walked over to Siobhan. He was speaking Serbian, Ricky had applied an advanced translator to the text.

"Hold on a second, guys," he said as he slid buttons and bars across the rendered image on the screen, the voice suddenly becoming English. Ricky stopped the video and slid the footage back.

"Look at this little slut, all the way from England. Though she's Irish, look at this face, dial in tomorrow when she meets the gang. Twenty blue-balled studs that will tear her pussy apart."

They watched her be thrown into the pit, and the footage ended with a webinar link to join the broadcast the next day.

"We have to find this place, Simon," Alex said.

He nodded.

"He's been on an arrest warrant since the Balkan war, the authorities have failed more than eight times to apprehend him." Ricky said.

"Let's not use the usual channel then?" Broadstone suggested.

"Who you gonna call?" Ricky asked.

"Not Ghostbusters, my friend, best you don't ask. Give me a couple of hours to see what covert agencies we have on the ground. Be prepared to move on him."

They nodded.

"In the meantime, we need to deal with the shitstorm

that's happening out there. Get your game faces on and get this De Jong in one of our interview rooms."

"GUYS?" They turned, the door was opened, and one of the fresh-faced operatives had poked his head around. "You need to come."

They filed into the operations room adjacent to the Vestry. The big screen was a hive of rich media being streamed to the team in SIS.

"It's getting out of control, police are drowning, people attacking each other, we are going to have to speak to the Home Secretary and get the military on the streets," said the watch commander, an experienced operator from the Intelligence Corps.

Broadstone was letting the information sink in and ferment briefly in his mind while he saw people go about their business, watching the catastrophe unfold through the news media.

"RIGHT, LISTEN IN!" Broadstone said, standing in front of everyone in the control room. "This is going to sound very weird. But you're going to have to trust me on this. I want you to hand your smartphones and personal tablets over to Alex, she's going to be stood at the door with a box. When this is over you can get your devices back."

This caused a stir. The feedback loop was alive and well even in the security services.

"Why?" said one guy.

"Listen, guys, if you don't hand them over, I'm going to have to ask you to leave the building and go home. Please, I wouldn't ask you if I didn't think it was necessary."

Reluctantly people stared at each other, reaching for their devices and walking to Alex.

"If you can contact your loved ones, friends, whoever, through the landline and tell them to switch their devices off," Broadstone added.

"What's wrong with the phones then?" A voice said.

Broadstone looked at the watch commander, then to Alex, who nodded.

"Okay, listen in, and official secrets remains in force even after what I'm about to tell you."

Five minutes later, the team was fully informed. A look of shock and disgust filled the room. Oddly, the mood became buoyant, the team were now driven to find a solution for what was happening outside.

Broadstone went to the watch commander. "I want armed guards at the door. If this group of people out there know we are onto them, who knows what they'll do."

"Roger that."

Broadstone turned to Alex. "We need to get to the Houses of Parliament. We need to have a chat with the Home Secretary."

Alex nodded. The last time she had seen him was immediately after Broc had disappeared and her daughter was taken. He knew Broc well when he was a young doctor finding his way around the sex scene, he almost made Alex feel sorry for him.

"I'll get the car."

"No need, Alex," Broadstone said.

She looked surprised. "I don't think walking there would be good. We have a security issue being outside, I think."

"We're not going to walk, we're going by train, well, a monorail."

Alex stopped, looked about, her mind trying to figure it out. There was no such thing in London.

Broadstone laughed. He pointed to the floor, underground. "We are connected to the Houses of Parliament. Why do you think this building was placed here?"

"You mean we can access Parliament by going under the Thames?"

"Yes!" He said, matter of fact. "Let's go."

"I understand, I will get Jamal to sort it out, thank you, Mr Blunt."

Jamal looked up from the desk. "Something up?" he was concerned that his brief conversation was already rumbled. Jamal knew that the security services would now be asserting Jamal's credentials, and stacking up the evidence now mounting throughout the country.

"That was Mr Blunt. The intelligence services have caught wind of what we are up to, of course, they don't know the full details, however, he needs us to provide some security," Veshausen said, sitting heavily in the chair.

"How does he know?" Jamal said, nonchalantly typing away on the computer.

"He has someone on the inside of a group called B5, idiots!" Veshausen said, equally as nonchalant, checking his phone.

Jamal knew that was Alex's outfit.

"When you say security, what do you mean?"

"Those people, Mr Broadstone and Ms. Brown are to be eliminated from this process. Can you organize someone to deal with that?"

Jamal was puzzled. "When you say eliminate, you mean kill, right?"

Veshausen stopped scrolling on his phone, quizzically, he looked at Jamal. "What else did you think I meant, man, this isn't a quiz fucking show!"

He pocketed his phone and leaned over. "You know, what you have done so far is far worse than killing a couple of spooks."

Jamal nodded.

"Infect some people near to where they live and work and then have them..." he paused, smiled "... killed."

Jamal nodded, turned to his computer, and started to type. Veshausen had no idea what he was doing.

Just been told to have you killed, there is someone on your side that is spilling the beans, you need to sort your end out before we can do anything else, message me when you have done this. In the meantime, watch your backs.

21

Jongy entered the building – The Working Man's club in Esher. Esher wasn't the most inspiring of locations for the nerve centre of Asclepius. The spiritual meaning of the club was related to the Blackshirt Oswald Mosley, a Hitler supporter and leader of the far right fascist party during the 40s and 50s. The speech about immigration and the rivers turning to blood was written in this very place. This was as close to Hitler as you were going to get. In fact, it was the sole reason why Jongy was now living in the UK.

He went through the bar area to the rear. A large muscular man was standing there, the man stopped him, and ran a security device over his body like a comb. Finally, he placed Jongy's hands on a fingerprint recognition pad. He checked the screen, confirmed the face.

"Hey man," Jongy said, the big guy smiling.

"How are you, brother?" he said in a thick German accent.

"Is the boss in?" Jongy asked.

"Ja, he is waiting for you." He opened the door through the myriad of security parameters. The door hissed as it opened, and a dark corridor about twenty meters long revealed itself. The carpet was plush to walk on, and the walls were adorned with images of the Third Reich, swastikas, and images of prominent neo-Nazis that have filled the boots of the Fuhrer since his demise back in '45. Jongy felt a stiffening in his loins, this was his home.

He walked down, the smell of tobacco and wood omnipresent in the air. The sensation walking into this building was electric, his goose-bumps bounced all over his body. His hair was even standing on end.

At the end of the corridor, there was a door that led to a large open space. It was tastefully appointed, with big red leather couches, and wingback chairs. Paintings that went missing during WWII were here, alongside antiques that were also still missing from the war, with Jewish antiquities that stood on pedestals. A reminder of the Aryan might. This was no homage to Germanic customs, but a working environment where racism and Nazism lived side by side for a cleaner world.

"DE JONG!" boomed a voice from the back. The eyes in the room turned. All men. They were in tailored suits, smoking big cigars and swirling cognac. This was no club you could just join. For some people it was a birth-right, others had to pay the huge fees to join, and suffer an initiation ceremony that was fairly unpleasant. The likes of De Jong, their membership was automatic through pedigree and his overt views and core beliefs. He was a Nazi through and through. His mission was to cleanse the world where Hitler had left off.

He turned to the sound, Van Der Meld was sat, facing him. He was talking to someone.

He walked over, clicked his heels. "Sit Jongy, eh."

He walked around the chair and sat, facing the person sitting in front of him.

Instantly Jongy stood up, rigid. The Duke of Devon smiled, and waved in an almost dismissive way.

"Sit, man," said the Queen's nephew. The man was a

legend in the ranks of the WA. Jongy had seen him speak in Soweto nearly twenty years ago. The man was the natural leader of the fourth Reich, a true German, direct lineage from the Kaiser himself.

He seemed to be smaller than Jongy remembered. Even so, the mere stature of the man was a dream come true for Jongy. Gingerly he sat, staring at the Duke.

"I've been hearing a lot about you… Jongy." The nickname was difficult for the Duke to say.

"All good I hope, eh?" Jongy said.

"Of course, a real trooper if ever I saw one, Himmler would have been honoured to have a man like you serve in the SS."

Jongy's heart began to swell.

Van Der Meld leaned in. "Now, listen, we need to deal with the intelligence services, they are already on the trail. It won't take them long to start finding out things if you see what I mean."

Jongy nodded. "You said that some people came to visit you?"

"That's right, Jongy, eh, two spooks from the intelligence services, they need to be dealt with. I've already told Mr Blunt about them."

"What did he say?" Jongy said, he was stealing glimpses of the Duke sat next to him, smoking his cigar. The Duke was eyeing him intently, swirling the tip of the cigar in his mouth, his face slightly obscured by the smoke.

"He will try and leverage some influence in government to throw the scent off, but it's imperative to get these two taken out of the picture."

Jongy sat back, the leather creaking. The smell of the leather oozed credence and opulence, he felt a belonging like no other time in his life.

There was a silence, the Duke broke it.

"The cull is going better than we thought, Jongy. There should be close to two-thirds of a million dead by the end of the day. Undesirable people that choke the health service and community amenities. The cull will stretch deeper into the next five years, with only ten million people living in this great country, and spreading our joy to other parts of the world." He took a huge heave from his cigar, inhaled and then jetted the smoke out like an afterburner. "We could even wipe the Indian and Chinese population off the planet."

Jongy smiled. "That would be a utopian world Mein Herr."

"Indeed." The Duke studied Jongy, toying with the cigar in his mouth.

"Tell us what happened at the house, Jongy," Van Der Meld said.

He shrugged. "I don't know. I don't know why these people were there, nor do I know how my name came top in a police search, I was very careful, eh."

"Of course, of course," the Duke said, "even so, we need to tie this up, and I want you to deal with it," he continued, pointing with the glowing cigar.

Jongy curtly nodded. "I will get the kaffir to deal with them. We can use this technology to have them disposed of."

"The kaffir, you mean this Jamal?" the Duke said.

"Yes, sir."

"Can we use the software ourselves, and bypass the Untermensch?"

"No, I spoke with Mr Veshausen, the kaffir has placed so many security parameters on the software that if it were to be used without him physically operating it, the consequence is that we will be revealed," Van Der Meld said, crossing his legs.

"Can we find a way? If we can operate it, then we can really do as we want."

"If I may, sir?" Jongy said. "The kaffir is placated. He will do as he's told, we don't have to worry about him. He has the knowledge that he will be paid richly for his services, eh, but when we find the route to use the software ourselves, we will dispose of him."

The Duke took another huge pull on the cigar. "Excellent, Jongy." There was a pause. "You can go now, you need to deal with these intelligence officers, and deal with them quickly."

"Jawohl, Mein Herr." Jongy stood, clicked his heels and walked out.

"You trust this man?" the Duke said.

Van Der meld watched Jongy leave. "I trust him, implicitly, but do I trust his attitude and temper? Absolutely not, sir. The man is barbaric, a poorly-trained rottweiler, where his bite is worse than his bark, and the bark is pretty distasteful."

"Everyone has a purpose and a shelf life, Mr Van Der Meld."

Van Der Meld cut a look, it felt like a shot across his bows as a warning. "Does that mean me, sir?" he asked, smiling.

"It means even I, my dear friend."

Both Alex and Simon went through a series of security checks, and there, in the basement of SIS, was a monorail.

"This is like something out of a Bond film," Alex said. It wasn't a train as such, but like a golf cart fitted to a rail. The carts were controlled at each end, and each cart was meticulously videoed.

They climbed in, and Broadstone hit the green go button. Seconds later, the electric motors kicked in and the cart started speeding towards the Parliament building on the north side of the River Thames.

"How long has this been here?" Alex asked.

"I think it was Tony Blair that had it installed when the building was first opened. The government at the time wanted access to security services without using communication devices or being seen leaving either building. Politicians that need to know, as well as military and security operators, can freely move between the two buildings."

The rail snaked, passing other carts coming the other way.

"It was installed by the same company that did the Channel Tunnel, in true British economy style, they chose the French company, and not the British one. I have no idea what the cost was."

"It's incredible, to know about this and the rest of the world has no clue."

"It's also the escape route for the Houses of Parliament if the place was attacked or bombed."

In under five minutes, the cart had pulled up at its destination. The platform was a mock underground station, with the London Underground logo saying, Houses of Parliament. The joke wasn't lost on Alex, until she saw the army of armed officers.

"They're not police, by the way," Broadstone said winking.

A staircase led up into the main chamber through a security door. The opening of the door was made to look like the access to an office or chamber.

Entering the minister's chambers, the wooden panels were oppressive yet exuded the history of British politics. Three doors down was the Home Secretary's chamber. The door was ajar.

Simon knocked and walked straight in, Mr Bromilow MP was deep in conversation on the phone, he looked up and waved them in. Simon shut the door after Alex had walked through.

"I have to go, thank you for your call," he said on the phone.

Bromilow cut a very different figure from the person that Alex had met six months previously at his club.

Broadstone had sent Alex to meet him at his club Lolly's. The club labelled by the Zookeeper as a hotbed and meeting place for paedophiles. Nothing could be further from the truth. The place was, and had been for decades, a safe haven for the people in society that thought very differently. He had explained to her the world of kink and everything goes along with it. She discovered that the people were normal but just wanted a more diverse way of life and expressing themselves. He himself was a caged submissive and cuckold. And very gay to boot. Right now, the gay submissive man was absent. The dynamic statesman that she was more familiar with was now sitting across from her.

"Alex, please, my honour. How are you?" His voice was direct, educated yet empathetic. He cleared the screen of his computer, his fingers tracing across the keys, long and slender like a pianist.

"I am very well, sir!" Alex said.

"Please, you've seen me at my most vulnerable, I'm sure we can dispense the formalities," he said with a nod and a smile.

"Mr Broadstone, report?" The smile vanished.

Simon filled Bromilow in with what was happening, leaving nothing out. He even included the incident with Broc, which piqued his interest.

"How did this make you feel, Alex?" Bromilow asked, and Alex looked at him, surprised.

"Not sure really, concentrating on what's happening with Hypnos. I didn't see Broc coming, but I guess I'll have to deal with that after this!"

He pursed his lips and gave her quizzical look. "Forgive

me, Alex, I know Broc very well as you know, how did he make you feel when this incident unfolded?" he leaned in his chair, engaged. Alex felt Broadstone shift in his chair, he was desperate to speak.

"Angry," Alex said, Bromilow nodded "Upset, scared." He smiled slightly. "Terrified, actually. I feel a strong connection with Siobhan."

Bromilow cut in. "The woman you met at this club?" Alex nodded, and Bromilow leaned back and thought for a moment. He turned to Broadstone. "After this shitstorm is finished, I want Broc made an intelligence priority."

Broadstone nodded.

"You will have whatever assets you need to take the son of a bitch out. This man isn't to face trial, I want him put in the ground."

"Sir, but–" Broadstone said.

"There's no but. I'm not having this man flout the law and affect one of my own servants in such a way, his opportunity for due process and the rule of law ended the moment he took Alex's daughter, and now this. Broc is mocking the fabric of our laws, it ends."

Broadstone smiled. "Understood, sir."

Someone knocked the door. "ENTER!" Bromilow said. The door opened and in walked Mr Blunt MP.

"Here is the Health Secretary, my learned friend, Mr Blunt." Simon and Alex stood, shook his hand.

"Hello," Blunt said. He sidled next to Bromilow. Alex felt it. She felt an instant dislike to the man, he seemed cold, calculating, slippery. That could have been a bias from the negative press he had received, squandering the money of the National Health Service and carving up the assets of the organization. He looked down, smiling sardonically at Broadstone and Alex. Alex tapped Broadstone's foot, she caught him nodding in her peripheral vision.

"To be honest, Stephen, I don't see the need to include the intelligence service. I think the police are adequately equipped to deal with what's going on in the health service. We have seen an unprecedented amount of deaths, granted, but what's your correlation?"

There was a pause, Broadstone didn't really know what to say. He wasn't sure of Blunt's intelligence clearance. It didn't matter anyway, Bromilow spilled everything.

After a few minutes of the Home Secretary explaining, Blunt was still smiling and nodding, catching a glimpse at both Alex and Broadstone, widening the faux smile.

"This Jamal character, what's his story?" Blunt asked. The question seemed contrary to the discussion. He asked a few times about Jamal, and the questions seemed too probing.

Alex was watching the three men talk, each one measuring the size of their dicks with each sentence, although Bromilow's penis was probably still in a chastity cage, even so, Alex was transfixed on Blunt. She pondered for a few seconds, when there was a break in the conversation. She fixed her gaze on Blunt. "Any one of you know of an organization called Asclepius?" she left it there, hanging in the air. Bromilow was searching, slowly shaking his head, Broadstone cut an angry glance at Alex, but Blunt absorbed it. He was off guard, the comment had knocked him off kilter.

"Mr Blunt?" Alex pushed.

He shook his head, but it was already too late, Mr Blunt would firmly be on Alex's hitlist. It was Broadstone's tap of the foot this time that told Alex he had noticed it too.

"What is this organization, Alex?" Bromilow said, looking around the room.

"We're not sure at this stage, but the name has come up in our investigation," Broadstone said.

"Does it mean something?" Blunt said, it was a half-arsed comment. He knew, Alex just had to prove it.

"Okay, Simon, what do you need from me?"

Simon didn't say anything, he was looking at Blunt.

"Don't worry about Mr Blunt, he's cleared at the top of the secrets tree, I trust him."

"We need to switch off the mobile network, stop all phones from transmitting and receiving data. And that includes computers, sir."

"IMPOSSIBLE!" boomed Blunt.

Bromilow glanced at the Health Secretary, then looked back at the two of them across the table. "My learned friend is right, I can't dial the UK back to 1990 without a good cause. Now I know you've mentioned about this Hypnos, but I have no evidence to support this."

"Can you at least stop the police and the army from using smartphones and the mobile internet?"

"What's the army got to do with it, Simon?"

"That's another reason for coming to see you, we need to enforce the military aid to the civil power."

"PREPOSTEROUS, SIR!" Blunt exclaimed.

"That would mean a conversation with the PM, which in turn would mean she would have to have a conversation with the Queen, not to mention the electorate, and on what grounds do we activate MACP?"

"You have police officers downing tools and refusing to work, in fact, some officers have been seen assaulting members of the public," Broadstone said.

"I had been hearing reports of this too, Mr Blunt, would you second this in Parliament, before the commons?"

Blunt paused. "Maybe we ought to take counsel from…" he looked at Alex and Simon "…a more reliable agency?"

"Indeed, you're right," Bromilow said, tapping his fingers on the leather inlaid surface of the desk.

"Would you mind awfully waiting for me in the commons, Geoffrey? Matters of national security."

"Of course, sir," Blunt said, he nodded, looked at Broadstone and Alex again, and left without saying another word. The door closed.

Before Broadstone could speak, Bromilow beat him to it. "I know what you're going to say, Simon, I will speak to Colonel Beard, chief military man in COBRA. For due process and parliamentary approval, I need his opinion more than yours."

Broadstone nodded. "I know him, he's a good man. Give him my regards, won't you?"

"I will, and convey your thoughts to add weight. If it's any consolation, I think you're right, the military needs to be on the street. This epidemic is going to cause widespread pandemonium if the reason gets out." He leaned forward, eyes piercing and deadly. "You need to cut the head of the snake off, and you haven't much time."

Alex phone beeped, she pulled it out and read the message from Jamal.

Just bin told to have you killed, there is someone on your side that is spilling the beans, you need to sort your end out before we can do anything else, message me when you've done this. In the meantime, watch your backs.

22

Not far from the East End of London, Jongy and Errol sat in a car. The car was stolen, a 1999 Vauxhall Omega, the engine jangling unhealthily like an old bag of spanners. The engine still had some guts under the hood, but it was old enough to stop prying eyes.

The front door opened, and the two men instinctively hunched their shoulders to avoid detection. More habit than actually being an effective technique.

Three men and a woman left the house, Alex's husband Simon was standing there, seeing them off. His face was puffy and red, he was clearly upset. The group of people filed into a large SUV, with blacked out windows. The engine roared and left the street, swirling the fallen leaves and dust across the road.

"We wait twenty minutes, then we go, eh?" Errol nodded.

The sun was setting on the spring sky, the leaves beginning to bud from the bare trees. Jongy exited the car, not slamming the door. It clicked shut. He walked with purpose to the front door and knocked, Si opened it. His eyes smiled at the visitor then tracked down the Beretta 9mm pistol with a silencer fitted, his face dropped in an instant, like he was having a stroke, and his skin crawled.

Jongy walked in, Si walking backwards, kicking the door

shut with a backwards kick. They kept walking towards the kitchen when Si stopped. Errol was stood in the threshold of the kitchen, having left the car five minutes earlier, and made his way to the back of the property. Si snapped around to see. The Zulu that had a seen a world of pain was stood there, a cocktail stick in the corner of his mouth, the smell of body odour overpowering, his eyes bloodshot and bulging like boiled eggs.

"You get used to the smell, eh," Jongy said. "I grew up around kaffirs, they generally stink, Errol is no exception, eh."

"Who are you?" Simon said, the nerves distinct in his voice.

"Come to the kitchen, Mr Brown. Can I call you Simon?"

They walked into the kitchen, Jongy pulled a chair out and forced Si onto it.

Errol walked around the back of the table, behind Simon, and grabbed his hands and tied them to the chair with a cable. Simon tried to resist, but the pistol whip across his face insured his compliance.

Simon, his face smarting from the smack, felt the swelling around his jawline. His tongue darted over the bruise inside his mouth. "Who are you?" he demanded.

"I want to know where your wife is, Simon." He pulled out a chair opposite Si, Jongy sat, he put the pistol on the table and reached into his pocket. He pulled out a large manila envelope, tipping the contents out on the table. Large elastic bands of varying widths littered the surface, industrial types.

"I'll correct myself, eh, I know where your wife is, I just need her to stop what she's doing, and that's where you come in."

"You want her to stop what?" His tongue now felt a definite lump in the sidewall of his mouth.

"We don't want British Intelligence meddling in our business," Jongy said.

"You know we're not together anymore, right?"

"I heard that, but I still think you have a special place in her heart, eh."

"Are you going to film me, get me to say something ridiculous?"

Jongy looked over his shoulder, Errol was shuffling around the place setting up a tripod and camera.

"Don't mind Errol, eh, just a kaffir going about his business. I don't need you to say anything, by the way."

"Oh," Simon said, puzzled.

"We're going to send a message to the people that your wife…" he paused, "I mean, ex-wife, works for."

Jongy pulled his phone out, opened it, launched YouTube, found the video he wanted and clicked play.

"Watch this eh, very funny."

The video played – a couple of teenagers, British, playing around with a watermelon. The melon was on a table and they were taking it in turns to apply an elastic band. Within a few minutes the melon had distorted, a few minutes after that, one of the boys placed the final band over the fruit and it exploded everywhere.

Simon and Jongy both jumped when it popped. Laughing, Jongy said, "It always makes me jump that, eh." He licked his bottom lip.

Errol shuffled in wearing a forensic boiler suit, goggles and a face mask, throwing a more sinister picture in the kitchen. He threw Jongy a packet containing the same.

"You see, Simon, the message has to be strong enough to provoke a reaction, just shooting you isn't going to cut it with these people."

"You're going to kill me?" Simon asked.

Jongy stopped, looked at Errol, he smiled, and then

burst out laughing. "Yes, we are. Then we go after your daughter."

"My daughter was kidnapped six months ago by Dale Broc."

Jongy stopped, took a seat. "What do you mean, kidnapped?"

"Alex was working on a case, Dale Broc, he took her, he has had her since."

Jongy was nodding. "Ah I see, I see," he said thoughtfully. "Was this the reason for your split?" he asked.

"It didn't help," Simon said ruefully.

"But you have a son too, eh?" Jongy asked. The trauma of the last six months completely going over his head.

Jongy nodded to Errol, he shuffled around and placed a large ball gag in Simon's mouth, he tried to fight, but his bonds were too tight.

"We kill you then go after your boy," Jongy said, unpacking the boiler suit.

Simon was fighting against the gag, retching, his shoulder fought against the plastic ties. Terror was spreading across his face.

"Hey, calm down, eh, we'll make this quick, just take shorter breaths, eh."

Si bucked against the bonds, Jongy reached across and grabbed his hair, Si cried out. "Settle the fuck down, eh, shallow breaths and we'll be quick as a flash."

Tears flowed from Si's face, the torment of the last six months now crescendoing into this horror show with Jongy and Errol.

Jongy made sure the camera was on, focused it and got closer to Simon, but far enough to be away from the explosion that was going to happen.

He stood behind Simon, wearing a gas mask to hide his face, and he delivered his message.

"To British Intelligence, this is what you get for meddling with Asclepius. There will be more bloodshed before the week is out."

Simon was sucking through the ball gag, sweat running down the sides of his face, and he was trying to blow hard through the gag. The bruise on his right cheek was swelling horribly.

The first band went around Simons heard, over the bridge of his nose, the band biting into the skin. The second band went over the top of that. Simon grunted in pain through the gag. Blood started oozing from where the band was cutting into the skin, pain was scathing across his face.

The third band, the fourth…

With the tenth band, Simon's head was becoming distorted, herniating from the sides, as though the brain was trying to escape. The eleventh, the camera picked up cracking as the skull was giving way to the pressure.

Jongy stood back, his head canted, he picked up the twelfth band as he was going to place it over the head too, but suddenly the head popped, blood and brain matter splattering everywhere, covering Jongy with blood and gristle.

"Fuckin' hell, Errol, did you see that, eh?" Simon's body slumped against the chair, the heart still pumping blood out of the tangled mess of tissue, the blood arching over the camera in spurts.

Errol shuffled to the camera, unphased by what he had just witnessed, and switched the camera off.

Jongy went into the front room, sent a text to Van Der Meld and uploaded the video to the dark web, knowing that the security services would pick it up. On the tags, he typed Asclepius, B5, British Intelligence, Alex Brown. He thought for a moment, then he typed Dale Broc.

"Are we ready to go, Errol?" he shuffled in, nodded, then shuffled out and opened the front door. Jongy hit publish and walked out of the house. The sun had already set, and the street-lights were now turned on with a warm glow. The earthy damp musky smell of the spring air filled Jongy's nostrils, taking him back to the veldt, on wet spring days. He didn't look back and the gate to the front garden thumped shut.

Ricky was sitting at his desk, running algorithms and checking any correlation to see if they could anticipate an uploaded person. His messages box beeped, which was odd, because it was from the dark web.

He looked over his shoulder to make sure prying eyes weren't looking. Opening the browser to the dark web meant he would have no idea what the first image was.

It was a video, with a keyword search of Dale Broc, and other keywords that were familiar to Ricky, he clicked the link, and sat back in concern. His friend, Alex's husband was sitting in a chair, restrained. A bright red ball gag was wedged in his mouth, preventing him from speaking. The swelling on his cheek told Ricky there had been a struggle. The camera picked up De Jong, wearing a gas mask, but the voice gave him away, the thick South African accent was unmistakably Jongy.

Ricky watched the fifth band go over Simon's head, he stood and banged on the window when he saw Broadstone walk by. He came straight in.

"What's up?" he asked.

The video had paused, he stood behind Ricky. "This isn't good, boss," Ricky said.

He dialled the slider back to the beginning and hit play.

"Have you seen it to the end?" Broadstone asked.

"No," Ricky said as Jongy was delivering his speech.

"This isn't going to end well, is it?" Broadstone said.

More bands were slipped over Simon's head. His eyes were bulging in terror and pain. The ninth band, thicker than most, obscured Simon's eyes, his head horribly herniated. Finally, just before the twelfth band, Simon's head popped. It made a sickening sound, like a wet mop on the floor, and Ricky recoiled. "Jesus." He bent over and started to retch. Broadstone tapped his back. "I need to tell Alex."

"I've known Simon almost twenty years, dear God, he didn't deserve that."

Broadstone pulled his phone out, remembering it was an old Nokia. He reached for the desk phone.

"I need to team to get round Alex Brown's house, the house needs to be treated as a crime scene." Broadstone was listening to the voice on the other end. Alex walked in, and Ricky hit escape, the video disappearing.

"Understood, I want the team processing the scene armed, roger that?"

"Every time I come into a room, you guys are talking in secret."

"Alex, I need you to sit down."

"I got another text from Jamal."

"Alex, please," Ricky begged. "It's Simon, I received a video, he's been killed."

"I got this text from Jamal, he said that we have someone in here that–"

Broadstone cut her off. "Alex, did you hear what Rick said?"

She looked at Broadstone, tears glistening her eyes, she held up her phone to show Simon the text. He took the phone from her and gave it to Ricky "I have a team going over to your house now, they're going to process it. As soon as we find out more, we'll deal with it."

"Who?" Alex asked.

"De Jong, we believe. It's a message to call us off, he used Asclepius. I'm sending a team to your son's university, to place him in protective custody. We're dealing with a fast-moving multifaceted enemy. Broc, and now these guys."

Alex slumped against Broadstone. The case that nearly broke her. Broc, then Devon. Splitting from Simon, finding someone like Siobhan, then she's taken and now this. "When is this going to end?" she said calmly, detached, emotionally spent.

"Ricky," Broadstone said, he was distant. "Ricky!" He snapped out of it.

"I need you on point here, find anything you can on Asclepius. Also, the message Jamal sent to Alex, we have a mole our ranks. I suspected it. Nothing leaves these four walls, and trust no one."

Ricky nodded. "I'll start with everyone that's working here on the case."

Both Stubblebine and Statham walked past the window, looking into the office.

"Don't leave those chaps out of the equation either, in fact, start with them. They're the only ones that haven't been vetted by our own screening process."

Ricky nodded. Broadstone touched his shoulder. "I know Simon was a mate, but we really do need you to focus, Rick." He nodded again, wiped his cheek and began typing on his computer.

"Mr Blunt," Jongy said down the phone. "I believe we may have solved your problem, eh."

"How so?" he replied, eyes darting around the parliamentary chambers, watching for prying ears and people that might be suspicious of his activities.

"The woman in the intelligence cell, we dealt with her husband."

"What do you mean dealt with her husband?"

"It's a warning shot across the bows, they'll back off now, eh."

"Have you done something to stir the hornet's nest, Mr

Van De Jong?" Blunt said, turning to the wall to shield his face, and lowering his voice even further.

"Well, of course, sir, we killed the husband."

"Are out of your fucking mind, Jong?" he glanced over his shoulders, the swearing causing raised eyebrows amongst his learned friends.

"I was instructed to deal with the potential mess and get the intelligence service off our back, eh, I did that."

"You were supposed to get the intelligence agencies off our backs by using dialogue, discussion and persuasion, the sort of thing that politicians do. Why one Earth would it be okay to go and kill somebody, somebody that means a lot to the very people we want to throw off the scent, have you told Van Der Meld?"

There was a pause. "I thought I'd tell you first."

"There will be no chance of quelling the intelligence services now, you absolute idiot Jongy, go back to the house and wait for further instructions."

Blunt ended the call, and Jongy stood looking at his phone. Errol shuffled up, eating a burger, the relish dripping down his wrist and onto his polo shirt.

"That went well, Errol," Jongy said, looking him up and down, Errol shrugged, and offered a bite of the burger to Jongy. "Really, look at the state of it, eh, I can't take you anywhere, filthy kaffir."

Blunt scrolled through his phone, found the Van Der Meld and Veshausen group chat on WhatsApp.

De Jong has done something that may complicate things, he's executed one of the intelligence agent's husbands, I won't be able to divert attention at my end, someone needs to sort Jongy out.

Van Der Meld replied

The plan is going ahead nicely, let's just see how this pans out, what's our contact in SIS said???

Blunt considered the comment, he hadn't heard from his man on the inside for a while. Surely they couldn't be on his tail yet. They will, but they must still be on track.

He scrolled his contacts, found the name, hit message and typed, *report*.

23

Jenny, the therapist, had been called in to manage Alex's downward spiral. The house had confirmed that Simon, Alex's husband, had been killed, and how he was killed was graphically conveyed to the Ops room. The mood was sullen, upset, as one of their own had been affected in the most brutal of ways. A service that mainly operated in the shadows was now in the clear sights of an organization that knew they had the upper hand.

The watch commander approached Broadstone.

"The Home Secretary is inbound, he'll be here in five minutes. Simon, he's requested a meet with you and Alex."

"Does he know about Alex's husband?"

"He mentioned it, he's throwing everything at the investigation. I think he has a bit of a soft spot for her," Broadstone said.

The armed guards were making a commotion outside, and Broadstone went to the secure door, the Home Secretary was giving a dressing down to the police officers.

"Simon, tell these men that I need to have my phone on me at all times."

Broadstone frowned. "Stephen, please, you know why. We have to have total sterility in the Ops room."

Bromilow wasn't going to back down, so Broadstone

stepped out. "Look, I can get one of my guys to sit with your phone out here and report on any messages that you get."

Reluctantly, Bromilow agreed. "There's a national emergency on, I need to be contactable."

"I understand," said Broadstone, "we don't take these measures lightly."

"Is there somewhere we can talk?" Bromilow asked.

"Of course, this way."

Broadstone led the Home Secretary into an office.

"This is nasty business, Simon, I don't really know what to make of it?"

Broadstone perched himself on the edge of the desk, and Bromilow sat in a chair.

"Did you speak with Colonel Beard?"

"I did, he cannot utilize the military at this point," he said with a sigh.

Broadstone's shoulders slumped, and he looked up to the ceiling.

"I know that's not what you want to hear, Simon, but unless I get his blessing, I can't move forward with it."

"Okay – why else have you come?"

"I came to see Alex, is she okay?" Bromilow asked, leaning forward in the chair.

"She's with her therapist right now, I don't think she can stay on task with what's happening in her life right now."

"She's a tough cookie, I know this will motivate her."

"What else do you want to share with me, Stephen?" Broadstone sensed there was something else.

He paused, considered his words carefully. "How secure are we here?"

"Why do you ask?" Broadstone asked, puzzled.

There was a pregnant pause, the question needed answering, and not with another question.

"We have a suspicion that there is someone in this organization that we can't trust. We're looking into that, why do you ask?"

"I did some digging, regarding this Asclepius. It makes for some worrying information."

"Oh, what have you found?" Broadstone leaned into his words.

"You know the origins of Asclepius?" Bromilow asked, and Broadstone nodded.

"Even the medical profession today uses the Staff of Asclepius, with the two snakes," Bromilow said.

"There is a closed-door group, which I thought was a quango, but it runs much deeper than that. I need you to dig deeper, I just don't have the resources at hand to check things out."

"What have you found out, Stephen?"

Bromilow looked over his shoulder instinctively, reassuring himself that there was no one else in the room.

"The world is overpopulated, the organization is a fraternity of billionaires, movers and shakers in political circles that want the world to be sustainable, there are even tenuous links to the far-right neo-Nazis, which I'm not so sure about."

Broadstone pulled a face. "What was that?" Bromilow asked.

"This De Jong, he's linked to the South African neo-Nazi group the WA, that could be our link."

Bromilow leaned back and thrusted his hands into his pockets. "The organization runs deep, and their tentacles have slithered into many avenues of the government and military. The use of Hypnos fits their remit, if indeed there is something behind the smoke."

"We need to find this De Jong, we can lift him for Simon Brown's murder, so plod can have a carte blanche looking for him and breaking doors down."

Bromilow nodded. "You must bring him here, he isn't to be interviewed in a police station."

"Understood," Broadstone said.

"My sources in Spain have told me that Broc is in Salamanca."

"Salamanca," Broadstone said.

"Yes, I want you to go there as soon as this is tied up and finished with, and I think you should take Alex."

"This Asclepius, what are your suspicions, Stephen?"

He thought for a moment, "The hushed voices in the Commons make me nervous. I don't trust anyone in the building as it is, who knows. This could stretch to the highest echelons of power, and we are not just talking about the United Kingdom," Bromilow said.

"Who have you actually spoken to?"

"It's not who I've spoken to, old bean, it's the people that aren't saying anything that worry me."

"I see," Broadstone said.

"Take care of our Alex, will you?" Broadstone nodded. "And find this swine, Simon, find him and wring out whatever information you can get out of him." Again, Simon knew exactly what that meant.

The door knocked, and Ricky walked in. "We have a hit on De Jong, boss."

Bromilow stood. "You'd better go and catch the beast, Simon." He turned to Ricky. "And how are you bearing up, old bean?" he asked.

"I'm okay, sir, we have a mountain to climb, I'll reflect when it's all over."

"Indeed, indeed, gentlemen, to the breach, and call me if there are any developments please." Bromilow walked to the door, Ricky opened it for him, and then he stopped and turned. "I shall be checking my end, if there are any preverbal lying in the woodpile, then, of course, I shall be in touch." He looked at Ricky. "No offence, old bean."

"None taken, sir."

Broadstone was on the job with Ricky, De Jong had been spotted buying some food at a service station on the M25. The cameras were loaded with software, and once they had identified the target, the target's journey would be observed, providing that there were cameras following.

Jamal was no fool, using this technology for his own gains in his previous life. With triggers within the system, the security services were onto Jongy. A rueful smile crept across his face, Veshausen was messing with his smartphone – Angry Birds or something. He was oblivious to the multitasking Jamal was doing, taking no notice to what was occurring on the screen. Every time he looked up, Jamal was quick enough to slide the panel away and reveal something more appropriate.

Ricky had Alex's phone, and Jamal was feeding locations to him via text. Ricky picked up the video that Jamal was using as well.

"What have we got, Rick?" Broadstone asked

"He was at Clacket Lane services on the westbound carriageway of the M25. He travelled to the M4 exit and drove into Hounslow. Currently, he's parked outside the Tesco Express just down the road from the Texaco garage by terminal one."

"Okay, do we know why he's there?" Broadstone asked, grabbing a chair.

"No, but working on it. There's a flight coming in from South Africa in thirty minutes, but I can't confirm that, I have no intel to suggest that's on task."

"Good work, Rick, you have Jamal feeding you this too?"

Ricky nodded, he was running algorithms working out the exit routes that Jongy could possibly take.

Broadstone stood. "I have a plan." His athletic frame strode out the door, pulling his phone out.

Ten minutes later, Ricky's phone rang, it was Broadstone.

"Speak to me, boss," Ricky said.

"Right, en route to Jongy, keep this on the knock, no one is to know, roger that?"

"Roger," Ricky said. He stood and closed his door, locking it.

"Okay, on task with some SO19 boys that are glad to help. If he moves, ping me, and we'll follow him."

Ricky was working the cameras, he pinged Simon's location. "Roger that, I have you, don't say your location over the phone." Broadstone was impressed.

"I'm going to upload the best route to your satnav, I'm switching off the cameras to your target location, so we can stay covert."

"Roger that, Rick, I'll call you when we're on task." The line went dead.

Ricky selected and primed the cameras to be switched off, they would momentarily switch on as their convoy vehicles approached the camera and then switch off again as they passed. This gave Ricky time to contact the convoy if there was something happening up ahead, he also targeted the vehicles that the gun teams were traveling in, so the traffic light favoured their vehicles, each light always green – the traffic flowed seamlessly. There was no way of knowing who would be watching.

As the cameras switched on, it became clear to Ricky the full impact of Hypnos. People were lying in the street, cars abandoned, fires burning out of control. Emergency service vehicles were everywhere, trying to cope with the disaster happening in their communities. He shook his head, and tried to remain focused.

Broadstone was two minutes out, he disabled the mobile communication network on the street Jongy was on. Ricky zoomed in to see how Broadstone was going to deal with the lunatic sitting in the car.

The black Ford Transit followed by a blacked-out Range Rover came into view, the Range Rover close and unsighted by Jongy. Jongy had seen the van as he was looking in his wing mirrors, shoulders hunched.

As the van pulled up, the Range Rover mounted the pavement, four heavily armed guys got out and pressed against the doors, the van parked so close that the doors on the driver side couldn't open. A weapon was drawn, but too late. The back window went in, followed by a sonic grenade. The white flash and the white smoke plumed instantly out of the shattered window for the percussion blast. Ricky saw Simon in the back of the van reach inside, and pull the car occupant out with a noose around his neck. Like the dog pound finding a rabid dog, Jongy was fighting, arms flailing, half naked from the fracas. Another hand came out of the van, holding a cattle prod. Ricky winced as he saw the flashing cackle rip through Jongy's body, suddenly becoming flaccid. His prostate body was dragged out of the car and into the van, the van doors closing and driving off, leaving the scene. Some uniformed local plod turned up and started directing traffic – the whole episode had taken less than thirty seconds. The blacked-out SO19 officers were exchanging words and then leaving in the opposite direction to where the van had gone.

Jamal was also watching from the garage, Veshausen trying to catch peanuts by throwing them in the air, no idea his bully boy was now a rag doll for the British security services. He smiled as he closed the applications that fed both him and Ricky the images.

De Jong was lying on the floor of the van, the noose still around his neck, his eyes darting around, looking for an escape. Broadstone sensed his stiffening. "Hit him again."

Broadstone's accomplice bent down and zapped him again, he stopped. "Hit him again," Broadstone demanded.

The guy complied, the crackling horrible, intrusive, the smell of singed skin, like carbon. "Keep it on him, count to twenty." The officer smiled as he did, counting out loud as Jongy bucked, shook, and vomited.

"Okay, restrain him, make sure he's tight."

Jongy was breathing heavily, anger in his eyes. "YOU CAN'T DO THIS TO ME!" he demanded to Broadstone, shouting through gritted teeth. "I HAVE RIGHTS!"

Broadstone took a knee to the nape of Jongy's neck. "Do you, indeed," he said, he bent down, close to his ear. "And was Simon Brown shown any remorse, mercy or fucking rights when you killed him?" he seethed.

"You haven't got any evidence that I killed him."

"Let's find that out when we get to my manor, sunshine, let's see how tough you really are, De Jong."

"When the powers that be find out you're holding me, they'll make you understand me," he said.

"Really, well, no one knows I have you, and by the time I've finished with you, you're gonna tell me your fucking bank card numbers, let alone what your weird organization is up to."

Jongy laughed.

Broadstone turned to the officer securing Jongy's feet. "Hit him again, this time, fry his bollocks."

Broadstone pulled out his phone, hit dial to Ricky. "En route back to you, make sure you're ready, we might not have much time with him."

"Roger." The line went dead.

Broadstone looked at his phone, hearing the cackling

behind him and the screaming of Jongy, spitting and bucking on the van floor. He thought to text Bromilow.

I have De Jong, taking him to SIS now.

Broadstone waited for the dots, they came, and he got the message that he wanted.

I won't tell anyone, get as much meat off him as you can, then dispose of the carcass when done, he never existed.

24

The basement of SIS was adjacent to the monorail that fed the decision-makers of the land, and it served as a temporary prison and interrogation unit. The walls hadn't been finished since the building was completed. There was no finesse here. The environment was unpleasant, unwelcoming and lonely for those that sat in there, often for weeks on end.

There was a large square room with three doors coming off the walls, a square metal grate bordered by a single course of bricks. He was suspended above the grate, on his tiptoes. His hands were tied behind his back, and suspended by a pulley on one arm. The only respite Jongy had from the searing pain in his shoulders was shifting his weight on each foot. He was naked, ice cold water cascading down on top of him. The temperature was taking his breath away, the sheer volume of water coursing down and adding to the asphyxiating effect. Brilliant white light strobed in time to the beat of the music. Slipknot's Essential Hits on replay. Not only could he not breath properly, the music and strobing light was interfering with his thoughts.

Today, De Jong was going to understand how Britain became Britain and that due process of law only extended to those that deserved it. Who made that decision was down to the keyholder at the time and Broadstone knew how to play the system. A system he believed in.

The music stopped suddenly, as did the water. The air was thick with the smell of the workings of the building. The room was acoustically tuned to zone out all ambient sound. If you sat long enough, you could hear your own heartbeat. It was an intimidating place for the staff, terrifying for the accused.

Jongy moved, his body aching as though he had been beaten up, the ropes and restraint getting worse. His sinewy muscular frame was red and bruised, his lips swollen from involuntary biting down as he was tazered earlier.

The door opened. Due to the environment, Jongy heard nothing other than the air change and then footsteps. He moved then felt it, a blow to the kidney, knocking out the little wind he had left in his body. "GET UP!" His body was being pulled with a chain placed around his neck, the chain made him choke. His shoulder felt overwhelmingly relieved from the suspension.

The person, who was clearly strong, kept pulling, and Jongy realized that he was wearing a sandbag. His eyes were open, but the familiar smell of the hessian sacking from his military days was strong in his nostrils. It's a smell no soldier forgets. Again, the hands pulled at him, and choking, he managed to get to his feet.

"String him up," the familiar voice of Broadstone said. Jongy heard the cranking of a pulley, then felt the chain around his neck lift, and the tension of the chain tightened. Jongy had to lift onto his toes again to follow the chain. Cramp bubbled in the soles of his feet, and he screamed. As with all chains, it suddenly came to an end, the collar getting tighter as the pulley made it to its limit. He felt the air in his lungs diminish, the pain around his throat stopping any normal air flow. His body tried to drag more air in by pulling on other muscles, but it wasn't working. His accessory muscle was trying to help the normal breathing muscles contract, his toned belly seesawing, a blow to the solar plexus stopped it.

Suddenly, Jongy's eyes closed in pain as the bright light flooded in when the sandbag was pulled off his head.

He went to lash out, but there was nothing to lash out to. The chain caused more pain as his arms tried to grab the nearest person. He counted three. Broadstone he recognized, a coon that he couldn't place, and another man. The man seemed familiar but he couldn't place him. He felt hands behind him grab his own hand. There were four, hands, strong and skilled. Before he could lash out, the hands were subdued in cable ties by the thumbs only. He knew that trying to wriggle out of thumb ties was hopeless, he'd have done it this way as well.

The familiar zip and they closed, biting into the skin. Specifically designed for law enforcement, a bigger aperture and bigger teeth meant the applier could do it quickly without fear of injury by the person resisting. Now Jongy couldn't use his hands to steady himself on the chain, only his toes could stop the chain from choking him, and they were already starting to cramp.

"You can't do this," Jongy said, struggling to speak.

The man in the suit came forward. "What do you mean I can't do this? You're a racist Nazi hellbent on ruining my country."

Jongy recognized the man. "Stephen Bromilow, the Home Secretary," he hissed, saying everything out loud. The interrogation would be recorded, his death was not going to be covered up.

"The rule of law doesn't apply to the likes of you, old bean, my colleague…" he turned to Broadstone "… is going to ask you a series of questions, how long that takes and to what extent you are prepared to suffer is up to you. But if you want that rule of law to apply to you…" he stepped closer, now looking up at the stretched out South African, "I suggest you start singing like a miner's canary."

"Fuck you!" He tried to spit at Bromilow, but the impotent attempt only fell onto his chin. "Fuck you, you kaffir-loving cunts," he spat. He tried to kick but the chain instantly placated his efforts by biting further into his neck. The pain thumped through him as the skilled hands behind pummelled his kidneys again, the pain so intense that Jongy's bladder voided.

Bromilow jumped back and started laughing. "Piss yourself, Mr Van De Jong? By the time these men have finished with you, you're probably going to shit yourself too." Bromilow turned and walked out, passing Broadstone. "Make him scream."

British Intelligence knew how to interrogate. They had been doing it since John Andre and the American Revolution very effectively – none of this waterboarding nonsense. Pressure positions, white noise and good old-fashioned beatings and digital amputations were enough to secure information.

Broadstone walked up to Jongy. "Talk to me." His hands were on his hips, waiting.

"Fuck you!" Jongy said. "When people know I'm here, you'll have to let me go and then we'll see who the man is, eh?"

Broadstone laughed. "You think you're going to be rescued? I admire your ignorance, Jongy, but you're a bottom feeder, do you know what that is?" Broadstone said, walking around his sweating naked body. "It means you're plankton, just a goon with a head for sadism, the whole Hypnos thing is one thing, Simon Brown puts you in a very difficult and unpleasant position my friend."

"You have no evidence that I killed him, eh." His eyes were desperately trying to see where Broadstone had gone.

Ricky stepped forward. "Your voice on the video matches my voice recognition software. People's voices are like fingerprints, you're a 99% match."

"Fucking kaffir!" A blow to Jongy's flanks again, he screamed.

"I don't tolerate any form of racism in my presence," Broadstone said.

"Like I said," Ricky continued, "your voice is a match and that places you at the scene."

Broadstone came back into view. "We also know you're involved with Hypnos and this organization, Asclepius."

Broadstone nodded to the guy behind, the chain slackened and Broadstone kicked one of the chairs over to Jongy, his legs too weak to carry him, so he slumped into the chair.

Broadstone grabbed another chair and sat opposite. Nothing between them, Jongy considered his options. He wanted to lunge, take him out, at least take another non-believer down with himself. Broadstone would be banking on it, the noose was still there and the meathead was still in the shadows, any false move would result in more pain.

"Tell me about Asclepius – who are they? What are they about?" Broadstone repeated.

"You have no idea what you're messing with." Jongy spat, trying to lean forward. The sweat poured off his face and down his naked chest.

"Then enlighten me?" Broadstone said, leaning back in the chair.

"Fuck you!" He said with a laugh.

"Tell me about Hypnos, where are you controlling the software? We know you have this Jamal character."

Jongy looked at Broadstone, disbelief shot across his face.

Broadstone laughed. "We know because we've been talking to him."

"Impossible," Jongy said, his face changed, a thousand questions darted across his eyes.

"We have, and for a few days now, no honour amongst thieves, you know. He knows where his bread is buttered."

Broadstone leaned forward and pulled a manila file from the small desk behind him.

His legs crossed, he opened the file and leafed through some of the pages.

"Joost Van De Jong, known as either De Jong or Jongy to his mates, can I call you Jongy? Makes things a bit easier for you."

Jongy looked stony-faced, he gulped, the choker reminding him of his bondage.

"You were a promising soldier but too right wing even for the apartheid regime." Broadstone leaned further forward. "Seriously, Jongy, how does a racist pig like you get booted from an already heinously racist organization such as the South African Army during the apartheid regime? That's a real accolade, I think." Leaning back again, Jongy shifted slightly and spat on the floor.

"You're a prominent member of the Afrikaner Weerstandsbeweging, or WA for short… really?" It was a question, Jongy was still stony-faced. "You were disciplined by the WA for violence?"

Shaking his head, Broadstone carried on reading. "Then you disappear, come to the UK and work for the SA consulate." Broadstone leaned forward again.

"This is what confuses me, you have this rap-sheet that in this country would lead you to a prison sentence, so how do you end up working in this country for the SA consulate?"

Still stony-faced.

"Asclepius," Broadstone said again, "that's how."

Broadstone stood and flipped the file back onto the table. "Tell me who the organization is, where they're based, where you're running Hypnos from and we will get you that lawyer."

Jongy laughed. "You think that would make it okay? Dying in here would be a better option for me, eh, these people are everywhere."

Instantly, Jongy was hoisted into the air, his throat nearly giving way. Broadstone stood, and punched him squarely in the solar plexus, Jongy screamed out his air.

The skilled man slid a knife behind, Jongy's hands coming free. He tried to reach out, but a cattle prod placated him again. They grabbed him and fastened him to a metal chair, the steel cold on his already freezing body. His hands were grabbed and cable tied to the arms, his feet secured in the same way. His hands were placed in malleable metal hands, his fingers stretched out.

"You see, Jongy, my favourite technique for extracting information isn't to pull the finger nails off, that's too crude." Broadstone lifted a small pair of black-handled scissors, tapered at one end.

"These scissors are called tenotomy scissors, but that probably means nothing to you" Broadstone operated them in front of Jongy. "In fact, I don't know the difference between a normal set of paper scissors and a pair like these, but to a friend of mine, a surgeon, these are particularly good for avulsing the nail off the finger, shall we try?" Broadstone asked.

Fear shot across his face. Fingernails, toes and crocodile clamps on the testicles always made the sternest of men quiver with fear. Jongy tried to get a grip of his emotions.

"The questions throughout the whole process remain the same, feel free to answer them." Broadstone pointed upwards, Jongy looked over Broadstone's shoulder towards a large flat screen secured behind some reinforced Perspex, which displayed the questions Broadstone had asked.

Who is Asclepius?

Who works for Asclepius?

Where is it based?

Where are you running Hypnos from?

Jongy smiled. He looked at Broadstone, his face rock solid. "Do your fucking worst, eh, I won't say a fuckin' thing!"

Broadstone leaned in, grabbed the forefinger, and in his other hand the point of the scissor touched the nail edge, slowly, while still looking at Jongy, pain was already shooting across his face in anticipation, the pain struck home. The scissors smoothly slid through the hyponychium, the thin membrane keeping the outside world out of Jongy's body, the prongs of the scissors sliding all the way down to the half-moon. Broadstone opened the jaws of the scissors, the pain searing through Jongy's finger, up the arm and into his brain. As the scissors reached the side wall of the nail bed, the nail popped off. Only a little bleeding, yet the pain was fierce. Jongy screamed more as the nail popped off, the gorilla pulled hard on the chain, choking him further. Broadstone sat back. "Another nine, look at the questions." Hands gripped Jongy's head like a vice as his head was directed to the screen.

Through his teeth, he seethed. "Fuck you." Tears involuntarily cascaded down his face.

Broadstone leaned forward, and grabbed the middle finger, repeating the torture.

"Once we get through with your fingers, we shall start removing your teeth."

"Teeth are overrated," Jongy said.

Ricky came in and recoiled slightly when he saw the state Jongy was in. Broadstone walked over, still carrying the scissors.

"Death toll has officially hit half a million."

"Fuck," Broadstone said.

"Some good news, though, maybe put it to him." He motioned to the face staring at them with hatred.

Broadstone looked at Ricky, inviting him to speak. "I've been tinkering with his phone, triangulating both his and Van Der Meld's, a property owned by the Royal family in Great Missenden."

Broadstone suddenly focused. "The Royal family?"

"Missenden Hall, in Hertfordshire, home of the Duke of Norfolk."

"I didn't know we had a Duke of Norfolk?"

"Nor did I, so I did some digging, turns out that Queen has nothing to do with him. He seems to be the black sheep of the family, he has spent much of his time in the African Veldt, but now resides between here and the USA. He does live at the house when in the UK."

"So, what has Van Der Meld and Jongy got on the Duke of Norfolk?" Broadstone said, "I'll see if I can use that with him." He thumbed in Jongy's direction, still staring at them, trying to hear what was being said.

"Another thing about the Duke of Norfolk, he was schooled with Jeffrey Blunt." Broadstone frowned, looking at the floor. "Coincidence that the Health Secretary is implicated?" he asked.

"I always default to Alex's option about coincidences," Ricky said.

"Which is?"

"There's no such thing."

"So, the current Health Secretary is a potential member of this organization, makes sense. That's how I would play it out."

Broadstone pulled his phone out and found Bromilow's number, hit message.

How well do you know Mr Blunt?
Dots…
For a while now, not a fan, but a good minister, why?
Broadstone thought for a second.
You had better drop by SIS NOW!!!

Ricky had made his way back to his desk. He went to pick his coffee cup up, the fluid was stone cold, but he drained it anyway. Typing away, Alex came into his peripheral vision. He stopped and watched her walk down the corridor to the main office that he was in. She was resolute, purpose in her stride. He really didn't know how much more she could take.

Coming into the office, Alex's face was swollen, people snatched glances at her as she walked through the desks. Ignoring them, she was focused on Ricky. He stood waiting, and she just embraced him. She slid her arms around his and buried her face into his barrelled muscular chest.

Their relationship was purely platonic. They had had been partners and friends for many years, so there was no awkwardness in the embrace, Ricky just enveloped her, and she disappeared in his enormous frame. The embrace lasted for at least a minute when she broke free, and in the meanwhile her eyes had welled up again. She smiled up at him. "Thank you."

Ricky smiled, turned and grabbed the nearest chair, and helped her into it. "Why don't you go home? Let us deal with this."

"Go where? I can't trust anywhere, Broc is watching me everywhere, I can't go home, I don't think I can ever do that ever again," she said.

She looked around the room, Ricky staring at her intently, waiting to react to whatever she wanted.

"My home is here, Dillon is safe, you need me here!"

Ricky shook his head. Dillon, Alex and Simon's son. Taken from university and into protective custody. He felt a huge sense of loss, he had watched the kids grow up and develop into awesome young adults. Things like this really change you. He could see the anger in Alex, she wasn't going to sleep until she had seen this through. Ricky's computer beeped suddenly and he turned.

Moving the mouse, he got closer, it was something that he wanted to see.

"What is it?" Alex said.

"Christmas." He reached and grabbed the phone. "Get me Broadstone, now" He turned to Alex, tapping the screen. He picked up the phone "We have a hit on Dragoslav and his safe house." Ricky plaid the receiver in the crook of his neck and typed with both hands, waiting.

"You're kidding?" Alex said, wheeling herself closer to the desk. "What's Simon up to?"

Ricky realized that Alex wasn't aware, he snatched a glance at Alex, she clocked it.

"We have Van De Jong!"

"WHAT?" Alex said.

"Yeah, Simon is doing his James Bond shit on him, he has lost his fingers already, it's pretty grim down there."

Broadstone came to the phone, he sounded out of breath. "Yes?"

"I've got a hit on Dragoslav and his location, boss."

"I'm coming up." The line went dead.

"What do you mean 'James Bond shit'?" Alex asked.

"Bromilow wants whatever measure done to get the information from Jongy, whatever it takes, the death toll has tipped over half a million, Alex." Ricky accessed the cameras around Chiswick and Richmond park. Normally a bustling interchange of people, public transport and pedestrians. Bodies were lying on the floor, cars abandoned. The image was an apocalyptic movie scene rather than anything real, what was happening outside the doors of SIS.

The door burst open, and Broadstone strode in, clocked Alex, a broad smile beamed across his face. "Alex," he said, nodding.

"Talk to me, Ricky."

"I've put tracer software in all the communication networks in Eastern Europe. It was a punt to just use Eastern Europe and I have a hit. Just let me dial into the cameras on the hit."

There was a pause as the software sifted through multiple images and video, then suddenly the image froze with the word MATCH flashing above.

"I can't pronounce the place, Slovenia, though."

Broadstone looked up, scanned the room. "Rowan, over here." A man in his forties turned away from his screen, nodded, and came over. "Guys, this is Rowan, he runs the Slovene desk for Interpol."

They nodded.

"Look at the image, where is that?" Broadstone said. Rowan bent and took a look. 'It's the Carrefour interchange hypermarket in a small town called Slovenska Bistrica, about twenty miles south of Maribor."

"Anything we should know about this place?" Alex asked.

"Just a small rural town, the military have a base there, artillery I think," Rowan said.

Rowan took another look. "Hold on, is that Dragoslav?"

"Yes, 100% match on the software." He tapped the screen behind. "Who is that?"

The three of them looked closer. "Well, bugger me with a pitchfork," Ricky said.

"Broc!" Alex hissed.

"Indeed," Broadstone joined in, standing and pulling his phone out.

"Mr Bromilow, please." He waited, looking at the screen.

Bromilow came to the phone immediately. "Better be quick, Mr Broadstone, about to go into a COBRA meeting."

"We've got a positive hit on Broc and one of the most-wanted men in Europe, Dragoslav," Broadstone said.

"Excellent, Mr Broadstone, congratulations, do you want a Blue Peter badge or something?" he said, clearly not in the right mind space.

"Can we hit him?"

"No," Bromilow said. "The country is facing one of the biggest disasters to humankind, Broc will have to wait!"

Alex slumped, she knew he was right.

"What if we sent a team, a close observation team, keep close tabs on them, and when the time's right, we can take them out?"

They could hear chatter in the background, Bromilow was thinking, the pause became uncomfortable.

"Okay, I'll sanction a special forces team to infiltrate, draw it up now, and execute, Broadstone. I trust your skills and integrity. Do not, under any circumstances make a move on Broc or Dragoslav until I have sought counsel from the right people, understood?"

Broadstone paused. "Understood, Mr Broadstone," Bromilow insisted.

"Roger that, sir."

"I take it you haven't gleaned anything from our guest?"

"No, sir," Broadstone said.

"Okay, keep me posted." He hung up.

He turned to Alex and Ricky. "It's on, guys, let me call Hereford." He turned to Alex "Let's go, we need to speak to some people."

25

The police car screeched to a halt, blocking the exit road out of SIS. Both Alex and Simon's eyes were darting left and right, he wanted to reverse, but the ram-proof door was already closing.

He instinctively fingered his Glock, Alex doing the same, they both undid their seatbelts and waited, their minds racing.

"What the fuck?" Alex exclaimed, pulling her service pistol out, placing her right hand through the denim jacket she was wearing. If the bounce came, the guy coming at her window would get three rounds, no messing!

The police car had grey livery and flashing lights, indicating it was armed response. The seconds passed, Simon considered mounting the pavement, but he noticed other police cars, unmarked, to the left and right of their access.

"Cover left, Alex." Simon said.

"Roger that," Alex said.

After what seemed like an eternity, the back door of the police car opened, and a plain clothed man stepped out. He stood momentarily, looking up and down the street. An amateur, he was checking his own hired guns were in position, this was a kill zone. Either they had to comply or be killed in the process.

"Be cool," Alex said.

The man, thin, smug and repulsive looking, was wearing a heavy black woollen dress coat, pinstripe three piece under. The lapel pin had a Union Flag attached. He looked at the Range Rover and smiled sardonically, stepping forward. Alex checked her phone, as she suspected, the mobile comms was jammed. Broadstone reached and tried the radio, again, just static, even on the SIS emergency frequency.

"Standby, if this guy gives me the willies, I'm slotting him. Exit rear and get to the rear of the vehicle, roger that?"

Alex nodded, she took the slack up on the trigger of the Glock, realising that the trigger travel was tiny on the Glock, not like the trusty Brownings when she was in green. She released the slack.

The man reached the rear of the Range Rover, he tried the door, but it was locked. Simon looked in the wing mirror, raising an eyebrow. He knocked, and smiled, the thin lips giving his true personality away. Alex was fighting the urge to look over her shoulder, her training and skills told her to keep looking left, marking everything that was happening in front of her. The world still carried on. The Number 32 bus still trundled past, cars going about their business, and the train on Vauxhall bridge pulled into the station and then left. The only difference today was that there were hardly any people around. Some smoke twirled above the sky, which was odd as this was London in the 21st century.

"Let him in?" Alex said. "We have no game plan, you don't do as you said, we're dead." She stole a glance over to him.

There were a few seconds, and she could feel Broadstone thinking. His answer came in the guise of the central locking unlocking, the car thumping. The rear door opened, and in stepped the man.

Alex could feel the suspension and Simon shuffling in his chair. "I've got the arcs," Alex said, as she shifted her piercing stare from only the left aspect of the Rover, to both the left and right of the car.

The man smelt of tobacco. Not the cigarette type, the smoky expensive aftershave tobacco. Simon broke the silence.

"I take it with all this drama that you're Asclepius."

The man looked around and crossed his legs. He looked tiny in the massive rear seats. Smiling, he adjusted his spectacles.

"I represent the organization that you mention, my name is David Frederickson." His voice was English, not your average Joe English but entitled, rich, Oxford or Cambridge, one or the other but it didn't matter.

"I come with an olive branch so to speak." he said, still looking out the window. The task was onerous and irksome, under instruction or command from a higher power.

"Who is Asclepius?" Broadstone said.

The man laughed, more a snigger. "More than you can ever imagine at this point, personally, I see you as a threat but my chain of command thinks that you need a meeting, a parlay."

"Tangos left and right approaching," Alex said.

Simon turned and looked, plain clothed mutt heads fingering the trigger guards of H&K carbines hanging around their cars, staring into them.

"Don't worry about them, they're just simple folk, well-trained rottweilers." Again, the laugh.

"You could have just called."

"This creates more impact, don't you think? We like the drama."

"What do you want?" Broadstone asked.

"We want you to just hear us out, listen to our side of things, maybe come to an informed opinion."

"You want us to join your organization?" Broadstone asked.

"It's a one-time-only deal!"

Alex turned, she was angry. "So, you're comfortable with this…" she searched for the right word, she found it, it sounded worse coming out of her mouth. "…genocide."

Fredrickson laughed. "You think this is genocide? This is for the preservation of man, the world is dying," he said, looking directly at Alex.

Alex chuckled to herself, looking him up and down. "And what does this organization base their theory on?"

Fredrickson studied Alex. "I am of the understanding that things haven't turned out so well for you, Mrs Brown."

"What's that got to do with this?" Alex snarled, he had touched a nerve. The grin stretched across his face again.

"We can help you with that," he said.

"The rule of law stands firm as far as we're concerned," Broadstone said.

"Does that rule of law stretch to our colleague and friend, Van De Jong?" he quickly said.

Broadstone looked at Alex.

"You still haven't told me on what you have based your theory?" Alex looked at him, she turned to make herself more comfortable, getting ready for the conflict that was going to come.

"The world is overpopulated. There isn't the food or the energy to service a planet that will house over two billion people in the next five years, Asclepius will reduce that number to two billion over the next five years." Fredrickson looked pleased with himself.

"But where has this come from, Mr Fredrickson?" Alex asked, she wasn't going to let it go.

"These are well-known facts, Mrs Brown."

"It's not really true, is it?"

"How do you come to that conclusion?" he said.

"While it's true that we're overpopulated, in five years the world will see an abundance of energy, the scientists are talking about *squanderable energy*. GMO food that will literally feed the planet. Technology that has educated the world. Ten years ago, most Africans didn't even have a bank account, now three billion of them have smartphones, accessing top-level education and using online banking such as PayPal. Your opinion is bigoted, outdated and follows an American model of narcissism."

Broadstone sat back, raised an eyebrow, Fredrickson sat there, blank.

"And what do you base your theory on?" he asked.

"It's not a theory. These are facts that are happening as we speak. Your actions will see the world back twenty years, not to mention the millions of deaths. And while we are talking about deaths, or I'll rephrase, murder." She paused to let the word 'murder' sink in. He shifted in his seat. "Who decides on who dies? By joining your organization, does that mean we get the golden ticket to Willy Wonka's Chocolate Factory? What about our elderly parents? Are they euthanized to suit the organization? Is there a degree of blackness that gets to survive? You know we have to have the token black person. What about the professional people that work in the city that are social alcoholics? Do they get to be killed too?" Alex waited for the answer.

"It's a complicated process, Mrs Brown, but the terms 'murder' and 'killed' are a strong reference."

Alex laughed and looked at Broadstone. He was looking up the street, but he was listening, she knew.

"I haven't much time, you have twenty-four hours to give me your reply, you can get me on this number." He offered Alex a business card, she took it.

246

"Call the number, you have to exactly this time tomorrow, remember that as well as the cull, we have an army of people that will do anything for the cause."

"You mean you have infected thousands of people to do your dirty work. Saying that you have people that are willing to do whatever you want are not the correct words," Alex said.

"As you wish, this time tomorrow." He opened the door.

"Mr Fredrickson, I'll see you arrested and tried for this, make sure you feed back to whoever grinds that organ of yours and tell them that I will also see them clamped in irons and standing trial for crimes against humanity." The door closed. Fredrickson nodded to the hired guns on the street. They waited until he got in his personal police car. The engine grunted and drove off, and the hired help followed.

Alex picked up her phone, she had signal, scrolled, found Ricky's number and hit dial.

Ricky answered immediately. "Thought you went off-grid, so I geotagged your last location, chucked a drone up," Ricky said, watching the cars speed down toward St Thomas'.

"And?" Alex said.

"Geotagged the suit that was in your car, the drone is following him. Tap the link, you can follow too. As soon as he stops, I'll get pinged."

"I legit love you," Alex said.

"I know, you're just not my type." Alex smiled. "You're defo not my type now," he added.

Broadstone was accessing his own phone. "Ricky?" he asked, raising his phone to his ear.

"Yeah, he's got a drone following Fredrickson"

"Good man," he said, "oh, Davey, the meet will have to hold, mate. Get the guys bombed up, I'll deal with everything on the sat-vid so you guys can get on task ASAP," he said done his phone.

Alex went to climb out of the car. "Where you going?" Broadstone asked.

"We have a twenty-four-hour free pass, nothing is going to happen to us. I'm going to get a salad baguette, want one of your cardiac-blocking bacon rolls?"

Broadstone smiled. "I'll park the car, get the coffees in as well, may as well enjoy the ceasefire," he said.

Alex got out, the air felt chilly, but refreshing. The street on the Albert Embankment was clear. The smell of smoke was everywhere, the sound of sirens more ubiquitous than normal. The offices were empty, she noticed. The café that they went to almost daily was thankfully open.

Waiting in the queue, Broadstone caught up with her. "Have you ordered?" he said.

"Not yet."

"Might go for a *gypsy's kiss*, be a couple of minutes."

Alex waited. "Excuse me," said a voice behind her.

Alex turned. A well-dressed businesswoman was stood, back suit, nice heels, carrying a cardboard takeaway cup. She was attractive and young. The pause was too long.

"Can I help?" Alex said, furrowing her brow and canting her head.

"Alex, this is Jamal," she said. The words sounded incongruous to the person the voice should have belonged to.

"Sorry?" Alex said.

"This is Jamal, I've managed to upload my digital IP address into this woman."

Alex looked around the room. The people were oblivious to what the woman was saying. Broadstone came up. "What's going on?" he asked.

Alex spotted a free table. "Come on, let's sit down, Simon, buy the coffee." He pulled a face.

"I thought you were getting them in?"

"Just do it!" Alex said.

She steered the woman over to the table, sat her down. "Jamal…"

"It's me," the woman said. "She has no idea that I'm in her head."

"I'm slightly freaking out right now!" Alex said, looking around the room.

"Well, that makes two of us."

Broadstone sat, placing the drinks on the table. He offered his hand. "The name's Simon."

"It's Jamal," Alex said in a hushed voice.

Broadstone sat back. The woman was stunning, he looked confused. "I thought Jamal was a dude?" he said.

"He is."

"I am," the woman said. He slowly eyed her, stirring his coffee equally as slowly.

Alex leaned into Broadstone. "He's inside her head!" He stopped stirring.

"And the day couldn't get any weirder?" Broadstone said, the woman laughed.

"What's it like?" Alex said, looking at the woman like she just stepped out of a UFO.

"It's very strange, I can feel everything Linda feels, I can feel her anxiety about her failed business proposal this morning, I feel the afterglow of her night with her boyfriend last night. Do women really feel like this?" he asked.

Alex smiled. "Yes, normally we're in touch with our emotions, makes things feel a bit differently."

"Have you… you know?" Broadstone said.

Alex shot him a glance. "What do you mean?"

"Well, you know…" He whistled.

"Really?" Alex said

"Really?" Jamal said.

Alex repeated the really again.

"I can give you the location, we're in Great Missenden in Hertfordshire."

"The Duke of Norfolk's residence," Broadstone said.

"I don't know, all I know is that I'm here, in the main garage. I haven't left the place."

"Who's with you?" Alex asked.

"There's one of Jongy's comrades, a mute Zulu called Errol, and another guy called Veshausen. I've been visited by the Health Secretary as well, Mr Jeffrey Blunt MP."

Both Alex and Broadstone looked at each other. Broadstone pulled his phone out, scrolled, and found Bromilow's number. He texted, *Blunt is implicated, DO NOT TRUST, I will be in touch.*

He hit send.

"You also have a traitor in your midst, I don't know his name but he's an American that's visiting." Again, both Alex and Broadstone stared at each other. It was Alex this time that grabbed her phone, found Ricky, hit dial.

"Hold on, Veshausen's coming." The woman's head shook from side to side. "What the fuck happened, who are you?" she said.

Broadstone smiled. "You joined us for a coffee, Linda," he said.

She looked confused, looked around the café, people still ignoring them. "You okay?" Broadstone asked.

"Yeah, um, I think I have to go," she said, she got up and nearly tripped across the table. "Sorry, shit."

"Take your time," Broadstone said, she looked down and smiled.

"Ricky, the Americans, isolate them and get them in the interview rooms, one of them is the mole," Alex said.

"Roger that, boss." The line went dead.

"Something you said?" Alex said, motioning to Linda

making her way out of the café. She drained her coffee and grabbed her food. "Lets go, we have some fish to fry."

"WHAT ARE YOU DOING?" Veshausen said, striding over to Jamal. He clocked him on a chat net. It wasn't the normal software panel that Jamal was usually on. It disappeared quickly as he approached.

"Put it back man!" He clouted Jamal on the back of the head. "Did you not hear me, kaffir? Get that panel back up."

"It's gone," Jamal said.

"Bullshit, out of my way." Veshausen wheeled Jamal out of the way, clicked file, and hit backwards on the screen that the panel was on. The chat software came up, Jamal wasn't sure that the chat would expire and delete as it was shut down. His heart sank when he saw it was still there.

"FUCK!" Veshausen said, he stood, and with the back of his hand, struck Jamal, the slap hurt like hell. Veshausen grabbed his phone.

"We have a problem." He walked off, talking into the phone.

Jamal thought quickly, he grabbed the chair, sat and was typing in one moment. As insurance, he had noticed that Errol was a big fan of Fruit Smash. For the last twenty-four hours, Errol had been under the influence of Hypnos. He had no idea.

He quickly accessed the Hypnos database, found Errol. He typed quickly, Jamal's fate was being discussed. "YOU, GET AWAY FROM THE TERMINAL," Veshausen shouted. Jamal ignored him, carried on typing. Jamal didn't look up, like an athlete focused on the gold medal, it was over when it was over, he heard the steps. "KAFFIR, GET AWAY FROM THE TERMINAL NOW!" Jamal heard the sound of a click. He hit return, the screen disappeared.

"We've just been on the phone to my paymaster, he told me to dispose of you, your worth has expired, eh."

The door opened and in walked Errol, his headphones in, head bouncing from side to side. There was a spring in his stride as he walked. He was whistling 'More than a Woman' by the Bee Gees, Jamal could hear the high-pitched tones of Barry Gibb through the earphones. Errol reached into his pocket and slid out the shiny machete. He walked towards Jamal and Mr Veshausen, smiling, with a swagger in his step. He stopped short of the two of them, Veshausen telling him to kill Jamal, but he couldn't hear. Jamal closed his eyes, expecting to feel the blow of the machete. But if didn't come. He opened his eyes, and Errol had turned to Veshausen, now the blade of the machete was stuck in Veshausen's neck, blood spurting across the room, eyes filling with terror. Errol raised his right foot and kicked the blade off the tall South African. Veshausen stumbled, his fingers trying to staunch the blood, blood was running out of him like a broken water main, Jamal quickly hit the terminal again.

Veshausen was on one knee, Jamal could hear him sucking for air, he looked over the monitor and Errol had hold of his hair, with one slice, the head came clean off. His massive smile, with yellowed teeth, held the head high with blood hosing out of the brain, the eyes twitching. He saw the body crumple to the floor, legs kicking out as they received the final signal for the central nervous system. Errol let go of the head and kicked it across the garage. Jamal hit return.

Errol's eyes lowered to Jamal, murder in them, the smile drifted away, then suddenly, the smile came back. Errol wiped the blade, and walked to the door, placing a chair by it. He sat, still whistling the Bee Gees tune.

Jamal blew out the relief. The 'protect me at all cost' message received and now performed by the lunatic Zulu.

Jamal notice Veshausen's phone was still ringing, he reached and answered it.

26

Alex and Broadstone made it back to SIS. Ricky was waiting at the Vestry entrance, his face was full of questions and concern.

"You managed to separate them?" Alex asked, taking her coat off.

"Yeah, Stubblebine was okay about it, he didn't really ask any questions but Statham was toxic, he took their phones too."

"Awesome, Rick, and?" Alex asked, knowing that Ricky would have been through them.

"Nothing on Stubblebine, and?" he raised his eyebrows, Alex waiting with baited breath. Someone walked past, he paused. "Nothing on the gobshite's phone, either."

"Damn," Alex groaned. "Listen, I spoke with Jamal."

"You spoke with him?" Ricky asked.

"Yes, it was very weird."

Ricky looked at her, puzzled. "How so?"

Alex led him to the corner. "He had uploaded his digital self to a woman called Linda."

"What?" Ricky said, looking shocked. "How did he do that?" he realized that the question was lost on Alex, Broadstone joined them. "Tell Ricky about Linda."

"She already has, incredible."

"Weird as shit, you mean," Broadstone said.

"Anything on our American friends?"

"Nothing, apart from the dubious early days of Hypnos, both are clean American boys, not so much as a parking ticket."

Alex's phone rang. It was a number she wasn't familiar with, her finger hovered over the reject button, but something was telling her to answer. "Hold on, guys." She hit answer.

"Alex Brown?" A few seconds later, Alex was snapping her fingers to dial in the guys, she hit speakerphone.

"… anyway, I've managed to secure the computer room where I'm running the software."

"I've just put you on speakerphone, my compadre Ricky and my boss Mr Broadstone are here!" Alex said, looking at them.

"Oh, hi," said the voice on the other end of the line nonchalantly, Alex mouthed the words, Jamal.

"Repeat what you just told me," Alex said.

"Oh, okay, yeah, um, this guy Veshausen was looking after me, he caught me using Linda to communicate with you. He phoned some chap who I think ordered him to kill me. So I headed him off at the pass. I had uploaded Hypnos into Jongy's partner in crime, Errol. He came to the rescue and chopped his head off."

"Beg your pardon?" Alex said.

"Yeah, pulled his blade out and proper fucked him, kicked his head across the floor."

"Are you safe?" Ricky asked.

"Yer bruv, I have my own Zulu bodyguard looking after my rear."

"Okay, more pressing, we have the American in our interview rooms, we need to know which one is feeding Asclepius the information?" Broadstone asked.

"That's easy," Jamal said.

"How?"

"I have Veshausen's phone, I'll ring him"

The three of them looked at each other in the corner of the corridor. Alex smiled and raised an eyebrow.

"By the sound of your silence, you're wondering why you didn't think of that, that's because I'm shit hot – which brings me to my terms."

"Go on," Alex said.

"Full immunity, and protection. My dabbling in the criminal world is over. I legit have a target on my back now." He paused. "You need me."

Broadstone brooded for a moment, he called it as it was. "You survive this, Jamal, you're hired, immune and under the British Intelligence's protection. I will have to run that through my boss though, understand?"

"Mr Bromilow, the gay dude?" Jamal asked.

Broadstone looked at Alex and Ricky. "Yes, that's the man!"

It took a couple of minutes to grab the phones, and make a plan. The phones were identical, with no distinguishing marks or photos of loved ones on the home screen.

"Did you not want to bag the phone, Ricky?" Broadstone said.

"I only had five minutes, then it was too late."

Broadstone entered one of the interview rooms. Stubblebine was sat looking pensive as the door opened. His hands were wringing together, he appeared nervous.

"Can I ask why I'm being held?" The old man croaked.

Broadstone came up to the table. "Just a precaution, you know how it is Mr Stubblebine, listen, we've decided to give your phones back. I think our decision to take them was a little churlish." Broadstone offered the phones, like a magician producing a deck of cards. Stubblebine looked at both of them and took one, he opened the phone. "This is mine?" he said. A large grin came across his face. "Thank you, can I phone my wife?" he asked. Broadstone looked down, he liked him. A genuine old America patriot.

"We shouldn't be too long now, as soon as we're cleared up, we will get you to your hotels, and then you can get back to the States. Your commercial flights are cancelled, so the RAF will be taking you to Bolling Air Base probably in the morning."

"Mr Broadstone, you're a gentleman, thank you."

Broadstone left the room, Alex was waiting on the outside. "Definitely not the old timer," she said.

"I know, right, but you never know, these old spooks, cold-war trained and all that."

Broadstone entered the second interview room.

"YOU HAVE NO RIGHT TO KEEP ME UNDER LOCK AND KEY!" Statham shouted, he stood and thumped his fist on the table. "I demand to see a representative from the embassy!"

"Pipe down, mucker, just bringing your phone, when things settle, we'll be taking you back to your hotel room, chill your beans, Mr Statham."

"This is an outrage, how dare you do this to a member of the United States," he said.

"We have to take all the precautions that we can, you, sir, are no exception. Now please just be patient."

Broadstone left and closed the door. Ricky was waiting at the end of the corridor; he was already on the phone. "Call the phone," he said.

It took a couple of seconds but the phone in Statham's room began to ring. Broadstone looked through the single-view glass. "Bingo."

Broadstone entered the room with Statham. He was looking down at the ringing phone, looking puzzled.

"Going to answer that? Please don't let me stop you." Broadstone slid a chair out. The metallic scraping drowned out the sound of the phone. Statham hit the green button, his hand shaking as he raised the phone to his ear.

The voice, clear, spoke, "Pass the phone to Mr Broadstone," said the voice.

Statham looked up, his face pale and confused, still looking at Broadstone. He passed the phone to him. "It's for you," he said, his voice not the confident mouthpiece it had been previously.

Broadstone smiled and snatched the phone from him. "Hello?" he crossed his legs, smiling. "Of course."

Broadstone hit end and placed the phone on the table. His fingers paused for a moment, then table-football flicked it across the table. Statham's eyes followed it.

Broadstone studied the American briefly, then broke the silence.

"Do you understand the significance of that call, Mr Statham?"

Statham shrugged, he looked weirdly beaten. His confident frame was slightly slumped against the chair, looking at the table. Like the cross had been removed, the burden lifted.

"Should I?" he said.

"We have access to Jamal, the hacker who stole Hypnos, taken by an organization called Asclepius." He paused, letting it sink in. "You know this though, right?" Broadstone leaned forward, clasping his palms together in front of him. "Jamal had told us that there was a mole in my building. I was pretty sure that the mole wasn't one of my guys. Which left you and the old man, Mr Stubblebine."

Statham looked at Broadstone, a smile edged from the one corner. "You think you have it figured out, don't you?" he said.

"No, actually, we don't. We are making progress one step at a time, but you will tell me who the *grand-fromage* of Asclepius is, and the rest of the crooked lunatics that think they are the master race."

"You think this is about race," Statham said, he chuckled. "It was never about race, it was about survival."

"That's ridiculous, Statham, have you seen it out there? The death toll is on the fast lane to over one million, where does it end? And who decides what's going on?"

He looked at the floor speculatively. "I won't answer anything, you will have to kill me. And when my superiors realise that I'm here, they will force you to release me."

Broadstone smiled and turned to the window, he nodded. Seconds later the door opened.

The skilled man from the basement entered, dragging the prostate, broken body of Jongy. His naked body was bruised, bleeding and ruined. He was barely conscious.

Statham stood to see. "You can't do this, this isn't legal," he said, pushing the chair back. "I demand that you release him!" His American accent was getting stronger.

Broadstone nodded to the man, who then approached Statham. Statham tried to protest but the big man grappled him to the chair and restrained him, without much resistance. Statham was a weak man who lacked anything requiring moral fibre. A person of privilege and influence. A daddy's boy now facing the harsh realities of British intelligence.

"Please, I can't tell you anything, I just can't," he whimpered. The skilled man placed some earphones in his ear, the kind that sportsmen wear. Duct tape was stretched out and placed over the aperture of the ear, they were then plugged into a smartphone.

"You see, Mr Statham," Broadstone said, coming into view. "We don't need unnecessary interrogation methods, you have created the best tool possible. It struck me like an epiphany, why not use the software to make you sing like a canary?"

Statham realised what he meant. "No, you can't use Hypnos on me, you can't do this." Fear was etched in Statham's face, his body began to tremble.

On the three large LCD screens on the wall, Fruit Smash was being played, a 90's playlist was selected for no particular reason, they hit play. The skilled man pivoted Statham and forced his eyes open, it took less than eight-seconds and Statham's head snapped back and shook three times. His demeanour didn't change, he still looked pathetic and weak, yet there was a fire in his eyes.

Broadstone wasted no time. "Who's in charge of Asclepius?" Statham pondered for a moment whether the conscious mind was trying to stop the flow of information, his lips pursed then blurted out, "The Duke of Norfolk is the puppet of the Bilderberg group, ultra-right-wing. They see a different world to the world that we are in now. They want a secular group based on science and knowledge with an abundant world." He stopped, his conscious mind was trying to stop him, his masseter muscles pulsated on the jawline like a heartbeat. "Your Prime Minister is part of this, your Health Secretary, Minister for Defence. Fuck, most of your fucking Royal family are implicated, I mean, involved." Statham clamped his lips shut and tensing all of his muscles, he screamed.

Broadstone looked at the window, knowing who was behind there. Alex was with Bromilow, the watch commander and Ricky. A drawing pin, if it fell from the notice board, would have echoed around the room like a bass drum. Bromilow simply said, "Shit!"

Broadstone was unphased. "Who else? Your president? What about your side of the pond?" he asked.

"At least twenty percent of congress is involved, not the president though, though every member of the European Union is involved. The whole parliament in Brussels has an invested interest in seeing how the model goes in the UK."

"Can we rely on our military?" Broadstone said, Statham nodded his head. "The British military is untouched, we thought about hitting the law enforcement first, then the military."

Broadstone looked at the window again, telepathically sent the message to Bromilow. On the other side of the glass, Bromilow received the message loud and clear, he pulled his phone out and hit dial, the other end of the phone was the military head of COBRA. "My good man, mobilize the army, I'm declaring a national state of emergency, General Beard, the prime minister is to be placed under arrest immediately, contact me the moment this is done." There was a pause, Bromilow, the sexual submissive from his club was showing the side that Parliament feared the most. His acerbic, sharp-witted intelligence and quick-thinking that disgusted the back benches of the commons but made the wider public love him.

Alex stole a glance at him, she respected him as well as trusted him. He pocketed his phone and looked through the glass again. "This will put a cat amongst the pigeons, by God!" He said.

Broadstone left the interview room and entered the viewing room. "Where do we go from here?" he said.

"We still have the military, you have to appreciate that this organization has been waiting for some years to do this. This is a very well-versed plan. We cannot trust a bean, unfortunately, including Her Majesty and her clique of free-loading siblings."

Alex took in the information, she was struggling with what was happening. "Tents are being erected in hospital grounds to deal with the influx of patients that are falling ill, is there any way that the effects can be reversed?"

"How do you mean?" Bromilow said.

"It started as a software upload, can we not upload a fix the same way into the brain and stop the spread of whatever is happening to them?"

"It's worth a call," Ricky said, "to Jamal, to see if this is feasible."

"Make it so," Bromilow said, his phone rang, he hit the green.

"Bromilow?" he stood nodding, the gravity of the situation and whatever he was being told was spreading across his face. "The Queen and her staff are to not be trusted, General, I understand that this goes against all your sensibilities as an officer and gentleman of Her Majesty's army, but they are also to be supervised in the minutest of details, do I make myself clear? Very good, keep me posted."

Broadstone looked, Bromilow nodded. "It looks like I'm the prime minister at this moment in time, and telling the Chief of Staff and head of COBRA to more or less arrest the Monarch is quite possibly the worst thing that I've done." Broadstone agreed.

"I need something more here than this nutter Errol to protect me," Jamal had said to Ricky.

"I'll get you out of there in a jiffy, mate, but first we need to discuss reversing the effects of Hypnos, do you think it can be done?" Ricky said.

Jamal paused on the phone, Ricky could hear tapping. "I'll use your man in the interrogation room to help you," Jamal said.

Ricky was stood in the corridor between the interview rooms and the viewing room that the crew was stood in. There was a knock at the door from the room Statham was in.

Ricky opened it. "It's Jamal here," Statham said. Ricky just looked in amazement. "That's so freakin' weird." Ricky studied him closer.

Alex came out of the viewing room. "What's going on?"

"I just spoke with Jamal, he's now using Statham as a means to communicate." Broadstone and Bromilow filed out, hearing the conversation. Bromilow looked closer. "Are you sure this is Jamal in there?"

"Pretty sure," said Statham. "Maybe this might be a good time to discuss my terms?"

Bromilow smiled and looked at Broadstone. "Mr Broadstone filled me in, I think the Crown can accommodate your immunity for the greater good. There is a caveat, though, you are to work for this organization when this debacle is over."

"Deal! Now, Ricky, can you get me to a computer terminal? I can access all manner of data in Mr Statham's head, maybe you should use Mr Stubblebine as well?"

"Mr Stubblebine left, went to the hotel. After the phone rang in Statham's room, we sent him to his hotel," Alex said.

"Why, what's the deal with the old timer?" Ricky asked.

"You're kidding, right?" Jamal asked, it was still weird to be coming out of another man's mouth.

"Stubblebine's involved, you gave Statham his phone, he switched them. Saw your plan a mile off guys."

"So, both of these guys were involved?" Alex said.

"No shit, Sherlock, I can tell you're old bill, even I would've figured that out."

Broadstone reached for his phone. "Anderson is taking him to the hotel down the road, I'll get him." He hit dial.

Alex reached for the phone on the wall, hit security. "Has Stubblebine left the building?" she said, she was listening. "Okay, go and check, NOW."

The phone was still in Broadstone's ear. "Stubblebine left

the building literally five minutes ago, alone, in one of our cars," Alex said.

"And Anderson?" Broadstone said. "Security are going to the carpool to check."

Ricky and Statham, controlled by Jamal, had disappeared. Bromilow turned to the two of them. "This is the only place I can trust right now, this will be the centre of government, I need a large room and place to gather the people, I need to manage this broken country."

"Of course, sir," Broadstone said. Alex left to find Ricky and Statham.

Ricky and Statham were sat at a computer terminal, websites flashed up, spreadsheets contact, government organizations, all connected to Asclepius. Ninety-three billionaires live in the United States alone, twenty-three of them were implicated. Russian oligarchs, all were connected, as were some of the Chinese elite.

"We can probably reverse most of what's happening here," Statham said. His hands were typing like a ballerina pirouetting across the keys.

"Where's the nucleus in this country?" Alex asked, leaning across the desk. Statham stopped, he looked to the side, he carried on typing. "Esher Working Man's Club."

Alex stood frowned. "Why? Such a random location to have a Bond-like villain operating."

Ricky starting clacking the keys of his computer. "Not really, Sarge," he said.

"What have you found?" she asked.

"Home of the National Front, Oswald Mosley had his nerve centre there for the fascist right during the war, in the back rooms of Esher Working Man's Club."

A smile crept across Alex's face. "Bosh," she said, reaching for her phone.

Broadstone answered. "We've located the nerve centre

of this whole thing, it's not in Great Missenden, it's in Esher."

"Esher?" Broadstone said. "Why?"

Alex explained, Ricky had searched the deep web for any other references to National Front activities since Mosley's demise. There was some traffic on the net, but the club was now in the hands of the Duke of Norfolk, and had been for nearly thirty years.

"To good to be a coincidence," Broadstone said.

"I don't believe in them, Simon," Alex said. "Generally, coincidences are impossible in our reality, if it looks like a dog and barks like a dog, it generally means that it's a dog, you feel me?"

"Anderson, by the way, has been found, throat has been cut, and Stubblebine didn't turn up at the hotel, so he's in the wind, Alex."

"I never saw that coming," she said. "We have to find him, he was clearly involved from the beginning."

"Have the guys found a way to reverse the effects of Hypnos?" Broadstone asked.

"I guess that should've been the first thing that we discussed, looks like they have. They're just finalising the data."

Broadstone heard Ricky call Alex.

"Got to go."

She turned to Ricky "That drone I fired up to follow Fredrickson?"

"Yeah," Alex said, dialling into the screen in front of her.

"He made a couple of car changes, but he left a car and walked into here."

Alex bent down and looked closer. "Esher Working Man's Club," Alex said, smiling even more. "We have to hit this place hard, and fucking hurt them."

27

The Working Man's Club lay off Broadhill Road, adjacent to the high street in Esher. The club was a regular haunt for the working man, the bar opened at 8 am and stayed open until 1 am, so the shift workers could get their cheap booze in before going home. Kids hung around out the front religiously, from time immemorial in the hope of scoring some fags or a cheap carry-out of some tins. Most of the new generation didn't know Mosley and his fascist organization, which was disguised as a political party during the Second World War, nor was it even known that the 'Rivers of Blood' speech was first penned at the mahogany bar still standing at the back of the saloon.

The sun was setting, Broadhill Road deserted. The calamity happening to the country was keeping people indoors, scared with a perverse curiosity of what was happening in the news. The last time the street was this quiet was when the World Trade Center imploded in on itself, Islam declaring war on the West. Or so the politicos of the West tried to make us believe.

Charlie-fire team from three troop, A squadron of the Special Air Service, run by a tyrant of a sergeant called Declan Maws. A dedicated fire-pisser and close friend of

Broadstone, deriving first in the Household division. Doing the hard times on the *sickners* in Brecon with Brodstone, badging at the same time. This was a fight Maws would be most up for.

Maws eyed his team in the back of the high sided IVECO transit van. Seven men, all veterans of Iraq and Afghanistan, not a man amongst the troops that would turn down a gunfight. Maws felt sweat drip down the sides of his face, the van was horrible to travel in, and he was slightly nauseous from the traveling with no window for nearly three hours. The brief had been quick and succinct. He expected nothing less from his old comrade, Broadstone. Hit the club hard, take down the tangos, make a *two-way range* and secure the suits hiding in the back. Some of which the troops involved were sure to recognize. It was mission-critical to not be on mobiles, tablets or laptops. Any political opinion or allegiances had to be set aside until each man was de-briefed after the Operation.

He fingered the safety on the HK416 assault rifle, up, down, up, down. His preferred short cannon for breaching buildings in the urban environment. The gat silenced, as were all the weapons under the instruction of Broadstone. With ten magazines of thirty rounds of 5.56mm ammunition plus two Glock 9mm service pistols, Maws was bombed up for a small war.

The team eyed him, respected him, loved him. He was fearless, formidable and utterly merciless in combat. It would be the first time he had drawn blood this year for the good of his country. The smell in the van was thick with sweat, deodorant and gun oil. The weapons were facing down, muzzles resting on the toe caps of the men, hands resting on the butts of their chosen blasters.

"Five minutes!" Came the word from the front. Maws nodded, and, with the heel of his fist, he punched his wingman in the chest. "Lock and load motherfuckers, time to get amongst it!"

The men were instantly out of their slumber, checking rigs, mags, guns, and webbing. Rechecking to the point of obsession. One man was chewing gum, the guy next to him fished in his mouth with his fingerless gloved hand, his teeth stopping the whole ball from being removed from his *muckers* mouth. Fingerless mitts chucked the other half in his mouth, he bashed his mate's helmet in thanks. The van stopped. Maws was going through the floor plan of the building. Back at Hereford, the teams quickly mocked up the floorplan with white tape outside the deployment hanger. The steps were counted, every inch of the building visualized in the very short time they had. All Maws was now waiting for was the top-cover, the loners with the long guns cutting off any escape from the front and rear aspects of the building. Bromilow had given the 'weapons free' order, so any unfortunate soul not part of Asclepius who was innocently running from the cataclysmic event that was about to happen would be slotted where they stood on the street. Delta was in position, the radio static crackled, Maws' oppo, Dinger boomed in his ear, "Delta in position, long guns locked in, building ready on your mark, over."

"Wait out!" Maws said. He pulled an old Nokia phone out – he hadn't seen this phone for almost ten years. When Maws had dug it out of his attic at home in Hereford after that conversation with Broadstone. He switched it on and smiled. There was still a quarter of the battery left in the charge. 'How on Earth did these phones end up in the bin?' he thought.

The only number in there was to Broadstone, he hit dial.

"Dekkars, sitrep, bro?" Broadstone said.

"All teams in position, what's your location, Si?"

"Opposite newsagent, both me and my partner Alex are

in there waiting. We entered from the rear as you pulled up."

The mic boomed in Maws' ear, one of the long guns on the roof spoke. "Tango coming out, sparking up a smoke, positive ID he's WA, he's clocked your van, walking over to you, standby?"

"Si, tango outside, I won't speak, can you see?" Maws said.

"Roger that Dekkar, right outside, walking around your van to the side door."

Maws hit the pressel of the radio. "Gun Bravo, clean shot, over?"

"Gun Bravo, roger, open your door and he's toast!"

Maws nodded to one of the guys next to the side door, with his thumb, finger, then the third digit nodded, the guy opened the door. Tango looked startled, staring at eight bombed-up special forces troops smiling at him. The startledness was the last thing that he felt as he went to grab his Tec-9 machine pistol. Maws heard the buzz whip past as the 7.62mm black-spot round entered the right temple and exited out the left with a fist-sized hole with a cloud of red mist making a popping sound, even darker in the failing light. The guy waited briefly for most of the detritus exiting out of the tango's head to fall away. As the body started to slump, hands from inside grabbed him and dragged him into the van, a plastic hood rammed over the bleeding head and secured around the neck as he was hauled in. The door shut silently, with the faintest of clicks as the lock engaged. They hung onto his body as it jerked violently the plastic bag filling with blood, the men not saying a word.

"Tango, secure!" Maws said, looking at his men, all smiling back at him. The fight was on.

Broadstone and Alex watched through the window of the newsagents. The glass was littered with For Sale signs and local amenities notices. The van lay motionless at the side of the road. Alex watched as the tango was dropped. "Fuck!" she whispered when she saw the van door open. The whole thing happened in slow motion, the head snapped to the left, the exit of his cerebral contents, and then being grabbed into the van. In the space of just a second, the man had disappeared. She looked at the mess on the sidewalk, and spatter along the side of the van. Broadstone spoke into the phone.

"Proceed, Dekkars, see you on the other side, bro." He pocketed the phone, looked down at Alex. "We go in as soon as the shooting stops."

"If there is any," Alex said.

Simon stopped and frowned, then smiled. "Rules of a gunfight, Alex, bring a gun, preferably two guns, and bring all your friends who also have guns."

The van door slid open, Maws led, a big, nasty-looking face wet with sweat, the men filed out silently afterwards. One filed to the front, the other filed to the rear.

The long guns spoke, "Clear." Maws squelched the radio, static pinged in all the earpieces. The team made their way to the front. The front door to the club was covered, the first sign of anyone leaving was dead.

"On my mark," Maws said as the team was stood against the wall to the club. "All callsigns, at this point we are weapons free, standby."

The door opened, another tango, the team had disappeared against the dark shadows of the wall, Alex saw slight movement, a crack. A long gun spoke, the round tore through the tango's head, catapulting him into the doorway.

"BREACH BREACH BREACH!" Maws shouted down the radio. Alex and Broadstone watched as the team entered. A percussion from the rear as the security door was blown off the hinges. There was shouting. A small window on the front aspect opened, and a face appeared. The long gun tormented this soul as they thought they were free from the invading tac team, he squeezed through the window, forward rolled and stood. He had the audacity to brush himself off when the crack of two rifles intersected his escape with one round each, ripping his head off. His body was left twitching on the pathway.

Maws entered first, his HK on the shoulder, eyes on stalks as he searched the corners, the door saying MAIN BAR was kicked open. A casually-dressed idiot stepped forward with a broken bottle, Maws dropped him and the team fanned out, dropping anything that moved. The calmness of their entry in comparison to the utter chaos they were looking at was electrifying to Maws. People were opting to just lie on the floor and avoid a brush with a 5.56mm bullet. This wasn't a local gang muscling in on the local talent, these guys were mustard!

The door to the corridor mentioned in the brief was solid. Maws felt it, like smoothing his hand over a freshly plastered wall, he knocked. Solid.

"Blow the cunt," he said, sweat dripping off his nose.

One of the guys sprang into action, slapped a mouse charge onto the door lock, the team filed against the wall again, "FIRE IN THE HOLE!" The guy said, a crump and the door buckled, then fell to the floor. Another guy lobbed a nine-banger around the corner. The percussion charge fired nine times with a sonic fizz disorientating anyone in the corridor. There followed was a spray of Tec-9 rounds, quick and angry like a wasp. Maws nodded to the grenadier again, this time he chucked a *mixed-fruit pudding*, two nine-bangers followed by a fragmentation. The cacophony of flashing lights and fizzing was overwhelming, even for the room not in the immediate vicinity, then the cooked fragmentation grenade gave a sickening crump as it went off. Shrapnel exited out of the blown door with a billow of smoke, catching one of the bar drinkers with a wall of high-velocity white hot metal shards, ripping him to shreds, sounding like a bag of nails being thrown across the floor. The sound of groaning filled the room, Charlie was inside the target corridor.

"GO!" Maws shouted, the team filed in. The corridor was dark, so night vision goggles were fitted, the soft glow of the optic catching as the heads turned and scanned the room. A tango insured, he didn't get an option to surrender, round to the back of the head, next tango, on his knees. Ears still ringing, Maws approached, without thought or blinking, drilled three rounds into him. Another door. Maws listened, nothing. "Delta, locstat, over?"

"Rear of the main room, over," he said.

"Roger that, we are on the opposing side, let's synchronise our entry."

There was a pause. Delta team commander squelched in, "Ready, over?"

"Roger that, on my mark. Three, two, one." The detonators smashed through the doors, showering the room with splinters and masonry, and the team entered. People scurried about, the team made their way through the room, slotting anything that moved.

People on the ground universally meant that they were either a non-primary target or surrendering. The natural response for anyone in that position was to either stand and fight or lie on the floor, the room was now secure.

Maws went up to one of the suits. "Who's upstairs?"

"Fuck you!" Came the reply. Maws pulled out a taser, jabbed it in the man's neck and fired, he crumpled to the floor. He walked to the next one. "Who's upstairs?" The man was shaking. "I know you, don't I?" Maws said. The man's featured hardened. "I'll see you punished for this outrage!" The man said.

"Tough guy, right? You get the zap in the Jacob's." Maws

kicked his right knee out, the knee made a popping sound as the man fell. The man lay on the floor screaming, Maws stood on the bad leg, bent it and jammed the taser in his groin, he paused and smiled. "This might hurt!" He said and fired. The man passed out.

"Okay, *sludge-gulpers*, I want to know how we get upstairs. The first man gets a 'get out of jail' pass. A hand raised, and pointed to the opposite wall, Maws looked over and smiled. The wall was the same colour but the paint was a different shade, like it was worn."

Maws nodded to the Delta team lead. "Breach it."

He nodded, rallied his men, the wall was blown, revealing a staircase. The team filed up, pepper-potting their way up the staircase. Maws heard some shouting followed by a couple of nine-bangers and the spray of bullets. The report was not Tec-9 but conventional weapons, the radio crackled and the Delta team leader declared it clear.

Maws surveyed the tangle of people, all in stress positions, bloodied and terrified.

He reached for his radio. "Building clear, approach with caution, get the plod in to process the non-combatants, no one comes in here, all callsigns, roger, over."

Maws radio reverberated with every radio hand agreeing. "Long guns stay in position, weapons no longer free, over." It meant that they were not to shoot unless they had Maws' permission.

"Roger out!" They said.

Victor Cranson, the famous record producer now business mogul and billionaire was trying to hide his face, as was Oskar Smirnov, the Russian oligarch. A couple of other faces were there that he couldn't place. He walked over to Cranson. "You're in a bit of bother mate!" Maws said.

"My barrister will see me freed, this is an outrage!"

Eighteen people were still alive and unhurt in the room.

"We'll see about that, treacle, your current prime minister might have a different opinion about that, and your prime minister that you're thinking of is in jail. So, you have metaphorically fallen into a bucket of shit, and now a very fat man is going to take a shit on your head."

Maws pulled back the cocking lever of his HK, still a round in the spout, he clocked Broadstone walking through the destruction. Glass was crunching under his feet, trying to avoid the broken furniture, the good looker following. Alex was wearing tight jeans, knee-length boots, and a tight quilted Barbour jacket done up tight, accentuating her curves like an hourglass.

"Sitrep me?" Broadstone said.

"Building clear, twelve fatalities, all hired guns, these *tards* have kept their fingers clean." Maws look around the room. "This looks like an all-night party ready for *HELLO!* magazine, there's a veritable who's who."

Broadstone nodded, also surveying the room. "And your men?"

Maws nodded. "All good." He placed his hands into the sides of his assault vest, leaving the HK to dangle by his side, he was looking at Alex. Broadstone noticed. "Sorry Dekkars, this is Alex Brown, my oppo."

He smile and his blackened face augmented a brilliant white row of teeth. "Pleased to meet you, Ma'am!"

Alex smiled. "Alex will do." She walked off, the glass crunching under her feet. The air was thick with the smell of carbon from the weapons, mingling with the scent of a gentleman's bar, smoky and sweet.

Maws watched her go, he felt a blow to his chest. The back of Broadstone's hand thumped him in a friendly gesture. "You go there, bro, I'll shoot you myself."

Maws looked at him, thought for a second. "Roger that, boss, I'll stand down."

Broadstone came up to Alex. "Get all of these separated, they're not to talk to each other, understand?"

The uniformed officers of the police had arrived to clear up the mess. All the participants of the club were being processed.

"Excuse me?" A voice said, Alex chose to ignore it, she turned to Broadstone. "MADAME, EXCUSE ME!" The voice said again, and Alex turned. She was staring at the Duke of Norfolk, accompanied by an officer.

"Sir," Alex said.

"You will address me as Your Majesty, I am a Duke, a knight of the realm, and the nephew of your monarch!" He looked her up and down in a supercilious way. "I demand that you show patronage to your royal."

Alex placed her hands on her hips. "And?" she said.

The Duke looked perplexed. "What do you mean *and*, one thinks my instruction to you was clear enough, methinks?"

"You, sir, are neither of the things you claim. No monarch in this country would behave in such an abominable way." He went to interject.

"I AM SPEAKING, you over-inflated shit-cunt, your rights as a gentleman ceased when you got into bed with these lunatics, I will see you charged and dealt with in the appropriate manner!"

"I am not subject to the laws of the land," he said smugly.

Alex laughed, looked at Broadstone, then turned back. "Get in line, now!" Alex motioned to the officer. He yanked at his arm and was led away.

"How does the world wake up to this image, Simon?" Alex said.

They both stood and looked at the wall. The line-up of some of the richest men in the world stood there, looking dejected and broken, a couple of politicians and a royal. The swag bag of movers and shakers was going to upset the apple cart.

Broadstone's phone rang, it was Bromilow. "Sir?" he said, answering. He turned and looked to Alex, smiled, "Roger that, sir, we are leaving right now." Broadstone hung up.

"Let's go, there's a C130 turning and burning at City Airport. It's taking us to Aviano in Italy. We have the green light to take out Dragoslav, let's bring her home," Broadstone said. He didn't finish the sentence; Alex was already moving out the door

Jamal was sat watching the event unfold on his terminal. A message window popped up in the top right of his monitor. It was Ricky.

Standby for extraction, choppers inbound. They will be landing on the lawn adjacent to the garage. Let the teams sweep clear the whole estate. They will then come find you – they know who you are.

Jamal went to reply, then he heard the whoop whoop of rotors, the whole estate was basked in bright white light. Other lights in the air were darting around, locating landing sites and targets. Errol stood, he walked to the window. He looked out, then turned to Jamal, pulling the machete out. He gestured with it that they should make their escape.

"No, Errol, you go, I'll stay, I have to stay with the program." Errol looked over his shoulder at the terminals, then eyed Jamal suspiciously. There was no one to tell him what to do. It was as though it was the first time that Errol had to make a decision himself. He shook his head, pushing Jamal.

Jamal turned and typed into the terminal, telling Errol to leave, flee. He stood and turned, Errol was still standing there, weighing up his decisions. He walked past Jamal, past the terminals and out of the door. Jamal skipped to the window, he saw black-cladded armed officers running, hunched over, eyes on stalks staring over the sights of their weapon systems.

Jamal notice movement to his right, it was Errol. He had stripped to his boxers. They hung off his body like a ten-day-old cadaver, he was still wearing the trademark snake-skinned shoes. He stood there stamping his feet in an apparent Zulu war chant, wailing a blood curdling chant, the machete smashed against his chest as he stared down his foe. Jamal grabbed his phone and hit record on the camera.

"ARMED OFFICERS, PUT THE KNIFE DOWN NOW!" Was all that Errol got. The gun team were almost creeping towards him. He stopped stamping his feet, in a half crouch, he spat on the floor and swept it away with his foot. He then broke into a run, leaving behind those ruined snake-skinned shoes. Raising the machete above his head was the last thing that Errol ever did. Ten rounds rang out as they slammed into his chest, launching him backwards onto the floor.

"Wow, fuckin' hell," Jamal said, jumping back. Two of the officers approached, Errol's arm moved slightly then jerked violently as one of the gunners fired three rounds into him, not stopping except to kick the machete away from his bloodied body. The door to the garage suddenly blew off its hinges.

Two bodies entered the room. "JAMAL?" the nearest man shouted.

Jamal nodded. "Mr Broadstone sent us!" The guy said.

"Thank you, officer, I was wondering when the police would show up," he said, grabbing his things.

The man grabbed his arm and led him out of the garage. Jamal realised that it was the first time that he had inhaled clean sweet air since being taken. As he skirted Errol's body, the officer looked at Jamal. "We ain't police, mate!"

As Jamal was being led to the helicopter turning and

burning on the lawn, Jamal heard thumps and bangs. His eye were drawn to the main house, with flashes coming from the rooms like a camera flash. The house was being cleared.

As they got to the chopper, a blue Dauphin 2, the smell of aviation gas was heavy, Jamal paused at the door, hands grabbing. He had to shout over the sound of the rotors. "WHO ARE YOU THEN?"

The man smiled. "WHO DARES WINS, MATE, WHO DARES FUCKIN' WINS, NOW FUCK OFF!" He threw him into the back. Immediately, the engine pitched and the chopper suddenly swayed, almost weightless. The nose dipped frighteningly forward and the engine pitched again as the vehicle gained height. Jamal was pushed into the back wall, the cabin hot, gnarly and unpleasant. The normal world passed at 200kph below. Two heavily-armed men sat there looking at him. Their faces weren't changing, one was chewing gum. Jamal said something, the men just looking at him, he said it again. One of them reached for a row of headsets suspended from the ceiling of the heli and threw a set to Jamal. He slipped them on, the sound drowning out instantly.

"What did you say?" The voice in the ear said, he looked up, one of the guys was talking to him. He spoke again, the man opposite lifted the oblong box, in which the wire was fitted. Jamal understood. He pressed it and then spoke, "Where are we going?"

The guy nodded, he said something in the mic that was inaudible to Jamal, another frequency, he thought.

The voice boomed in. "London, mate, you're gonna be debriefed by the spooks. You're getting your bollocks electrocuted, mate, I would say bye-bye to them!" He broke off laughing, his mate next to him started laughing as well.

Jamal brought his knees up, suddenly he had become more terrified.

28

The flight time from Avian was just over two hours. The pilot was a seasoned special forces transportation pilot who was used to ferrying around clandestine military types all over the world. After fifteen years, he had stopped asking why.

The Hercules sidled up to the Merlin waiting, the rotors already turning. The two fire teams climbed in, grabbing Alex by the shoulders and hurling her to the rear of the chopper. Broadstone leapt in with ease. The back of a Merlin had been a second home for many a year for Broadstone. He eyed the team commander, who was called 'Cabbage.' A nickname he received when he first joined the army. A giant Cornish man, wide-eyed and chubby cheeks with chubby hands, resembling a cabbage patch doll. Nervously, he noticed Broadstone looking at him. He knew Broadstone when he was still *in-green*. So well known within the ranks of the regiment that having a veritable celebrity on a mission was an honour and a privilege. They nodded at each other. Simon had checked him out. The head shed at Hereford said that he was the man for the job, and he trusted that advice.

Both Alex and Broadstone put on their earphones, the roar of the three Rolls Royce Turbomeca engines pitching and lifting the heavy load to its destination. The net was awash with radio jargon, Alex too tired to try and think back to her radio voice procedure training to decipher the phonetics and call sign indicators, she was sitting on the cold floor, watching the airbase disappear beneath them.

"You okay?" Broadstone's voice boomed into Alex's ear. She turned and nodded, he nodded back. He reached for the team commander, and they shook hands. "What's your QBO's, Cabbage?" Broadstone asked.

The team commander swivelled on his chair, a swell shot through him – Simon Broadstone knew his name. "My quick battle orders are, Delta will repel onto the roof space, hit 'em from the top. The observation team will provide fire support at close quarters." He pulled out an aerial photograph. "We land here, they can't escape as there are two gun teams with interlocking arcs at the rear, we go through the front, slotting anyone that wants a gunfight."

Broadstone was studying the photo. "Where do you want us?" The team commander shrugged. "You can stay on the chopper that will provide IR overwatch at two hundred feet or get off and hold back til we've cleared it."

"Okay, we're getting off!" Broadstone said, the team commander looked over Broadstone's shoulder and looked back at Broadstone. "Don't worry about her, Cabbage!" He said. "She's mustard, she's been around the block, ex-military and all that!"

"Okay, sir, I trust your judgement, I don't want to bring any civilians back in a body bag, I've been told that you're the gaffer on the ground and I respect that, she's your responsibility, though."

"Understood," Broadstone said. "What's the flight time?"

Cabbage looked at his watch. "Twenty-five minutes, sir, there's no FRV, we land on the target and smash the shit out of it, as soon as we're on target, the fire support is going in!"

Broadstone was still looking at the photograph. "How many tangos?"

"It's unclear at this point sir, but there is a count of at least thirty, mostly tracksuited, lightly-armed wannabes that have no discipline. We have two .50 Barretts with incendiary rounds to take their cover away, drones painting targets and the gun teams have six thousand rounds of link ammo with a couple of barrels. We're bombed up to fuck, so they won't stand a chance sir!"

Cabbage's radio went, information that Broadstone wasn't privy to. He acknowledged it and turned back. "I was told this is a No-Russian situation, sir, you okay with that?"

Broadstone looked over his shoulder, he wasn't sure of Alex's views on this edict, the *No-Russian* jargon was from the Call of Duty computer game, when in one scene Makorov orders his men to shoot everyone, including civilians. It meant no one leaves alive.

"Yeah, I think humanity isn't going to miss these scrotes, tear them to pieces, Cabbage!"

Cabbage smiled. "Roger that, sir!" He tapped Broadstone on his chest. "And put these on so the fire support doesn't blue on blue you." Broadstone took the baseball caps, the caps were fitted with infrared strobe lights that only specialized optics could see. The optics being used tonight were for fire support.

The flight time was busy, the chopper contouring the lay of the land. The sea was replaced with mountain, lush green, even in the moonlight. Alex felt sick, the smell of aviation gas thick. She checked her watch, five minutes to target. The pilot concurred, the chatter on the net becoming busy. The men in the back started checking their gear – cocking weapons and checking their pouches on the chest rigs. One guy crossed himself, looking up to salvation. The air was thick with gun oil and sweat, the wash of the rotors changing as the as the target came into view.

The compound on the outskirts of the town in Slovenia was shut off by the authorities. Industrial and ugly. As soon as the merlin pitched and swayed, the pilot was looking for the best place to drop Delta fire team, tracer rounds erupted from three sides of the compound. The fire support was battering the windows and doors. The chatter of the engines mixed with with the cyclic chatter of the 7.62mm rounds were shredding the building. Some sporadic firing was being returned, met by the boom of the .50 Barrett vectoring the opposition with incendiary munitions, blowing huge sections of wall and metal work away. Alex watched as Delta hooked up to the line, the loadmaster vibrating on the mini gun strafing where the first man was landing, in seconds they were gone. The Merlin pitched and swayed, tracer ammunition bouncing off the target and zooming off into the air past the chopper. Red smoke indicated where the Merlin needed to land. The pilot wasn't hanging around, the wheel bounced, the loadmaster turned and screamed at Charlie fire team, "GO GO GO!" The team sprang into action, exiting the sides, and instantly adopted their well-drilled stances. Broadstone grabbed Alex, and pushed past the loadmaster, he nodded.

They jumped down, lying on the floor. Alex closed her eyes, the noise of the ensuing battle ahead was intertwined with the acceleration of the Merlin, it lifted off, tracer rounds flying everywhere. Cabbage was kneeling, his voice loud over the noise of the gunfire. Dragoslav's men were putting up a good fight, but every time a gun appeared at a window, the Barretts returned fire, destroying the gunner and the surrounding area.

The building was decrepit, full of mangled ironworks strewn from years of neglect. Windows smashed, doors came off their hinges. High-end German performance cars and SUVs littered the car lot.

Alex joined Broadstone at the entry point and knelt, covering the rear. Sweat beads were on his forehead. He felt comfortable in the environment, Alex could sense it. She felt safe with him among the sound of chaos. Men were dying horribly.

Charlie fire team wasn't taking any chances, each room and corridor received a mixed fruit pudding of a two nine banger's and a frag grenade. The wounded were left battered and disorientated by the explosions, left to the mercy of the special operators, systematically shooting each one. The report of low-velocity rounds rang out, more of a thump than a bang, Alex knowing that each shot counted as another tango sent to the pearly gates.

The smoke billowed out the top of the door, the smell of cordite and carbon. Broadstone sucked it in. "Love it!" He said. Alex felt her heart beating faster, the surge of adrenaline coursing through her veins. She suddenly got a hero complex, pulled her Glock and stepped over Broadstone. "Fuck it, in for a pound!" Alex shouted over the din of the battle.

"ALEX?" Broadstone screamed, she was gone, through the door, towards the clatter of guns and dying men. "Fuck you Alex!" Broadstone hissed under his breath. "Charlie, Delta, friendlies coming through the rear now over," he shouted into the radio.

"Roger that, make sure your strobes are on, or you're gonna get a .50 through the swarde, out."

Broadstone scampered through the door, Alex was waiting at the other end of the corridor. He skidded up to her, peering around the corner, a few bodies lay on the floor, one moving. His bloodied hand was reaching for God, shaking.

"Fucking hell, Alex, you die here, I'm in front of the big man!"

"He's still alive," Alex said, motioning to the injured man.

Broadstone peered again. "No-Russian, stay on my six, you got a round in the spout?"

"Locked and loaded!" Alex said.

They moved, coming to the injured Serbian, Alex went to administer first aid, but Broadstone beat her to it, the report of his side arm sounded, a round to the side of the head. The spent cartridge bounced off the corridor wall, hitting Alex in the shoulder.

"Simon, he was injured, that wasn't necessary!"

Broadstone shot her a glance. "Exit is that way if you can't stand it, otherwise grow some minerals and lock and load, sergeant, the only people leaving here alive is us and Siobhan, roger that?"

Alex paused. "Roger that," she said reluctantly.

He turned and crouched as they approached the opening of a doorway, the link gunner from Charlie was waiting for them.

"Okay, sir, stay on my six, the main part of the studio is about to breached."

They filed in. The smoke was hanging heavy at the top of the room. The floor was littered with battlefield confetti of empty cases, spent nine bangers still smoking, and the bullet holes in the bodies of the dead. How people exposed to a violent death got half-dressed and lost their shoes was always a mystery to Alex!

One man moved and groan, the gunner double tapped from his 5.56mm minimi belt fed the machine gun. His body jerked then went rigid. His bladder voided then he suddenly went limp, his agonal final breath audible over the shooting in the adjacent corridor.

"What's a swarde?" Alex whispered to Broadstone, a little too loud, the gunner heard, smiled. "Means swede, as in the bonce!" He said, tapping his head.

"Ah, not heard that one," she said.

"It's an infantry term for head!" Broadstone said.

The radio crackled, the voice was high-pitched, fuelled with adrenalin, it was Cabbage "BREACHING, BREECHING, BREECHING!" He screamed.

There was a loud boom, the building shook and dust seemed to sweat from the walls with the reverberation. The suppressive fire from outside intensified, the build being hammered from all sides. The element of surprise and fire control was robustly in the hands of the special operators – and they were loving it.

"Let's go, DOUBLE!" shouted the gunner.

The three of them rounded the corner, ran the short way and entered the main studio. It was too early, the gun team was pepper potting their way across the floor, coming across intensive fire from the rear wall. The spectators of the sick regime were putting up a valiant effort, but their minutes were numbered!

Alex saw Siobhan, tied up on a cartwheel naked. She was battered, bruised and bleeding. "Oh my God!" Alex screamed pointing. Broadstone followed the finger, he saw her, she was in the crossfire.

Alex pushed Broadstone out the way, almost knocking him to the ground, it was pointless stopping her, she was going to die trying whatever. He grabbed his pressel, "SUPPRESSIVE FIRE, SUPRESSIVE FIRE! Friendlies in the open." Delta joined the fray, opening a large door connecting the two hangars, they now had the advantage of a pincer movement to the right of the enemy positions, everyone clocked Alex running. The weapon system's intensified, empty cases spitting out everywhere, the opposition beaten to hide behind whatever they could find, they inched further, passing Alex. She had vaulted over tables, chairs. Grabbed a bin lid, a man sat up, blood spurting from his neck, he raised a pistol and fired, the round whizzed past like a wasp. Alex threw the metal lid, hitting him square in the face, with her Glock, without even thinking, she operated the trigger, the top slide bounced back ejecting the spent round. The round smashed in the Serbian's face, the 9mm round obliterating his face, her momentum faster than the special operator. She reached Siobhan, tears flowing from Alex's face, she pulled her Leatherman, flicked the blade out. Alex felt the bash of a body, it was Broadstone, he had picked up a Kalashnikov, the rattle of it ringing out as he laid down more suppressive fire.

Siobhan opened her eyes. She looked broken, ruined. Her naked body was smeared in oil, dirt mixed with the bruises and blood. She looked thinner from when Alex had first met her and that was only days ago. Alex cut the ties, her arms came free, gripping around Alex's neck, Alex struggled but she managed to cut the legs free, she fell to the floor in a crumpled mess. Alex was caught up in the twist of arms and legs. Broadstone raced over to a metal table, kicked it over. Using it as cover, the gun teams made their way closer to the target.

"Alex?" Siobhan said, she burst into tears. "I knew you'd come, I knew you'd come!" she whimpered, gripping her twin flame even tighter.

Alex couldn't stop, she shuddered with relief. "I'm so sorry baby, I'm so sorry!" She said.

"It's not your fault, don't leave me again, promise me you won't leave me again."

Alex stopped and looked into Siobhan's eyes. The battle raged on, tracer rounds pinging off the wall and flinging to the ceiling, the ricochet and low hum of bullets trying to find something to hurt. It wasn't the bullet with your name on, it was the one that said to whom it may concern you had to worry about. Men were screaming to control the battle. None of it mattered, Alex wiped Siobhan's face with her hand, smearing the dirt away from her face. "I promise!" She said. She kissed her, time stood still, the world slowed down. Alex's heart skipped a beat, pulling her tighter into herself.

Alex was rocking her as Siobhan's body shook, she was cold, hungry and in shock. Alex quickly checked her over, no entry holes or exits. Her bleeding was subcutaneous, nothing major that needed urgent medivac. She felt her pulse, it was rapid, her breath was short and quick, and her face was swollen from the beatings, bruises all over her body.

"CHECK YOUR FIRE, CHECK YOUR FIRE!" the radio boomed, the shooting almost stopped instantly. The odd pop, and the odd scream from an injured Serb which ended with another report of a weapon.

Broadstone had disappeared, and returned covered in dirt and blood. Alex shot him a glance. "I'm okay, you should see the other guy!" He said, smiling.

He crouched. "Siobhan okay?" he asked, Alex shook her head. "We need to get the fuck out of here, Simon."

"On it!" He said, standing.

The special operatives were busy. Cabbage came over, his face had blood on it, and he was wet with sweat. He crouched next to Simon's feet. "She squared away, Alex?" he asked.

"Roger that, Cabbage, can we go?" Alex said.

"No dramas, just have a clean up and we'll bounce, the Slovenes are gonna do the tidy up, we're inbound into Aviano in figures ten." Figures ten being ten minutes in army speak.

A civilian-clad man stumbled up, wearing a suit and gimp mask, he struggled at first. He stumbled to the floor and managed to stand, he turned and then tried to run, his leg had a bullet wound in it, it wasn't going to work anytime soon, and he stumbled again.

"SIMON!" Alex screamed, he turned and saw what she was looking at.

Broadstone wandered over. The man was laughing. "Fuck you, pig!" He spat, his accent heavy and menacing. Broadstone grabbed the man by the mask, pulled him over to Alex, and knelt him down. The face was swollen under the mask, blood oozing from his mouth, making his features all the more macabre as bulged from the mouth and eyes.

Broadstone pulled his tactical knife, in one action he sliced the back of the mask off, it fell away revealing the swollen face. "Jebi the kurvo." He spat.

Broadstone slapped him across the face. "That's no way to speak to a lady, Dragoslav!"

Dragoslav eyed Broadstone. A smile crept to the corner of his mouth. "You filthy pigs, you have no jurisdiction here, I will sue!"

"You've come to the end of the road, your warrant for arrest expired three hours ago!" Broadstone said, Dragoslav looked at him. "So, let me go, and I won't kill you and your filthy fucking family."

"Can't do that I'm afraid!" Broadstone said, he stood looking at him, a few of the special operators walked over, the muzzles of their rifles still smoking.

"Who's this chopper?" One said.

Dragoslav looked at all of them. "All of you are dead men standing, that whore and her bitch will die a thousand deaths!" He went to spit again.

"I've had enough of this!" Broadstone said and pulled his Glock out.

"You haven't got the balls to shoot me!" Dragoslav spat.

"You see, this is where you think that I'll torture you, and take you to England, and the government will give you protection. You may even face life in prison after The Hague finds you guilty of crimes that need answering."

He laughed. "Hand me over to the Dutch, I will be sharing my cell with Ratko Mladic."

"Wrong." Broadstone held the gun to Dragoslav's face, operated the trigger, the smile faded as his head snapped back. The body almost paused as the muscles tried to stop the rest from falling over. His eyes turned inwards, his life extinguished, the back of his head violently exploded out the back, spreading across the floor behind. His body crumpled to the floor. The legs kicking out as the last of the autonomic messages faded to nothing. Dragoslav went how he deserved.

Cabbage walked up to his body, pulled his gun and fired. The body jerked. "I saw those videos at the brief, what a horrible little cunt!"

Cabbage surveyed the destruction. "Right, let's get frosty, we have a chopper to catch, let's move gents…" He went to move, stopped "… and ladies!" he said with a smile.

Alex looked at Dragoslav, and looked down at Siobhan, her face buried in Alex's chest. Broadstone bent, and picked her up off Alex. Alex stood, her knees creaking, her feet sending the brass empty cases clattering across the floor. she pulled her coat off, wrapped her up into Broadstone's arms. Siobhan's hand came out, and grabbed Alex.

"I'm here, Siobhan, I'm here, we're going home."

The team cleared the way back to the landing site, the snipers already at the landing zone, guarding the arcs. Alex looked at her G-Shock, the operation had taken a little over forty-five minutes. The Slovenian army were waiting at the gate. The load master grabbed Siobhan, and then grabbed Alex. She wasn't launched into the back this time. She settled next to Siobhan, she tried to smile but erupted into tears. Alex cradled her as the combat medic was inserting a line for fluids.

Broadstone slid over as the chopper pitched, the engines

roaring suddenly becoming weightless in the massive beast. The guys fist bumped as they left, sharing gum and clearing their weapons.

Alex put on the earphones, stroking Siobhan's bruised face, she was already fast asleep.

"Cabbage was very complimentary about you, Alex," Broadstone said.

Alex smiled, not taking her eyes off Siobhan, wondering what the future held for them. But right now it didn't matter. "How so?" she asked.

"Well, I think he said that Alex is fucking nails, which for Cabbage, is a compliment."

Alex looked and smiled. "But seriously, don't pull a fucking stunt like that again, understand?"

Alex let the cursory bollocking sink in, she deserved it, and he had to say it, he put his arm around her, and kissed the side of her head. "Good job, sergeant, fucking outstanding."

29

Broc was sitting on the fly deck of his Fairline Squadron cruiser in the Harbour at Falmouth in the southwest of England. He had only just made it back to the UK from Slovenia.

The video link to Dragoslav's studio was a mixture of horror and fascination, and Broc had settled in to watch the proceedings. It was presented like a television game show, the hooded man pranced about the screen, shouting ineligible words. The Irish girl was strapped to a cartwheel, tonight she would die. 'This should tip that bitch over the edge,' he thought of Alex.

The sun had already set, middle-classes and the rich wandered to the clubhouse to swig Pimm's and measure the lengths of their dicks in boat sizes while waiting for a substandard pig to finish incinerating on the BBQ. Broc couldn't risk being in public at this point, but that didn't stop envious eyes looking the squadron boat up and down. A seventy-five-foot luxurious beast of a boat that housed five bedrooms, two kitchens and a medium-sized bar on the fly deck. Maybe the choice of cruiser should have been a bit more... *Cornish*, he thought looking about the marina.

Ji-Yeon sat on the aft deck, watching the revellers go to their destination, she couldn't watch the show Broc was

290

watching. "Go to the clubhouse Je, I think I'll be okay here," Broc said.

She stared over, frowned, and then looked back to the stern of the boat. Broc watched her momentarily, pursed his lips at the thought 'What goes through that mind? I could just do a dissection now.'

The show ramped up, the hooded man started to flog the Irish girl. Her body trembled before each whip, bringing welts up in the skin, the camera closed in while the hooded man's tongue grotesquely licked the welts on her legs and midriff. She was screaming through the ball gag, her back arching with the pain. "I wonder how she's going to die?" he asked out loud.

The talking was now subtitled, she was spun around like a Catherine Wheel. The cart creaked as she spun. A lucky contestant in the crowd was chosen, he ran over and pulled his trousers down. The ball of the gag was removed, the metal frame keeping Siobhan's mouth open. She was upside down when the man inserted his penis and roughly fellated her mouth. Siobhan gagged twice, retching, trying to be sick, her veins standing out on end trying desperately to hold the chyme down. For her insolence, as the subtitles said, she received more whips, more pain, and more welts. The man receiving the fellatio punched her hard in the stomach while his penis was inside her mouth, causing the back of the mouth to close around the glans, increasing the sensation. With a thumbs up, he roared in front of the camera.

Suddenly, the votes were in, the Irish girl was to be burned alive with blow torches. The crowd erupted. 'Obviously a favourite to these in-breds,' Broc thought. The money on the right side of the screen was flashing. "Sweet lord, Je, Dragoslav has made over three million dollars," Broc said

"Sweet ride," a voice said form the quay below, Broc

looked over the rail, he nodded to Ji-Yeon, she stood and vaulted down and onto the quay. "Okay, love, just admiring the boat, keep your knickers on," he said as his partner tugged at the arm. "Fucking hell!" Broc hissed, "keep the locals under control please."

Ji-Yeon nodded and stood by the gangplank on the quay like a bouncer in a club.

Shooting caused Broc to snap back at the screen, the camera swung around and the door had been blown off. He sat and watched the rescue of Siobhan and the annihilation of the entire room and the execution of Dragoslav by Broadstone.

"Well, well, well, our friend Alex Brown has rescued her lover," he said over to Ji-Yeon, she looked up from the quay, emotionless, as always. "We should just kill them!" she said.

An old man was walking down the quay, and Broc noticed him. Seemed weird. Boating was a sport for the rich and middle classes that were fit. This man seemed to be out of place. The old timer approached the boat and doffed his cap to the Korean. The powder blue slacks and chequered shirt gave the impression he wasn't English.

He said something, Je-Yoen nodded and let the man up. She had to help him as his bones were too weak, as were the muscles attached to them. "Thank you, you're very kind," he said. "Oh, would you mind? Thank you." More grunting.

"I say, old bean, what are you doing on my boat?" Broc said, meeting the two of them on the stairs leading to the fly deck.

The old man removed his cap. "Hello, Mr Broc, my name is Stubblebine, Channing Stubblebine, you may have heard of me from our mutual friend, Mr Ng."

Broc furrowed his brow, searching the data banks of the conversation with Tao Ng. He knew Ng, and the man knew where he was. He at least had to hear what he had to say.

"I don't recall," Broc said, moving out the way, allowing the old man to enter the fly deck.

He sat, blew air out, puffing his cheeks. "That was more of an ordeal than driving here, you Brits ought to drive on the right side of the road, by the way. Did you not want to buy a smaller boat, Mr Broc?"

"So many questions. We do drive on the *right* side of the road," Broc said. "The left!" He smiled and poured a whiskey.

"It's a single malt, judging by your accent old bean, you might like something more acidic like bourbon?" The old man smiled.

"I don't have that, I'm afraid, only British spirits, you can pretend it's horrible if you like, I won't take offence, just don't drink it all."

Stubblebine took a slow and long drink, he savoured it in his mouth, looked at the amber liquid against the subtle lights on the fly deck. "That's simply beautiful," he said.

"Not to be rude or anything old bean," Broc said, leaning back and crossing his legs.

The old man placed the glass on the table, the sound of cut crystal rang out.

"Have you heard of me?" he asked again.

"I confess I haven't, which must come across as rude, apologies."

"None taken."

The man shuffled in his seat, looked around the deck, he smiled again at Broc while trying to find the right words. "Tao Ng was working for the CIA on many missions. A supplier of bona fide intelligence that always stacked up. It helped NATO militarily and the USA corporately. In return, we turned a blind eye to his business practice, in truth we protected him, he told us all about you and your operation."

Broc leaned in, fascinated. "Are you serious?" he said.

"Completely," Stubblebine said, picking up his drink, draining it a little more urgently now. Broc instantly filled it, and a little higher in the glass, Stubblebine noticed and smiled.

"Ng is in prison in China and my operation is suspended, most likely definitely at this rate," Broc said, disdain in his voice.

"Which is why I'm here... old bean," he said, smiling.

"Go on?" Broc said, draining his glass.

Have you heard of the Human Potential Movement and the StarGate Project?"

"The goat-staring lunatics in the 50s," Broc said. "I saw the film."

Stubblebine smiled again. "I've been involved in the project since my twenties. I worked alongside my father for many years. The project was actually a front for something a little more sinister but necessary for the future of human potential and longevity."

"I'm still listening?" Broc said, mirroring Stubblebine and leaning back as well.

"Have you seen what's been going on in your country over the last few days?"

"Yes, the media haven't elaborated, but as a doctor and a surgeon, it all seems a bit suspicious," Broc said.

"That's because it is, suspicious that is. An organization called Asclepius has triggered a culling of the world's population to only two billion, currently British Intelligence is about to stop it in its tracks." He smiled. "A friend of yours, no less."

Broc scowled. "Who?" he demanded.

"Ms Brown and Mr Broadstone"

Broc burst out laughing. "You're kidding me? Just for the record, I'm not going to kill three billion people for you, because if that what's you're here for, you're leaving. And by the nature of your profession it won't be from the same way you arrived." Ji-Yeon stiffened, her hand slid into the right breath of her jacket.

"Steady, the whole operation has been put on ice, the software we developed is now in the hands of British Intelligence, I would be surprised if they give it back. Although we are trying to take it."

"So, what do you want from me?"

"I mentioned about a front for something more sinister, have you heard of Unit 731?"

Broc searched the floor, eyes darting. "No," he was more interested and engaged. This was leading to something juicy, he felt it.

"Unit 731 was a Japanese human vivisection and bacteriology unit during the Second World War," Stubblebine let it sink in.

"What happened?" Broc asked, not phased.

"Well, General MacArthur knew of the orchestrator on the unit prior to the war. He had even spent time with Colonel Ishii Shiro of Unit 731 prior to Pearl Harbour and the war in the East, as the American Military attaché in Tokyo."

"General, and your President following the war," Broc said impatiently.

"That's correct Mr Broc, he was a dear family friend." Stubblebine thought briefly, a memory.

"The unit was moved to Fort Bragg, and then to the Mojave Desert in the USA, where it worked for many years, currently, and for the last twenty years, the organization, still called Unit 731, is working in North Africa under the guise of a food aid agency sponsored by the UN. We conduct drug trials and vivisection on live humans, basically carrying on were Shiro and his scientists left off. My job offer to you my friend, is a one-time-only deal."

Broc had to think for a moment. "So, let me get this

straight, the Americans rescued these chaps in wherever it was, brought them to the US and let them carry on their work?" He shook his head.

"The data collected was performed in a cruel way, yet the information was vital to the production of vital antibiotics and medicines we take for granted today," Stubblebine said, sipping more whiskey.

"How do you think the Ebola outbreak four years ago was quelled and eliminated? How do you think HIV has been cured, hepatitis? To name just a few."

Stubblebine motioned to the Garmin Radar. "The one-time-only deal."

Broc looked, the large blip on the screen had come to the southern tip.

"It's the USS *Gettysburg*, to pick us up or…"

Broc highlighted the blip, the call sign indicator of USS *Gettysburg* popped up then disappeared, the blip disappearing with it.

"Or what?" Broc said.

"…The *Gettysburg* is authorized to blow this vessel to smithereens, old bean, you have twenty seconds to make your decision."

"Do I get full protection from the USA?" Broc asked.

"Not from the government, but from the black ops wing. It comes under a presidential edict, just not a transparent policy. You are protected, though."

"And my role?"

Stubblebine smiled, replaced his cap and struggled to his feet, both knees cracked like a pack of dominos, as well as his spine.

"Your role is to do your job, cut people up in any way you want and make the data available for the scientists."

Broc took three seconds to decide. "I'm in, Ji-Yeon comes with me."

"Of course, but the girl stays... unhurt and alive. It was a cruel torture to remove the girl from her mother's side." Broc looked dejected, upset even, not a fan of criticism.

"Don't worry, Mr Broc, where you're going, you can *fuck* and *kill* any number of girls to your heart's desire!"

30

It had been a week since the teams returned with Siobhan from Slovenia. Alex sat by her bedside in the hospital all the while. She spent most of the time struggling to smile in the awake times.

Broadstone had given Alex the space she needed to be with Siobhan. Ray, Siobhan's husband, had come a few times. He seemed genuinely pleased that she was okay. Although in tow with another man, his attention was directed elsewhere.

"I think he's finally decided to get out of that closet and be the person he should be!" Siobhan said. Her voice was tinged with sadness. Not only was her dignity, her body and soul defiled, she had returned to her husband probably leaving her. Her eyes drifted to Alex.

"What about us?" Siobhan said.

Alex grasped her hand, eyes still glistening from the endless crying that she had done, so unlike Alex.

"I have never felt like this before," Alex said, "about anyone, I'm actually so confused."

Siobhan smiled, the muscles in her face not used to smiling. She edged herself in the bed. "Nor have I," she said. Alex felt relieved that she'd said it.

"We can make a go of it? I feel so complete when I see

you, smell you. You slot into my life like the missing jigsaw piece I've been looking for," Alex said.

Siobhan nodded, a tear dripped from her eye, and rolled down her cheek, she caught it before it fell.

Alex looked around the room, the armed officer stood, his back to them. "Hey?" Alex said. The guy turned. "Go find us something to eat?" he frowned, looked her up and down. Alex opened the side of her jacket, revealing the butt of her Glock. He smiled. "I'll give you guys ten minutes of peace." He sauntered off, boots squelching on the vinyl floor.

Alex reached and grabbed both hands. "The confusion I feel is marred by Si, and how he died. Devon and her kidnapping. Am I going to feel the same way three months down the road?" she looked across the ward, the sun was setting over the Thames, the top of Big Ben just visible, her lip quivered.

"I think I'm the patient here," Siobhan said, smiling. She squeezed Alex's hands back. "Look, I don't know what this is, but let's just see where it takes us. If we want to kill each other in three months then we'll deal with it, if we spend the rest of our lives together then, holy shit, I'm good with that." Siobhan's Irish accent was soft, lamenting and compassionate.

There was a pause. "You mentioned in Slovenia, at the hangar, about twin flames?"

Alex smiled. "My therapist is a spirit guide and medium as well as my *shrink*. I couldn't understand how I felt after I first met you, she said you're my twin flame!"

Alex regaled the story to Siobhan, she was gripped. She loved how Alex spoke, so English, dynamic and gentle with an underlying badassness about her. Some of the words were going in but mostly she sat mesmerized by her love. This twin flame made sense. She had never fallen for a woman before, always a sucker for a black man, but never a middle-class white woman that carried a gun.

Alex's phone rang. "Another thing you're gonna have to get used to," she said, waving her phone. Siobhan shrugged. She didn't care, she watched her walk off answering, loving the swag of her tight ass in Levis.

It was Broadstone "Alex?" she said.

"Where are you?" Broadstone said.

"At Tommy's, fifth floor on Harold Ellis ward, why?" Looking over her shoulder at Siobhan, she could feel her eyes boring into her, it made her tummy twinge, she liked it.

"We've found Devon!" Alex dropped the phone, legs falling beneath her, Siobhan screamed.

It had taken a few nurses, a junior doctor and a passing ODP to help Alex. Siobhan was still in too much pain to help. After getting her senses together, and Siobhan speaking to Broadstone on the phone, a car was sent for Alex.

Outside SIS, Broadstone met her. "She's okay, Alex, just a bit dehydrated." Alex was coming out the car like her life depended on it.

"Where is she?" Alex said, fighting against her boss trying to get to her. "They're in the garage, the doc has looked at her, she needs to go to hospital, ALEX," Broadstone said, snapping her out of her panic.

Alex stopped, she cupped her face, and buried herself into Broadstone's massive frame, he squeezed. "She's safe, let them do their thing, let's get her to Tommy's and get her checked out."

The blacked-out van squealed up the ramp, turned left and roared down the Albert Embankment. British Intelligence had their own entry point into Tommy's, again this was no coincidence on the placement of SIS. The first left to the building took you to a ramp that opened on a basement floor. The medical team was already waiting when the van arrived. Devon was lying down, supine on the trolley, still awake but almost catatonic.

Broadstone and Alex followed.

It was an agonizing wait in majors in the ED. A tall Indian chap in scrubs came into view.

"Alex Brown?" he enquired.

Alex stood, threw the third cardboard coffee cup into the bin, she nodded. "That's me!"

"Hi, Doctor Arjun, I'm the senior consultant on the floor today." He offered his hand, Alex took it. It was a bit limp, but Alex didn't judge him for it.

"We've checked Devon out, physically she's fit. But there are some other issues to consider." His accent was overly thick, the last letters of every sentence emphasized.

"Like what?" Alex said, looking over Arjun shoulder.

"She's in a bit of a catatonic state, we have her on a dopamine infusion currently to raise the dopamine in her body that…" Alex cut him off.

"I know what that is."

Arjun stopped, considered for a moment. "There's evidence of abuse and sexual abuse as well, can you confirm her age for consent purposes? And we also have her on some retrovirals as well as antibiotics, prophylactically, of course."

"She's nineteen, she has capacity, but if she's unresponsive, I do consent for you to run tests, what are her blood results?" Alex said.

Arjun was taken aback, he flipped the chart. "U's and E's okay, liver functioning normally as well as the GFR. White cells are high, as well as the CRP, something we would expect, no?"

Alex was nodding as he was reeling off the results. "Would you like to see her?" he said.

"Yes!" she said, already breaking into a walk, Broadstone stood, not knowing to follow or stay. Alex grabbed his hand and led him to the curtained-off area.

Alex entered the bay. Devon lay on the trolley not moving, a drip in the arm fed through a cannula along with the syringe driver feeding her a concoction of drugs. She was staring at the ceiling and not moving, hardly blinking. Alex felt her hand. She felt cold, clammy and damp. "Oh, baby," Alex said, she dropped the side rail and climbed on to the trolley, and snuggled up to her. The doctor went to say something but the nurse stopped him. "Let's leave them!" he said.

Devon felt rigid, hurt and broken. Alex started singing her the song she would sing when Devon was a baby. "*Sing me a song of a lass that is gone. Say could the lass be I. Merry of soul she sailed on a day, over the sea to Skye.*" A tear ran off Alex's nose and fell onto Devon's face. The water seemed to spread life through the young woman, she blinked, then again, and then again. Her head turned slowly, almost afraid of what she was going to see. Their eyes met, tears welled like fresh puddles and then erupted and flowed from Devon's face, the bond of a mother and child so strong, even the evil of Broc couldn't break it. "Mummy," she said and the tears flowed.

"Yes, my love, you're safe now." Devon buried her face into her mum's chest, the sobbing echoed around the busy ED. Arjun poked his head around the curtain. He nodded his approval, Broadstone suddenly felt like he was the third wheel and slipped out the side, something had caught his eye... he thought!

Siobhan was standing in the corridor. "Is she okay?" she said, carrying her drip. "The nurse on the ward said you guys were down here."

Broadstone nodded. She walked past Broadstone, slipped

through the curtain. Siobhan needed to be with her new family. Broadstone heard the trolley creek, Siobhan had climbed onto the other side, sandwiching Devon between her and her mother.

Broadstone's phone beeped, it was Bromilow, He answered.

"Broadstone?" he said.

"We need an urgent meeting at the vestry, Simon."

"Roger that, sir, be there in fifteen minutes."

"How are the patients?" he asked.

Broadstone looked at the curtain, he could hear the sobs and the crying. "It'll take some time, but Alex is as tough as they come, she will make it through. Though the cross hairs are firmly at Broc's head right now!"

"We will make sure that Alex, her partner and her daughter are well cared for Simon. With regards to this Hypnos debacle and the very brief discussion about Broc, this meeting cannot wait, I'll see you in fifteen minutes, old bean!"

The line went dead. He motioned to two armed officers, they took their positions at the bay. He popped his head around, the three of them half asleep on the trolley, Alex poked her head up, face wet from crying, yet her eyes sparkled. She looked happy, Broadstone thought.

"Vestry with the boss, stand down, I'll brief you afterwards!" Alex nodded. Broadstone was gone.

Bromilow was already at the Vestry, he stood when Broadstone entered, the rest of the team was there, including Jamal, who was working with Ricky.

"How's the arm?" Broadstone said. Jamal brandished it like a cricket bat. "Good for a *six*."

Ricky leaned in and said something, Jamal pulled a face, looked at Broadstone. "Sir!" He said, sheepishly.

Broadstone smiled. 'He'll get there,' he thought.

"Sir," Broadstone said to the Home Secretary, he nodded. "I suppose the formalities are in order, Mr Greer." Jamal was still talking to Ricky. "Mr Greer?" Ricky nudged Jamal in the side with his elbow, motioning to Bromilow.

"Oh, sorry, not used to being called Mr Greer, let alone my name actually being used.

"Stand up, boy!" Bromilow snapped.

"Considering the facts, all misdemeanours that you or may not have done in the past are now considered admonished, as long as you work, and only work for Her Majesty's Government?"

There was a pause, Broadstone leaned across the table. "He needs an answer."

Bromilow was smiling, Jamal nodded. "I agree, sir!" he said.

"Right now that nonsense is over, down to business, and may I say, what a fucking disaster this has been."

"I have the lock-up downstairs full of some of the richest men in the world as well a fucking royal, how the hell am I supposed to tell the electorate what the fuck has gone on?"

"That's why you're paid the big bucks, sir!" Broadstone said.

Bromilow pursed his lips. "And a heavy burden it has become, old bean. They will be dealt with in accordance to military law, as the military aid to the civil power was activated at the time of their arrest, meaning that time is under Queen's regulations."

Broadstone frowned. "What does that mean?"

Bromilow looked at the general, surveyed the room and then back to Broadstone. "Treason old bean, treason. Under Queen's regulation with MACP being activated, they face a firing squad."

The general nodded. "Holy shit," Broadstone said, "and will the public react to this?"

"Well, that's quite simple, the public, like the Hypnos bullshit, will be unaware of it. Your office will leak the deaths slowly over the next two years, of natural causes. All of their assets, down to the penny will be seized to help pay for the catastrophe they have caused." Bromilow went to sip some coffee. Coffee, Broadstone thought, he stood and went to the coffee station.

"The estimated value of assets is in the regional of two trillion dollars," Ricky said. "Mr Greer is in the process of draining their bank accounts."

"I have to go cap in hand to the Eurocrats and ask for their help, as well as the bloody *Yanks*, can't tell you how difficult that's going to be. We've literally just stopped paying the Americans for the fucking war!" He added, sipping more coffee.

"The software, can we be sure it's offline?" Broadstone said.

"Er, yes," Jamal said, still deep in typing one-handedly. "The software is totally offline, both Ricky and I managed to reverse engineer some of the nano-bots, so the accumulated deaths of most people should stop."

Bromilow nodded. "And the military are helping medically, general?" he said. The general sat forward and nodded. He was going to go into his spiel about numbers and the sort, Bromilow cut him off. Someone not interested in the piffle of budgets and accountability.

"This chap Broc, seems to have made an alliance with the American Secret Service."

"WHAT?" Broadstone said, eyes of the room boring into the new prime minister.

"Thought you might react like that."

"Can't you speak with the president?" Ricky said.

"Sorry, old bean, my hands are tied. Since 9/11, the secret service is a law unto themselves, the president pretty much told me to sling my hook."

"That's unacceptable," Broadstone spat, standing. The chair nearly toppled over.

"The president told me that he will be supervised and guarded at all times, I wasn't sure if that was to appease me or a warning to not try and grab him," he said, smiling.

"What do I tell Alex, sir?" Broadstone said.

"Alex." He shrugged. "You tell her nothing, that's my job, old bean. My experience in these sorts of matters is that they sort themselves out…somehow. Broc is neatly out of the spotlight for now, there's nothing that we can do, he will turn up again, I'm sure of that."

He stood, buttoned up the single-breasted Armani.

"Can we use the software to locate clandestine operatives working against the UK?" Ricky said, looking at Broadstone.

"In what way?" Bromilow enquired.

"We have Jihadi groups working in the UK, can we isolate them and turn them against their own regime, or Russian and Chinese agents working here?"

Bromilow nodded. "I think we ought to worry more about our American brothers first, but I take your point." He looked at Broadstone "I'm not sure about the legalities of that or the morals, and considering the moral compass in dealing with those unmentionables in your lock up, I suppose it's an impotent thought, yet, as prime minister… for now, I have to work in the best interest of the country." He considered for a moment. "I will leave you to formulate and execute a plan, Mr Broadstone."

"Understood, sir!" he said.

"Now, I have to address the nation and explain why more than one million people have died in the last four weeks, more than one million families are mourning the death of a loved one, just let that sink in for a second, chaps."

He turned to the general. "Stand-down the troops,

general, and convey my thanks to every man-jack of them, and women, of course." He went to leave, before leaving he turned to the room.

"The people watching this so-called game show by Dragoslav, you can find these people?"

Ricky and Jamal nodded, looking at each other. "Good, find them, as this crime was committed against one of our subjects, and under MACP, have agents deal with them in a way that they are trained to, regardless of who they are in society!"

Broadstone nodded, he smiled. A mission that his unit would relish in. Bromilow was gone.

31

The months following Hypnos and Asclepius had flown by. Alex was settling into a routine with Siobhan and her daughter, Devon. All three of them were undergoing analysis from Jenny.

Ray had agreed to a divorce and was living close by with a barrister called Paul; they'd all agreed to stay in each other's lives. Saturday night was game night, followed by a meal at a restaurant that was reviewed in the Standard the previous day, it was the distraction Alex needed. To finally have a social life and be around people that genuinely loved her. The summer had been glorious in London. Idle dinners, walks in the park and a great night vibe on the doorstep. Life just couldn't get any better.

Making a life with Siobhan was hard. She was flighty, provoking and combative. It was made worse by her experience at the hands of Dragoslav, although surpassing it and being too stoic by Alex's standards. Things would bubble over and a tremendous fight would erupt out of the slightest of incidents. Three independent women, all driven, dynamic and outspoken yet damaged by their life experiences. A solidarity coupled with the anger of their emotional processing gave way to a toxic atmosphere. But in the main, the apartment felt calm, peaceful… clean.

Broc became a nagging ache in the back of Alex's mind whenever she thought about him. Sometimes that was when Devon would throw a certain glance. Alex couldn't identify exactly what, but it was fleeting. With the coping mechanisms that Jenny had given, the isolation lasted no more than thirty seconds or so. Broc certainly wasn't going to win.

Hypnos had been used extensively by British Intelligence, the software had uncovered numerous corporate infringements that had affected British import and export as well as espionage. Diplomats expelled and loops closed without bloodshed, friendships that spanned decades over diplomacy ruined; but new friendships forged in the light of truth, honesty and profit.

Bromilow required updating every Friday morning at the SIS. As the non-elected prime minister, but with the support of the party, the clean-up process was long and arduous. Having medical aid delivered by the European member states did nothing for the Brexit debate still ensuing, even with the calamity that Hypnos had caused. The public's thirst for independence was still unquenchable. The economy for this fateful five days had run into the tens of billions. The assets seized by the government had more than made up for the deficit. But the fate of these people was unsure. Investigative journalists had tried to uncover the truth, but Hypnos had come into play again.

The truth was Bromilow couldn't bring himself to have these people executed. Incarcerating them away from the public and away from business associates was the tough question.

9/11 had seen an unprecedented change to the dynamics of the world. The coupling of technology and a resistance to globalisation was going to pose an even bigger problem. Asclepius was just the start to the problems of the twenty-first century. Bromilow and his advisers had a clear understanding of this, from where the threat came next was anyone's guess.

"Got to go, Simon's outside!" Alex said. Both Siobhan and Devon looked up from the breakfast bar, both deep in conversation about which bag looked great on Meghan Markle. They nodded and went back to *Grazia* magazine.

"Byeee," Alex said again. Siobhan clocked it, she snapped herself out of the moment, and ran over, her bare feet slapping on the wooden floor. She wrapped her arms around her and kissed her square on the lips. "Eww, get a room!" Devon shouted from across the kitchen.

"There's this yummy recipe in that mag," Siobhan said. "Linguine with prawns and creme fraiche dressing." She looked at Alex, her love had felt no bounds when she gazed into those pale blue eyes. "Don't be late home, I want to enjoy it with you, text me when you leave, honey."

"I will, have a great day, and tell me about your session with Jenny today, leave nothing out, just chasing paperwork up the road, you will be a light relief."

Siobhan stuck her bottom lip out. "You know my head forgets stuff." Her soft accent tickling Alex, she loved it.

"We're doing lunch, mummy," Devon shouted. "If you're free, we can eat together"

Siobhan held Alex at arm's length. "Gee, that would be swell, why not?"

The door knocked, then opened, it was Broadstone, the girls were all now used to Simon walking in. He enjoyed it. They would cluck around him while he caught up with the headlines from the sports channel, he felt like John Bosley from *Charlie's Angels*.

"Hey?" Siobhan said, looking over Alex's shoulder. "Hey, Simon," Devon shouted from the kitchen.

"Good morning ladies," he said. "Are we good to go?" he said to Alex.

Alex nodded, blew a kiss to Devon, she caught it and blew one back, Alex hand cupped the side of Siobhan's face, pulled her in and kissed her again. "Love you!" Alex said, turned and left with Broadstone.

They hadn't said a word as they left the apartment block, the concierge on the door doffed his cap. The concierge changed every day. Some considered the post irrelevant, others, knowing the pedigree of Broadstone in special forces, had volunteered. Today was Frank, a six-foot-seven ex-Royal Marine, six months after completing the selection process. Broadstone knew that under that uniform was a bombed-up badass, snarling to kill anything that crossed him.

Police cars zoomed past, ambulances. Five, six, then seven.

"Wow, what's going on?" Alex said, her phone rang, so did Broadstone's.

"Alex?" she said, it was Ricky.

"Get your ass back to SIS now, the shit's hit the fan, boss!" Alex closed her phone, Broadstone's conversation was longer. More sirens. The fire station down the road erupted to life, the doors sliding open. All four vehicles were leaving, but two going in opposite directions.

He ended the call.

"Bromilow?" Alex asked.

"Yeah, there's been major incidents at all the main London railway terminals and in all the capitals in Europe. Multiple fatalities and injuries. Europe has been placed by NATO in a state of emergency."

Broc had woke, drenched in sweat. He hated the heat. The smell of body odour ubiquitous. The place was his own version of hell. Then his rusty bed creaked. His feet hit the floor, he felt the fine grains of sand and gravel under his feet. "How did I get here?" he said out loud.

"You made your choice," the Korean voice behind said. He looked over his shoulder, Ji-Yeon was standing on her head. Some weird yoga position.

"If I tried that I think I would have a stroke!"

"You have stroke because you fat, Mista Bloc!" She said, still not pronouncing those 'R's', face stony straight, still on her head.

Broc looked down. He had gained some timber, he rubbed his not-so-flat tummy with his hand. He stood, his back creaked. The request for a decent bed had been ignored. He was going to bring it up again.

The compound in South Sudan was in the guise of a food aid warehousing station. How, under the United Nations mandate for humanitarian aid, there were armed Caucasian guards, sporting high end assault rifles, and ripstop cotton gabardine clothing was anyone's guess.

Local militia had rusty AK-47's that were made on the first batch by Kalashnikov himself, so well used, the black steel chassis of the rifle had a silver appearance. These guys were normally bare foot with rags as clothes. The reason was that the food was continually pilfered by the locals.

The compound was a front. Behind the facade was a biochemical, bacteriology and virology lab that used the human displacement of thousands of people for its own ends. The people were lured in with the promise of food and shelter. When, in fact, they got the opposite. The lab tested all organically-cultured viruses, such as Ebola, avian flu, HIV, all the hepatitis as well as influenza, common colds. The lab also ran more sinister testing such as anthrax, nerve agents novichok, tabun, sarin, cyclosarin and VX. Blood agents like arsine, cyanogen chloride.

The viruses were bred into fleas. The fleas were exposed to the world's best courier of anything toxic, a specially bred rat that didn't require the same amount of food and water as the indigenous rats did.

For the poor humans, viruses and toxins were exposed to different parts of the body, surgically exposed and infected with anthrax, Ebola and other horrible diseases. The subjects were then dissected. These dissections led to live vivisection as the modality of injuries was also scrutinised.

The Ebola in Sierra Leone was one experiment that got out of hand. Rats were stolen from one of the Unit 731 compounds and consumed by the perpetrators, causing a world-wide panic. Unit 731 already had the cure, sitting on it for a sufficient amount of time became painful for the paymasters of the organization. A cloak of secrecy shrouded the state side offices as they needed to find a delivery system. The molecular design was given to two pay-rolled graduates of the non-profit Albert Einstein College of Medicine in upstate New York. Not for their excellent research studies, but because the world wouldn't really give a shit about this small laboratory. Harvard or the Mayo Clinic seemed too obvious, Cern in Switzerland too focused on colliding particles for the media to not ask award questions.

The lab had been in operation since WWII. Started by a lunatic medical research scientist called Shiro Iishii. He worked out of Manchuria and was responsible for the systematic culling of millions of people. Mainly Chinese and Korean. Some allied prisoners of war had been vivisected, but that was never corroborated. The level of crime made the likes of Josef Mengele look like a first-aider. Pregnant women were dissected without anaesthetic, people tied to posts and shot or blown up. This was a two-fold experiment. To see how effective the munitions were, and the second was to understand the mortality and morbidity of the injuries on the subjects.

At the end of the war, Unit 731 was surely going to face a

criminal war crimes court like the Nazis in Nuremberg. General Douglas MacArthur, under advice, saw this as an opportunity. The world was spared the horrors of Unit 731, unlike the liberations of the concentration camps across Europe, Unit 731 was never going to have the same consequences.

The whole operation was bartered for immunity by Iishii to give over all the data of the findings. MacAthur went a stage further, he moved the unit to the USA and carried on their work. In the late 40s, and throughout the 50s, the Americans developed chemical weapons to protect their shores from the possible threat of Soviet invasion. Mexicans, Native Indians were used by Iishii and his henchmen. During the 70s, the notion of free love and an ever-intrusive press. The organization bounced into the Mojave Desert, and then, under Carter, the CIA moved the operation to South Sudan. The scientist and lab rats could have their pick of a salient majority. People desperate for food water and shelter. The absolute most vulnerable humans in the modern world were manipulated and exploited, from babies right through to the elderly. Their fate assured the moment they walked through the gates of the compound.

Three thousand hectares of land, mostly covered from the blistering sun, fed the compound. The fertile soil fed with the ground-up bones of the victims.

This was where Broc came in. The vivisection of the specimens was conducted by him. The subjects were held down by chained refugees, Broc would open them up like a can of worms, and strip their organs out, placing them into sealed jars so the scientists could analyze the proliferation of the infection. Cure and vaccines would then be sought from the findings.

"Mr Broc, you are needed, sir," a voice said at the door. The soft American accent grated on Broc. "I'll be there is a minute!"

"Sir, the controller has said to me to inform you that your attendance is most urgent, in that he requires you in the ops room immediately, sir."

Broc boiled. "WHY THE FUCK DO YOU YANKS USE SO MANY WORDS?"

"Sir, I am so sorry, maybe I wasn't clear for you, may I be…" he was cut off.

"Fuck off, I'll be there IMMEDIATELY!"

Ji-Yeon sprung to a standing position, she walked with a slight swagger to the door, the young man suddenly feeling intimidated, "I'll tell him you're on your way, sir!" The door creaked and slammed, he was gone.

Ji-Yeon looked through the window, there was activity. Something was up.

"Mista Bloc, something is up!" She said. Broc walked over, his body glistening with sweat. Although he had gained a bit, he still cut a fine figure of a man. He stood naked at the window, a small but pleasing draught, the venturi effect coming through the opening licked over the bronzed muscles. Ji-Yeon looked up and down the compound. "You dress!" she said. "Something serious!" Motioning to the outside.

Broc nodded. He wandered over to the chair that served as the clothes-horse. Put the same clothes he had had on yesterday. White rings of sweat betrayed the cleanliness of them.

"You coming?" he asked. Ji-Yeon considered for a moment, looking up and down the compound.

"No, I stay, call the room if we need to move, I'll be waiting!" Broc nodded and walked into the blazing sun. He was tired.

There was a series of high-tech entry systems to negotiate, each manned by a 'civilian' guard. The guards themselves were armed to the teeth and not once broke a smile.

The ops room was, dark, blissfully cold. The air-con state of the art and silent. The room was dark apart from the low light of computer terminals. It was busy, the large screens flashing different orders and news annulments.

The ops officer was Grant Ballard. He was the CIA operator and all-round piece of shit.

"BROC!" He shouted. "Over here."

Broc acknowledged him, he walked over, avoiding the people darting about in front of him.

Chewing gum far too loudly for his own safety, Broc considered how he should kill him just on the jaw action. "Shit's hit the fan, Broc," Ballard said, nodding to the main screen.

"What's happening?" Broc asked, not quite figuring out the frenzy.

"Isopescu, the scientist that absconded just before you arrived," Ballard said, checking his phone and pistol. "You knew him, right?" he said, stopping expecting an answer.

"Sure, he was a gifted pathologist, I must admit, I was surprised that his name was mentioned to me when I arrived."

"Why's that?" Ballard asked.

"Well, he was certainly going to get a Nobel for his work with malaria and mosquitoes, I had heard…"

"I haven't got time for your lamenting bullshit, Broc, the only reason that sonofabitch was here was because he owed over three million dollars in gambling debt, we paid it so then we owned his fucking ass, all of you psychopathic motherfuckers, although brilliant in your chosen fields, are flawed. His was gambling." He stood looking at Broc, the hate in his eye bore into him.

Ballard was a big man. Muscular and a sharp thinker, Ballard had no time for flimflam or small talk. He only spoke in open-ended questions with the air of violence in everything that he said. The right man for a place such as

Unit 731, commonly called the *Crate*. He despised every-thing about the place. But a good patriot and devoutly Christian, he did his duty to the letter. He expected noth-ing less from the Crate's inhabitants. A rag tail bunch of lowlifes. Good at their jobs, yet incompetent to behave in the real world. Ideal subjects for the legacy of Ishii and Unit 731. He didn't get involved in the clinical research of the job, he chose to ignore it.

Broc nodded ruefully, still looking around at the chaos. "And me?" he asked.

Ballard stopped, considered the question, he picked up a cup of something, drained it. "You're just a sick mother-fucker that needs puttin' down, but unfortunately for me, Fort Bragg has decreed that you are protected, which means I can't shoot you!"

"Oh, was that on the cards then?" he asked.

"For sure, some of the assets that we no longer need have already been executed, you and a few others have been spared. You are to carry on your work here, I have to leave and get my ass to Bragg for a debrief." He carried on clear-ing his desk.

"Tell me what has happened," Broc asked. Ballard pointed to the screen. "Yo, Gunther, get the news headlines up on the screen!" He shouted. Broc looked for Gunther, he couldn't make him out in the melee, it didn't matter, the giant screen went blank, then the BBC headline came up.

Five minutes in, Broc uttered, "Isopescu?"

Ballard broke the trance. "Yeah, Isopescu. The ASU's failed to locate him, we estimate the fatalities run into the hundreds of thousands, the shit has truly hit the fan. The only locations hit have been London, Paris, Berlin, Madrid and Rome."

"Has America been hit?" Broc asked.

"Not to my knowledge. Now keep on with your work,

my replacement is coming on the plane I'm leaving on. His name is Bingley."

He went to leave. "Have a safe trip," Broc said.

"I'm flying on a plane that has only one window, and that's the pilot's, and I hate flying. Make sure you don't do anything that I have to clean up Broc, you feel me?"

Broc nodded. "I feel you!" He said emphatically but awkwardly, following him out.

"And Bingley makes me look like Mother Teresa!" Ballard said, throwing his gear into the back Landcruiser.

The dust was thick, Broc heard the engine fire, he placed his neckerchief over his face. When the dust finally settled, the SUV was long gone.

32

The blacked-out Range Rover screeched to a halt outside the main steps to Waterloo. People were spewing from the victory arch and down the main steps. They seemed to take on the appearance of rats. At the top of the steps, sinister figures stood, armed, wearing vacuum-sealed chemical protection suits.

"What the fuck is going on?" Alex demanded, nodding out of the window to Broadstone.

"I don't know, Alex, but I feel we're going to find out."

Broadstone got out first, Alex followed. Mine tape had been stretched across Mepham Road. "You can't park there!" A suited police officer said, unsure who he was talking to. Alex stepped out, wearing her trademark door-kickers, Barbour jacket cutting her hourly figure. She fished into her inner pocket, the butt of her Glock coming into view. The officer smiled, she had to be, he thought. She showed her card.

"B5 Intelligence and Interpol, where's your incident commander? We need to speak with him urgently."

He turned, his suit bulky and awkward. "Over there, Ma'am!" The vacuum becoming louder when he turned.

"Thank you!"

"You need to suit up, Ma'am." He motioned to the London Fire Brigade Scientific Unit.

Broadstone had come around. "We need to suit up, Simon," Alex said. They made their way to the truck, a portly cockney in blue fire brigade fatigues measured them up. He was sweating. Alex surveyed the scene, this was probably his busiest day that year.

They made their way through the throngs of scientists, paramedic HART and USAR specialists, the police and the army as well.

Broadstone and Alex could feel their phones vibrating in their pockets. The mine-tape funnelled the traffic to Platform 8.

Alex looked about. This was probably the quietest Waterloo had been since the revamp in 1922. People scurried about, the incident commander's desk was sat at the mouth of Platform 8.

It was Johnny Drinkwater, known to his friends as Quench, Alex was one of them.

"Well, well, well, if it isn't the *ledge* that is Alex Brown?" They exchanged handshakes.

"Quench, how are you?" she said.

"I would hug you, but," he held out his hands in an almost curtsey.

"I'll forgive you."

"I heard you went to the dark side, started at SIS, down the road?" he eyed Broadstone, trying to catch a glimpse.

"We like to call it Interpol," Broadstone said, offering his hand.

Quench looked him up and down, then over to Alex. "Is that right?" he said smiling.

He turned, went to wipe his face, but realized that his whole body was covered, he grabbed a clipboard. "Then what does Interpol need from my crime scene?"

"What have you got?" Alex asked, walking to the barrier.

"Something very weird, guys, I just need to check your clearance, you know the score."

"Sure, call the Prime Minister's office," Broadstone said. "He's the one that sent us here."

He eyed them, turned and spoke into his radio. It boomed to life, the voice carried with too much static for Alex to make out. Quench was screwing his face up to listen to the voice. "Okay, you can go down the platform. Rules, chaps, do not open the train, no matter what. And no photos."

Alex puzzled her brow. "Okay!"

Both Alex and Broadstone walked down to the train. It was eerily quiet. The swish of the chemical suit and the whoosh of vented air took up the noise of the station. "This is very weird, I don't have a good feeling about this," Alex said.

The first carriage had no one in. Menacingly, soldiers in green chemsuits patrolled the train both sides. A plastic tent was being erected at the furthest end.

There was a thump at the window, it made Alex jump. She looked into the second carriage, the word PLEH was written into the window. It took a few seconds for Alex's mind to flip the words in her mind, "HELP!" She said.

Broadstone had caught up with her. "What did you say?" he said.

She pointed to the window. "Help, it's written inside, in blood, I think."

Another thump, Alex gingerly walked up to the window, the carriage was black. She pulled out a Maglite from the suit's accessory pocket, she tried to figure out how to use it while Simon watched the soldiers, gats in the shoulders. "No Russian?" he muttered.

The light flicked on, making Alex jump. "What did you say?" she said, looking at his gaze up the platform and looking into the bright flashlight, she managed to figure out.

"No-Russian!" He repeated leaning into Alex, their suits clashing like balloons, rubbing together. They stood watching, another thump. Alex jumped back. Things were getting frosty, she didn't like it.

She shone the light into the carriage, a small child, a girl, of about six or seven was stood by the window, bloodied. Crying. Soundless. The glazing and the ambient noise blocking out all the sound the child was making. Alex's heart broke into pieces. The flashlight switched on, she shone into the carriage, people lay dead in their seats. Blood spilt from every hole. The carriage was awash with blood, faeces and mucus. The death masks of the passengers showed no peaceful death, the deaths harrowing and upsetting. Alex stood back, her skin crawling. The goose-bumps mixing with her own sweat and the harshness of the chemo suit. "Holy mother of God!" Alex whispered.

Broadstone took the flashlight, shone it into the carriage. "What the fuck?" he said sweeping the light up and down the walkway. He spent a second or two on each haunting face. The light shone onto the girl. Her crying was prolonged. Her face mixed with her tears and the blood of the others, she was cuddling her bunny rabbit, it was matted with the clotted blood of the passengers.

"YO, THERE'S ONE ALIVE IN HERE!" Alex screamed. She ran up to one of the soldiers. "WE NEED TO GET IN THERE NOW, IT'S A CHILD." He stood, just looking at her, faceless, no emotion. His wiry lips dry and chapped from the forced air suit, his strong hand pushed her away. Alex stumbled in her suit, Broadstone caught her.

"We can't get involved, Alex."

"That girl is alive, Simon, we have to get her out of that fucking hellhole."

The flashlight darted around inside, suited people were

entering the carriage from the front of the train. Broadstone nodded to the window.

"Thank God," Alex said, Alex trotted over, knocked on the window loudly. "OVER HERE, OVER HERE!"

The small girl's hand touched the glass, Alex tried to smile, she raised her hand. Alex could almost feel the warmth transmit through the glass as she placed her hand next to the girl.

The girl's eyes were like saucers filled with water. Distressed and upset. A woman was slumped across the seats, blood had vomited out of her, still oozing. Blood was coming from her eyes, her groin soaked in blood, her skin horribly mottled. The veins were ruptured, she had bled out. Alex looked at the girl again. Suddenly, the girl's head snapped back, and recoiled forward. The report of the pistol came second. The girl's head smashed against the window, and crumpled onto what Alex thought was the girl's mother.

"NOOO!" Alex screamed, she looked into the carriage. Three suited men stood there, reloading their low-velocity pistols. They held a pistol to the head of the girl's mother, a shot rang out. Alex jumped as the corpse of the woman slumped. She stood back.

Broadstone had experienced a lot of things. But watching a government employee execute a small girl, kind of went against the grain.

Quench came running up. "You guys have to leave, the prime minister needs you at Number 10, there's a car waiting, they've been on the blower."

"Quench, what the fuck?" Alex said. "What is this?"

He looked into the carriage. "The day of reckoning Alex, it's time for us humans to pay the ferryman."

"Is this the only place?" Alex asked.

Quench turned. "No, Paddington, St Pancras, Victoria, Euston, Manchester Piccadilly, Birmingham New Street.

There are reports that a load of European capitals were targeted as well."

"You say targeted?" Broadstone said.

"The *biffs* in the labs have said this is off the record. It's a weaponized virus."

"Shit," Alex said. They had made their way back to the decontamination unit. Changed.

"Weaponized virus?" Broadstone said.

Alex pulled her phone out. Ten missed calls from Siobhan, three from Devon. And one from her son at University.

She found Siobhan, hit dial.

"Hey babes, you okay?" Siobhan's smoky accented voice came on almost immediately.

Alex fought to keep herself under control, her voice broke only once through. "Yeah, kinda messy, can't say much."

"I understand," Siobhan said.

"Can we rain check the prawn linguine?" Alex said, a tear rolled down her cheek, she sniffed.

Siobhan laughed. "We have the news on, they're not saying too much, and we saw you being whisked off in that blacked-out SUV. We will be here when you're done, honey, know that I love you and be strong. "

Alex paused. "You didn't pull your Angel card, this morning," Siobhan said.

"Shit, I didn't." Alex hit her forehead with her hand.

"Shall I pull one for you?" Siobhan said.

Alex nodded. "Sure." She heard shuffling.

"You got the chimpanzee, means that you need to use your intuition and intellect to solve problems and get to the bottom of your questions, you are protected by a higher purpose, so stride forwards." Alex knew what it meant…

There was another pause. "This is your calling, Alex, don't worry about Devon and I. Your home will be warm and loved for when you return."

"Thank you, Siobhan," Alex said.

"We have to bounce," Broadstone said.

"I have to go, baby," Alex said.

"You're safe, save the world and come back home, whenever that may be, I will always be waiting for you baby" Siobhan's said.

The line went dead. Alex got into the car. A sadness descended on her, a heavy cloud that had become a friend. She thought she was free of it after Hypnos.

"You good?" Broadstone said, looking over to Alex.

She nodded, she felt the familiar warmth of her friend Renton, she acknowledged him by her side, she shivered and felt her heart swell, his spirit strong and reassuring, genuine. Alex looked at Broadstone, threw two sticks of gum into her mouth.

"Let's rock and roll!"

The End

Author's note

People ask me where I get the inspiration for Alex Brown. It took me a few moments to analyse who I was basing my character on, and then I realised that the character is in fact my wife, Samantha.

She always wanted to be a spook or in law enforcement but I came along and ruined all that. Nonchalantly I gave Alex Brown her name when in fact Alexandria is Samantha's middle name, which is my favourite name. And Brown is Samantha's maiden name. Alex is sexy, driven and passionate, just like my Samantha, and knows how you use both her intellect and sexuality to maximum advantage. I know she won't mind me saying this. It's weird because I'm married to my character, and I didn't see it and makes it more interesting as a writer to develop that character.

Alex's daughter Devon is the same name as my daughter Devon. Why I used her name in this series is still a mystery to me. At the time when I was completing Harvester, my daughter was going through some challenges at university, and was in the forefront of my thinking all the time, when the need for a characters name was required, Devon was the first name that I plucked out of the air. I think maybe because as a parent, so entwined was I the story line at the point I tried to feel how Alex would feel seeing her daughter being kidnapped. I remember it giving me goosebumps and the hair stand up on the back of my neck.

Anyway, writing this book and any of them in this series has been a real pleasure, there are more in the pipeline, and hope to carry on reading these books.

Click the link to the Harvester listing on the website, follow the links from there to my author profile on Amazon and buy yourself the first book Harvester in this series.

https://jonbiddle.uk/books/harvester-3/

If you have enjoyed this book, you will enjoy other books in this series along with standalone books. Click the link to join my mailing list to receive special offers, FREE short stories, newsletters and access to content on my website. The link takes you to the FREE novella that I have on the site which you can download on any device. If you already have, hold back and thank you for the add.

https://jonbiddle.uk/get-my-free-book-troll/

The story in the prequel to my first book, Harvester, where we introduce Alex and her team to the story.

Lightning Source UK Ltd.
Milton Keynes UK
UKHW011405240220
359232UK00001B/191